THIRTY TURNS OF THE SAND

THIRTY TURNS OF THE SAND

Book Two of
THE ELDORMAAR

DAVID MACKAY

Cover design by Melanie Moor. Melli M Designs

ISBN: 9798470687210

At The Point Of Forever Literary Creations

www.atthepointofforever.com
www.theeldormaar.com

CHAPTER ONE

A storm was coming.

An ominous gathering of black clouds darkened the sky.

The wind battered the high plateau. Its obvious craving to throw him to its mercy was becoming more desperate by the minute. Bracing himself against the onslaught, he watched as the appearance of the mountain changed in response to the sudden shift in daylight.

The landscape was familiar but something about it felt different, as if he viewed it all from a new perspective. The curved summit ridge rose gently from the sprawl of trees blanketing the lower slopes. He followed its gradual ascent up among the staggered spears of rock until the mountaintop succumbed to the elements and disappeared behind the clouds.

Shifting his gaze, he caught sight of a windswept figure some distance away on the plain. Moving steadily towards him, its progress seemingly oblivious to the harsh conditions, it closed the gap between them at an almost unnatural speed.

'A blustery day.' The new arrival, an imposing figure wrapped in a rust-hued greatcoat, called out his greeting as he came to a stop only a few paces away. 'Forgive me if it appears I'm shouting, but the wind...' A calloused hand waved a gesture of dismissal. 'In truth, I find it all rather invigorating.'

Brushing aside a tangle of greying hair, the stranger pointed in the direction of the mountain. 'Beyond the forest there is a settlement. By my reckoning, you will reach it by nightfall. When you arrive there, you will know what to do.'

'Why are you telling me this?'

'It matters not. You will go there, and you will know what must be done.'

'Who are you?'

'Think of me as a messenger. Nothing more.' With a parting nod, the stranger brushed past him. 'Until we meet again.'

Puzzled by the odd encounter, he watched the jacketed figure until it merged with the rolling clouds.

With a shake of his head, he dismissed the chance meeting as little more than bad luck.

Turning to the mountain, he hunched his shoulders in defiance of the wind and began walking towards the forest.

CHAPTER TWO

With the failing light of dusk, the weather had taken a turn for the worse. It was raining harder than he'd ever seen it rain before. In only a matter of minutes the torrential downpour had turned the dirt road into something more resembling a squelching bog. Wiping the rain from his face, he entered the settlement of Creek.

He kept to the shadows as he moved cautiously among the disjointed rows of timber shacks. Didn't seem any reason to change the habits of a lifetime now. And in times of uncertainty, it was best to stick with what you knew.

Picking his way through the muddle of rain-drenched lanes and alleyways, he found her slumped in a doorway. By the looks of her blood-stained shirt, she'd had a run-in with the sharp end of a blade and come out second best.

Gasping for breath, she looked up as he approached. Panic flashed across her face. Her eyes flickered wildly, darting frantically to the far side of the lane and back again. Turning quickly, he saw the source of her distraction kneeling over a motionless body. At the sound of his boots slopping in the sludge, the bending figure got to his feet and swung around.

'About time!' The man splashed angrily towards him. 'This is on you,' he snarled. 'If you'd been here sooner there might've been no need for bloodshed. They wouldn't have put up a fight if there'd been two of us as we'd planned. Doesn't feel like you've earned your share of this.' Brandishing the leather pouch, he shoved him aside. 'Lucky for you I'm a man of my word. I'll just put her out of her misery and we'll be on our way.'

He didn't hesitate, not even for a second. Reaching inside his jacket, his fingers closed around the handle of his hunting knife and with one swift effortless motion the deed was done.

The blade flashed through the air.

He watched as his target fell face down in the mud.

It was no lucky strike. It appeared the messenger had been right. He'd known what had to be done, and how to do it.

Retrieving the knife, he wiped the blade on his victim's sleeve.

Seemed like their partnership was dissolved. Didn't seem like he was about to shed any tears over it either.

Lifting the money pouch, he retraced his steps and leaned over her. Didn't seem like she had much time left. He'd seen injuries like this before, plenty of them, and the outcome was rarely good. Knowing his efforts would most likely be in vain, he ripped the torn sleeve from her shirt, bunched it tightly in his hand, and pressed down hard on the wound.

He covered her mouth with his hand as he applied more pressure. Surrounded by bodies, the last thing he wanted was her crying out and drawing any attention.

As he lifted his hand away, her ragged breathing eased slightly. He cut the other sleeve from her shirt, tied it round her, best he could, and pulled it tight. The colour drained rapidly from her face. Her eyes rolled skyward and, with no sound or protest, she slipped from consciousness.

It was done. Getting to his feet, he surveyed his handiwork.
He was no surgeon. It would merely delay the inevitable.
Lifting her onto his shoulder, he took one last look around and slipped back into the shadows.

The hours of darkness passed in a blur.
It felt like he'd walked all night through the pouring rain, and the trees had offered little respite. The first light of dawn found him at the edge of the forest looking out over an open stretch of moorland. At least the rain had finally stopped.
He eased her from his shoulder in the shelter of a great fir tree. She hadn't regained consciousness; he doubted now that she ever would. Bending to inspect the wound, his eye settled on the small silver pendant around her neck. He examined it closer.
The inscription meant nothing. He rolled it in his fingers for a few moments, contemplating its value, before letting it go.
Didn't feel right to take it. Seemed like she'd lost enough already.
He pressed his hand against her forehead. Her skin felt cold as ice. Didn't seem much point in examining the wound again.

He cast his gaze across the moor as the first rays of sunlight pierced the ghostly veil of mist and cloud bringing the promise of a fine day ahead. Stretching with a yawn, he sat down against a tree, closed his eyes, and fell asleep.

When he woke sometime later, he found that he was alone.

The woman was gone.

CHAPTER THREE

A chill hung in the air. Stirred by the new day's first glimpse of sunlight, the early morning dew danced on a network of intricate cobwebs. Moving steadily through the hushed forest, Dragon Slayer Ten Six Nine paused and held her breath as a procession of deer crossed the trail a short distance ahead. As they slipped from view beyond the rise, she continued walking.

Her concerns for Twelve Seven Two were growing. Something had happened to trigger his new-found obsession with this place, but what was it? Why did he keep coming back here? His unusual insights had been met with derision by their fellow Slayers for so long he was now less than willing to talk openly, but something had happened to him here. She knew it; the unspoken bond they shared made it impossible to ignore.

Rubbing the dull ache in her shoulder, her hand settled on the thin cord around her neck. Her fingers moved to the smooth metal of his identification tag. Why had he taken it off and left it above the fireplace?

As the trees thinned, she came to a sudden halt.

This wasn't right. There was no road in the Eastern Forest.

She moved from the safety of the trees to investigate. The old cobblestoned surface was losing its battle with the encroaching moss and grass. The sound of falling water beckoned her forward. Rounding a corner, she paused at the sight of a waterfall tumbling down a great rift in the mountainside. Thundering onto the rocks, it surged into dark swirling pools before disappearing beneath a bridge carrying the road to the far side of the yawning ravine. Though time-worn and overgrown, the bridge still made for an impressive sight and as she moved towards it she felt a glimmer of recognition. She'd been here once before.

The Bridge at Callinduir.

This definitely wasn't right. The bridge was more than a full day's ride north of Enntonia's city boundary. She'd left her horse at the Eastern Gate and headed east on foot. How could she possibly have arrived here? Pondering her inexplicable lapse in navigation, her eyes followed the Old North Road as it began its long journey towards the Old Kingdom.

The sound of laughter echoed suddenly from the forest. Leaving the bridge, she edged carefully down a steep grass embankment and skirted the edge of the churning water. Once more among the trees, with the rumble of the waterfall fading behind her, she climbed to the top of a grassy knoll.

Sitting by a pool of crystal-clear water, a young dark-haired woman looked up at her and smiled. 'Hello. Would you like to join us?'

Ten Six Nine eyed the scene warily. 'Us?'

'Forgive me, I do not mean to deceive you. I am not alone. My friends, however, can be shy, elusive even. Do you not see them?'

'I see you, but no one else.'

'Come down. Perhaps they will show themselves when they see that you mean them no harm.' As Ten Six Nine made her way down to the pool, the woman rose to greet her. 'My name is Elemi. What's yours?'

'Ten Six Nine.'

'Oh! How exciting.' The young woman's eyes sparkled brightly. 'A Dragon Slayer. I've never met one before, but I've heard lots about you.'

'None of it good I'll wager.'

'On the contrary. I've read all about the history of the Order and friends that talk of you have only good things to say.'

'Sounds hard to believe. Your friends, are they the ones you claim were here just now?'

'No,' she winked mischievously. 'The small folk don't gossip.'

'Small folk?' Ten Six Nine scoffed. 'Fairies? Sorry, I don't believe in all that nonsense.'

'They're as real as you and me. Living creatures, just like us.'

Ten Six Nine rolled her eyes. 'I still don't believe in them.' She rubbed her shoulder.

'That's probably why you can't see them,' the woman replied softly. 'Your shoulder, is it troubling you?'

'An old injury, looks like I'm stuck with it.'

'Perhaps I can help.' She clicked her fingers excitedly and began rummaging in a colourful canvas bag decorated with floral designs. 'We'll need ginger, some black pepper, and a splash of rosemary.' Taking several little bottles from the bag, she arranged them carefully on the ground at her knees.

'What are you doing?' Ten Six Nine eyed her curiously.

'I'm making a remedy for your shoulder.' Carefully shaking three drops of oil from each bottle into a little ceramic bowl, she began stirring them together. 'So, what brings you to Dipper Mill Forest? We've never had a Dragon Slayer visit us here before?'

Ten Six Nine frowned. 'Dipper Mill?' She'd never heard of it. 'You are mistaken. This is the Northern Forest. Enntonia's Old North Road passes through it.'

'No, it is you who are mistaken. This is Dipper Mill Forest. You have my word on it.'

The woman's response was indignant. Ten Six Nine decided against challenging her further. Something strange was going on. Her unexplained arrival at Callinduir was evidence enough of that.

'Right.' Elemi's smile returned as she got to her feet. 'It's ready. Would you like me to apply it for you?'

'Okay.' Ten Six Nine removed her coat.

'Ooh, that's really nice.'

'Sorry?'

'Your identification brand. It's more subtle than the books suggest.'

'You've read about them too?'

'Yes. The Dragon Slayer is identified by either a branding somewhere on their person or by wearing a small metal identification tag. I see that you have both.'

'Oh, the tag on the cord is not mine. It belongs to a friend. I was looking for him in the forest.'

'He is missing?'

'No.' She hesitated. 'At least, I don't think so.' She felt the soothing effect of the concoction begin to take effect. 'What did you say your name was?'

'Elemi.'

'So, you are an apothecary? Herbalist?'

'No, not really. I just love experimenting. Salves, potions, ointments. I also make teas and tobaccos.'

'What about red wine?'

'No, I haven't dabbled in that area yet.'

'Pity. So, where do you find all your ingredients?'

'Most of what I need grows wild in the meadows and on the hillsides, but I have a secret garden for my own special varieties.'

'Why is it secret?'

'I used to be troubled by mischievous little spirits who caused havoc in my garden, so I asked a friend to help. He comes to visit me now and again and is particularly fond of my Silver Birch Leaf tea. Some folks might refer to him as a wizard. He placed an enchantment on my garden to protect it.'

Ten Six Nine sighed inwardly. More nonsense.

'There, that's you done.' Elemi clapped her hands in satisfaction. 'How does it feel?'

'It feels good.' Ten Six Nine stretched. 'Best it's felt in a long time. You should come to Enntonia City. You would be a welcome alternative to Old Hunchback the herbalist, and your results are better. What do I owe you?'

The woman shook her head. 'No charge.'

'Really?'

'The ingredients belong to nature. They are not mine to sell.'

'But what about your time and expertise?'

'There's no need. I'm glad it helped.' She poured the rest of the ointment into a small bottle and sealed it. 'Take this with you. It should last you for quite some time. It doesn't look much, but appearances can be deceiving.'

Ten Six Nine caught the glint in her eye but chose to ignore any further inferred reference to enchantment. 'Thanks. A fine remedy and at no charge. You should definitely come to the city.'

'Thank you for the invitation. I'd like to go there one day, if I can.'

'Let me show you the way.' Ten Six Nine picked up her longcoat. 'It's the least I can do. I'll take you to the bridge. From there, you just follow the road south.'

'Bridge? There is no bridge near here.'

'The Bridge at Callinduir,' Ten Six Nine replied dismissively. 'It spans the gorge at the great waterfall.'

'Oh, the waterfall.' The woman's tone became hesitant.

Ten Six Nine turned to face her. 'What is it? What's wrong?'

'I know of no bridge, but the folk of Dipper Mill and the surrounding area stay away from the waterfall.'

Ten Six Nine sighed. More superstition. 'Come on, there's nothing to fear. I can't believe you've never seen the bridge before. It's a sight worth seeing.' Nearing the top of the slope, having heard no response, she looked back. The woman had vanished. And there was no sign of the pool.

'Elemi?'

No response. Was she being tricked?

'Elemi!'

Nothing.

Hissing her annoyance, she continued to the top of the climb.

Stopping mid-stride in disbelief, Ten Six Nine gaped at the dramatic change in her surroundings. In place of the ravine, the land had slipped several hundred feet to a flat arid plain.

In the distance, a jagged white mountain ridge sparkled in the hazy sunshine. The Northern Forest and Enntonia's Old North Road were gone, and the bridge at Callinduir was nowhere to be seen.

CHAPTER FOUR

'I think we should go back now, Reen. They might be wondering where we are.'

'You go. If anyone asks, tell them I won't be long.'

The sounds of his disapproval faded gradually as the distance between them widened. Reaching the top of the gravel-strewn slope, she stopped to catch her breath and looked back down. There was no sign of him. She smiled. She loved her little brother, but sometimes he acted more like a nagging parent than an inquisitive fellow explorer.

Eager to make the most of her time alone she forged ahead, her bare feet guiding her assuredly over the rocky terrain. Weaving her way through a field of boulders, some so big they almost dwarfed her, she came to a series of eroded ledges. The rock was dry and offered a good grip. She clambered hurriedly up the short ascent until the ground levelled again.

And that was when she saw it.

A column of rock nearly three times her height, brilliant white in colour and speckled with dashes of silver. At first sight, from the plain far below, she had thought it was a trick of the light; an illusion that might disappear at any moment. Up close, it was more captivating than she could ever have imagined. Drawn to its beauty, she approached it excitedly.

The stone seemed strangely out of place, its appearance starkly at odds with its location. She reached out tentatively. It felt cold to touch. Strange markings were etched into the surface. As her fingertips traced the outlines of the weather-worn symbols, she heard a noise coming from the far side of the stone. A ringing sound, so beautiful, like nothing she'd ever heard before.

She took a deep breath and ventured forward to investigate.

As she rounded the stone, her jaw dropped open in astonishment.

As far as the eye could see, a vast expanse of water sparkled in the sunshine.

Reen's mind raced with excitement.

Could it really be the ocean? It had to be. Clasping her hands together in delight, she marvelled at her discovery. The enormity of her find was staggering. All she knew of the seas and the oceans was confined to the folklore of her tribe.

'Who are you?'

Startled by the unexpected challenge, she spun round to see a blue-cloaked woman striding towards her.

'Who are you?' The woman repeated. 'And what are you doing here?'

Reen's eye darted to the sword swinging by the woman's side. 'My name is Reen...'

'Why are you here? Are you of the Fifteen?'

'The who? I don't understand.'

'If you are not of the Fifteen, then who sent you? Why have you come here?'

Reen fought the urge to panic. Edging slowly backwards, she readied herself to run. 'I'm sorry, I don't know why I'm here. I don't understand what's happened. I'm sorry for disturbing you. I will leave now.' Turning on her heels, she ran back around the stone. Her hopes of escape were quickly dashed. It seemed the ocean was everywhere. She was surrounded by it.

Where had the great plain gone? She turned in frustration. The woman had followed and was standing over her, looking down disapprovingly. Reen swallowed uncomfortably.

'Where am I?' she asked tentatively.

'The Watcher's Stone. And your presence here must be explained. You must come with me. The Warden will want to speak with you.'

'The Warden?' Reen took a cautious step backwards. Panicking suddenly seemed like an increasingly good idea. She was running out of options. 'Who is the Warden, and what would he want with me?'

'He must be informed of your arrival. He will want to know why you are here, and who sent you.'

'No one sent me,' she replied indignantly. 'Why would you say that?'

'You must either have been sent or been summoned.' The woman eyed her suspiciously. 'And we were not told to expect anyone.'

Reen glanced around warily. 'But where are we? Is that the ocean?'

The woman's expression changed to one of surprise. 'The Sea of Lucidity. You have not seen it before?'

'Never heard of it.'

'Then I fear you are not very perceptive. Come; we must go.'

'Go where?'

'The Haven. To see the Warden.'

'Do I have to?'

'Yes.'

Her tone left little room for negotiation. Reen sighed her dismay. 'Very well, but I can't stay long.' The woman stared at her inquisitively. It struck Reen right at that moment that she might just be the most beautiful woman she had ever seen. She wondered momentarily if she was a dark-haired angel, like the ones in the camp-fire tales. She decided against asking. Instead, she nodded and offered the faintest of smiles. 'I'm ready.'

'Good. Follow me. And don't think of running away.'

Reen followed, hesitantly at first, but as they wound their way through a field of lavender, her mood lifted. Excitement and expectation grew in tandem as the adventure unfolded. This was a proper adventure. The best she'd ever had.

The track came to a sudden end as the grassland gave way to a pebbled shoreline. Above the rhythmic sound of the waves, a flurry of birds hovered and cried overhead. The breeze whipped her hair to life. Reen's senses danced with the new sensations.

As they rounded a rocky outcrop, the view changed as the pebbles surrendered to a curving stretch of golden sand. The sand felt soft beneath her bare feet. Her heart soared as she gazed along the beach and out to sea. This place, wherever it was, was beautiful.

Up ahead, on a grassy bank, a grey-stoned structure stood watch over the bay. As they approached, the ringing sound she had heard at the tall stone called again invitingly, clearer, and more beautiful than before. As they drew to a stop, Reen's eyes settled on its source.

Swinging freely in the breeze, a succession of cylindrical metal pipes hung in the lee of the overhanging roof. Knocking gently against each other, they chimed melodically. She listened intently, spellbound by the enchanting sound.

The building was of modest construction; a single storey of grey-coloured stone topped by a grass-covered roof. A row of small arched windows, spaced evenly apart, stretched the length of the building, their balance upset by what appeared to be the only way in or out; a sun-bleached, wooden door.

Reen eyed the door warily. Was she expected to go inside? The idea didn't appeal. As if sensing her trepidation, the woman offered words of reassurance as she opened the door.

'It's safe. You are meant to be here. There is no other explanation.' She stepped inside.

Reen followed hesitantly. They moved along a candle-lit passageway. To her relief, the gloom didn't last for long. As they entered a large circular room, daylight flooded in from above. She looked up in wonder at the blue-skied gap in the roof. An ornamental stone structure at the centre of the room appeared to be a source of free-flowing water.

The dark-haired angel gestured towards it. 'It is customary to drink from the fountain.'

Reen cupped a handful of water and raised it to her lips. She sipped it cautiously. It tasted wonderful. 'It's so refreshing.'

'When you are ready, follow me.' The woman crossed the room and entered another passageway.

Quickly taking another mouthful of water, Reen hurried after her. She'd just caught up when the woman came to a sudden halt as a short, balding man with bushy sideburns and little white whiskers emerged from a doorway to their left.

'Good day to you, Shadow.' He smiled. 'Back from your vigil so soon?'

'Yes, Druan. My day took an unexpected turn.'

'So I see.' The man turned his attention to Reen. He had a friendly face. His eyebrows twitched inquisitively. 'And who do we have here?'

'I found her by the Watcher's Stone. She claims not to be of the Fifteen.'

'Not of the Fifteen? Now, that is interesting.' He rubbed his chin thoughtfully. 'What is your name, child?'

'My name is Reen, and I am not a child. I'm nine. Nearly ten.'

'I beg your pardon,' the man chuckled. 'I did not mean to offend you.'

'That's okay,' Reen shrugged. 'Grown-ups do it all the time.'

The man grinned widely. 'They do indeed. It is a most unfortunate failing.' He adjusted his stance. 'But I am intrigued. Tell me, Reen, if you are not of the Fifteen, where did you come from?'

'The Plain of Elsor.' she replied boldly.

'Incredible!' His face lit up. 'The Aaskrid?'

'You know of us?' Reen's eyes widened with surprise.

'Yes, I do,' he nodded. 'Seyk herders. An old and noble tradition. It is an honour to make your acquaintance.' Reen giggled as he gave an elaborate bow. 'The mystery deepens, and the plot thickens,' he continued. 'How did you come to be by the Watcher's Stone? Can you tell me what happened?'

'I'm sorry, Druan.' The woman interrupted. 'We should be going. I must take her to the Warden.'

'Please, Shadow,' he clasped her by the arm. 'Can I talk to her first? Just for a few moments.'

'As you wish. A few moments more.'

'Thank you.' The little man turned once more to Reen. 'You were saying?'

Reen returned his stare blankly. 'I don't know what happened, I really don't. But before I say anything further, maybe you could explain some things to me. Where am I? How did I get here? And what is this Fifteen you both keep talking about?'

'Splendid answer,' he grinned. 'You'd make a fine diplomat, Reen of the Aaskrid. Begin the negotiations as you mean to go on. So, in a show of good faith, I will endeavour to...'

'You said a few moments, Druan.' The woman smiled apologetically. 'I'm sorry, but we must go to the Warden...' She hesitated at the sound of footsteps.

A blonde-haired woman appeared suddenly from the gloom of the passageway. 'Your Warden is dead,' she announced coldly. Her focus settled on Reen. 'And the girl is in danger.'

CHAPTER FIVE

At the sound of the waves, Sanna Vrai drew to a stop.

She shouldn't be anywhere near the ocean. She'd headed inland from the coast at the old hill fort several hours ago.

Her progress had been good until the mist had descended. It had formed quickly and without warning, hiding all clues of her surroundings.

Certain that her sense of direction could not have led her this far astray, she put her hand to her hair. It felt different, much shorter. A fleeting glance sideways was all she needed.

With her suspicions confirmed, she continued walking. She had drifted between realities; she was certain of it. The mist now concealed all manner of unknown threats to her safety, dangers that might reveal themselves at any moment.

She didn't have long to wait. The sound of voices echoed eerily in the mist. The ghostly veil cleared, as quickly as it had formed. With no time to prepare, she found herself standing only a few paces away from three men huddled in conversation. Two of them were cloaked in blue, a uniform of sorts. The third, the one doing most of the talking, wore a plain black jacket.

Sanna reached instinctively for the handle of her sword. At any moment they would turn on her. She held her breath, poised to defend herself but, to her amazement, they didn't even look her way. They continued talking.

'Find the girl.' The speaker was a black-haired man with a bitter-looking face and a presence that reeked of ill intent. 'She is with a woman. They were seen near the Watcher's Stone.'

'Shadow is on duty at the Stone.' The blue-cloaks exchanged glances.

'Then find her and bring the girl to me.'

'She will already have taken the girl to the Warden.'

'No. That's not possible.'

'What do you mean?'

'The Warden was riding the coastal path above the cliffs. His horse lost its footing, and he fell over the edge.'

'He's dead?'

'He would have little chance of surviving that drop.' The man gestured impatiently. 'Enough talk. Find the guard and bring the girl to me.'

'What do you want with her? Who is she?'

The man scowled. 'You're wasting time. Get it done. Bring her to me.'

Sanna looked on in disbelief as the men dispersed. Not one of them seemed aware of her presence. How had they failed to see her? As she backed away slowly, the ground opened up suddenly beneath her. She landed, feet first, on a stone floor some distance below. She quickly scanned the circular room. It was empty, save for the oddity that stood at its centre. A pillar of shining stone, carved with strange markings, carrying a running flow of water. Looking up she saw that a large section of the ceiling was open, revealing a wide expanse of blue sky.

As her gaze settled on an opening in the far wall, she moved quickly towards it.

The narrow passageway was lit on either side by sporadically spaced wall sconces, each flickering a nod of recognition as she passed them by. Once again, the sound of voices brought her to a stop. She held her breath and listened carefully.

As the conversation unravelled, her options quickly diminished. She knew what she had to do. She stepped boldly from the gloom and confronted them: a small balding man, a blue-cloaked woman, and a young girl.

'Your Warden is dead,' she said grimly. 'And the girl is in danger.'

The man's expression twisted. 'Whatever do you mean? The Warden is fine. I spoke with him last night, just before supper.'

The man had a friendly face, but Sanna had no time for pleasantries. 'The girl is in grave danger.'

'What kind of danger?' The woman's hand hovered over her sword. 'And who poses the threat?'

Sanna eyed her warily. 'Two men wearing the same colours as you,' she replied. 'And a third. He was dressed differently but appeared to be the one issuing the orders.'

'What did he look like?'

'Like the kind who would push someone from a clifftop. I'd say he is responsible for your Warden's fate, and he wants the girl brought to him.'

'Why me?' The girl asked anxiously. 'What does he want with me?'

'He did not say.'

'And we don't know who he is.' The blue-cloaked woman added.

The little man cleared his throat. 'Or where he came from. An arrival at the Watcher's Stone is a rare event. For one to be followed so quickly by another, rarer still. If there is a third, it is unprecedented. We must act quickly.' He frowned in Sanna's direction. 'I will take steps to authenticate your claims regarding the Warden, but the girl's well-being is the top priority. Her sudden appearance at the Watcher's Stone may have triggered this chain of events. Until we know why she is here, we must do everything we can to ensure her safety.'

'I will see to it.' The blue-cloaked woman placed a hand on the girl's shoulder.

'I'm afraid that won't be possible,' the man frowned. 'If her claims are true, the girl is not safe here.'

'Then I will take her somewhere else. Somewhere safe.'

'No, Shadow. You cannot leave the island. Your oath of service forbids it.'

'I will do it.' Sanna's offer came without hesitation.

They both turned towards her. 'You?'

'It appears you have no other choice. I will see that she is safe. I will take her with me.'

'And where will you take her? We don't even know who you are, or where you came from.'

'She speaks the truth, Shadow,' the man conceded. 'She is our only option.'

'But we don't know who she is. Or if she can be trusted.'

The man gave a sudden smile. 'I pride myself on being a

decent judge of character.' He eyed Sanna keenly. 'I believe you. Your appearance here must be connected to the girl's. It is meant to be. Shadow, accompany our new friends to the Stone. I will endeavour to make sense of things here.' He clasped the girl by the hand. 'Reen, you must go quickly. You will be safe. I promise you.' He then turned his attention back to Sanna. 'Things are in motion. Shadow will take you to the Watcher's Stone. From there, fate will lead the way.' He wheeled around quickly. 'Hurry, Shadow. I'd take the direct route if I were you.' The door slammed shut behind him.

Sanna frowned. 'The direct route?'

'Follow me.' The woman took the girl by the hand and entered another of the narrow passageways. Sanna followed closely behind. Turning a corner, they came to the bottom of a stone staircase. 'Up here.' The stairs ended abruptly after only a dozen steps.

Standing on the flat slab of stone, Sanna peered over the edge into darkness. 'What now?'

'Now, we jump.' The blue-cloaked woman pulled the girl close and disappeared over the edge. The girl's scream faded quickly. Sanna took a deep breath and followed.

The fall lasted only a matter of seconds, barely time to prepare for the inevitable impact. To her amazement, the landing was soft. A stretch of golden sand glistened in the sunshine. Sanna leapt to her feet.

Standing by her side, the girl stared up at her, eyes wide with wonder. 'What happened?' Her gaze shifted to the sky. 'How did we get here?'

Sanna shook her head, 'I don't know.'

'Hurry.' The woman prompted them onwards. 'There's no time to explain.'

Leaving the shoreline, they made their way across the grass-covered flatlands. A tall slab of silver-grey stone, set vertically in the ground, loomed suddenly into view.

As they approached it, Sanna saw the striking resemblance to the great standing stones at Sumarren. 'This is the Watcher's Stone?'

'Yes. This is it.'

'Can I go back home now?' The girl's expression was a mix of fear and confusion.

'That depends.' Sanna's response was non-committal.

'Depends on what?'

'On lots of things. We don't know why you are here, or what will happen next. But don't worry, you will return home soon... when you are meant to.'

The girl eyed her suspiciously. 'You don't belong here either, do you?'

'No.'

'Then, why are you here?'

'Believe me, I do not know.'

'Has this happened to you before?'

'Yes. More times than I could ever count.'

'We have company.'

Sanna looked over her shoulder. Two riders were crossing the plain towards them.

'What do we do?' The girl asked anxiously.

'We walk around the stone.' Sanna took her by the hand.

'But where will we go?'

'Fate will lead the way. That's what the old man said.' Sanna turned to the blue-cloaked woman. 'Are you going to be okay?'

'Yes. Just keep your word. Keep her safe.'

Sanna felt the girl's grip tighten as they moved around the stone. The landscape changed quickly and as the great ocean faded from view, the girl gasped in wonder.

They stood on a stone bridge spanning a wide gorge. Close by, a thundering waterfall tumbled down the mountainside before crashing noisily on to the rocks. Sanna drew a deep breath as she took in the surroundings. She almost whispered the words as the pieces fell into place.

'The bridge at Callinduir.'

'Where are we?' The girl looked up at her questioningly.

'Enntonia,' she replied. 'We are in Enntonia.'

CHAPTER SIX

Shadow waited as the two riders dismounted and walked towards her. Raddan and Aksel; both fellow members of the Seers Watch. Were they who the blonde-haired woman had seen talking to the stranger?

'You should not have let them go, Shadow,' Raddan glowered disapprovingly. 'They should have been held for questioning.'

'Druan told me to escort them to the Watcher's Stone,' she replied firmly. 'And to let them go.'

'Under normal circumstances I'd be wary of questioning Druan's judgement,' Raddan sighed. 'But this is a grave matter.'

'The Warden. Is it true?'

'It appears so. They are searching the waters beneath the cliffs, but I hold slim hope.'

'How could this have happened?'

'We don't know.'

'The stranger. The dark-haired man. Was it you he talked to?'

'We know about him,' replied Raddan. 'Aksel was on patrol with Falk when they were approached by the stranger. He claimed to be an envoy of the Messengers. It was he who told them the news of the Warden's fate. Could be he's the only one who truly knows what happened.'

'And most likely he's the one responsible for it.' Shadow

echoed the blonde woman's thoughts. She turned to Aksel. 'What did he want?'

'He said there was a girl here on the island who wasn't supposed to be here. We were to find her, take her to him, and that he would then deal with her.'

'And you believed him?'

'Didn't seem any reason not to. At least, not to start with.'

'Their suspicions grew when he told them about the Warden,' Raddan interrupted. 'They then ignored his instructions. Aksel came to me, and Falk went to the cliffs to help in the search.'

'Where is he now? Did you find him?'

'No, I expect he has gone. Just like the others. But we will keep searching. If he is still on the island, we will find him.'

'Who was the woman?' Aksel changed the flow of the conversation. 'Did she accompany the girl here?'

'No. I was taking the girl to see the Warden. We were chatting to Druan when she appeared and told us what had happened. When Druan said that the girl must be protected, she volunteered.'

'And what made you think she could be trusted?'

'Druan!'

'His wisdom will be in much demand,' Raddan sighed. 'There's nothing more we can do here. Let's return to the Haven and see what news awaits us.'

Sitting on the sand, she watched the sun fire the evening sky with its orange glow as it dipped towards the sea. It was a routine she followed each night before turning in. The calming sound of the water meeting the shoreline and the feel of the cool air on her skin. The quiet solitude of the island. But tonight, her thoughts were troubled. The tranquility of the island had been disturbed. She couldn't recall anyone ever coming here before. Today, not one but three had come. She wondered what it all could mean.

'Druan wishes to speak with you, Shadow.' The voice startled her. She turned to see Aksel standing behind her. 'Sorry,' he continued. 'I didn't mean to interrupt your meditation, I thought you would have heard me coming.'

'No, I didn't.' She got to her feet. 'I was deep in thought.'

'It's been a strange day.'

'You can say that again.' She regretted judging him so harshly. 'About earlier,' she began, 'I didn't mean to...'

'There's no need to apologise, Shadow. I can't believe we were so easily fooled. To think we could have apprehended the stranger right there and then.'

'Best not to dwell on it. Is there any news of the Warden?'

'Nothing yet.' Aksel shook his head. 'The search will resume in the morning.'

'We can hope.' Shadow smiled. 'I'd best not keep Druan waiting. Sleep well, Aksel.'

'And you,' he replied.

'Come in, Shadow.'

She smiled as she opened the door and entered the room. He always knew it was her, before she even had the chance to knock. She'd never been able to understand how he did it and despite her many requests, he had declined to offer any explanation.

'I have a little something brewing,' he grinned. 'Would you like a cup?'

'Of course. What is it tonight?'

Druan sniffed the contents of the pot suspiciously. 'Some herbal concoction.' His whiskers twitched. 'A favourable aroma. Let's see how it tastes.'

They took a seat either side of the wooden table and sipped their tea quietly.

'Aksel said that you wanted to speak with me.'

'Yes, I wondered if you had any thoughts on today's events.'

'Thoughts and questions.' she replied. 'Lots of them.'

'Such as?'

'So many, I wouldn't know where to begin.'

'Unexpected events can have that effect. But if we talk it through, perhaps we can make some sense of it.'

'The most obvious question is, how did they come to be here? If they were not summoned, then why were they here?'

'Do we know for certain they were uninvited?'

'Did you know of their coming?'

'No, I did not.'

'Then that confirms it.' She offered a smile. 'You know everything that goes on here, Druan.'

He grinned in response. 'Not always, it seems.'

'The laws of the island are clear,' Shadow continued. 'None can come here without being summoned. Unless...'

'Yes?'

'Perhaps one of them was of the Fifteen. Obviously not the girl. She genuinely didn't know what we were talking about. But what about the others?'

'A possibility, but unlikely.' Druan eyed her carefully. 'What do you know of the Fifteen?'

'Only what I have learned in my studies.'

'And that is?'

'They are the Guardians of the Gateways.'

'And what of their history? Their origins?'

'Sometimes also referred to as the Wise Ones, their origins lie in an ancient circle of learned minds who discovered that all worlds were one.'

'And what did they do with this newfound knowledge?'

'They pledged to keep it safe, to protect it from becoming common knowledge, at the same time vowing to deny any such claim as heresy.'

'Very good, Shadow. And where did they hide all proof of their findings?'

She stared at him blankly. 'I... I don't know.'

Druan gave a wry smile. 'No. Such information was never to be shared. Their findings had to be recorded so that the knowledge could be passed on to those considered worthy. The Scribes poured their heart and soul into their task, etching the wisdom onto parchment, and when it was deemed appropriate, a destination was chosen; a place where the knowledge could be kept safe.' He leaned in close until his voice was little more than a whisper. 'They hid it here, on the island.'

'Here?'

'Yes,' he replied. 'The scrolls are here. Safe... for now at least.'

Shadow nodded as things fell into place. 'And the Seer? He is the keeper of the writings?'

'Yes, I suppose you might say that.' Druan smiled. 'He formed the Seers Watch to guard the island and to protect its secrets.'

'That is why we are here? That's what we are guarding?'

'Yes, amongst other things.'

Rising from the table, she walked to the window. The moon had appeared, casting its calming reflection on the glass-like sea. She didn't recall a life before the island. It was all she remembered. Playing on the beach as a child, exploring the meadows and valleys, climbing the hills, and scaling the mountain peaks. All the while she tended to her daily routine of study and guard training, fully dedicated to fulfilling her dream of joining the ranks of the Seers Watch. It suddenly occurred to her that in all those years she had never questioned its true purpose.

She turned from the window. 'Then that must be why they were here,' she said, thinking aloud. 'If they weren't summoned, they must have been sent. Sent by someone who knows about the scrolls. The three of them must be connected.' She sat down again and met his stare. 'Who other than the Fifteen could know about the existence of these scrolls?'

His cheeks puffed in response. 'Such a question is beyond my reckoning, but perhaps we are arriving at the wrong conclusion.'

'What do you mean?' she eyed him carefully.

'Perhaps there is some other reason for their coming here.'

'What other reason could there be?'

Druan sat quietly for a moment, as if considering his response. He smiled reassuringly, as he often did before delivering his words of wisdom. 'You said it yourself. None can come to the island without first being summoned. It can be the only explanation.'

'But you said…'

'Forgive me, Shadow. I was merely talking things through. They were summoned, I am almost certain of it, yet I knew nothing about it.'

'The Seer? Why would he bring them here? Why would he put the girl in danger?'

Druan considered this for a moment. 'It is not my place to question the will of the Seer.' He rubbed his chin in quiet contemplation.

Shadow replayed his words in her head. 'You said amongst other things. What did you mean by that?'

Druan snapped back to attention with a jolt. 'Yes, yes. Well, it's not called the Seers Watch for nothing. As you know, before coming to the island, the Seer and his followers studied at Sumarren, where he honed his craft, drafting great literary works of his own. The Scrolls of Sumarren. Some were etched into the great stones that stand guard there, whilst others remained hidden in the underground vaults. The rest, he took with him here to the island. And here they still are, safe under the watchful eye of the Seers Watch.' As he rose from the table, a determined look flashed across his face. 'Come with me.'

Shadow followed. They moved silently along the candlelit corridor. The moon shone brightly through the open roof as they passed the fountain. The sound of the trickling water did little to calm her mood. Leading the way down a short series of stone steps, Druan came to a halt at a wooden door.

Shadow drew a breath in expectation. She'd never been here before. Pulling a key from his pocket, he unlocked the door and motioned her inside.

She gasped as the wall sconces flickered to life. The walls of the room were lined with high bookshelves, each one filled to overflowing with books and scrolls.

'This is it,' Druan waved a hand. 'The Seer's secret horde. With any luck we will find what we are looking for in here.'

'There's so much of it,' gasped Shadow.

'I've documented a lot of it already,' he smiled. 'I've been working on it since I came to the island.'

Shadow's heart skipped a beat. An opportunity to peruse the writings of the Seer. 'I'd like to help,' she tried to hide her excitement. 'If you think I can be of use?'

'I was hoping you'd say that.' Druan grinned. 'We'll make a start tomorrow when you return from your vigil at the Watcher's Stone.'

CHAPTER SEVEN

The forest had wakened to a dusting of fresh snow. As sunlight pierced the canopy, an icy drip fell from the branches overhead. All was quiet, the peaceful slumber of the trees disturbed only by the sound of the twigs snapping beneath his boots.

His breath lingered in the air. It was still very cold but as the daylight gained momentum, the morning frost scampered hurriedly for the shadows. Nearing the old fence that marked the boundary line, Messenger Two Cups drew to a stop. He sensed he was not alone.

'And where would you be off to on this fine morning?' A stooped figure came into view from behind an age-old, twisted pine tree.

'Hello, old friend,' Two Cups beamed. 'What a nice surprise this is.' Bounding forwards, he shook the old man's hand firmly. 'Deelightful!'

'Not all that much of a surprise, Scaraven, is it?' The man gave a roguish grin. The dog accompanying him gave a quick scratch to its hindquarters and yawned.

'And how are you, my good fellow?' Two Cups ruffled the dog's ears playfully. 'Eh? Eh? Looking well, I see. Seems to me you never look any older...' He raised his glance. 'Either of you.'

The man groaned.

'Try telling that to these creaking joints of mine.'

Two Cups snorted his amusement. 'Nonsense, you're both still young pups. This calls for a brew.' He began rummaging for his flask. 'Can I tempt you?'

'Tea? No, I prefer my tipple to be of a stronger variety.' The man dismissed the offer with a frown. 'I saw a man in Farnwaar Forest,' his tone grew serious. 'By the old footbridge. Looked like he might have lost his way. Did you come across him?'

'Yes, our paths met.' Two Cups sipped his tea.

'Did he mention seeing me?'

'Oh, yes, he was quite a perceptive fellow.'

'And what did you tell him?'

Two Cups grinned. 'I told him all about old Breck the Indentation and his faithful companion.'

'And he was content with that explanation?'

'Yes, he appeared to be.'

'Good.' The old man leaned forward on his stick. 'So, I take it you are on your way to meet with the Representatives?'

'Yes, indeed.'

'You know my thoughts on them, Scaraven. I don't trust them.'

'I know you have your concerns but, strange as their ways may seem, I believe their cause to be true.'

'Maybe so, but no man, mortal or otherwise, has the right to deny knowledge to another. That's too much power for anyone, and power corrupts. It's a fact. Old ScriptScratcher had it right. Never give power to those who seek it.'

'Ha! Indeed.' Two Cups chuckled his agreement. 'Oswald D

was right about a lot of things. I'm glad he's passed much of his wisdom on to young Token.'

'Young? He's nearly as wrinkled as I am myself.' The withered features broke into a wide grin. 'How is he? Does he still have his head buried in books and parchment?'

'Yes, as always.' Two Cups hoisted his pack onto his shoulder. 'Still, such is the calling of the Scribe.'

'Studies and libraries,' the old man grimaced. 'Not healthy. I much prefer the fresh air and besides, it's out here that the real knowledge is to be found.'

Messenger Two Cups grinned as they shook hands.

'Take care, my friends, until we meet again.' He patted the dog fondly. 'Here's hoping it won't be too long.'

'We'll meet when we are meant to, Scaraven. After all, aren't you always telling us that time is irrelevant?'

'Indeed, I am, old friend,' snorted Two Cups. 'Indeed, I am.'

CHAPTER EIGHT

The boundary line fence was in a bad state of repair. Years of neglect had taken its toll. At the edge of the Harlequin Forest, it deteriorated further; to the point where Messenger Two Cups found it hard to detect any trace of it. Relying on his instincts, he continued across the open moorland, all the while whistling contentedly, until the ground gave way in a sudden and precipitous drop.

On the far side of the gorge, nestled among the trees, stood the Hall of the Representatives. A terraced structure of blueish grey stone and weather-bleached timber, with towers and turrets aplenty. Two Cups took a moment to marvel at the grandeur of the place. His visits here were now few but the sight of it still never failed to impress. A myriad of windows looked down on him as he began the precarious crossing.

The footbridge spanning the gorge was in no better condition than the old fence. The rotting timber boards presented a seemingly endless succession of alarming gaps, offering worrying glimpses of the river surging noisily through the rocky chasm far below. Two Cups tentatively negotiated each in turn, clinging tightly to the handrails as if they were his very lifeline.

The crossing, nerve tingling as it was, took little more than a few minutes. With his feet back on firm ground, he began the ascent of the stone stairway leading up to the Hall entrance. Once again, he sensed he was not alone. His approach was being closely watched. As he reached the top of the stairs, his suspicions were confirmed. As the great doors swung slowly open, a deep voice boomed from within.

'Enter, friend. If that be your wish.'

With a grin, he walked into the marbled hallway as the doors closed behind him. A little man, shorter even than the Messenger himself, stood waiting to greet him.

'Hello, Shroo,' Two Cups smiled. 'It's wonderful to see you again. How are you?'

'Greetings, Scaraven.' The little doorman rubbed his hands together excitedly. 'I'm well, thank you,' he squeaked. 'It is good to see you again. It's been too long. The Representatives bid you welcome. This way please,' he waved a hand towards the sweeping staircase. 'If that be your wish?'

'It is my wish, dear fellow.' Two Cups hid his amusement at the change in the doorman's tonal quality. Shroo had clearly been given a lesson or two in the art of voice manipulation since the Messenger's last visit. 'Lead on.'

His boots clicked noisily on the polished floor. Again, he felt his movements being monitored by unseen eyes and he knew well who was watching. The Acolytes of Sycamore Glade; the servants to the Representatives. Poorly paid servants, it had to be said. In the pursuit of learning, the little people had given their oath of service in good faith and whilst it could be said that the envoys of the Wise Ones shared some of their knowledge, it was considered scant offerings by many and there was little doubt who had benefited the most from the ill-matched alliance.

The spiral staircase twisted and turned high above their heads as if reaching for the clouds but as they reached the first floor, Shroo stopped and motioned to their right.

'Visitors today will be received in the west wing conference room. This way.'

Two Cups grinned as he followed. Such pomp and ceremony. Today's visitors. As if there would be any other than himself. He chuckled at the thought.

Shroo led him along a grand hallway offering stunning views of the gorge. Two Cups cringed at the sight of the footbridge. From this viewpoint, the crossing looked even less appealing. They came to a stop before a large oak door.

'We are here.' Shroo pulled on the steel latch and pushed the door inwards. 'Follow me.'

The room was bright and airy. Sunlight spilled in through a row of large circular windows on the far wall. Looking up as he walked across the polished marble floor, Two Cups studied the carved wooden beams spanning the high ceiling. Ancient texts: some he recognised, some he did not. A gallery of randomly spaced hangings mottled the brilliant white of the walls, each depicting strange and wondrous landscapes: a pictorial treasure trove of distant worlds. 'Please be seated, Scaraven,' Shroo gestured towards the long wooden table. 'The Representatives will be with you shortly.' He bowed as he retraced his steps. 'We can chat more when your business is concluded.'

Thanking him, Two Cups crossed the room and took a seat. The three chairs on the far side of the table appeared to be elevated. He peered under the table and chuckled. A raised pedestal; perfect for further enhancing a sense of superiority. Beyond the chairs, a second door in the far corner of the room caught his attention. It held his gaze as he toyed with his whiskers. His thoughts drifted. He was just about to reach for his flask when the door opened, and the Representatives entered the room.

The woman seemed familiar, perhaps he'd seen her on a previous visit. Her long blonde hair tumbled down over the shoulders of her dark blue gown; midnight blue, if he wasn't mistaken. Two men followed her. One had a beard, white as snow, that almost covered the entirety of his face and reached down to his waist. His green hat sat propped on his bushy eyebrows. Two Cups liked him immediately but the same could not be said for the other fellow. He was taller and leaner than the first and had a face that resembled that of a wolf. His cold stare put Two Cups instantly on edge. He watched as they took their seats. He'd forgotten how tall they were.
He stifled a chuckle at this. Compared to his own height of three feet and nine inches, most folk seemed tall.

'Welcome, Scaraven of the Messengers.' The woman sat directly opposite him, flanked by her two companions. The blue of her eyes matched the shade of her gown. 'Many days have passed since you last sought our counsel.'

Two Cups drew a breath. It was a typical opening to the conversation. The Representatives always had this effect on him; he felt as if he were being reprimanded. He cleared his throat and composed his thoughts, reminding himself, as he always did, that they were merely representatives and thus perhaps had ideas above their station. A simple thought, he conceded, but one that always helped him address them with more conviction.

'Indeed,' he replied. 'Many days, but it is a pleasure to be here at the Hall once again and I thank you for this audience.'

'I'm curious, Scaraven,' the bearded man interrupted. 'The Days of Thunder prophecy. The Man of the Trees. Did he come through the Harlequin Forest as predicted?'

Two Cups straightened in his chair. The abruptness of the question and the tone of voice didn't match the fellow's laid-back appearance. This one was straight to the point. There would be no need to waste pleasantries with him. 'Yes,' he replied. 'Just as was predicted.'

'And what happened? Did you intervene?'

'I played my part in events, to the best of my ability.'

'And a stirring performance it was, I don't doubt.' The man with the wolf-like face entered the fray sarcastically.

Two Cups bristled in response. This wasn't an audience. It felt more like an inquisition.

'It was foretold that this man would bring answers, Scaraven,' the bearded one continued. 'Was this the case?'

Two Cups picked his words carefully. 'In truth, the Man of the Trees carried with him more questions than answers. However, he had in his possession a scroll and things became clearer when we arrived at Sumarren.'

'You reached Sumarren?' The surprise in the woman's voice lightened his mood.

'Yes, and we managed to translate the remainder of the scroll.'

He paused as the Representatives exchanged glances. 'It told of many things. The Land of Mirrors featured prominently, as did the Woodsman and the Sun Warrior. A fitting twist, given the circumstances.'

'And what circumstances would that be?' The wolf's stare hardened.

Two Cups was unable to hide his satisfaction. 'It transpired that I was with them both at Sumarren.'

The woman's eyes widened. 'They were both there with you?'

'Indeed, they were. Everything fell into place quickly, and then came the biggest surprise of all.'

'And what was that?'

'The Man of the Trees and the messenger from Nallevarr.' Two Cups grinned. 'He was the same person.'

His revelation met with suspicion.

'A brave claim, Scaraven,' the woman challenged. 'Can you be sure of this?'

'Yes, I'm certain of it.'

'And you are certain he came from the Frozen Lands?' the bearded man quizzed. His tone had lost its sharp edge.

'Absolutely! No doubt about it.'

'It makes sense,' snapped the wolf. 'Man of the Trees, Woodsman, both are obvious references to the same individual.' His expression soured as he reclined in his chair. 'And Sanna Vrai. The Sun Warrior.'

Two Cups held his silence as the Representatives conferred quietly. He'd clearly given them plenty to think about.

After a few awkward moments, the woman looked his way

again and smiled. 'So, the writings of the Seer Magister appear to become ever more relevant.' Her tone softened. 'You will forgive our eager cross-examination, Scaraven. You came to us seeking counsel. What did you wish to discuss?'

With a deep breath and a scratch of his forehead, Two Cups gathered his thoughts and began his pitch. 'Enntonia,' he hesitated, 'there was a bit of trouble, nothing too serious, but...'

'Our sources there keep us well informed, Scaraven.'

He frowned at the interruption. The Representatives were on the front foot again.

'Your intervention,' the bearded one continued. 'The illusion. Was such an arrogant display of sorcery really the best way to deal with the situation?' His bushy brows twitched animatedly. 'Was it necessary?'

Fired by the accusatory tone, Two Cups jumped boldly to his own defence. 'With Osfilian on the verge of unleashing the chaos of the Black Wing? And Ergmire's war party on our doorstep? Absolutely!'

'Ah yes, Ergmire. One could easily foresee trouble ahead there.' The wolf passed his judgement chillingly. 'It is likely they will seek reprise for their losses. Would you not agree, Scaraven?'

'I have taken measures to avoid such an eventuality,' he replied. 'I hope that we can resolve our differences diplomatically. My account of events elevated TrollGatten and his men to legendary status, and we all know how much Ergmire love their heroes. However, the responsibility for their demise lies with Osfilian and his confounded Raiders. It is my firm belief that something must be done to eradicate his threat.'

'Really? And what did you have in mind?'

'That is why I am here,' he responded cagily. 'To seek advice. My efforts to thwart him have not always been as successful as I would like. I wish to find a more permanent solution.'

'Osfilian has a role to play in the order of all things, Scaraven,' the woman replied calmly. 'The nature of balance; dark and light, good and evil. Remove him, and you create a vacuum. Have you considered this?'

'Yes, I have. But my mind is made up.'

'And in his absence, you would risk having something far worse take his place?' The bearded fellow appeared concerned by his response.

Two Cups held his ground. 'Fear of what may come can no longer be used as an excuse to do nothing,' he waved a finger. 'No excuse at all.' As his words hung in the air, the wolf-faced man leaned forward.

'Tell me, Scaraven. Where is Osfilian now?'

'Bog-Mire Towers.'

'He is in Bog-Mire?'

'In a manner of speaking.' Two Cups snorted his amusement. 'He's trapped in the realm beyond the mirror which hangs in the old banqueting hall.'

'Was that the best solution?'

'Seemed so at the time,' he pulled thoughtfully on his whiskers, 'but admittedly things were somewhat chaotic. I had to act quickly.'

The reaction from the other side of the table suggested his audience were far from convinced, and the exchange drew to a halt. Another awkward silence followed as the Representatives shared a succession of nods and frowns.

'We thank you for coming, Scaraven,' the woman brought their deliberation to a close. 'Your input has been enlightening, as always. We will retire to consider your concerns further. The Acolytes will provide you with refreshment while you wait. When we have arrived at our conclusion, you will be informed.' They rose silently and in unison.

Two Cups held his breath until the door had closed behind them then got to his feet and paced the room impatiently.

Never in all his visits to the Hall had he been made to feel so ill at ease. No introductions and worse still, no offer of tea to begin proceedings! He tutted his disgust at such neglect in the very basics of hospitality. As he paced and tutted, the door he'd entered through opened slowly and a small figure peered inquisitively around the room. Two Cups greeted the new arrival heartily.

'Hello, Moxi. How are you?'

Shroo's fellow Acolyte closed the door cautiously behind him.

'Are they gone?' he asked in a hushed tone.

'Yes,' chuckled Two Cups. 'They're gone. How are you?'

'I'm disillusioned, Scaraven,' grumbled the little fellow. 'Disillusioned and disheartened.'

'Now, now, we can't have that,' Two Cups patted him on the shoulder. 'What troubles you?'

'Them!'

'Them?'

'Yes. Them!'

'And who might Them be?'

'The Representatives.' Moxi whispered. 'Didn't you notice?'

'Notice what?'

'Evasive,' replied Moxi. 'Quarrelsome too. And they don't like their motives being questioned.'

Two Cups took a moment to ponder the observations and found himself, reluctantly, in agreement. But before he had time to respond, the door opened again and Shroo entered. He eyed them both suspiciously.

'I hope I didn't interrupt?'

'Nope, not at all.' Moxi adjusted his stance. 'Just telling it like it is.'

'Please excuse him, Scaraven. He shouldn't be bothering you with his idle gossip.'

'It isn't gossip if it's the truth, Shroo, and you know I'm not the only one saying it. Perhaps Scaraven could help?' He aimed a hopeful grin in Two Cups' direction. 'Maybe you could put in a good word for us?'

'I'm not sure I follow?' Two Cups raised an eyebrow.

'It's nothing, Scaraven,' Shroo shook his head apologetically. 'I think what my mischievous friend is hinting at is that some of the more impatient among us small folk are perhaps a little disappointed with our arrangement here at the Hall.'

'More than a little disappointed,' fired Moxi. 'They share nothing with us, Scaraven, aside from trivial voice enhancements and such like. Petty pranks, no more. We came here to learn, to gain knowledge. That was why we freely offered our service.'

'And a noble gesture it was,' agreed Two Cups. 'But I have to agree with Shroo. Whispers behind closed doors rarely achieve anything. I'm sure if you raised your concerns in the correct manner, they would listen and take your views on board.'

'Really?' Moxi threw his arms in the air animatedly. 'Let me ask you, Scaraven. Do you feel that they listened to you in an unbiased and helpful manner?'

'Well, um…'

'Moxi!!!' Shroo snapped his annoyance. 'I don't believe it. Were you eavesdropping on the Messenger's audience with the Representatives?'

The little fellow became flustered. 'Well, no… at least, not on purpose. I was… just passing the door… and…'

'Enough!' Shroo silenced the floundering denial with a simple command. 'How embarrassing. I can only apologise, Scaraven. Please forgive my colleague's misguided behaviour.'

Two Cups quickly brushed the appeal aside. 'There's no need for apologies or forgiveness here, dear friends. In fact, I can honestly say that I sympathise with your dilemma, although,' he scratched at his forehead, 'I'm not sure that there is much I can offer in the way of assistance. The Representatives did not appear to be in the most congenial of moods. I'm not sure that my requests would hold much influence with them.'

'They've changed, Scaraven.' Moxi found his voice again. 'In fact,' he glanced towards the door before lowering his voice to a whisper. 'There's some here among us who now question their authenticity.'

'Moxi!!!' Shroo's face reddened. His eyes darted nervously round the room. 'Not here! Walls have ears… and eyes… and heaven knows what else. Ignore him, Scaraven, he has taken leave of his senses.'

'Have I, Shroo?' Moxi scowled his displeasure. 'I'm merely asking the question. Are they true representatives of the Wise Ones?'

Two Cups drew a breath. Shroo was right. You never know who might be listening, especially here. 'Ah, well now, I'm certain such allegations are unfounded.'

'Yes, I agree wholeheartedly.' Shroo waved aside further deliberation. 'Return to your duties, Moxi.' He ushered his friend towards the door. 'You can start by preparing some tea for our honoured guest.' He smiled apologetically in Two Cups' direction.

'Tea would be very welcome. I'm parched.'

A disgruntled Moxi left the room announcing that tea would be ready shortly. 'Will I serve it on the balcony, Scaraven?'

'That will do nicely,' he smacked his lips in response. 'Very nicely indeed.'

Shroo led Two Cups along the hallway and out into the sunshine. 'Excuse his outburst, Scaraven. In his eagerness to learn, he sometimes forgets his place.'

Two Cups chuckled. 'No need for explanations, Shroo. He has always been a slightly overzealous soul.'

'Yes, but that is no excuse for listening in on your audience with the Representatives.'

'No harm done,' Two Cups waved the concerns aside. 'Truth be told, Moxi is not the first to share his doubts about our learned friends with me in recent days.'

'Really?'

'Yes,' chuckled Two Cups, recalling his exchange with Breck in the Harlequin Forest, 'but, with great knowledge comes great responsibility. Such is the burden of the Wise Ones, and you know the old saying, you can't please all the people all the time.'

'A fool's errand.' The blonde woman's silent approach took them both by surprise. 'The Wise Ones,' she mused, 'to my knowledge, the Guardians have never referred to themselves in such a manner. An unwanted mantle, I can assure you, bestowed upon them by others.'

'Indeed.' Two Cups noted his agreement.

'Of course.' added Shroo.

'Forgive my interruption,' she smiled half-heartedly. 'I will get straight to the point, Scaraven. Enntonia troubles us. The winds talk of change, we hear it in the whispers of the trees.'

'Change?' Two Cups raised an eyebrow. 'For good or for bad?'

'The answer to that question has yet to present itself. You asked for counsel, Scaraven, and it is our opinion that Osfilian would be best kept where he is, for now. Until we know the nature of the coming change.'

Two Cups pondered this for a moment. 'A prudent approach, one with which I would be tempted to agree. But we must remain vigilant. Mistakes of the past must not be repeated. Bog-Mire will be protected, I will see to it.'

'Your diligence is of great comfort, Scaraven. Never doubt it. Journey safe, friend.'

'I will,' Two Cups bowed. 'And thank you for your counsel.'

As she took her leave a momentary silence descended on the

balcony, broken by Moxi's return with a fully laden serving tray.

Tea was served to a backdrop of blue sky, sunshine, and birdsong. Laughs and memories were shared, and stories, old and new, were told and re-told. Two Cups had always considered the Acolytes to be among the finest of hosts. He'd spent many happy times with them in the Glade before the great floods had swamped the landscape, forcing them to flee their homeland. When they had re-settled in the woodlands to the east of the Hall of the Representatives, many of them had been happy to accept the opportunity offered by their new neighbours.

As for the Representatives, given their elusive nature, it was said that not even the Acolytes knew how many of them were present in the Hall at any one time.

The sun had disappeared behind a cluster of clouds and the air had turned cool when, having refuelled the big teapot three times, Moxi announced that he would have to return to his chores.

'Yes,' agreed Two Cups. 'And I too should be on my way.'

'Will you be leaving by the footbridge, Scaraven?' asked Shroo as they accompanied him to the main entrance of the Hall.

'I think not,' he chuckled. 'One crossing of that monstrosity in a day is more than enough excitement for me.' He grasped each of them firmly by the hand. 'Take care, my friends, until next we meet.' Pulling the small glass globe from his jacket pocket, he held it up level with his eyes.

'So, destination Enntonia?' quizzed Shroo.

'Yes, but with a small detour on the way. Your tea was delightful, dear friends, and it has reminded me of a very

important task that I have been neglectful in attending to.'
He winked mischievously as he patted his pack. 'My old flask is
in desperate need of a re-charge. A visit to Dipper Mill Forest is
long overdue.'

CHAPTER NINE

'Enntonia. What a beautiful name. It's very pretty here.'

Dragon Slayer Ten Six Nine eyed the young girl dubiously.

'Is everyhing okay?' The girl smiled. 'You seem troubled.'

'Where did you go?'

'I don't know what you mean. I didn't go anywhere.'

'Right.' Ten Six Nine's suspicions peaked. The girl looked very different. This wasn't the same person she'd sat by the pool with. She looked younger, much younger. Her clothes, her hair, her face. Everything about her was different. 'I see you changed.' Her words sounded ridiculous.

'Sorry? I... I haven't changed at all.'

'Really? So, what did you do?' Ten Six Nine scowled her displeasure at being duped. 'Tricks and illusions. Very good. Well, if the show is over, I'll be on my way. It's a long walk back.' Scanning the trees, she debated the prospect of retracing her route back through the woods. It didn't appeal. The deceptive forest, the momentary glimpse of strange landscapes, and now the morphing apothecary; she'd had her fill of the bizarre and the unexplained for the day. The road seemed like a better option. 'Perhaps we will see you in the city one day.'

'Aren't you taking me with you?'

'What?'

'Aren't you taking me with you? You said you would.'

'You said you couldn't go… because of the waterfall.'

'Waterfall?'

'Never mind.'

'So, I'm coming with you?'

Ten Six Nine shrugged. The girl's behaviour was strange, but she had made the invitation even if she was now beginning to regret it. 'If that's what you want.'

The girl nodded eagerly. 'Yes. It is.'

Ten Six Nine waited. After a few moments, her patience dwindled even further. 'So, are you going to take anything with you?'

'No.' The girl frowned and gestured with open arms. 'This is all I have.'

'Really?'

'Yes.'

'Very well, let's go.'

'Good.' The girl grinned. 'So, where are we going?'

'To the city.'

'The city. How exciting. Is it far?'

'A full day's ride, at least. I don't suppose you could conjure up two horses?'

The girl laughed out loud. 'This is going to be such fun.'

Ten Six Nine didn't share her enthusiasm. 'It's different, I'll say that much.'

'I'm Reen. What's your name?'

'Ten Six Nine,' she replied warily. Reen? That wasn't her name. It was something else. But what was it? 'I think we already did the introductions.'

'No, I don't think so.'

'Yes, I'm sure we did. You knew that I was a Dragon Slayer.'

The girl laughed. 'You're funny!'

'Nothing funny about it.'

'You are a dragon slayer? Really?'

'Only in name, obviously.'

'Obviously?'

'It's difficult to slay something that hasn't been around in ages.'

The girl whooped with delight. 'You are so funny. You truly are. This is the best adventure I've ever had.'

Ten Six Nine stared at her with growing unease. 'What did you say your name was?'

'Reen.'

'Reen? You're sure?'

'Of course, I'm sure.' she giggled. 'I do know my own name.'

Despite the girl's infectious laughter, Ten Six Nine wasn't ready to dismiss her suspicions. The girl was up to something. Was it merely a good-natured prank or was it something more sinister?

'Let's get going,' she said dryly. 'It's a long walk. Maybe when your legs get tired, you'll change your mind about summoning those horses.'

CHAPTER TEN

Enntonia's streets bustled with normality.

It seemed inconceivable that the unusual events of recent weeks had been so quickly forgotten. Dragon Slayer Twelve Seven Two found it odd that nobody appeared to want to question the unlikely turn of events, or to even pass comment on the bizarre manner in which they had unfolded.

The High Council no longer held power. They'd been stripped of their authority by the Defender of all Enntonia, a figure from legend and folklore whose sudden and inexplicable appearance had come only days after rumours of impending gloom had spread through the city like wildfire.

In the High Council's stead, the Dragon Slayers were now charged with the upkeep of law and order; an arrangement that didn't sit well with the good folk of Enntonia. Whilst the scowls of contempt and the glares of mistrust were clear for all to see, none were willing to incur the wrath of the Defender by openly challenging his enforced changes.

A mythical figure who, according to legend, had once saved the land from an evil wizard, the Defender was both greatly revered and feared. If he was real, and not some wicked deception, his ability to defy the passage of time was a feat that surely belonged in the realms of sorcery. As unlikely as it seemed, Twelve Seven

Two found it no harder to believe than the things he had seen and heard in the forest beyond the Eastern Gate.

The folk of Enntonia appeared content in their ignorance. He suspected things would be very different if they knew the threat that lurked on their doorstep. Not that he would be the one to tell them. There was only one person he felt comfortable enough to share his experience with, but he hadn't seen her for several days. The nightmares that had troubled him for weeks had stopped, but he knew that the threat was real and that its source was to be found in the Eastern Forest.

Breaking into a gallop, he arrived a short while later at the Eastern Gate. Dismounting, he walked through the yawning gateway and looked up at the age-old towers; the stone sentinels guarding the ghosts of days gone by. If only the walls could talk. What secrets could they share?

The moments passed by in silent contemplation.

Dreams, disturbing as they were, could be easily dismissed, but the fact he had experienced being pursued through the forest by a winged beast, the kind heard of only in myth and legend, could not so readily be denied.

As unbelievable as it seemed, he had seen it with his own eyes. The Slayers gathered at the Gate had seen it too; their shouts of horror were all the confirmation he needed.

Dozens of them had watched on in terror, yet when he had reached the Gate, he found only three were waiting for him, each scoffing their denial and dismissing his claims as ridiculous.

He hadn't imagined their initial reaction. Why then was he the only one to remember it, and what did it all mean?

Returning to his horse, he sighed in resignation. As unsettling as they were, the events of the past were of no real concern. He was more troubled by the prospect of what might lie ahead.

Navigation of the Eastern Forest proved difficult. Here and there glimpses of poacher's tracks offered fleeting moments of false optimism before disappearing from view, concealed by the overgrown vegetation. Guided by the sun at his back, Twelve Seven Two scoured the forest for evidence of his monstrous pursuer. There should have been an abundance of broken trees and snapped branches, but he found nothing. No trail of destruction left in the wake of some thundering apocalyptic beast.

The hours slipped by. Afternoon gave way to evening. As the sun dipped from view beyond the treetops, he came to the forest's edge at Willowbrook. Crossing the river at the wooden bridge, he arrived at the cluster of thatch-roofed cottages.

The balding farrier grudgingly agreed to stable his horse for the night and offered his recommendation for lodgings reluctantly.

The curse of the Dragon Slayer. Despised wherever you went.

'End of the lane,' scowled the farrier. 'Inn is called The Night Owl.'

CHAPTER ELEVEN

The Night Owl Inn was quiet. A welcome change from the raucous nature of the city's hostelries. Sitting by the window, Twelve Seven Two watched the daylight surrender slowly to the encroaching darkness. His stew and ale were served by a young woman of nervous disposition. The guise of the Dragon Slayer often had that effect, weaving its contemptible charm everywhere it went. When the Innkeeper came to clear the table, he offered at least a little more in the way of conversation.

'Your room is ready for you. Room three. Upstairs.'

'Much obliged.'

'Scouting?'

Twelve Seven Two nodded. 'Something like that.'

'Your patrols are regular; I'll give you that. Had two of you in here, night before last,' he hesitated. 'Slayers, I mean.'

Twelve Seven Two caught his gaze. Had Ten Six Nine come this way? 'Was one of them a woman?'

'No. Two fellas. Heading north they were, told them they were wasting their time.'

'And why would that be?'

'Ain't much between here and The Barrens, unless you count fields, trees, and bushes. And besides, if you wanted to know anything about that area, for a price, that fella over there could tell you all you want to know.'

Twelve Seven Two followed his gesture to the slender figure sitting at a table by the fireside. 'And who is he?'

'They call him The Weasel. Doesn't look much, does he? But he's the finest scout this side of The Barrens. You want to know anything about these parts, he'd be the one to ask.'

'Is that so?' Twelve Seven Two rose from his seat. 'I'll have another ale by the fire. And another drink for him.' He crossed the room and stopped by the table. 'Mind if I sit here?'

The lean-framed character looked up from his drink with disinterest. 'I got no say over who sits by the fire.'

'I'm told you're a scout.'

'May be that I am.' The Weasel was well named. His small, rounded face twitched nervously as Twelve Seven Two sat down. The black eyes watched him studiously as the Innkeeper arrived with the filled tankards.

'I'd like some information,' Twelve Seven Two continued. 'I can arrange more drink if need be.'

The man hissed his annoyance. 'I can pay for my own drink.' His jaw gave an audible crack as he spoke. 'You want information? You pay for it with coin.'

'Fair enough.' Twelve Seven Two placed his money pouch on the table. 'What's your price?'

The Weasel's eyes twinkled in the light of the fire. He sat forward as he rubbed his hands in anticipation. 'Depends on what you want to know?'

'The Eastern Forest.'

'What about it?'

'Do you know of any strange things that happen in there?'

'What kind of strange things?'

'I'm paying you for information, not questions.' Twelve Seven Two pulled three gold coins from the pouch and pushed them across the table. 'Is there anything strange about the Eastern Forest or not?'

Spindly fingers reached out to push the coins away. 'Keep your money, Dragon Slayer. I'm guessing you already know the answer to that, otherwise you wouldn't be asking.'

Twelve Seven Two changed tact. 'Okay,' he pushed the coins back again. 'If we both know the answer, how about I pay you for an explanation?'

'You wouldn't believe it.' The Weasel took a noisy slurp from his tankard and wiped his whiskers. 'Then you'd want your money back, and then we'd have ourselves a problem.'

'I'd give my word but I'm guessing that wouldn't hold much sway with you?'

The Weasel gave a short cackle of amusement. 'Only one thing in all Enntonia with a more dubious reputation than the old Weasel, and that's a Dragon Slayer.'

Twelve Seven Two pulled another three coins from the pouch and pushed them across the table. 'In that case we are in good company. I'll double your fee. You tell me what you know, and I'll leave you in peace.' The Weasel eyed the money hungrily. 'Take it,' urged Twelve Seven Two. 'It's yours, no debate.'

The Weasel gathered the coins together eagerly, slipped them into his coat pocket, and took another mouthful of ale. Twelve Seven Two watched and waited. The cunning looking fellow wiped his mouth on his sleeve and cast an eye round the inn before speaking.

'Gateways.'

'Gateways?'

'Yup! The forest is riddled with them. And the land north of Willowbrook, all the way to The Barrens. And beyond, most likely.'

'Gateways to where?'

The Weasel snorted. 'I told you that you wouldn't like it.' He sniffed and rubbed his nose. 'Gateways to anywhere, I'm guessing. But from what I've heard, you've not much control of where you might end up.'

Twelve Seven Two supped his ale. Gateways? He quickly considered the possibilities. Was this the explanation to the strange events in the forest?

'Seems like you've some thinking to do.' The Weasel drained his tankard noisily and rose from his chair. 'If our business is concluded, I'll leave you to it.'

'Can you take me to one of them?'

The Weasel stopped in his tracks. 'Now, why would you want to go to one of them? You want proof?' His features twisted. 'You don't believe me? I knew it. You want your money back.'

'No, I don't want the money back. In fact, I'm willing to pay you more. I'll hire your services. Take me to one of these Gateways.'

The Weasel clicked his tongue. 'Ah, now that might be expensive.'

'Name your fee, I'm sure we can negotiate.'

'That's not what I mean.' The Weasel appeared offended by the insinuation. 'Them things are not easy to find. You can't just walk up to one of them. Problem is, they usually find you… when you are least expecting it.'

'I'll take my chances,' Twelve Seven Two raised his tankard. 'I'm in no hurry, I don't care how long it takes. Besides, you said the place is littered with them. Can't be that hard to find. And I've got the best scout this side of The Barrens guiding me. What can possibly go wrong?'

The Weasel eyed him suspiciously. 'And money is no object?'

'None at all.' Twelve Seven Two tossed a second pouch onto the table. It landed with a clunk. 'There's another ten dragyr in that one. I trust that is enough to be going on with?'

The Weasel licked his lips in anticipation as he lifted the pouch from the table and peered inside.

'Well now, isn't this an unexpected turn of events.' Clutching the pouch tightly in his fist he gave a quick nod of his head. 'It looks like we have ourselves an agreement. I'd suggest we shake on it but as neither of us has a shred of honour, we'd be wasting our time.' He grinned fleetingly. 'You'd best finish that ale and get some rest, Slayer. We leave at first light.'

CHAPTER TWELVE

Token ScriptScratcher, the Scribe of Bog-Mire Towers, frowned as he looked up from his journal. Callers after nightfall were unusual, and rarely carried good news. The knock at the front door came again. Drawing on his pipe, he blew a circle of smoke towards the ceiling and waited for his assistant's response.

'On my way.' Elfin Fingle's footsteps hurried along the hallway. Token watched the candle flames dance as he sipped his brandy. The fire cracked in the hearth. A moment later, following a murmuring of voices, Elfin's face appeared round the door.

'Who is it, Elfin?'

'A Dragon Slayer and a young girl, Scribe.' Elfin replied cautiously. 'The Slayer says she needs to talk to you.'

Token's eyebrows furrowed. 'Very well, show them in.'

As Elfin led the new arrivals into the room, Token took a quick draw on his pipe. 'Be a good lad, Elfin, and alert Mrs Burrows. Our guests look in need of refreshment.'

Standing by the fire, pipe in hand, Token studied his late-night visitors closely. The girl munched heartily on Mrs Burrows' baking, all the while commenting favourably on the wondrous flavours and textures. The Dragon Slayer appeared somewhat less at ease. Seated at the head of the table, she twirled an empty brandy glass idly between her fingers; a glass she had already emptied three times. Her demeanour suggested she was keen to be getting on with business. Elfin Fingle loitered near the door, ears primed, anxious to hear the reason for the unexpected arrival of their visitors. Token smiled at his inquisitive assistant and then turned his attention to the matter at hand.

'We don't often have callers after dark,' he began, 'but you are welcome.' He hoped he was not about to be given reason to regret such words. 'So, how can I help you?'

The Dragon Slayer pushed the glass away and rose from the table. 'We are travelling south,' she began, gesturing towards the girl. 'We met only a few hours ago but from our conversations on the road, it's obvious something strange is going on.' She hesitated. 'I'm not sure how to describe it. The girl says she is not from Enntonia, she says that she comes from another land.'

'And do you believe her?'

'I don't know what to believe. At first, I suspected a deception but too many things don't add up. Things just don't make sense… for either of us. That's why I came here.'

As Token drew again on his pipe, his eyebrows twitched with interest. 'Go on.'

The Slayer picked her words carefully. 'I met her not long after dawn, at least I thought it was her, by the bridge at Callinduir…'

'Callinduir?' Token frowned. 'What business took you that far north?'

The Slayer's expression soured. 'I didn't mean to go there. I was scouting the Eastern Forest…'

'The Eastern Forest?'

Her frustration was obvious. 'Yes and as if arriving there inexplicably wasn't enough, I met a young woman in the forest near the bridge. She claimed to be some kind of apothecary. She made me a potion for my shoulder,' she hesitated. 'We spoke for a short while. I was going to show her the bridge, I turned away for a few seconds and when I looked back she was gone.'

'Interesting.' Token did his best to hide his surprise. 'And then?' he prompted. 'What happened next?'

'The landscape changed completely. It was like a different world. I remember it vividly, but it only lasted a few moments. When everything returned to normal, we were standing on the bridge,' she pointed a finger towards the girl. 'But she looked different.'

'I see.' Token took a moment before turning his attention to the girl. 'And what about you?'

The girl swallowed a mouthful of cake before responding. 'It wasn't me she met in the woods.' She smiled towards the Slayer. 'I'm sorry, but it just wasn't me. I know nothing about potions.'

'Elemi!' The Slayer snapped her fingers.

'Sorry?'

'Elemi. It just came back to me. That was the woman's name. The apothecary.'

'I know of a young woman called Elemi.' Token puffed on his pipe. 'She is well known in some parts for her herbal concoctions, but you shouldn't have found her anywhere near Callinduir.'

'I shouldn't have been anywhere near there either,' the Slayer replied defiantly. 'But that is where we met.' She fixed Token with a stare. 'What more proof do you need that something strange is going on?'

'Something appears to be amiss.' He tapped his pipe gently on the mantlepiece. 'That much is obvious.' He turned his attention back to the girl. 'Tell us more about your recollections of things. If you are not from Enntonia, then where do you come from?'

'The Plain of Elsor.'

'By all the stars!' Token's jaw dropped in wonder. He glanced fleetingly at the girl's bare feet. 'Seyk herders. The Nomads of Aaskrid.'

Elfin Fingle gave a gasp.

The girl's eyes widened. 'You know of us?'

'You know who she is?' The Dragon Slayer pounced on the revelation. 'You know where she came from?'

'I've read of you in books,' Elfin chipped in excitedly. 'I thought you were just a myth.'

'I'm as real as you are.' the girl countered assuredly.

'Where does she come from?' The Slayer's patience thinned.

'Far, far away,' Token marvelled. 'Another world, another plain of existence.'

'Another world?' The Dragon Slayer circled the table. 'What is going on? How can any of this be happening?'

Gathering his composure, Token refuelled his pipe.

'Satisfactory explanations may still be some way off, I'm afraid.' He stretched out a hand towards the girl. 'I am Token ScriptScratcher. What is your name?'

'I'm Reen.' She smiled as she took his hand. 'You remind me of the nice man on the island.'

'The island?' Token raised his brows. 'And what island would you be referring to?'

'The island I found myself on.' She took a biscuit from the plate. 'I was exploring, high above the Plain. I'd found the most beautiful pillar of rock. Taller than me it was, and the colour was amazing. Anyway, next thing I knew I was surrounded by the ocean. Water as far as you could see. It was beautiful.'

'Shifting landscapes again.' The Slayer gave a shake of her head.

'And what happened then?' Token urged the girl to continue.

'A woman confronted me. By the look of her uniform, I'd say she was a guard or sentry or something like that. The pillar of rock was there too, but it looked very different. The woman called it the Watcher's Stone. She took me to a quaint little building by the seashore, said that someone called the Warden would want to see me. Then we got talking to the nice old man and then she,' she motioned towards the Slayer, 'appeared from nowhere. She told us that the Warden was dead and that I was in danger.'

Token's mouth worked anxiously on his pipe. 'Then what happened?'

'The old man said that they had to take me somewhere safe but that the guard woman couldn't leave the island because of her oaths. That's when she volunteered to help me.' She smiled at the Slayer. 'She said she would take me with her… and here we are.'

'How did you leave the island?' Elfin asked.

'I don't know,' she shrugged as she munched on the biscuit. 'We slid down some dark tunnel and landed on the sand near the stone pillar. We walked round it, then found ourselves in the forest by the big bridge.'

'It's incredible.' Token eyed them keenly. 'Do you recall anything else about the island? Either of you?'

'I don't think so.' The girl smiled.

'I don't remember anything about any island,' scoffed the Slayer. 'Far as I'm concerned, I was never there.'

'The girl's testimony clearly implies that you were,'

The Slayer's expression softened slightly. 'With all that I've witnessed in the last few hours, I'm willing to accept that her claims might be genuine. But if I was on that island, why can I not remember anything about it?'

'I honestly don't know. I'm afraid my attempts at explanation would be little more than conjecture.' Token ScriptScratcher had much to consider. He puffed silently on his pipe, drawing deeply, in search of inspiration. Elemi was a familiar name, yet Dipper Mill Forest and Enntonia shared no common connection. They were worlds apart in every sense of the term. The Aaskrid girl and the Slayer's experience on the island raised issues beyond his comprehension. There was, however, one person on whom he could call for help. One person who knew about such things. Token blew a circle of pipe smoke into the air and turned to his assistant. 'Prepare a bird, Elfin. We need to send a message.'

The Dragon Slayer looked at him questioningly.

'Is there sorcery at work here?'

'Sorcery?' Token returned her stare cautiously. 'What would I know of such things?'

'There are some that say you conspire with wizards.'

'Humph! Tittle-tattle and gossip. Don't believe a word of it.' Token shrugged his disapproval as he moved towards her. 'I don't think we have been properly introduced,' he held out his hand. 'Token ScriptScratcher, the Scribe of Bog-Mire.'

'Ten Six Nine.'

'She says she is a Dragon Slayer,' the girl offered knowingly. 'That's why she has a strange name.'

Token smiled at the girl. 'She is a loyal servant of Enntonia and if she has offered you her protection, you have a worthy ally at your side.' With a nod, he turned to his assistant. 'Make ready the envoy, Elfin, and have Mrs Burrows prepare beds for our guests.'

As Elfin left the room, Token turned to the Slayer and the girl. 'You are welcome to stay the night. In fact, I must insist on it. I am sending for help, and my learned friend would be very annoyed with me if I let you leave before he arrives.'

Left alone with his thoughts, Token ScriptScratcher poured a large glass of brandy and settled into his chair by the fireside. As he watched the dying embers of the fire fade, he contemplated the evening's strange twist.

CHAPTER THIRTEEN

'Two Cups!' Jumping the little stream, she bounded towards him and threw her arms around him in a tight embrace.

'Elemi,' he wheezed. 'What a lovely welcome.'

'It's so nice to see you again.' She kissed him on the cheek. 'It's been so long. Where have you been?'

'Here and there,' he chuckled. 'Here and there.'

'How's the flask?' She planted a hand on her hip.

'Well, funny you should ask,' he grinned. 'It just so happens…'

'Then you have come to the right place,' she smiled. 'I have a supply of Silver Birch Tea ready and waiting for you. But first, let's go and put the kettle on.' She took him by the arm. 'You can tell me all about your adventures over tea.'

'A splendid plan, my dear. A splendid plan indeed.'

Two Cups sighed contentedly as they strolled side by side through the forest. 'Ah, the wonder of Dipper Mill. I do miss the old place. You know, it always feels like home.' He grinned as they reached the picket fence surrounding the little white cottage. 'And how is your garden? I trust you are no longer having any problems with the little rascals?'

'Not anymore, thanks to you.' She led him up the path and pushed open the door. 'Let's get that cup of tea.'

'It all sounds such fun.' Elemi bustled at the cluttered worktop. 'Scary and dangerous too, I imagine… but it must be so exciting to visit all those different places.'

Two Cups had been regaling her with snippets of his adventures and travels. 'Yes, I suppose it could be seen that way.' He noisily drained his fourth cup of tea.

'There we go, all done.' She placed his flask on the table. 'All filled up again. Even allowing for my secret ingredient, I still don't know how you make it last so long.'

'Probably the most important trick I ever had the good fortune to learn.'

'I had a bit of an adventure too.' She sat down next to him and refilled their cups. 'I didn't go anywhere, but something very unusual happened.'

'Now, that does sound interesting.' He winked playfully. 'Tell me more.'

'We had a visitor,' she began excitedly. 'A Dragon Slayer.'

'Here? In Dipper Mill?'

'Yes, although she didn't seem to think she was in Dipper Mill. She acted as though she'd never even heard of it.'

'That much is true. She shouldn't have.'

'As far as she was concerned, she was in Enntonia's Northern Forest. She was adamant about it, and I think she was annoyed with me for saying different.'

'How intriguing.' Two Cups considered this for a moment before continuing. 'Did she say where in the Northern Forest?'

'She mentioned a bridge, spanning the gorge at a waterfall.'

Two Cups snapped his fingers. 'The Bridge at Callinduir.'

'Yes,' Elemi nodded. 'I think that is what she called it. I told her that there was no bridge near here, but she seemed convinced.'

'Tell me more,' Two Cups prompted enthusiastically. 'How did events unfold?'

'It happened one day whilst I was sitting by the fairy pool. She just appeared from nowhere. We had a nice chat. She had a sore shoulder, an old injury she said. So, me being me, I made a lotion remedy, I even applied it for her. She said my skills would be well sought after in Enntonia.'

'That would go without saying.' Two Cups smiled. 'But please continue, what happened then?'

'She offered to show me the bridge, as proof I suppose. I watched her climb the slope from the pool and then, when she neared the top, she just vanished.' Elemi pursed her lips. 'She was convinced she was in Enntonia, and she claimed to have never heard of Dipper Mill Forest. It's so obvious now, I don't know why it didn't occur to me before. She didn't mean to come here… did she?'

'It would appear not. You make a fair assumption.' Two Cups hesitated for a moment before continuing. 'Ah, now that is interesting.'

'What is it?'

'I think someone is calling me.'

'Two Cups?'

'I'm sorry, Elemi,' he quickly finished his tea and placed the cup down on the table. 'I'm afraid I will have to cut my visit short.' Getting to his feet, he pulled her into an embrace. 'Thank you for replenishing the flask, my dear. I don't know what I'd do without you. I will come and visit again soon, I promise.'

'What is it? Is everything okay?'

'I expect I'll find out shortly,' he grinned playfully as he opened the door. 'I'm being summoned. Someone is waiting for me at the Cairn of Scaraven.'

CHAPTER FOURTEEN

The track narrowed as it wound its way among the crags. The terrain had changed quickly, the grassy slopes giving way to scattered scree. Moving on foot, they led the horses through the eerie landscape.

Twelve Seven Two scanned the rocks overhead, watching for any sign of movement or sudden change in surroundings. The Weasel had offered little in the way of explanation for the strange phenomenon they sought. His insights were limited and whether this was down to his secretive manner or the fact he knew little about them was anyone's guess.

Content that the lure of coin was enough to hold his guide's attention, Twelve Seven Two followed his lead resigned to the hope that he was not being led on a meaningless search.

The lack of conversation had at least given him plenty of time to consider the possibilities.

The gateways opened and folk saw things that weren't usually there to be seen. That was how The Weasel had put it and, as unlikely as it sounded, it seemed a fitting explanation for Twelve Seven Two's strange experience in the Eastern Forest.

The Weasel came to a halt with a wave of a scrawny hand. A short distance ahead the ground sloped down to a flat area of coarse grass, sheltered from the sun by the overhanging rocks.

'Down there,' he pointed. 'We'll leave the horses here.'

Without waiting for a response, he began zigzagging among the scattered boulders. Twelve Seven Two followed warily into the shadows. Reaching the bottom of the slope, he waited for a cue from his guide. What were they looking for? Was he missing something?

The Weasel sniffed the air suspiciously.

'Heard some tales told about this place,' he began. 'Never seen it for myself mind, but I've heard things.'

'What nature of tales?'

'Folk saw things here, things that just appeared from nowhere.'

'What things? What did they see?'

'The rocks changed shape and appearance. It was as if they were looking into another world, a window if you like. Story goes that one fool, a sheepherder as I recall, was daft enough to investigate and was never seen again.'

Twelve Seven Two eyed the rock face warily. 'And you believe it?'

The Weasel shrugged his lean shoulders. 'I've seen enough on my travels to know my place in the order of things. And some things are best left alone.' He frowned as their eyes met. 'Why are you so interested in all of this? What did you say you saw in the Eastern Forest?'

'I didn't.' Twelve Seven Two ignored the thinly veiled inquisition. His guide had made several similar attempts since their first meeting. Twelve Seven Two wasn't about to share his reasons.

'Fair enough.' The Weasel gave a sigh. 'Problem is, we could sit here waiting for days, weeks even, and see nothing. These things don't have no rhyme or reason to them.'

'Then let's go looking for another one.'

'You sure about that?'

'Yes, I'm sure.'

'Right you are, Chief.' The Weasel gave a sly grin. 'Back up we go. There's a good viewpoint not far ahead. We can make a plan from there.'

CHAPTER FIFTEEN

'Do you see anything?' Twelve Seven Two sipped from his water pouch. The Weasel was squatted by the rocks at the edge of the drop, scanning the rugged landscape below. Pulling his spyglass from his jacket, he lifted it to his eye. Something had caught his attention.

'There's someone down there.'

'What are they doing? Are they following us?'

The Weasel pulled himself to his feet. 'They ain't doing much,' he pressed the spyglass against Twelve Seven Two's chest. 'Have a look for yourself. I reckon it's one of yours and by the looks of it, they're dead.' Twelve Seven Two hurriedly put the glass to his eye. 'Rocky ledge by a stand of spruce trees,' continued his guide. 'There's a cave. Body's lying below that.'

Twelve Seven Two drew a breath. The Weasel was right. It looked like a Dragon Slayer. Handing back the spyglass, he made towards the horses. 'We need to get down there.'

Credit where credit was due, The Weasel was good. He weaved effortlessly among the scattered trees, bushes, and boulders. Negotiating the steep slope quickly, they crossed the flat scrubland and found their target without any difficulty.

But their help had come too late.

Twelve Seven Two gently turned the lifeless body.

'Know him?' The Weasel picked idly at his teeth.

'Well enough.' Twelve Seven Two rose to his feet. 'Who could have done this?'

'I know who did it.' A tall broad-framed figure stepped into view from among the rocks. He held his hands above his head. 'I am unarmed.'

'Strike me down!' The Weasel gasped. 'A boar-man!'

Twelve Seven Two's hand reached for his blade. The Weasel was right again. The newcomer's features left little room for debate. The rough-textured skin; the elongated jawbone, the accented snout, and the stubby pointed ears poking up from the closely cropped mane of black wiry hair. He stood a good foot and a half taller than them. This one was from Ergmire. There was no doubt about it.

'That's far enough.' Twelve Seven Two shouted his warning.

'I don't trust him.' The Weasel hissed as he scanned the trees and bushes nervously. 'I don't like this, Chief. It feels like a trap.'

'It is no trap. I am alone.'

'Don't trust him.' The Weasel snapped. 'To the Hells with this. You can stay if you want to, Dragon Slayer, but I'm not hanging around to get my head bashed in.'

Twelve Seven Two caught him by the arm. 'You're staying. I'm paying you, and I say you're staying.'

'You're not paying me enough for this. I don't recall discussing any danger allowance.'

'Don't worry, I'll make it worth your while.' Twelve Seven Two released his grip and turned to the man from Ergmire. 'You can lower your hands, but don't try any fast movements. What happened here? Is Ergmire to blame?'

'Yes, and no.' The accent was strange, but the words were easily understood. 'They are men of Ergmire, but they are a rogue element. They call themselves the Hounds of Ergmire.'

'Why are you even listening to him?' The Weasel spat his annoyance. 'We need to get out of here, Chief.'

Twelve Seven Two ignored his pleas. 'Why are men of Ergmire here in Enntonia? And who or what are the Hounds?'

'A splinter group, intent on stirring up trouble to gain support for their cause.'

'And what cause would that be?'

'To gain political standing, their aim is to one day seize power. They are led by one called Carlon. He, along with several of his cohorts, claims to be illegitimate offspring of Ergmire's nobility.'

'How many in number?'

'Several hundred and growing, though only forty came here.'

'And you are one of them?'

'I rode with them but am not part of their cause. I was ordered by our High Chancellor, Raust, to infiltrate their ranks and to gather intelligence on their movement.'

'A spy.' The Weasel gave a sneer of satisfaction. 'Told you he couldn't be trusted.'

Twelve Seven Two shook his head and prompted the boar-man to continue. 'Carry on.'

'Ergmire's leaders are concerned about the growing support for the Hounds. I've been working undercover from within their ranks. When I learned of this planned excursion, the High

Chancellor ordered me to volunteer for it. Understandably he wants to avoid any possible confrontation with Enntonia, at least until diplomatic efforts have been exhausted.'

The Weasel snorted sarcastically. 'Might be a bit late for avoiding confrontation now.'

'Why would diplomacy be necessary?' Twelve Seven Two quizzed. 'What crisis needs resolving?'

'Many in Ergmire question Enntonia's account of events surrounding the fate of General TrollGatten and his men. The Hounds are feeding on this and using it to fire their own agenda.'

The Weasel frowned. 'General who?'

The boar-man's tone darkened quickly. 'You would claim to not know the name of our General? The one who fell alongside his men, whilst coming to your rescue? Enntonia's indifference is worse than we thought.'

Twelve Seven Two glowered at The Weasel. Something peculiar was going on and it was obvious neither of them had any clue what it was. It seemed best to keep their thoughts to themselves. He hoped that his scout understood the hidden message in his stare.

'Forgive my friend's lack of respect,' he addressed the man from Ergmire. 'He is only a scout. He spends most of his time in the wilds of the north. He knows nothing of what goes on down here.'

'Yup!' The Weasel chimed his agreement. 'I know nothing.'

This appeared to placate the boar-man. Twelve Seven Two seized the chance to regain control of the conversation.

'How did you get here? Did you ride through The Barrens?'

'Not a chance,' hissed The Weasel.

'No. We rode west from Ergos, Ergmire's capital. Avoiding the wastelands of The Barrens, we then followed TrollGatten's route south.'

'So, what happened here? Was it an ambush?'

'It wasn't planned. It was meant only to be a scouting mission. We weren't expecting to encounter anyone. When the Dragon Slayers confronted us, the situation spun out of control. One of Carlon's hot-headed sidekicks struck him and he fell from his horse. The fatal injury happened when his head hit the rocks on the ground. It was an accident.'

'Wait!' Twelve Seven Two seized on his words. 'You said Slayers. How many were there?'

'There were two.'

Twelve Seven Two paused. The Innkeeper had mentioned two Slayers, it had to be them. 'What happened to the other one? Where is he?'

'The Hounds took him. He is still alive.'

'Where are they taking him?'

'I do not know. I think he is just a bargaining tool, to help them negotiate a safe passage from Enntonia if they are challenged.'

'Nah! I don't like this.' The Weasel frowned. 'Something smells off here, Chief.' He pointed an accusatory thumb at the boar-man. 'Won't your friends be looking for you?'

'My guide makes a fair point.' Twelve Seven Two agreed. 'Why did you come back here?'

'Someone had to stay behind to deal with the body, to hide

the evidence. I volunteered, that way I could see if there was anything I could do to save him. But my hope was in vain. I hid in the trees when I saw you moving among the crags.'

Twelve Seven Two sensed truth in the man's words, but it didn't matter. The Weasel was right. 'If you take too long, they will send someone back to check up on you.' His thoughts shifted quickly to the missing Dragon Slayer. If the Hounds questioned him and realised that he knew nothing about Ergmire's fallen heroes, it would add further fuel to their cause. Twelve Seven Two had to find him before they carried out an interrogation.

He turned to The Weasel. 'It looks like we have a change of plan. He's going to help me track them, and you're going to Enntonia City.'

The Weasel's face twisted. 'And why would I be wanting to do that?'

'Because I said so. You'll take this Slayer's body home and inform the General of what is happening out here.'

'By the stinking bogs of Tonduur I will.' The Weasel crossed his arms indignantly. 'This ain't my fight.'

'Really? You don't want to defend your homeland?'

The Weasel scowled. 'I owe allegiance to none but myself, Dragon Slayer.'

'Then do it for money. I'm sure the Defender will see you are suitably rewarded.'

The Weasel laughed sarcastically. 'You must be soft in the head if you think that fraud in your city is really the Defender of all Enntonia. It just ain't possible.'

'His authenticity is irrelevant. Right now, he's the one holding power in Enntonia, not to mention the keys to the Treasury. Might be in your interest to get on his right side?'

The Weasel rubbed his chin thoughtfully. 'Now, there might be something in that. Might be that you're right.' Nodding his agreement, he gestured at the Slayer's body. 'Fair enough, Chief, but you'll have to put him on the horse for me. He looks heavy, and I'm prone to problems with my back.'

Twelve Seven Two lifted the body onto the horse then pulled The Weasel close. 'A word of warning just in case it's on your mind to ditch the body and run. Make sure you do as I ask. Fail me, and I will hunt you down.'

The Weasel's nose twitched nervously. 'Wouldn't dream of it, I'm hurt that you'd think such a thing.' He tapped his chest. 'Hurts me right here.' With a grin, he mounted up. 'Be assured, Chief. You can count on the old Weasel.'

'I'm sure I can. Stay safe, my wily friend.'

Watching him ride from view beyond the trees, Twelve Seven Two turned to the man from Ergmire. 'The Hounds. Will you help me find them?'

The boar-man agreed without hesitation. 'Carlon and his men do Ergmire a great dishonour. Their presence here has caused much damage. I will help you. We will find them, and I will try to convince them to release your friend.'

'Do you think they will listen?'

'I fear they have travelled too far down the wrong path to listen to reason, but we have to try. Some among them may be regretting the way events have gone and whilst they would never usually dare to challenge Carlon, this might work in our favour.'

He didn't seem at all convinced. He eyed Twelve Seven Two with a look of trepidation. 'I cannot say for sure what will happen if we find them.' He turned his horse with a nudge of his heel. 'They rode north.'

Twelve Seven Two nodded. 'North it is then.'

CHAPTER SIXTEEN

The Sea of Lucidity sparkled gloriously in the sunshine.

From her viewpoint on the crest of the great stone ridge, the water stretched as far as the eye could see.

Sanna Vrai sat by the Cairn of Scaraven and closed her eyes. Calmed by the warmth of the sun on her skin, her thoughts drifted.

Memories flashed through her mind. Scattered fragments of dreams; glimpses of a forgotten past now stirring to life. Visions of home and her loved ones; those gone but never forgotten. Asyllyar, her elder brother. She still clung to the hope that he was alive, somewhere in the sprawling myriad of worlds.

Her thoughts shifted to Taro Brook. They had sat here in the sunshine with Scaraven; strangers thrown together by the twisted hands of fate. What had happened to Brook after they had parted at Sumarren? Scaraven believed they were destined to play their parts in an ancient prophecy. Had events played out in some distant reality as had been predicted? And where was Taro Brook now?

At the sound of footsteps, she opened her eyes.

The approaching figure waved his stick in the air animatedly. With a grin, Sanna jumped to her feet and waved her response.

'It's wonderful to see you again, Scaraven.' She put her arms around him and held him close.

'It is delightful to see you, Sanna, my dear friend.' Taking her by the hand, he motioned towards the cairn. 'My flask is fully charged. Let's rest these weary old legs of mine and enjoy the sunshine.' He patted the stones fondly and greeted the cairn in his familiar manner, as if he were reconnecting with a long-lost friend. Dropping his stick to the ground, he threw his arms open wide. 'Just look at that view.'

They sat side by side as Two Cups poured the tea. 'I have fond memories of the last time we met here,' he smiled. 'The Woodsman, Taro Brook. You were thinking of him?'

'A little.'

The Messenger placed a hand on her arm. 'The two of you shared a strong connection. Do you remember anything about what happened? Did you find him?'

'I don't know. I remember him leaving, when he went back above ground, but after that… nothing. Do you know what happened to him? Have you heard anything?'

'No, not since we parted at Sumarren.'

Sanna nodded, then noticed something in his expression. 'What is it? What are you not telling me?'

'I spoke with him after you left.'

'He came back?'

Two Cups grinned. 'Truth be told, he never left.'

'What do you mean?'

'You remember the bearded fellow?'

'The man from Nallevarr? Yes, I remember. What about him?'

'It was him.'

'Taro Brook?'

'Yes, the rascal. Imagine that, eh? The Woodsman was the man from Nallevarr.'

Sanna took a moment to process the unexpected revelation. 'He gave no clue. I'd never have guessed it.'

'There was no deception on his part. He was no more aware of the connection than we were.'

Sanna held her silence. She had questions she wanted to ask; questions that, for now, would have to wait. There were more pressing things to be discussed. As if guessing her thoughts, Two Cups poured more tea from the flask.

'I knew that you were here,' he said reassuringly. 'I came as quickly as I could. I know that you have your concerns about the Woodsman, but I sense that something else is troubling you. Why did you send for me? What can I do to help?'

Shielding her eyes from the sun, Sanna scanned the horizon but saw no sign of the floating island. It lay hidden somewhere, obscured from view by the haze. 'The Seer's island,' she began slowly, 'I think I've been there.'

Two Cups looked up from his tea. 'Really?'

'I think so. The more I think about it, the more convinced I become.' It felt good to give life to her thoughts, as if hearing the words gave them credence. 'I drifted; I wasn't myself, but I remember everything about it.'

'Never doubt that which you know to be true. Tell me it all, Sanna.'

She quickly recounted the events leading to her arrival on the island. The enveloping mist and the three men who had, inexplicably, failed to see her. The strange access to the underground passageways and the water tower. Her recollections of the events were vivid. The old man, the blue-cloaked woman, and the young girl; the girl she had suddenly felt compelled to save from danger. She described their strange exit from the underground dwelling and their arrival at the Watcher's Stone.

The Messenger listened intently, never interrupting her flow. When she finished, he seemed lost in a trance. His eyes were fixed on the far horizon. After several moments he turned to her, his expression filled with admiration.

'I have never been to the island so I can't say for certain, but there are many correlations between what you've told me and other accounts I've read. I believe that you were at the Haven.' His eyebrows furrowed. 'You say the woman was bound to the island by her oaths?'

Sanna nodded. 'That was what the man said.'

'Interesting. By your description, I think it's safe to assume the woman belonged to the Seers Watch. The Watcher's Stone lies at the north of the island and its purpose is clear.' Two Cups fell quiet for a moment, then continued with a click of his fingers. 'All these things point towards confirmation but one thing we know for certain about the island is that to go there, one must first be summoned. If we are to assume that you were on the Seer's island, then we must ask why? When you drifted you say you weren't yourself? Any clues as to your identity whilst you were there?'

'I know who it was.' Sanna couldn't have been surer of

anything. 'I was aware of her presence once before, in Enntonia. The Dragon Slayer with the blonde hair.'

Two Cups' eyes widened with excitement. 'And where did you drift to when you left the Watcher's Stone?'

'Enntonia,' she replied. 'To a bridge by a waterfall. The Slayer called it Callinduir.'

'Enntonia, I knew it!' The Messenger clapped his hands in delight. 'I don't suppose you recall meeting a girl in the forest, by a pool?'

Sanna shook her head. 'I don't think so.'

'No matter, I have just spoken with a friend in Dipper Mill Forest. It appears the Dragon Slayer,' he hesitated, 'you, are jumping worlds with some measure of regularity. Enntonia has come to the attention of the Wise Ones. They are concerned that some kind of change is imminent there and it has them worried. We have to consider the distinct possibility that Enntonia and the events on the island are connected.' Two Cups took a mouthful of tea. 'In fact, I think it is almost certain.'

Sanna nodded. It made sense. 'How can I help?'

'Your connection with the Slayer is unprecedented. Your presence is already there in Enntonia. All I can ask is that you try to connect with her as much as possible. Let your thoughts become one. Be with her and guide her as best you can.'

'Guide her in what way? What is her role to be?'

'I'm afraid I haven't worked that out yet. Just do what you always do. Use your intuition. I suspect your intervention on the island will have given her cause for confusion. It is likely that she will remember nothing of being there and will be wondering who the young girl is and where she came from.' He clambered to his feet. 'And she is not alone in that.'

Picking up his stick, Two Cups slung his pack over his shoulder. 'To Enntonia, then. By good luck I was on my way there when you called. Once there, I will do what I can to help.'

A mischievous grin flashed across his face. 'I wonder if I'll recognise you?' He reached into the pocket of his faded coat. 'This is going to be very interesting. Farewell for now, Sanna.'

As he clutched the sphere tightly in his hand, his image faded. Seconds later he was gone.

Beginning her descent of the mountain ridge, Sanna Vrai contemplated the task ahead. It wasn't going to be easy. She'd been in the Dragon Slayer's presence long enough to know that much.

CHAPTER SEVENTEEN

The rain had come on without warning, the downpour brief but heavy. When it passed, Dragon Slayer Twelve Seven Two's mood matched the brooding sky. The rolling clouds warned of more to come. Alongside him, the rider from Ergmire scanned the ground ahead with a grim expression.

'Tracking them will be difficult now.' His gnarled hand wiped the rain from his face. 'We will have to rely on the sense of smell. Luckily for you, the snout of Ergmire has its practical uses and is not just for attracting the ladies.' Twelve Seven Two grinned as the boar-man glanced his way. 'My name is Jaakar,' he thumped a fist to his chest. 'Tell me more about the enemy who faced TrollGatten and the Dragon Guard. Where did they come from?'

Twelve Seven Two gave his name and did his best to evade the question. 'We don't like to talk of it. They were a dark force, an unknown enemy who came from the shadows.'

'I understand.' The boar-man looked to the sky. 'Your nation would also have suffered heavy losses, and we all remember the dead in different ways. The fallen heroes of Ergmire have songs written in their memory.'

Twelve Seven Two sighed ruefully. No such glory was awarded to the fallen of Enntonia. 'We were fortunate,' he picked his words carefully, 'that your General and his troops were close at hand, but why were armed men of Ergmire here in Enntonia?'

'A show of force,' Jaakar replied. 'To prompt Enntonia's High Council to settle their debts.'

'Mining debts?'

'Yes.' The boar-man fell silent for a few moments. 'The Governors of Ergos have had time to dwell on their ill-advised plan. Ergmire has paid a high price for their impatience.'

'And Enntonia now has no High Council.'

'I believe matters are now settled. The Defender of Enntonia has dealt with the situation to Ergmire's satisfaction.' Jaakar hesitated for a moment before continuing. 'I'm glad I had the chance to talk to you, Dragon Slayer. You have confirmed what most of us in Ergmire believe. Our great General and his men fell in battle alongside our allies. It is Carlon and his followers who dishonour their memory. When I return to Ergos, I will expose their lies and all of Ergmire will know the truth.'

Twelve Seven Two rode in silence. Whilst he had no option but to lie to the man from Ergmire, the deception did not sit well with him. Questions had to be answered and on his return to the city he would make it his business to uncover the truth about what had happened. But for now, the search for answers would have to wait. There was a more immediate problem to deal with. He had to find the missing Slayer before the Hounds of Ergmire interrogated him.

Jaakar drew to a stop and jumped from his horse.

'The rain has beaten us,' he growled in resignation. 'We've lost their trail.'

Twelve Seven Two dismounted. 'Let's spread out to widen the search.'

'Very well. Don't stray too far. Call out if you find anything.'

The boar-man slipped from view beyond the scattered gorse bushes. He had been gone only a matter of minutes when he called out. Twelve Seven Two found him crouched low to the ground.

'There are tracks here, Dragon Slayer, lots of them.'

'Carlon and the Hounds?'

'Yes.' Rising to his feet, Jaakar sniffed the air.

Twelve Seven Two noted the sudden change in his expression. 'What is it?'

'Riders are approaching.'

Twelve Seven Two scanned their surroundings. 'We need to take cover.'

'There's no time.' Jaakar shook his head. 'It's them. Stand your ground. I'll do the talking.'

The riders of Ergmire presented a menacing show of force as they quickly formed a circle around them, barring any hope of escape. Twelve Seven Two counted a dozen in total. Jaakar had mentioned forty riders. Where were the rest of them? And where was the missing Slayer? He glanced to his left. With no inkling of what was coming, Twelve Seven Two had no time to avoid the blow.

Jaakar swung an arm and caught him in the stomach. As he doubled over, the boar-man kicked him to the ground. His fall met with a chorus of jeers and laughter. Jaakar circled him, revelling in the applause.

'I found another one, Carlon.' he boasted proudly.

Twelve Seven Two stared up at him in disbelief. The Weasel had been right again. It was a trap.

The leader of the Ergmire riders dismounted and stomped towards them. 'Good work, Jaakar.' Grabbing Twelve Seven Two by the collar, he dragged him to his feet. 'We have ourselves some extra insurance. Did you take care of the other business?'

'Yes.' Jaakar replied.

Twelve Seven Two eyed him suspiciously. What was he up to? Why was he not mentioning The Weasel? Was his reaction just a ruse to fool Carlon? Maybe it wasn't time to give up on Jaakar yet.

'Bind this one,' barked Carlon, shoving him to the ground. 'Let's get moving. The others will be waiting.'

Jaakar snatched the rope. 'I'll do it. I'll tie him.'

Twelve Seven Two took his chance. 'What are you doing?'

'I'm taking advantage of the situation,' Jaakar snapped angrily. 'I was willing to help you, Dragon Slayer, but things here do not add up. General TrollGatten was a great leader but a pompous loudmouth. He always ensured that any who came into his company knew his name, yet you and your friend had obviously never heard of him. How can this be? Were the Dragon Slayers there at all, or did the men of Ergmire stand and fall alone?'

Twelve Seven Two shook his head. 'I honestly don't know. But if you let me go, I will uncover the answers. I swear it.'

'Don't take me for a fool, Dragon Slayer. Enntonia will be held to account for its deception.'

'But I thought you wanted to take Carlon down?'

The boar-man bared his fangs with a growl. 'Oh, I do, and I will. His time will come but, for now, Carlon and I share a common grudge.' Binding Twelve Seven Two's hands tightly, he helped him onto the horse.

Jaakar's sudden change of plan was clearly no ruse, but something about it still didn't make sense. 'Why didn't you tell him about The Weasel?'

'I'm keeping my options open. I doubt that your scout will do as you asked. I think he will dispose of the body and deny all knowledge, something you Enntonians appear to be very good at.'

'And what if he does as I instructed? The information he carries could spark a reprisal. Things could escalate quickly. It could lead to conflict.'

'And perhaps that should be Enntonia's fate for their part in Ergmire's loss.'

'You don't mean that.'

'Maybe I do.' Jaakar's expression suggested he didn't care either way. 'If I'm wrong and he carries out your instructions, Enntonia will have proof of Carlon's savagery. It will be his undoing. A public execution in Ergos with representatives of both lands watching.'

Twelve Seven Two wrestled with his binds, but it was a futile effort. Quelling his resentment, he grudgingly accepted the sudden twist in circumstances. He could hardly blame the boar-man for his course of action; had their roles been reversed, he would have done the same.

CHAPTER EIGHTEEN

Twelve Seven Two sensed the growing discontent among his captors. The riders of Ergmire were becoming increasingly agitated. He reckoned they had good reason. The unfamiliarity of their surroundings had sparked his suspicions not long after the first light of dawn. It now seemed beyond doubt.

They were lost.

The ride north had led up into the foothills of the mountains bordering the western boundaries of the disputed lands known as The Barrens. They'd rode through the night.

Not long after dawn, four riders had been sent to scout ahead. As yet, none had returned. Carlon's aim to re-join the rest of his party was evidently not going to plan.

Twelve Seven Two felt torn. Whilst things were obviously not going well for the Hounds, the fate of the missing Dragon Slayer remained unknown. He looked again to the jagged mountain peaks in the distance. He'd no idea where they now were or how they could have become so displaced, but one thing was certain. This was not Enntonia.

Jaakar had ignored him since binding his hands. Twelve Seven Two wondered what the boar-man was thinking now.

The horses slowed as Carlon drew the riders to a halt. Scanning the ridge above them, he motioned one of his riders forward. 'Rangaar, take a rider with you and make for the high ground.'

'I'm not sure that's a good idea.' All eyes turned to Jaakar as he spoke. It was obviously deemed unwise to question their leader's command in such a way. Carlon growled his annoyance at being challenged.

'I'm not interested in your opinion, Jaakar. I want answers. I want to know where the rest of my party is. We should have caught up with them yesterday before nightfall. And now my scouts are missing.'

'Exactly my point,' Jaakar continued edgily. 'I don't think we should risk losing anyone else.'

'And what do you suggest we do?' Carlon snapped. 'Continue aimlessly wandering this forsaken land?'

'We should stay together until we learn more. The scouts could return at any moment.'

'A good plan.' A voice from within the riders grumbled.

'He might be right.' Another agreed.

'Quiet!' Carlon shook a fist in anger. Dismissing the protests, he barked his instructions. 'Rangaar! Take to the high ground and take Jaakar with you. That way he can't spread further dissent among these cowards.'

Twelve Seven Two sensed an unfolding opportunity. 'Your riders are right to be concerned, Carlon.' He gauged their stunned reaction. 'You are lost.'

Carlon of Ergmire bared his fangs in a show of anger. 'I don't recall asking for your opinion, Dragon Slayer.'

Twelve Seven Two stood his ground. 'I'm telling you; we're

lost. Those mountains, I've lived in Enntonia all my life and I've never seen them before.'

'Lies. You expect us to believe that?'

'You need to believe it. It's the truth.'

The groans of discontent echoed louder among the riders. Carlon acted quickly to assert his control.

'Quiet! All of you. Enough of this. Rangaar! Jaakar! Get up on that ridge, find out where we are.' He pointed a finger at Twelve Seven Two. 'And take this one with you. If he causes any trouble, throw him over the edge.'

CHAPTER NINETEEN

Flanked by the two riders of Ergmire, Twelve Seven Two held on to the reins tightly as the ground steepened sharply.

Drawing them to a halt, Rangaar dismounted and growled his instructions. 'We'll leave the horses here. It can't be too far to the top now.'

Stumbling up the slope, his hands still bound, Twelve Seven Two's patience waned. 'Your leader, he doesn't enjoy being questioned, does he?' He caught Jaakar's eye. 'Dangerous when things aren't going well. If you ask me, he's close to losing his authority down there.'

'Silence!' Rangaar turned on him with a snarl. Drool dripped from his open jaw. 'Nobody wants to hear your opinion, so shut your mouth.'

Twelve Seven Two ignored the warning. 'I know your thoughts on him, Jaakar,' he continued. 'This could be your chance. It wouldn't take much to bring him down.'

'Quiet!' Jaakar's warning came too late. The damage was done. Rangaar was quick to challenge him.

'What's he talking about?'

'It's nothing. Just more of his lies.'

'Tell him, Jaakar,' Twelve Seven Two pressed. 'Or I'll tell him for you.'

'Tell me what?' Rangaar moved towards them.

'There's nothing to tell.' Jaakar took a step backwards. 'He's trying to make trouble between us.'

'He's a spy.' Twelve Seven Two taunted the boar-man. 'He infiltrated your ranks at the command of the High Chancellor.'

'Lies.' Jaakar roared. 'It's all lies.'

'A spy?' Rangaar lunged forward in a rage, seizing Jaakar by the neck. 'I've had my suspicions about you all along. Is this true?'

'No.' Twelve Seven Two cut in. 'It's not true.'

Rangaar spun to face him. The anger raged in his sunken eyes. 'What are you saying?'

'It's not true. I made it up.'

'It's not true?'

'No. I just said it to distract you.'

Releasing his hold on Jaakar, the boar-man rounded on Twelve Seven Two. 'I've listened to enough of your lies, Dragon Slayer. I'm gonna rip your throat open.'

Twelve Seven Two stepped backwards. 'Now, Jaakar,' he yelled. 'If you want to survive this. Now!' To his relief, Jaakar reached out and struck his compatriot on the back of the head. Rangaar of Ergmire slumped to the ground at Twelve Seven Two's feet.

Jaakar's face twisted with anger. 'Why did you tell him?'

'Look around you. This is all wrong. I had to do something.' He pointed to the jagged peaks in the distance. 'Those mountains do not belong in Enntonia.'

Jaakar cursed as he stomped the ground. 'You will pay for this. You have turned me against my own.'

'Really?' Twelve Seven Two scoffed sarcastically. 'Seems that you double crossed me first. I'd say we are about even. And as for turning you against your own. Have you forgotten your mission?'

'I should not have struck him down.'

'You heard him. He already had his doubts about you.' Twelve Seven Two held out his hands. 'Untie me, we need to work together.'

'No. How can I trust you?'

'You can't. No more than I can trust you. But our options are limited.'

Hesitantly, Jaakar relented and cut the rope. He watched on guardedly as Twelve Seven Two worked the feeling back into his hands. 'So, Dragon Slayer. What do we do now?'

'We need time to think. Go back and scan the slope below. See if anyone is following us. I'll bind Rangaar.'

Jaakar nodded and did as instructed. With his attention diverted, Twelve Seven Two dragged the unconscious Rangaar to the edge of the cliff. He hated what he had to do next, but he had been left with no choice. As he eased the boar-man over the edge, Jaakar turned and ran towards him.

'No!' He bounded to the edge to see Rangaar tumbling down the hillside. 'Why did you do that?' Striding towards Twelve Seven Two, he shoved him in the chest. 'That fall may be the end of him.'

Twelve Seven Two staggered to regain his balance. 'It was either him or me.'

'Liar! I knew I shouldn't have untied you.' Jaakar held his head in his hands. 'You said you would bind him.'

Twelve Seven Two leapt to his defence. 'How did you think

this would go? He would have thrown me over the edge and that would have been a mercy compared to what they would have done to you.'

'They would not have believed your lies.'

'Your secret would have unravelled, Jaakar, even without my help …'

A sudden volley of shouts and screams echoed from below. Jaakar turned his head. 'What is happening down there?'

'Sounds like the rebellion is under way already.'

'No, something is very wrong. Listen to them. I need to get down there.'

'Jaakar. No!'

Twelve Seven Two's warning fell on deaf ears. He watched as the boar-man bundled his way down the slope, down towards the unfolding bedlam below. Left alone, Twelve Seven Two was free to make his escape. The steep face of the mountain offered no route ahead, there was only one way to go.

Back down to the horses.

The shouts from below ceased suddenly. The silence that followed was even more unsettling. Whatever had happened was over. There was no time to waste.

He descended quickly, his feet sliding down the loose gravel. The horses were gone, scattered by the sounds of the disturbance. Edging towards the cover of the trees, he heard a movement behind him. Spinning round, he gasped in horror.

A rider of Ergmire, barely recognisable, limped towards him. A flap of skin hung loosely, exposing a cracked jawbone and broken teeth. A hole had been gouged into the side of his head.

Twelve Seven Two stepped back as a mauled hand reached out despairingly.

'Help me.' Clutching his stomach, the boar-man of Ergmire fell to his knees. 'The trees…' He gasped for air. 'They came from the trees.' Blood ran from the gaping wound in his midriff. Something had ripped him to shreds.

Jaakar emerged from the trees, followed by two more of the Ergmire riders. Their faces were scratched, and their clothes were torn. They stared at their dying comrade.

Twelve Seven Two's thoughts of escape were now forgotten. 'Jaakar. What happened to them?'

The High Chancellor's envoy threw himself to the ground. His breathing was laboured. 'Something attacked them,' he began slowly, 'killed most of them.'

'What attacked them?'

Jaakar shook his head. 'They are making no sense.'

'They came from the trees,' whispered one of the men. His eyes held a haunted look. 'Appeared from nowhere. We didn't even see them coming.'

'Who? Who came from the trees?'

'They moved so fast,' the boar-man gasped. 'They had no shape or form. They moved like splinters of light.'

Twelve Seven Two struggled to make sense of it. What had these men seen? What had attacked them? 'Jaakar, did you see anything?'

Jaakar shook his head in response.

'I saw their faces.' A third member of the Hounds of Ergmire staggered from the trees. 'Saw one of them, at least.'

He limped forward. The horror of what he'd witnessed was etched on his face. 'Demons!' he spat. 'Demons with empty eyes. Eyes darker than the bowels of the Mines of Ergmire.' Dropping to the ground in front of them, he tore the sleeve from his ripped jacket. 'Demons!' He bound the gash in his leg. 'Nothing natural could move that quick.' He eyed them one by one. 'Are we all that's left?'

'We don't know yet, Garron,' replied one of the boar-men. 'Maybe others survived.'

'I doubt it.' He pulled himself to his feet with a groan. 'No matter. Expect we'll all be dead by nightfall.' He bared his fangs as his glare settled on Twelve Seven Two. 'I see this one is still alive. Why is he not bound?'

'I untied him.' Jaakar found his voice.

'Carlon will not be happy with you.'

'If he's still alive.' Jaakar turned to Twelve Seven Two. 'You say we are lost. Any clues as to how we find our way out of this mess? Which way do we go?'

Twelve Seven Two rolled his eyes. 'Your guess is as good as mine. This is not Enntonia.'

'Impossible.' Garron growled his response.

As unlikely as it sounded, Twelve Seven Two knew it was true. And, though he wasn't about to share it with the riders of Ergmire, he reckoned he knew the explanation for it too. They'd wandered through a Gateway, just like The Weasel had told him they might. Question was, how did they get back?

'I'm telling you; this isn't Enntonia.'

'Then where are we?' Jaakar cut in. 'Are we in The Barrens?'

'Definitely not.' Twelve Seven Two shrugged. 'I've no idea where we are. Reckon our only hope is to go back the way we came.'

'I don't trust this one,' growled Garron. 'We need to get out of here before those things come back and I suggest we do the opposite of what he says.'

A rider mumbled their agreement. 'He's bad luck if you ask me.'

'Yes,' chimed the second. 'Everything's gone wrong since we ran into them.'

'Is that the way of it then?' Garron prodded him in the chest. 'Have you cursed us, Dragon Slayer?'

'Leave him,' snapped Jaakar. 'This isn't helping any of us. He might be our best chance of finding our way to safety. I say we do as he suggests.'

'And since when did you become friendly with Enntonians?' Garron snarled at his countryman. 'Have you forgotten why we came to this stinking hole in the first place?'

Jaakar glanced warily at Twelve Seven Two before replying. 'No, I've not forgotten.'

'Then let's put it to the vote. Do we follow his lead? Or make our own way? If he's a bad omen, maybe our luck will change.'

'You can't let him go free. Carlon won't like it.'

'Carlon's out of the picture. He's probably dead. I say our priorities have changed. Let's vote.' He raised an arm in the air. 'I say we cut the Slayer loose and leave him to his fate. Who's with me?'

It came from nowhere. Twelve Seven Two saw the light ripple

and distort as the invisible assassin ripped through the air.

He felt the rush as it landed among them and began its attack. Garron's cries filled the air as his arm fell to the ground, separated from his shoulder in a spray of blood. The daylight warped again as more of the mysterious force moved from the trees.

Jaakar swung his arms in desperation but, with no visible target, his efforts were useless. The sound of slashing blades filled the air. Garron slumped to his knees as blood pumped from his shoulder. Twelve Seven Two watched on in horror as the boar-man's clothes were ripped to shreds by the unseen blades. As gaping wounds appeared in his arms and chest, Garron of Ergmire fell forward lifelessly. He'd been hacked to pieces in only a matter of seconds.

'Run!' Jaakar struck Twelve Seven Two on the arm. 'Run for your life.'

The noise of the slashing steel faded behind them as they ran into the trees. All sense of direction was lost in the chaos. All plans, good or otherwise, were thrown to the winds.

Twelve Seven Two ran. Tripping and stumbling on the tree roots, pushing the flailing branches aside, he ran until it felt like his lungs might burst. His head was filled with the horrors of the phantom enemy. What were they? Why did they have no visible form? What was he running from? As he ran, the visions from his nightmares came flooding back. Recollections of being chased for his life, pursued through the forest by some hidden assailant. These were no dragons, but had the dreams been an omen?

Had they been a warning of things to come?

The experience of being chased through the Eastern Forest by the thundering monstrosity had been very real. Yet when he had reached the Gate, there had been no sight nor sound of it.

The Weasel's explanation had made some sense of what had happened that day and it was the only explanation that made sense now. It explained why the landscape had changed so dramatically and why they were now being attacked by these other-worldly fiends.

He slowed his pace as the trees thinned. As he entered the clearing, he saw Jaakar and the two boar-men staring in disbelief at their gruesome discovery.

Carlon, the leader of the Hounds of Ergmire, was almost unrecognisable. Impaled on his own spear, his body dangled lifelessly a foot or so above the ground. The right side of his face had been ripped free from his skull. His entrails were hanging from the gaping gouge in his side.

Edging slowly towards them, Twelve Seven Two eyed the trees nervously. 'We need to move,' he prompted. 'Before the same fate comes to us all.' He led the way back into the trees. The boar-men from Ergmire followed without question.

The ground steepened. His legs ached as he clambered up the slope. His heart thumped in his chest as he scanned the trees on either side.

Then he saw a sudden twist of light, a movement in the trees.

'They're here,' he yelled. 'They've found us.'

His warning came too late.

A scream from behind signalled another attack. Looking back over his shoulder he saw the boar-man at the rear crumple to his knees, arms flailing in a desperate attempt to fend off his invisible attackers. His efforts were in vain. His screams ended as abruptly as they'd begun. The whole damned thing was futile. How were you meant to fight something you couldn't see?

'Run!' Twelve Seven Two shouted his instruction. But the ground was too steep to run. Changing direction, he led the desperate charge towards safety. He battered his way through the trees, heart thumping, sides aching, his mind racing. There were only three of them left now. But how much longer could they survive? Escape seemed impossible. There seemed no way out.

As daylight pierced the gloom of the trees, he reached the edge of the forest and came to a stop just short of a steep-sided ravine. Gasping for breath he waited, his eyes fixed on the trees.

Jaakar appeared moments later. 'I can't go any further,' the boar-man wheezed. 'I'm done running.'

'There's nowhere left to run,' replied Twelve Seven Two coldly. 'At least here, they can only attack from one side.'

As the last remaining rider stumbled from the trees, Jaakar walked to the edge of the ravine. 'There's no way across this. We are trapped.'

Twelve Seven Two nodded grimly. Trapped between the gorge and the forest, with only a distance of thirty feet between them and the trees.

'What in the name of all the Gods are those things?' The Ergmire rider gasped.

'I don't know,' sighed Twelve Seven Two, pointing at the trees. 'But whatever they are, they're here.'

It started as nothing more than a ripple in the air.

A blurring of shapes.

The ripple quickly became a wave that rolled ominously towards them. It was a chilling distortion of reality. Daylight danced on the advancing horde. How many were they? Hidden from view, they were impossible to count.

The swirling mass was almost within touching distance when it drew to a halt. The line broke suddenly as a sudden visible flash of steel cut through the air.

The last of the Hounds of Ergmire fell to his knees, his screams dying swiftly as the blades freed his head from his body.

With an anguished cry, Jaakar turned to Twelve Seven Two. 'I will not die like that.' Terror-stricken, he glanced towards the ravine. 'Good luck, Dragon Slayer. If this madness has left you with any sense, you'll follow.' He ran to the edge and jumped.

Twelve Seven Two stood mesmerised as Jaakar of Ergmire disappeared into the abyss. Was this to be his fate? Would he have to make the same choice?

Turning his back on the gorge, he saw the enemy materialise.

Taking form, they emerged from their veiled lair. A guard of tall wraith-like warriors cloaked in grey, standing statuesque only ten feet away from him. Twelve Seven Two drew a slow breath. Jumping into the gorge no longer seemed such a difficult decision to make. There were so many of them, too many to count.

He edged slowly backwards as one of the grey-robed fiends broke rank and moved eerily towards him.

The torn tattered cloak only partially covered its skeletal frame. Wisps of matted black hair hung limply from its balding skull. Its pale-skinned face was stretched and expressionless, its eyes were nothing more than empty black holes. Any semblance of jawbone was long gone; its toothless mouth hung vacantly open. Two narrow slits were all that remained of a sunken nose. Paralysed by fear, he watched the ghastly apparition approach. It stopped only a few paces away. The stench was almost unbearable. A bony finger reached out and jabbed him in the chest. Resisting the urge to throw himself over the edge, Twelve Seven Two held his nerve as the savage leaned in closer.

It sniffed the air suspiciously. What was it doing?

Why was he still alive?

Throwing back its head, the beast let free an infernal piercing screech. Spurred into action by the outburst, Twelve Seven Two threw his hands to his ears and stepped back. The demon followed; its blade held aloft high above its head. Stamping the ground in fury, it unleashed a further volley of screams.

Pressing his hands firmly against his ears to counter the deafening blast, Twelve Seven Two moved back towards the edge of the ravine. As if sensing his intention to jump, the beast swung its blade and launched itself towards him. It moved so quick he had no time to avoid the blow. The handle of its weapon cracked him on the side of the head, and he fell to his knees. The chilling shrieks stopped suddenly as the creature moved closer.

Head spinning from the impact, he looked up to see it standing over him. A skeletal arm lashed out and hit him again on the head. He fell to the ground and saw nothing more.

Dragon Slayer Twelve Seven Two slipped from consciousness with the screams of the ghoulish army ringing in his ears.

CHAPTER TWENTY

The Towers of Bog-Mire emerged slowly from the early morning mist. Crossing the stream at the old steppingstones, Messenger Two Cups paused as the dawn chorus echoed among the trees. His spirit soared with the sound of birdsong. The day promised much. Fresh dew on the grass, the prospect of a new adventure and, best of all, an empty stomach rumbling in anticipation of one of Mrs Burrows' famous Bog-Mire breakfasts washed down with lots of piping hot tea. And if luck was with him, a batch of freshly baked scones might well be awaiting his arrival.

It was a fine morning to be here. A much more enjoyable experience than his previous visit. Two Cups shuddered at the thought of it. It had been the foulest of nights. A night of heavy rain and gusting winds; a night of the darkest deeds imaginable. To think that Osfilian, the Black Wizard, had stalked the hallowed halls of Bog-Mire. He brushed the memory aside. It was foolish to dwell on it. Despite their worst fears, the night had ended favourably. Osfilian had been banished; his threat removed, for now at least.

Amidst a flurry of wings, a raven swooped down from the treetops and came to rest on an old tree stump by the path.

'Hello, Tok.' Two Cups grinned. 'Nice to see you, old fellow.'

The bird responded with a series of guttural croaks.

'You can let him know I'll be there shortly,' Two Cups nodded. 'And tell him to get the kettle on.'

With a ruffle of its feathers, and a short metallic 'toc', the raven took flight. Whistling contentedly, Messenger Two Cups continued on his way.

Arriving at his destination a short while later, he found the Scribe of Bog-Mire waiting to greet him at the main entrance.

'Greetings, Scaraven. Breakfast will be served within the hour. But there's a freshly brewed pot in the drawing room to be going on with.'

'Music to my ears, old friend,' beamed Two Cups, 'music to my ears. Deeelighted to see you again.'

'As I am to see you.' Token ScriptScratcher smiled. 'Let's get you inside for that cup of tea.'

As they entered the drawing room, the fire in the grate sparked to life. 'It's a fine morning,' noted Token, 'but there's still a chill in the air.' He reached for his pipe on the mantlepiece. 'Tok found you by the stream. He sensed that you had important business to discuss?'

'Indeed, I do.' Two Cups poured the tea as Token filled his pipe. 'Are you still on the beech leaf tobacco?'

'Yes.' The Scribe struck a match and brought the pipe to life. 'It's still my firm favourite.'

'I thought as much.' Rummaging in his pack, Two Cups took out a pouch of tobacco. 'Fresh from Dipper Mill,' he grinned. 'Elemi must have slipped it in my pack when I wasn't looking. The rascal.'

'She's an angel, that's what she is.' Token patted the pouch fondly and slipped it into his pocket. 'I'm in her debt, yet again.' Puffing on his pipe, he eased himself into the chair by the fireside. 'So, old friend, you were already on your way here. To talk about the mirror?'

'Yes, among other things.'

'That's a relief, it's been on my mind. I don't mind admitting it. You have spoken with the Representatives?'

'Yes,' Two Cups nodded. 'They advise that Osfilian should stay where he is for now.'

'Really?' Token's expression dropped.

'Yes, they have some concerns regarding Enntonia.'

'And what concerns would that be?'

'They are convinced that change is coming.'

'Change?' The Scribe peered over his spectacles. 'What kind of change? With Osfilian, his damnable Raiders, and that Ergmire business, I think Enntonia has had more than enough excitement lately.' With a puff he blew a great circle of smoke towards the ceiling. 'I know I have.'

'I couldn't agree more.' Two Cups supped his tea. 'But as far as Osfilian is concerned I'm inclined to agree with them.'

Token frowned as his mouth worked on his pipe. 'But is the mirror safe here? We have little in the way of security around the old place, not that we normally need it... but if there's change afoot, it might be bad news and the mirror might be part of it. What if someone has discovered its secret?'

'You raise a fair point. Perhaps we could have the Dragon Slayers keep watch.'

'An interesting thought,' Token nodded. 'And it just so

happens we have one here already.'

'You do?' Two Cups drew to attention.

'Yes, she's upstairs in the guest quarters. She arrived here late last night.' Token blew another circle of smoke. 'That's why I sent for you. She brought interesting news but was asking questions far beyond my reckoning.'

'What kind of news?' prompted Two Cups. 'What sort of questions?'

'She'd had a strange experience; one you will be familiar with. She'd been walking in the Eastern Forest when she found herself inexplicably on the Old North Road at Callinduir.' Token frowned. 'As you know, I'm not well versed in the mechanics of such events. I told her you'd be far better placed to help with her questions.'

'So she's here.' Two Cups gave voice to his thoughts. Sanna's Dragon Slayer was here.

'Yes, and she is not alone. She is accompanied by a young girl. A girl all the way from the Plain of Elsor.'

Two Cups' jaw dropped. 'The Aaskrid?'

'Yes, young Reen of the Aaskrid tribe. She claims that they met on an island, but the Slayer has no recollection of it at all.'

Two Cups could scarcely believe the pace at which everything was falling into place. The Aaskrid girl must be the one Sanna had told him about. 'Two souls from different worlds,' he mused, 'yet destined to meet.' He took a mouthful of tea. 'The Slayer's travels were not just confined to the island. She was also in Dipper Mill Forest. Elemi told me all about their meeting.'

'That's her. She mentioned it last night.' Token tapped his

pipe on the arm of the chair. 'What is going on, Scaraven? What was a Dragon Slayer doing in Dipper Mill?'

'I don't know, old friend.'

'And the island?' Token's eyebrows twitched. 'Do you think it was the Seer's island?'

'A fair assumption.' Two Cups hesitated as he planned his next move. He would speak with the Slayer soon enough but first, he had things he had to share with his old friend. Things he had kept to himself for too long. He drained his teacup and made himself comfortable in the chair.

'The Representatives didn't offer any clues as to the nature of Enntonia's possible impending change,' he began, 'but I'm beginning to have my suspicions.'

'Really? You think you might know what it is?'

'I think I might.'

'But you didn't share your thoughts with them?'

'No, but things have moved quickly since my visit to the Hall.'

The Scribe leaned forward in his chair. 'This sounds intriguing.'

'Token, there are things I must share with you. A tale from long ago that was best kept secret for the safety of all concerned.'

Token ScriptScratcher attended to his pipe. If he was surprised by the confession, he didn't show it. 'As ever, Scaraven, I bow to your judgement in such things.'

There seemed little point in further delay. Two Cups continued with his revelation. 'You will already know that when I first learned that the Black Wizard, Osfilian, had come to Enntonia, I followed, seeking an audience with the King.'

116

'Of course,' nodded Token. 'And the Defender of all Enntonia came to be.'

'Ah yes, but the historical accounts do not tell the full story of what transpired that night. I must confess that the extent of my intervention has never been truly told.'

Token's eyebrows twitched again. 'It's fair to say you have my full attention.'

'Starrin was a good fellow and a fine King.' Two Cups frowned. 'I took no pleasure in my actions that night, but the royal line was ending. Something had to be done.'

'You told him he would have no heir?'

'I had to. It was foretold in the writings at Sumarren. I knew it and I suspected that the dark forces at work knew it too. Osfilian's arrival was no coincidence. I drove a hard bargain that night. I demanded that Starrin gave me the power of authority in Enntonia. In return, I would defeat Osfilian and ensure that one day, when the time was right, a worthy successor would rule his beloved land.'

'And he agreed willingly?'

'He had little choice, given the alternative.'

'But surely… you would have protected Enntonia from Osfilian regardless of his decision… wouldn't you?'

'Yes, but he didn't know that. It was a vital element in my bargaining power.'

Token ScriptScratcher puffed silently on his pipe as he pondered the disclosure. 'This all happened a very long time ago, Scaraven. I can't help but wonder why you are sharing this with me now, unless…' His expression changed suddenly. 'You think the time has come, don't you?'

Two Cups struggled to hide a smile. 'I believe it has, old friend. In fact, I don't think there can be any doubt about it. And unless I'm gravely mistaken, our heir apparent is here, right now, in Bog-Mire Towers.'

Token's eyes opened wide in wonder. 'Here?'

'The scrolls at Sumarren guide us now just as they guided me that night long ago. I read it for myself; saw it with my own eyes. It foretold that change would come with the Guardian of Elsor.'

Token drew a breath. 'The Aaskrid girl.'

'Yes! The Aaskrid girl.' Two Cups sat forward as he clapped his hands together. 'We must prepare. We cannot delay. Synchronicity waits for no man. With the High Council deposed and the Dragon Slayers holding the peace everything is in place, but among the whispers of discontent there are troubling rumours. It's said that a few of the fallen Council members are plotting a return. This cannot be allowed to happen.'

'But the scale of what you're suggesting, folk will take a lot of convincing. There will be vociferous challenges against any newcomer's claim to the throne.'

'A fair point, but one easily dealt with.' Two Cups dismissed the suggestion with a wave of his hand. 'No great obstacle to those of us blessed with a gift for storytelling. It's the greatest tale of all; a kingdom in peril where, in order to save the land and his people from a terrible fate, the king reluctantly makes a pact with a wizard. The wizard comes to their salvation and becomes protector of the king's heir. The queen, who unknown to the realm was with child, is whisked away in secret, thus saving the

royal line, enabling a future heir to return and reclaim the throne.'
Token nodded his glowing approval as Two Cups continued.
'To give the story further credence we just add a generation or
two where necessary.' He stroked his whiskers with satisfaction.
'Everyone loves a good fairy tale, it can't fail.'

The Scribe of Bog-Mire beamed his admiration for the plan.
'I could draw up some papers,' he added enthusiastically. 'It
wouldn't take much work to make them look like historical
records, accounts of the time that were kept secret to protect all
involved.'

'An excellent proposition, Master Scribe. Excellent indeed.'
Two Cups grinned. 'And as we all know, history is written only
by the victors.'

Token ScriptScratcher struck a match and re-lit his pipe.

'We must be careful with the timelines,' he mused. 'The
details may be scrutinised closely. She would be Starrin's great-
granddaughter? Would that be right?' He frowned. 'Or great-
great-granddaughter? Does that add up? My goodness, it's mind
boggling.'

Two Cups chuckled. 'Worry not about the detail, Token.
Remember, the concept of time moves differently in different
worlds. A century here may be nothing more than a blink of an
eye in another world. It merely adds to the wonder of the tale. It
gives it an entirely otherworldly appeal.'

'It certainly makes for a wondrous story.' Token agreed with
a puff of smoke. 'For me, the truth behind it is even more
staggering. A new ruler for Enntonia; the royal line restored to
the throne. A girl from the Plain of Elsor. Who would ever have

thought it possible? And to think she is here, right now, in Bog-Mire.' He paused to draw again on his pipe then glanced towards the door. 'That was the front door. It appears we have another visitor.' A scuffle of footprints followed in the hallway. 'And it sounds like young Elfin is attending to them.'

CHAPTER TWENTY-ONE

Elfin Fingle could scarcely believe his ears. Crouched by the drawing room door, which stood slightly ajar, he listened intently, eyes wide in astonishment, mouth gaping in wonder. Cursing his laziness, he berated himself for not getting out of bed earlier. Moments like these came along rarely.

As was often the case, he hadn't planned to listen in on their private conversation. He'd only learned that the Messenger had arrived and was in conference with the Scribe when Mrs Burrows had sent him to inform them that breakfast would soon be ready. He'd just been about to knock on the door when he'd heard the Messenger talking about the concept of time and how it appeared to move differently in different worlds. About how a century in one reality might seem little more than a blink of an eye in another. If all the talk of other worlds wasn't interesting enough, what followed was even better.

'It certainly makes for a wondrous story.' Token ScriptScratcher agreed from beyond the door. Elfin held his breath as the Scribe continued. 'For me, the truth behind it is even more staggering. A new ruler for Enntonia; the royal line restored to the throne. A girl from the Plain of Elsor. Who would ever have thought it possible? And to think she is here, right now, in Bog-Mire.'

Elfin gasped in wonder. The conversation ceased suddenly. Had they heard him? At the sound of the front door opening, he wheeled round in surprise to see the Dragon Slayer enter the hallway. She stared at him disapprovingly. He'd been caught in the act.

Unable to hide his embarrassment, the colour rushed to his face. With his cheeks burning and without any thought for the consequences, he sprang to his feet and, arms flailing, rushed towards her.

CHAPTER TWENTY-TWO

Dragon Slayer Ten Six Nine sat by the stream, deep in thought. The gentle flow of the water did little to calm her troubled mind. She was torn. Unsure of the best way forward, and how best to find sense in the strange events of the last few days.

She'd wakened early from a restless sleep. Having paced the room until the creaking floorboards had threatened to betray her, she'd looked in on the girl who was fast sleep in the next room and then slipped out into the night. Mindful to keep the silhouetted towers in view, she'd walked among the trees until the first light of dawn had found her by the stream.

Flicking pebbles into the water, she contemplated her dilemma. The one person she knew could help her was missing, somewhere in the Eastern Forest. Or was he?

For all she knew he was already back in the city. Instead of waiting here with strangers, she could be back there, sharing her experience, exploring the possibilities with him.

But what if he wasn't there? What then?

Her own difficulties had started whilst looking for him.

With a sigh, she considered her alternative. The Scribe's response to her predicament had appeared genuine. She liked him. It would be difficult not to. She'd watched his raven take flight from the rooftop before she'd gone to bed, but who had he sent for? A learned friend he'd said, but who was it? Why hadn't she asked him? The answer, like all others, evaded her. Conceding that she was no nearer to a conclusion, she got to her feet and began the walk back.

As she approached the gardens of Bog-Mire, an opening in the conifer hedge caught her attention and a fitting distraction presented itself.

Her circuit of the hedged maze lifted her mood and focused her thoughts. Back at the entrance, she noticed a raven perched on a nearby fence post. It followed her progress with a beady eye as she walked up the gravel path, only taking flight as she opened the front door.

The Scribe's assistant was crouched by a door in the hallway. Turning to her, his face flushed quickly. Waving his arms in a futile protest of innocence, he sprang to his feet and bounded towards her.

'In here,' he hissed. Ushering her into a tiny room, he waved his hands frantically. 'You're not going to believe this.'

'What's going on?'

'You'll never guess who she is.'

'Who? What are you talking about?'

He looked like he was about to burst with excitement. 'The girl you came with…'

'What about her?'

'She's Enntonian royalty.'

'What?'

'I know!' His eyes bulged. 'Isn't it incredible?'

'Hasn't anyone ever warned you about eavesdropping?' she

scolded. 'It's never a good idea. Aside from being bad manners, things get mis-heard, misunderstood, and taken out of context.'

'I swear it,' he protested. 'I heard it clear as a bell. She's to be our next ruler. The Messenger is already here.'

'The Messenger?'

'Yes. Messenger Two Cups. The Scribe sent for him last night.'

'He's here already?'

'Yes, he is in there with the Scribe. They are discussing her right now.'

'Elfin!' A shout came from the hallway. 'Who was at the door?'

'Don't let them know that I told you.' He whispered as he opened the door. The Scribe shot them a look of bemusement as they stepped into the hall.

'It was the Dragon Slayer, Scribe,' Elfin Fingle looked up at her pleadingly. 'She's been out for a walk. I knew that you wouldn't want to be disturbed, so I showed her in there for a moment just until you were ready.'

'In the old broom cupboard?' The Scribe's face twisted. 'Elfin, in the name of the Mire, what possessed you?' He smiled wistfully at Ten Six Nine. 'I'm so sorry. Please excuse my assistant's misguided behaviour.' He waved her forward. 'Come in, come in. There's someone I'd like you to meet.'

Ten Six Nine shot a grin at Elfin as she passed. 'Told you it was a bad idea.'

A peculiar looking individual, wearing a sun-bleached coat and yellow hat, rose from a chair at the fireside. A grin swept across his white-whiskered face. His seemingly jovial personality more than compensated for his lowly stature. He bounded eagerly towards her as the Scribe made the introductions.

'Dragon Slayer Ten Six Nine; and this is my learned friend, Scaraven. The fellow I told you about.'

'Messenger Two Cups.' The little man beamed. 'Two Cups will do just nicely. It is an absolute pleasure to make your acquaintance.'

'Likewise.' His flamboyant greeting took her aback. It was rarely deemed a pleasure for anyone to come into contact with a Dragon Slayer, but he appeared genuinely pleased to meet her. In fact, it seemed he could barely take his eyes off her. 'So,' she began warily. 'You're the one with all the answers?'

'Ah, perhaps not all the answers,' he chuckled. 'I have my limits, the same as anyone else. Why don't you take a seat?' He gestured towards the table. 'The Scribe has been filling me in on things.' He sat opposite her. 'It's an interesting tale indeed.'

'And how do you explain it?'

'You jumped worlds.' His response was direct.

'Jumped worlds?'

'Perhaps drifted is a better term. If truth be told, all worlds are one. Our perceptions of them being all that differs.'

What was that? A hidden reference? If it was, its meaning escaped her. Ten Six Nine gathered her thoughts and returned his stare.

'So, I experienced a different reality?' As unlikely as it sounded, it was an argument she was willing to accept for her supposed visit to the island. 'That might explain some things, but how did I end up at Callinduir when I'd been in the Eastern Forest?'

'A very good question.' The Messenger grinned. 'But, when we drift it is not always just about the where. It is just as often about the when.'

'The when?'

'Indeed.'

'This looks fun.' The voice at the door brought the conversation to a sudden halt.

Ten Six Nine turned to see the girl grinning at them.

The little man jumped to his feet. 'Our gathering has another guest. Splendid!' He waltzed across the room and took the girl by the arm. 'Come join us, young lady. Messenger Two Cups. At your service.'

The girl giggled her delight. 'Two Cups? What a funny name.' She smiled at Ten Six Nine. 'Where did you go?' Without waiting for an answer, she turned back to the Messenger. 'I'm Reen.'

'Of the Aaskrid.' He gave a courteous bow. 'It is a pleasure to meet you. A very great pleasure indeed.'

Ten Six Nine glanced at the Scribe's assistant. He returned her stare blankly. Was there something in what he'd told her? Was there some meaning in the little man's bow? Her attention moved back to the girl.

'So, what did I miss out on?' She eyed them all with a mischievous grin. 'What were you all talking about?'

The room drew a collective breath. Only the Messenger appeared at ease with the unusual circumstances.

'We were discussing your exciting adventures,' his stare was fixed once again on Ten Six Nine. 'Perhaps we can continue over breakfast? I don't know about the rest of you, but I'm famished.'

'An excellent proposition, Scaraven.' The Scribe rose from the fireside. 'Elfin, you can inform Mrs Burrows that there will be five for breakfast.'

As the dumbstruck assistant trundled dutifully out of the room, the girl quizzed the Messenger. 'The Scribe called you Scaraven. But you said your name was Two Cups?'

'It's a long story, young lady.' He held out an arm invitingly. 'If you will allow me to accompany you to the dining room, I will share with you an abbreviated version.' Taking his arm, the girl giggled happily as they left the room.

The Messenger's infectious smile and obvious sense of fun had them all enchanted, Ten Six Nine included. His unnerving interest in her, however, had raised even more questions and given her even more to think about.

CHAPTER TWENTY-THREE

The Messenger held court at the breakfast table. A gifted conversationalist, he kept the mood light and entertaining, assuring both Ten Six Nine and the girl that, when he had filled his stomach and drained the teapot several times, he would endeavour to answer their questions to the best of his ability.

The girl giggled and chattered her way through the sumptuous feed. Ten Six Nine watched her with growing admiration. She was taking the bizarre nature of her predicament in her stride. For now, at least. Quite what might happen if Elfin Fingle's disclosure turned out to be true was anyone's guess.

Ten Six Nine dismissed the notion again. He must have misheard the conversation between the Scribe and the Messenger. She watched them closely, but their expressions gave nothing away. If they truly believed the girl was Enntonian royalty, they were hiding it very well.

The Messenger was a master storyteller, regaling them with his wondrous tales of distant lands and exciting adventures. Until recently, Ten Six Nine would have dismissed most of it as fantasy and nonsense. The events of the last few days had taught her to think differently. The more she listened, the more she wished Twelve Seven Two was here.

As the conversation switched to the subject of different

worlds, the Messenger's attentions centred on her once again.

'As I was telling you earlier,' he smiled. 'All worlds are one; our perceptions of them being the only difference. Your ability to sense the change is obvious; obvious in both of you.' He winked at the girl, then focused his stare again on Ten Six Nine. 'Drifters, as we like to call them, can navigate between realities with differing degrees of control, some becoming very adept at it.' He eyed her studiously. 'Now, to the so-called concept of time. I dismiss it as irrelevant. Drifters can transcend time in the same way that they transcend realities. And that, my friend, is your explanation for your experience at Callinduir. You were there before, and you will be there again.' He smiled broadly. 'I hope that makes sense?'

Ten Six Nine frowned. What did he mean by that? And why did he continue to look at her the way he did? 'A little.' It was a poor response, but it was the best she could muster.

'Splendid! A little goes a long way, I always say.' The Messenger suddenly drew his stare away. 'What about that now, young Master Fingle?'

The Scribe's assistant sat open-mouthed, his eyes bulging with wonder.

'I promised you that one day I would tell you all about the Drifters, didn't I?' The Messenger chuckled heartily. 'And now, here you are, sharing breakfast with three of them.'

Elfin Fingle said nothing. His expression spoke louder than any words ever could.

'Such explanation is simple enough,' continued the Messenger. 'Although the reason we drift is not always so easy to explain and is not always obvious or apparent.'

'What about me?' The girl interrupted excitedly. 'Do you know why I am here?'

Ten Six Nine drew a deep breath. The Scribe almost dropped his pipe with a wheeze, whilst his assistant spluttered a mouthful of tea down the front of his shirt. Reen giggled at the reaction. The Messenger appeared to be the only one unaffected by her outburst.

'It just so happens that I do,' he replied boldly. He turned his beady eyes on Ten Six Nine once again. 'And I suspect that I know why you came to her aid.'

A silence descended on the room as the Messenger drained his teacup. 'With everyone's permission, I would like to continue my deliberations with young Reen in private. Despite her buoyant mood, this must all be a very daunting experience for her.'

'Of course, Scaraven.' Token ScriptScratcher got to his feet. 'Might I suggest my study? On the first floor, you know the way?'

'I do indeed,' grinned the Messenger. 'Your study will be just perfect. Come along, young lady. Let's go and have a chat. See if we can make some sense of all this for you.'

Ten Six Nine got to her feet as they left the room. The Scribe's assistant stared at her in awe.

'I think I will finish this pipe in the drawing room.' The Scribe headed towards the door. 'You're welcome to join me, Ten Six Nine. I expect he will want to talk to you afterwards. Elfin, you can assist Mrs Burrows with the dishes.'

'I'll give him some help,' Ten Six Nine replied quickly. 'Then

I'll join you.'

'Very well.' The Scribe closed the door as he went out.

'I told you.' Elfin Fingle's face flushed. 'I bet that's what they have gone to talk about. The Messenger is going to tell her now. Do you think she knows anything about it?'

'I doubt it.' Ten Six Nine shook her head. 'And for what it's worth, I still think you've got it wrong.' The Scribe's assistant shrugged his dismissal and despite herself, as she helped him clear the table, her thoughts raced with questions. Was Reen the new ruler? If so, where had the royal line been all this time and why? And why was it being restored now? It soon became clear that she wasn't the only one with a lot on her mind.

'Oh, this is purgatory,' Elfin groaned. 'I wonder what they're saying now.'

She couldn't help but grin at his pained expression. 'You'd give anything to be in that room right now, wouldn't you?'

'Anything,' he grinned in return. 'Absolutely anything!'

With the table cleared, she left him to his chores and went into the hallway. As she neared the drawing room door, she saw the Messenger and the girl coming down the stairs.

'Aha, there you are.' His face lit up. 'I fancy some fresh air. Would you like to join me in the garden?'

'Yes. I suppose so.'

'Splendid!'

Ten Six Nine glanced at the girl as she passed. She seemed a little subdued. 'Are you okay?'

'Yes, thank you.' She offered a smile.

Less than convinced by the girl's response, Ten Six Nine

followed the Messenger outside. They sat side by side on a bench under a rustic archway.

'Is she all right?'

'Eh? What?'

'Reen, is she okay?'

'Oh, yes, she'll be fine,' he smiled. 'She has good friends around her.' He hesitated as if to emphasise his point. 'Much has happened to her in a very short space of time. It's a lot to take in, especially for one so young, but she is coping admirably. I've reassured her that everything will fall into place soon.'

Ten Six Nine held her breath. Did that mean what she thought it might? She waited silently. Was he going to share the revelation with her?

'I'm afraid I must ask something of you,' he watched her keenly as he continued. 'Something vitally important.'

Ten Six Nine felt her pulse quicken. 'What is it?'

'I must take my leave, there is something I have to do. I'll only be gone for a few days. I've made arrangements with the Scribe. Reen has a very important role to play in all our futures. She will stay at Bog-Mire until I return. It is safe here, but I'd feel even more at ease if I knew you were here too. Will you do that? Will you stay and watch over her while I am gone?'

Ten Six Nine hesitated. She had business of her own to deal with.

'I know it's a lot to ask,' he continued. 'I wish I could tell you more, and I will when I return.' He grasped her by the hand and held it firmly. 'Will you watch over her?'

Did she even have a choice?

'Yes,' she replied.

'Splendid.' He winked. 'I knew I could count on you. Enntonia is in your debt, as am I.' With a grin he jumped to his feet. 'Will you say goodbye to the Scribe for me?'

'You're not going to tell him you're leaving?'

'Oh, no, no,' he grinned. 'It won't come as any surprise to him. He is well accustomed to my comings and goings. Besides, I'll not be gone for long.' He hesitated as he turned. 'Oh, one more thing.'

'Yes?'

'Don't, under any circumstances, let those two young rascals anywhere near the banqueting room.'

'The banqueting room?'

'Yes. Young Fingle knows that it is out of bounds, but he can be a mischievous fellow and may well look for ways to entertain his guest.'

'Right. I'll make sure they don't go there.'

'Splendid! It's been delightful meeting you,' he beamed. 'Deelightful.'

Having offered her own goodbye, Ten Six Nine watched as he crossed the stream. At the forest's edge he waved farewell with his stick and merged with the trees.

Suddenly everything seemed so quiet. His absence created an unmistakable void. She liked him. It seemed everyone did. And there was something strangely familiar about him. Something she couldn't quite place. Something that made her feel like she could have told him anything. She'd thought about it but had resisted.

Her guard was up. These were strange times and not everyone

could be taken at face value. And besides, he hadn't been willing to share everything with her either. The truth would have been helpful. The next few days would be difficult enough as it was.

CHAPTER TWENTY-FOUR

Didn't seem like much had changed in the city of Enntonia since the last time he'd been here. There was no great surprise in that. In his experience, these places rarely changed and when they did it was never for the better. People, that was the problem. Too many of them gathered together in one place was bad news. Breed like rats they would. He didn't like rats, and he wasn't much keen on people either. Except those with money, he could always make allowances for them.

Nope, he didn't like crowds and this place was far too busy for his liking. Not a good environment for a fellow of his unsociable tendencies. As he rode further into the mire, the disapproving glances and gestures of unease increased. Still, riding into town with a corpse on the back of your horse was one sure way to draw attention to yourself.

Why had he let himself be talked into such a predicament? He shouldn't even be here. He should have left the body out there in the wilds. But here he was, carrying out the Dragon Slayer's instructions. What a damnable time to sprout a conscience. The least he could hope for was that it would end up with him being financially well rewarded for his troubles.

As he neared the old High Council chambers, he drew to a halt as two Dragon Slayers stepped out in front of him.

'Stop right there.' They eyed him suspiciously. 'What business brings you here?'

The Weasel held up his hands in a gesture of goodwill. 'Got a friend of yours with me,' he gestured over his shoulder. 'Who's in charge here?'

'Is he dead?' They approached warily.

The Weasel rolled his gums. 'Well, he ain't saying much. It's been a one-sided conversation all the way here and that's for sure.'

'What happened to him? Where did you find him?'

'No offence, but I reckon we'll all save ourselves a lot of time and trouble if you just take me to someone in charge.' The Weasel's jaw gave a crack as he sighed his disinterest. 'Is the Defender around?'

One Slayer gave a scornful sigh as the other circled the horse and quickly examined the body. 'There's no pulse.'

'Yup, that would do it.' The Weasel rubbed his nose. 'So, are we going to see someone in charge or not?'

The Slayers deliberated for a moment before consenting. 'Come with us,' nodded one. 'The General will be at The Twelve Bells.'

A small crowd was gathered outside the tavern. A big-framed drunkard was holding court, waving a pitcher of ale animatedly in the air.

'That your General?' scoffed The Weasel.

'That's him.'

'Right you are, let's get on with it.' He slid from the saddle and led his horse through the crowd. 'Move aside, folks. Make way for the dead.'

'What's the meaning of this?' The General's glare landed on him. 'What's going on here?' The crowd parted. The General's ale spilled free as he lunged forward towards the horse. 'Hells! What happened to him? Who did this?'

Dropping the reins, The Weasel was quick to distance himself from blame. 'Just so we're clear, I'd nothing to do with it.'

'So, who is responsible?'

'Well, for want of a better word; the misbegotten of Ergmire.'

'Misbegotten?' The General scowled. 'Of Ergmire?'

'Yup!'

'And how would you come to know this?'

The Weasel offered his explanation carefully. 'Stumbled upon one of them as he was about to dispose of the body.'

'Ergmire killed one of our own?' The General's face reddened. 'In our own lands? This will not stand.'

The mood of the gathering quickly turned hostile.

'Whoa! Hold on now!' The Weasel threw his hands in the air and appealed for calm. 'Before we all start polishing the armour and drawing up the battle plans, hear me out.' War. Hells, the last thing he wanted was Willowbrook being turned into a battleground. 'The riders responsible are a rogue element, working without the knowledge of Ergmire's government. They call themselves the Hounds. The one I talked with was trying to bring them down.' He gestured at the Slayer's body. 'This was an accident. Things just got out of hand.'

The General loomed over him menacingly. 'And where would this rider of Ergmire be now?'

The Weasel gave a sly grin. 'He was last seen riding into the wilds, north of Willowbrook.'

'You let him go?'

'Oh, he wasn't alone. He rode north with one of your lot.'

'A Dragon Slayer?'

'Yup!'

'It sounds right, General.' The Slayer standing next to them cut in. 'I sent two of them out on patrol, day before last.'

'Nope, not him,' sighed The Weasel. 'That one was taken captive by the riders of Ergmire.'

'Taken captive?' The General looked ready to explode. The veins on his neck bulged. 'This is an outrage.'

'Who was the other Slayer?' The General's sidekick pointed accusingly.

'Didn't get his name,' shrugged The Weasel. 'Not that I'd remember anyway. All that numbers. Damned confusing.'

'Well, what did he look like?' The General's tone grew darker still.

'Dark-haired fella he was. Held a distant look in his eye. Kind of vacant expression, like his mind was elsewhere. You know what I mean?'

The General slapped a hand to his forehead. 'Twelve Seven Two! In all the Hells! What's that clown up to now?' He turned to his second in command. 'Assemble a group of riders. Twenty, no more. Ride north. Find Twelve Seven Two and find out what's going on.'

'And the Ergmire riders. What do we do with them if we find them?'

The General threw his arms in the air. 'Use your discretion. Take them back for questioning if you can. If they resist… do whatever you need to. Just get it done.' He pointed angrily at The Weasel. 'And take this one with you. He'll show you the way.'

The Weasel drew a sharp breath at the unwelcome twist. 'Well now, the services of a guide? That could be expensive and besides, I'm a busy man.'

The General bared his teeth in a show of aggression. 'Enntonia thanks you for your service. How does that sound?'

'Not quite what I had in mind.'

The General's expression changed quickly. Grinning widely, he placed an arm around The Weasel's shoulder. 'I like you. Try not to get yourself killed out there.' Turning to the crowd, he roared his instructions. 'Would someone get that body down from that horse? Show some respect. And in the name of the Fallen Kings, someone get me another ale.'

In the ensuing confusion, The Weasel merged with the crowd and made his escape.

Finding a quiet alehouse, tucked discreetly down a winding lane, he made himself comfortable and planned his next move. The Dragon Slayers could find their own way out into the wilds. He'd only just got here and, as much as he loathed the place, he reckoned it would be best to hang around for a while. He couldn't just give up and go home, not yet.

Things hadn't gone to plan financially but there was no need to panic. He was nothing if not resourceful.

With his optimism fuelled, he signalled for more ale. There was no cause for concern. Everything would turn out just fine.

The keys to the Treasury might have been too ambitious, but there would be a host of other ways for a wily fellow like himself to make money in a place like this.

Patience. That's what was needed here. All he had to do was sit tight, relax, and wait for the opportunity to reveal itself.

CHAPTER TWENTY-FIVE

'Hendrick Stanner!'

'Never heard of him.'

'Now, that is strange. I have a poster folded up in my pocket. It's got a sketch of a man's face on it. Looks just like you.'

Stanner looked up from his stew bowl. 'Must be a coincidence. I'm eating. Shove off!'

The newcomer eased himself into the chair on the far side of the table. 'A coincidence? No, I don't think so. That would be mighty bad luck on your part. But then, you have been having a fair bit of bad luck lately. Haven't you?'

'Find another table,' hissed Stanner. 'There's plenty.'

'No, I'm quite content here thanks.' His uninvited company brushed a hand through his unkempt hair. 'You're a wanted man. Got a considerable bounty on your head.'

Stanner's patience thinned. How many warnings did people need? He dropped his spoon into the bowl. 'And I suppose you'd be thinking you'd be the one to collect it?'

'No, not me.' The man paused as a woman placed a bowl of soup on the table in front of him. 'I'm not interested in the price on your head,' he tore a piece of bread free, 'but the two riders headed this way might be a different story. They've been tracking you for the last three days. And they're close now.'

Stanner's alarm bells rang loudly. Was it a trap? He scanned the room, his fist clenched in annoyance. 'And how would you know about that?'

The stranger took a spoonful of soup. 'Hmm, not bad. Lacking a little salt, perhaps.' Staring straight at Stanner, the weathered face twitched with curiosity. 'Let's just say that I know things.'

'And why would you be feeling the need to share these things with me?' Stanner didn't trust him. Not one bit. Those eyes. Vitreous, and deep. There was something not right about them. 'Why would you be wanting to warn me?'

'Just helping an old friend out.'

'What friend would that be?' Stanner's suspicion peaked. 'Who sent you?'

'No one sent me, I came of my own freewill. You don't remember me?'

'No. Should I?'

'I wouldn't presume to suggest that you should but still, I thought you might recognise me.'

Stanner stared back. It wasn't the kind of face you'd easily forget. Unnerving, at best. But it triggered no recollection. 'Sorry to disappoint.'

'There's no need to apologise. We'll have plenty of time to get reacquainted. You'd best be on your way. Those riders are closing in fast.'

Stanner rose from the table. He'd had his fill of the fool and his cryptic ramblings. 'This better not be a trap, old man.'

'It's no trap.' The tone suggested a flicker of smile hidden among the scrawl of beard and hair. 'Farewell, Hendrick Stanner. Until we next meet.'

Stanner scowled. 'What makes you think there'll be a next time?'

'There's always a next time, Hendrick Stanner.' His tone grew ominous. 'There's always a next time.'

There was an unmistakable chill in the late evening air. The last throws of sunlight tinged the western sky.

Stanner shivered as he moved among the shadows. Having put a safe distance between himself and the inn, he watched and waited. The encounter had given him much to consider.

Who was the old man? Had they met before? If they had, why did he not remember it?

How did he know that Stanner had been having such rotten luck of late? He'd never been the luckiest, but recently things had been going from bad to worse.

Had the old man been following him? If so, why?

His instincts yelled that this was a trap. Instead of hanging around waiting, he should be making a quick getaway. But his curiosity had got the better of him. Part of him needed to know if there was any truth in the warning. The same part of him hoped that it was a trap; the alternative offered a far more worrying set of questions.

Why was the stranger looking out for him? If he wasn't hoping to claim the reward for himself then what were his motives?

And what was all that nonsense about getting reacquainted?

He didn't have long to wait. As the falling temperature

surrendered to the oncoming night, he watched as two riders came into view and dismounted outside the inn.

They were bounty hunters all right. And they weren't trying hard to hide it either.

Stanner waited until they'd gone inside, then made his way back to his horse. He scanned the shadows as he went, fully expecting the inevitable sting in the tail. But it never came.

Mounting up, he braced himself against the cold. It truly was a night to be indoors by the fireside but then freedom has its cost and a chilled night's ride under the stars was a small price to pay.

Gathering speed he rode fast across the barren wasteland, leaving the township far behind. As the terrain steepened, he slowed his pace and dismounted. The narrowing stream might well be the last he'd see for some time. Filling his water pouch, he watched the final faint traces of light give way to the enveloping darkness.

Surveying the land ahead, he readied his horse and began the climb. Picking his way among the crumbling spears of rock, he gained height slowly but steadily. Somewhere far below, shielded from his eyes in the gloom, the flatlands stretched to the distant horizon.

Hendrick Stanner rode into the night, keen to put his followers and the troubling encounter with the stranger as far behind him as possible.

CHAPTER TWENTY-SIX

The carnival had come to town, its unheralded appearance sparking a wave of excitement and expectation. Enntonia's streets were awash with colour; the air buzzed with anticipation and rang with the sound of merriment.

Mingling with the crowd, a rainbow-dashed mix of performers and wide-eyed spectators, Dragon Slayer Ten Six Nine led her two young companions through a succession of narrow side streets before emerging at the corner of Hawkers Square. Enntonia's age-old trading centre had been transformed by the travelling show's arrival. A jumble of brightly painted caravans were lined up around the square interspersed with a succession of canvas tents, each adorned with an array of banners and flags that snapped in the morning breeze.

Ten Six Nine stepped hurriedly aside to avoid a collision with a tall thin man who appeared suddenly from the throng riding a strange two-wheeled contraption. Reen screeched her delight as she skipped barefoot towards the caravans. Elfin Fingle followed close behind her. 'I wish Messenger Two Cups were here,' she cried. 'He would love to see this.'

Ten Six Nine followed with a sigh. She too was concerned by the Messenger's absence and her patience was wearing thin. He'd asked her to watch over the girl until he returned; a task she had at first been willing to accept and, given the unusual circumstances, one she would have found difficult to decline. He'd said it would be only for a few days, but four days and nights had now passed. The Messenger needed to return soon. Special circumstances or not, she was struggling with the awkward situation. Although nothing had been said, by either the Scribe, his assistant, or the girl, it was obvious an uneasy truth hung over them all.

'This is so exciting,' Reen smiled. 'I've never seen anything like this before.'

'It's just the carnival,' Elfin Fingle replied casually, trying to conceal his own excitement. Ten Six Nine reckoned he was doing a poor job of hiding it. 'They used to visit often,' he continued. 'But they haven't been here for a long time and as far as I know, no one knew they were coming.'

Reen looked up in wonder. 'Wow! Look at the height of him,' she gasped. 'He must be the tallest man in the world.'

'It's a trick,' countered Elfin. 'He's got wooden poles under there. They're called stilts.'

'Stop spoiling it.' Ten Six Nine scowled at him.

'And look at him.' Reen pointed excitedly as a tall figure in a long black coat and top hat emerged from the crowd and strode towards them. 'He's scary looking.'

The intricate design of a spider's web had been painstakingly sewn into the fabric of the man's coat. A white band ran around his black hat; at its centre was the image of a solitary black rose.

'The carnival leader,' whispered Elfin. 'What a costume.'

'Welcome, one and all.' A wave of jet-black hair spilled free as the striking figure doffed his hat. His mask-like face was painted white. Watchful eyes flickered from deep within the two black diamonds stretching from brow down to cheek. His blackened lips added further depth to the ghostly appearance. Long black-painted fingernails wrapped around his silver cane. 'Our humble company thank you for coming.' He waved a hand towards the caravans. 'Come join us. Feast your eyes on the wonders of the unknown and marvel at the secrets of the unexplained. Explore the darkest corners of your imagination. We have it all for you. Soothsayers, clowns, dancers, magicians...'

'Freaks!' A shout came from the crowd.

'Yes, yes. Freaks too, for all are welcome in our merry band. Come see for yourselves, come marvel at nature's little wonders.' His face widened in a ghoulish grin. 'Our performers await you. Let the Circle of the Black Rose transform your dreams into reality and bring your worst fears to life.' With a dramatic flourish he swivelled towards the caravans.

In his place, a woman emerged from the gathering. Her long dark hair swished in the breeze as her piercing gaze settled on the Scribe's assistant.

'Hey, little Mister,' she purred. 'Want to know your future?' Her bangles jingled as her painted fingernails beckoned him forward.

'No, he doesn't.' Ten Six Nine intervened. Elfin Fingle's face fell with a flash of disappointment. 'No distractions,' she continued. 'Remember?'

'I remember,' he replied grudgingly. He gave the woman a

longing glance as she retreated into the bustling crowd.

Ten Six Nine shook her head disapprovingly. Despite being a willing accomplice and doing his best to help keep the girl entertained, the Scribe's assistant was beginning to lose focus. It had been easy for the first two days but, as the time rolled by, his desperate need to know the girl's secret was becoming unbearable. For them both.

'And where in the Hells have you been?'

Ten Six Nine turned to meet the booming voice. 'General, I…'

'Never mind, you're here now. Get to work, Ten Six Nine. Need you to help keep an eye on this rabble.'

'Why? What for?'

'Something's brewing.' The General glowered at the crowd. 'Ex-Councillor Tauris is holding a gathering on the far side of the Square. He's stirring up trouble. Trouble for us, most likely. He's feeding on folks' discontent, hoping to turn it to his advantage.'

'They'll not listen to him.'

'People have a short memory, Ten Six Nine, and they don't like us being in charge. These are dangerous times, I tell you. Stay alert, we need to be ready for anything. It's all hands to the cause.' He scratched at his greying stubble. 'I'll be in the Twelve Bells if you need me.'

As he pushed into the crowd, Ten Six Nine eyed the scene dubiously. It wasn't going to be easy. She motioned Reen and Elfin to her side. 'I've got work to do,' she said firmly. 'Stay close to me. Okay?' She gave Elfin a hard stare.

They both agreed with a nod. 'What's going on?' asked Elfin. 'What was he saying to you?'

'Slayer business,' she replied evasively. 'Just stay close.' She began circling the crowd, glancing over her shoulder every now and again to ensure that they were holding to their word.

A troupe of dancers weaved back and forth in front of her. Brushing them aside impatiently, she reached the north end of the Square where a stout balding man on a raised wooden platform remonstrated with the crowd. Ex-Councillor Tauris.

Bellowing his rhetoric at the top of his voice, his face reddened as he saw her. Pointing animatedly, his rant reignited. 'Look, there's another of them. Come to shut my gathering down, have you?'

Ten Six Nine felt the glare of the crowd. The air was toxic. Tauris was right; there was no love here for the Dragon Slayers, but it seemed the former Council man wasn't getting things all his own way either. An object flew from the crowd, missing its target by mere inches. His startled reaction brought roars of laughter, which spiked his fury further.

'The Slayers should not be in power,' he screeched. 'They have no rightful authority. We must all demand that they relinquish their claim and stand aside.'

'And give the power to who? You and your old cronies?' The sarcastic response brought a round of jeers.

'Never!' The cries of protest rallied. 'Never again.'

'Things will be different,' Tauris roared. 'A new people's Council. That's the way ahead.'

'Never trust a politician.' Another shout was followed by a

chorus of derision. 'You're no better than a Dragon Slayer.'

Ten Six Nine felt the tension mount. The General was right. A volatile situation like this could deteriorate fast. Turning away from Tauris' sideshow, she scanned the crowd for her young companions. Where were they? Where had they gone?

With a groan of frustration, she saw them wandering off in the opposite direction, their attention fixed firmly on a trio of jugglers. Her shout died in the commotion. Even the carnival music was being drowned out by the noise of the growing unrest. Infuriated by their refusal to follow her simple instructions, Ten Six Nine barged into the swaying mass of bodies. She'd had enough of this. She was no child minder. When they got back to Bog-Mire, she was done. If he ever returned, the Messenger could make alternative arrangements.

As the crowd thinned, she saw a dark-haired man moving towards the girl. He looked familiar, but there was something about him that put her on edge.

Something troubling; something very wrong.

CHAPTER TWENTY-SEVEN

Sanna Vrai recognised him instantly.

It was him. The man from the island. The one she had seen talking to the blue-cloaks. The girl was in danger once again, and she had vowed to protect her.

She yelled her warning. Those standing closest to her stood aside quickly in response. Throwing the Dragon Slayer's coat to the ground, she ran towards him.

Alerted by the reaction of the crowd as she barged her way through them, the man swung round and thrust an arm up in defence. His elbow caught her in the throat as they collided, sending her spinning sideways into the horde. Grabbing hold of his arm, she pulled him with her.

The gathering reacted angrily. In the ensuing chaos she lost her grip, and he broke free. Pushed and shoved; kicked and cursed at, she hissed her frustration. Fuelled by adrenaline she regained her balance and, breaking free from the melee, she charged again.

Gaining ground quickly, she kept her eyes focused on her target. As the man neared the girl, he reached inside his jacket. Sanna called out but the girl stood motionless, transfixed by the unfolding drama. With a roar, Sanna launched herself forward.

She landed on him just as he came into touching distance of his prey.

Knocked from his stride, he swung out an arm in retaliation. Landing a lucky strike, his fist connected with her jaw. Fired by the blow, she caught hold of his jacket and brought her knee up into his stomach. As he folded with a groan, she swung out her leg. Her kick forced him to the ground.

Heart thumping fast, she stood over him.

But he wasn't done yet. Scrambling to his knees, he made one last desperate lunge for the girl. At the same time, his hand reached once again inside his jacket.

Was he reaching for a blade?

Left with no choice, Sanna threw herself at him and thrust the Slayer's dagger into his chest.

As his struggle faded, she released her grip and fell to her knees.

CHAPTER TWENTY-EIGHT

Kneeling, breathless, Ten Six Nine stared at the ground.

Her heart raced. Her head spun. Everything was a blur.

What had just happened to her?

Lifting her head, she saw that she was surrounded. The crowd stood a few paces back, as if keeping a safe distance. All eyes were fixed firmly on her. Her gaze shifted and settled on the body slumped on the ground next to her. Her stomach lurched at the sight of her blade planted firmly in the man's chest.

What had she done?

'What's going on here?' A Dragon Slayer stepped from the crowd and stared at her in disbelief. His eyes strayed to the body and back again. 'Restrain her! Someone go find the General.'

She was hauled to her feet as the crowd found their voice.

'It's Trask!'

'She's killed Ex-Councillor Trask.'

Their grip tightened. As the protests grew louder, she heard a familiar voice among the shouts.

'Leave her alone.' Elfin Fingle pushed his way through the crowd. 'Let her go. You're hurting her.'

'There will be much worse coming to her.' A hand shoved him aside. 'Get out of the way.'

Ten Six Nine watched on helplessly as he continued his pleas.

'She was just protecting the girl.'

Elfin's shout brought her much needed clarity. Freed from her confusion, Ten Six Nine scanned the crowd frantically. 'The girl. Where is she?'

'Move aside. Let me through.' A booming voice roared above the noise. 'Get out of the way, you rabble.' The General stormed into view and stopped dead in his tracks. 'In all the Hells, Ten Six Nine,' he barked. 'I only asked you to keep an eye on the crowd. What have you done?'

She couldn't answer his question. She had no words to explain her actions. She wrestled to break free, but it was useless. 'General, we need to find the girl.'

'What girl?' His expression soured even further. 'What are you talking about?'

'She was with the Scribe's assistant. We need to make sure she is okay.'

'The girl is safe.' A new voice cut through the air. 'She is right here with me. Clear the way.'

All heads turned in unison. As the crowd parted, Ten Six Nine felt a wave of relief as she saw the Messenger walking hand in hand with Reen.

'Release the Dragon Slayer,' commanded the Messenger. 'Release her now!'

'On whose authority?' A shout came from the crowd.

The Messenger thumped the ground with his stick.

'Whose authority would you like?' The anger in his voice was evident. 'The Defender? Would his word suffice? Or maybe Scaraven, the one who saved you all from the Black Wizard? Shall

I send word requesting their presence?' He stamped his foot. 'Do not provoke me any further. Release her! Now!'

The crowd retreated several paces. As Ten Six Nine stepped free from their hold, the girl broke into a run and threw her arms around her.

'What happened?' Ten Six Nine whispered.

'You saved my life…' Reen pulled back and smiled. 'Again.'

The Messenger eyed the gathering warily as he paced a circle around Ten Six Nine and the girl.

'I want an explanation, old man.' The General scowled. 'What in the Hells is going on here?'

Undaunted, the Messenger waved aside his demands. 'All will be explained, General, all will be explained.' An uncanny silence had descended on the Square. Even the sounds of the carnival seemed to have faded away.

The General stood his ground. 'And why would you assume authority here?'

'He is a Messenger.' Elfin Fingle was quick to respond. 'And the Messengers have the authority.'

'Indeed we do, Master Fingle,' the Messenger grinned. 'And this situation needs to be handled with some degree of common sense.'

The General sneered his defiance. 'Look here…'

'Enough!' The Messenger's tone darkened. 'I will not be challenged here. Cease with your groans and complaints, all of you, and I will explain everything.' He pointed at Ten Six Nine. 'This woman is not your enemy, but the one with her blade in his chest,' he gestured at the body on the ground, 'he is the one who should incur the full wrath of your hate.'

'What are you talking about?' The General frowned. 'That's Trask.'

'Yes, and the full scale of his treachery has just been revealed for you all to see.'

'What treachery?'

The Messenger paced impatiently. 'Ex-Councillor Trask is the one who would have left you all to a horrible fate. Only now, with his actions, have I truly seen it.'

A whisper ran among the crowd which must have now numbered a hundred, maybe more, and was growing by the minute. The Messenger had their attention and, for the moment, had scared them into a submissive state. But things could change quickly. How would they react when he revealed who the girl really was? Ten Six Nine bent to retrieve her dagger. Ignoring the looks of contempt, she pulled the girl close. As she scanned the gathering, she saw a man pushing his way to the front.

'What is going on here?' Ex-Councillor Tauris came to a sudden halt as he saw the body. 'Trask? What happened to him?'

'Ex-Councillor Tauris, thank you for joining us.' The Messenger pointed knowingly. 'You've saved us the trouble of coming for you. Seize him, General.'

The General stiffened. 'What?'

'Tauris. Have him restrained. Now!'

The General gave the command with a wave of his hand. Tauris protested angrily as two Dragon Slayers flanked him.

'What is the meaning of this?' He wrestled with their grip. 'What is going on? And what happened to Trask?'

'She did it.' A shout came from the throng. 'That Dragon Slayer killed him.'

'Why?' Tauris stared at her questioningly. 'Why?'

Ten Six Nine finally knew why she had done it. 'He was going to harm the girl.'

Tauris turned his attention to Reen. 'Her? Why would he want to hurt her? Who is she?'

'My thoughts exactly,' boomed the General. 'Who is this girl? If you're the one with the answers, Messenger, then tell us. Who is she?'

Messenger Two Cups grinned. 'It will be my pleasure, General. The girl is Reen of the Aaskrid, and I am in no doubt that Trask's intention was to harm her. And this is not the first time he has made such an attempt.'

The General's face twisted. 'Aaskrid?'

'You want proof of his intentions?' The Messenger continued. 'Have one of your charges look inside his jacket.'

'I'll do it myself,' growled the General. He stomped to the body and rummaged inside the jacket. He pulled free a small piece of linen and held it aloft. 'Nothing,' he bellowed. 'Nothing but this. Is this his weapon?'

Ten Six Nine drew a deep breath. A handkerchief? Was that all Trask had been reaching for? How could she have got it so wrong? She sensed an unwelcome change in the mood of the crowd. They were growing restless. Things were not going well, but the Messenger didn't appear to be worried. As the grumbles of discontent grew, he stood patiently, leaning contentedly on his stick, watching, and waiting, his expression calm and assured.

'Wait!' A Slayer standing next to the General put his hand up to his face. 'What's that smell?'

The General lifted the fabric to his nose and sniffed. 'Nightshade!' He threw it to the ground in disgust. 'Poison.'

The crowd gasped.

'There now, you have your proof.' Messenger Two Cups addressed the gathering in buoyant mood. 'Trask's intentions are clear for all to see.'

'But why?' The General stamped the cloth with his boot. 'Why would he want to harm her? Why is she here?'

'She looks like a vagrant.' sneered Tauris. 'Who did you say she was?'

'She is Reen of the Aaskrid.'

'Aaskrid?' Tauris pushed at his restraints. 'Folklore? Is that your explanation? This is nonsense. I've had enough of this.'

Shouts echoed around the square. A mix of disbelief and support for the Ex-Councillor's rally. Then, amidst the melee, one small voice took centre stage. Ten Six Nine looked on in growing admiration as Elfin Fingle stepped into the open circle.

'I have read all about the Aaskrid,' he began nervously. 'I know it sounds unlikely but if she truly is who the Messenger claims, there is one simple way to prove it.' He looked apologetically towards Reen as he continued. 'The Aaskrid can do magic.'

An audible gasp came from the mass.

'This is preposterous,' fired Tauris. 'This charade must stop. Now.'

The General slapped him on the arm. 'Shut it, Tauris. You have no authority here.'

'If she really belongs to the Aaskrid,' Elfin Fingle continued, 'she could show us now.'

Reen's face stretched in disbelief. She looked up worriedly at Ten Six Nine. 'I can't do magic,' she whispered.

'You can't?'

'I don't think so… I don't know. I've never tried.'

Ten Six Nine looked anxiously to the Messenger.

'I agree wholeheartedly with Elfin Fingle,' he beamed. 'It's a marvellous idea. The perfect solution to our dilemma.' He smiled at the girl. 'Go ahead, young lady. Why don't you show everyone what you can do?' Ten Six Nine watched on as the Messenger placed a reassuring hand on the girl's shoulder. 'She is understandably hesitant,' he addressed the crowd. 'Friends, the Aaskrid believe it wrong to display their gift without just cause. They shy away from such arrogance but I'm sure that with our collective goodwill, we can convince her that it would be okay to share it with us now. Yes?'

His exuberant challenge met with a hesitant response but, like every great showman, he was not to be dissuaded. 'Are we in agreement, friends?' he bellowed. 'Do we want to see magic?'

'Yes.' Once released from its shackles, the support quickly gathered pace. The shouts came thick and fast. 'Show us.'

Ten Six Nine hid her growing satisfaction. The Messenger had them right where he wanted them. For the moment, at least. She wondered what would happen when they realised the girl couldn't do magic.

'Get on with it,' roared the General. 'Or take your act back to the carnival tent.'

Ignoring the taunt, the Messenger put his arm around the girl. Smiling at her, he lifted his gaze to the sky. 'Go ahead,' he grinned, 'I think you'll do just fine.'

Ten Six Nine looked on in wonder as the girl raised her hand to the heavens and drew a circle with her finger. The crowd gasped in astonishment as a splinter of brilliant light pierced the grey sky. As the girl continued the circling motion, the crack in the sky grew wider. Shielding her eyes from the white light, Ten Six Nine saw the silhouetted shape of a great bird take form. The gathering in Hawkers Square watched spellbound as the winged wonder circled high above. Suddenly, with a snap of her fingers, Reen closed the rift in the sky, and the white light was gone.

Swooping from the sky, a raven came to land on Reen's outstretched arm. In its beak it held a tarnished silver chain and trinket. Tossing its head from side to side, the bird eyed its watchers warily. The chain and trinket fell to the ground as the raven took flight. Settling on a nearby rooftop, it watched over the Square.

The crowd's attention shifted to the silver trinket.

'Pick it up, Elfin.' Messenger Two Cups' expression remained calm.

As the Scribe's assistant moved to carry out the instruction, Ten Six Nine quickly glanced to the side where Reen stood wide-eyed staring down at her hands in wonder.

Elfin Fingle picked up the trinket. Turning it in his fingers, he examined it closely. 'It's a locket,' he began nervously. 'And it has an inscription.'

'And what is the inscription?' asked the Messenger quietly.

'What does it say?'

'It looks very old,' Elfin continued. 'It's quite faded. But I know my heraldry.' He looked up in surprise. 'You'll not believe this,' he gasped. 'It's the royal crest of Enntonia.'

The revelation rushed through the crowd.

'Impossible,' snapped the General. 'Let me see that.' Striding forward he snatched the chain from Elfin's hand and held it to his eye. 'The Scribe's apprentice is right,' he agreed grudgingly. 'It's the royal crest. A chained dragon sitting atop the Western Gate.' He dropped the chain and trinket back into Elfin's waiting grasp.

Excitement and expectation rippled through the crowd. Ten Six Nine studied the girl with concern. Had the moment arrived? Was the Messenger about to reveal her identity?

Reen didn't appear daunted by the prospect. She was too engrossed with her newly discovered ability. Ten Six Nine wondered how much of the illusion had been down to the Messenger. Was he still playing the crowd with his wizardry?

'Open the locket.' A shout came from the crowd.

'Yes,' cried another. 'What's in the locket?' The shouts echoed loudly across the Square.

Messenger Two Cups held his hand aloft to silence the growing appeals. 'Master Fingle, I think Ex-Councillor Tauris should open the locket.'

Elfin stepped forward and held out his hand.

'Why me?' Tauris scowled his contempt. 'What is going on here?' he snarled, pointing angrily at Reen. 'Why is she here?'

'Open it,' replied the Messenger. 'Perhaps then you'll have

your answer.'

Tauris snatched the locket. He studied it for a moment, checking the inscription for himself before clicking it open. 'It's a Dragon Slayer's identification tag.' He let the small metal tag swing on its silver chain. 'What is going on here, Messenger? This doesn't tell us why the girl is here.'

'On the contrary,' Two Cups grinned. 'It shows that the girl from the Aaskrid is here to play her part in changing Enntonia's future.'

Tauris' expression darkened. He clearly didn't like the idea. Momentarily freed from his restraints, he turned threateningly towards the girl. Ten Six Nine lunged instinctively and pushed him to the ground.

'Leave her alone,' she snarled. 'She is your queen!'

A deafening silence fell on Hawkers Square.

She knew, right in that moment, that things would never be the same again. Regretting her outburst, Ten Six Nine glanced apologetically to Reen and then to the Messenger. 'I'm sorry…' Her words came out little more than a whisper.

'Our queen?' The General stared at her. 'What are you talking about, Ten Six Nine?'

'What's going on here?' As Tauris struggled to his feet, the Slayers reclaimed their hold on him.

The General turned his glare to the Messenger.

'No more deception, old man. It's time you told us what is going on.'

'Yes, I rather think it is.'

Ten Six Nine watched on as Messenger Two Cups took the

chain and tag from Tauris. Studying it closely, a strange expression flashed across his face. An expression of mixed emotions; a look not only of surprise, but also of recognition. If he truly was the orchestrator of all these strange events, this part at least seemed to have taken him by surprise.

His distraction was only momentary. 'Tauris is correct,' he said loudly enough for all to hear. 'This is a Dragon Slayer's identification tag.' Turning to the crowd, he held it aloft. 'Before we continue, does anyone here need further proof of the girl's authenticity?'

No one spoke. If anyone had any doubts, they weren't about to share them. The silence gave the Messenger his answer. 'Excellent! Then we are all in agreement. Young Reen does belong to the ancient tribe of nomads known as the Aaskrid. However, contrary to the Dragon Slayer's claim, Reen is not your sovereign.'

Ten Six Nine drew a sharp intake of breath. The Aaskrid girl wasn't the queen?

She cringed with embarrassment as the Messenger walked towards her.

'I'm afraid I must ask you to bare your shoulder, Dragon Slayer.'

'What?'

'Bare your shoulder, please. I need to see your identification brand.'

Ten Six Nine drew a breath. 'Why?'

The Messenger gave a nod of reassurance. 'I need to see your shoulder. You're a lot taller than me so if you could bend a little too, that would help.'

Reluctantly, she did as he asked. Turning her back to him, she crouched down and bared her shoulder. She felt his fingers trace lightly across her skin.

'Just as I thought,' he mused. 'You can stand again, Ten Six Nine. Thank you.' Turning to the crowd, he tapped the ground with his stick. 'The identification on the tag is the same as the branding on her skin. Citizens of Enntonia. Bend your knees.'

Turning to her, his face a picture of triumph, he gave an extravagant bow.

'What's happening?' Her voice shook. She felt a hand close tightly around her own. She looked down to see Reen smiling up at her.

'I've been desperate to tell you,' she grinned. 'But he made me promise not to say anything. He told me at Bog-Mire Towers before he left.'

'Told you what?'

'I'm not Enntonia's new queen, silly,' she giggled. 'You are.'

CHAPTER TWENTY-NINE

Sitting cross-legged on the sand, Shadow watched the sun dip slowly towards the horizon. Closing her eyes, she listened to the calming sound of the waves breaking gently as they rolled against the beach.

'I thought I'd find you here.' A familiar voice broke the solitude of the moment. Not that she minded. She opened her eyes to see Druan striding, bare-footed, towards her. He'd rolled the legs of his baggy trousers up. She grinned at the comical sight.

'Long summer days in the sun,' he smiled. 'Without doubt, one of my favourite perks of immortality.' He dropped himself onto the sand beside her. 'Just look at that view. I never tire of it.'

'It's beautiful.' Shadow nodded as she shared her agreement. They'd discussed the concept of immortality many times but being only in her early twenties, in this lifetime at least, she hadn't given the subject much serious thought. She studied his expression closely. There was a definite glint in his eye. 'You've found something, haven't you?'

His grin widened. 'I might have done.'

'You have. What is it?'

'I'd planned to wait until you joined me tomorrow, but I couldn't contain my excitement any longer.'

'Tell me, Druan.' She pushed his arm gently. 'What have you found?'

'It is as I suspected,' he began enthusiastically. 'They were meant to be here. Whether summoned or not, it is just as the Seer predicted it would be.'

'What does it mean? And who are they?'

'Ah, I'm afraid I don't know the answer to that,' Druan winced. 'But I expect we will find out soon enough.'

'What is it?' She sensed his hesitation. 'What are you not telling me?'

'The time has come for one of us to go to him.'

'The Seer?'

'Yes. Although I suspect he will already know, it is our duty to inform him of the recent events.'

'But where is he?' She tried to read his expression. 'Is he here? On the Island?'

'Yes, to some extent.'

Shadow took a moment to consider his response. She wasn't sure she fully understood. She decided against asking. 'You will go to him, Druan?'

'Me? Oh, good heavens no,' he stifled a chuckle. 'My spirit may be forever young, but this aging shell,' he clapped his stomach playfully. 'I swear the cracks in my knees grow louder by the day.'

'Then Raddan will go?'

'No, not Raddan. He will be busy tending to his duties as our new Warden.'

'Then who will go?' She waited, but he didn't reply. He didn't need to. His expression said it all. 'Me?'

'Yes, Shadow.' Druan grinned widely. 'You will go. You will be our messenger. You're young, fit, and able, and besides, you must go. It's you he asked for.'

'I don't understand. What do you mean?'

Druan clambered to his feet. 'It's written in the scripts I've just uncovered. The writings of the Seer himself. A prophecy claiming that three would arrive on the distant shore and that when they did, Shadow's journey would begin. Come,' he held out his hand. 'I'll show you. You can read it for yourself.'

Lying in her bed, she listened to the gentle roll of the sea as the moonlight bathed the room in its ethereal glow. Sleep would be slow in coming tonight.

Her mind raced with the revelations of Druan's findings.

She'd read the scripts with her own eyes, yet still it seemed so unbelievable.

In only a few days she would leave the Haven, departing on a journey predicted long ago in a distant past. And, if the scripts were to be believed, at Journey's End, Shadow of the Seers Watch would meet with the Seer Magister.

CHAPTER THIRTY

Messenger Two Cups drained his cup and reached for the teapot. With a smack of his lips, he hurriedly refuelled. Fine china was all very well, but it held less tea than he would like. Supping at his refill, he looked across at the Dragon Slayer. She was troubled. It was only to be expected. She'd had quite a day and had a lot to think about.

The fire cracked merrily in the hearth. Beyond the window, the last light of day tinged the darkening sky. At the far side of the room, Token ScriptScratcher sat at his desk. Quill in hand, he puffed contentedly on his pipe before adding his thoughts to his journal.

Two Cups switched his focus back to the Dragon Slayer. He wondered if Sanna was aware of the unfolding events. If only he could connect with her directly. He had no way of finding out how much she knew, or the extent of her influence. All he could do was hope that she might be able to help Ten Six Nine better understand, and deal with, the enormity of her strange twist in circumstances. The Slayer didn't believe what he was telling her, that much was obvious, but something in her manner suggested that she wanted to.

As if aware of his attention, she swung her restless gaze in his direction. The glow from the fire highlighted the amber in her hair. 'I still don't understand how I can be this person you think I am.' She shook her head. 'There must be four missing generations, maybe more, since Starrin's reign. Where have they all been?'

Two Cups leaned forward. 'I won't insult your intelligence by lying to you.' Here it was, the crux of the matter. Sometimes truth sounded far stranger than fiction. 'The passing of time contrasts greatly between worlds. A decade in one reality can appear little more than a blink of an eye in another.' He paused for a moment, then continued. 'I for my part have a confession to make.'

'You have? What is it?'

'I came to Starrin long ago, in the hour of Enntonia's need. I will not bore you with the details. If you are interested, I'm sure the Scribe can let you see historical accounts of the time. Suffice to say Enntonia was in trouble, and I offered my services.'

'Your services? As what?'

'Folk have differing names for what I do, but I settle for wizard. And a wizard's work demands no small price.'

She eyed him dubiously. His claims were obviously testing her beliefs, yet she chose not to dismiss them verbally. 'Go on.'

'In return for saving Enntonia from a dreadful fate, I convinced the king to give me full authority of the land.'

'You?' Her brown eyes widened. 'You are the Defender?'

'Yes, I am.' He brushed the question aside as if it were irrelevant. 'In return, I gave my word to Starrin that I would ensure that a worthy and true replacement would one day again take the throne.'

'And you think I'm worthy?'

'Well, I expect we will find that out,' he chuckled. 'I would say that time will tell but, as I don't believe in such a concept, that would be foolish. Worthy or not, you are the one. Fate has played its hand.'

'So, do I have royal blood coursing through my veins or not? Am I truly Starrin's descendant?'

Two Cups took a mouthful of tea and wiped his whiskers thoughtfully. 'Now that is an interesting question,' he nodded. 'No, incredible as it may seem, given the circumstances, I'd say it's more likely to be the other way around. You are probably Starrin's ancestor.'

From across the room, Token ScriptScratcher gave a spluttering cough. The Dragon Slayer's jaw dropped open.

'Ancestor? How is that possible?'

'It is no stranger to explain than the alternative. King Starrin died with no heir. As you've already said, a very long period has passed with no heir apparent revealing themselves. So, either you have appeared from nowhere with no obvious connection to the royal line, or you are his ancestor, and you are drifting between realities. Such activity would explain the discrepancies in the timelines.' He snorted his appreciation. 'Makes sense, doesn't it?'

'It sounds plausible,' Token ScriptScratcher offered his thoughts. 'I must admit, I had wondered how the missing generations were possible.'

'All things are possible,' beamed Two Cups. He returned his attention to the Slayer. 'Either way, you need not worry. There will be unbelievers, there will be some who might even challenge your claim, but their opposition will not last. You have my word on that. I have my account of history and I will ensure that it is told throughout the land. In fact, it has already begun. The city's streets are already buzzing with the tale.'

'And the tale?' She asked warily. 'Your account of history. How does it go?'

'That the queen was still alive when I came to Enntonia as the Defender. It's true to say that, before her passing, she had been in poor health for some time and had not been seen much in public. And so, to the creative element of my story. I've let it be known that she was with child and that I arranged safe transit for her to escape the dark days facing Enntonia. As Defender, I had the power to decide when an heir would return to the throne and so I watched diligently over the royal line. When the right one came to be, and when conditions in Enntonia were favourable, I would ensure that the heir would return, thus fulfilling my promise to Starrin.' With a grin, Two Cups lifted his cup to his mouth. 'How does that sound?'

The Scribe was quick to share his appreciation. 'An excellent account, Scaraven. No one could take issue with any part of it.'

The Dragon Slayer remained silent. After a few moments, she rose from her chair. 'I need to get some fresh air.'

'Of course.' Two Cups jumped to his feet.

'I'd prefer if you didn't stand to attention every time I enter or leave the room,' she frowned. 'It feels wrong.'

'Don't be too ready to dismiss all I've told you,' he cautioned. 'As difficult as it might be to comprehend, it is true. You are of royal blood.'

'Then what of my parents? Did they know of their origins?'

She hesitated. 'I don't even remember them. Did they know who they were?'

'I wouldn't claim to know such a thing, but please do not dwell on it. The normal rules do not apply for the Drifters among us.' He watched her expression but saw no recognition of the name. 'We transcend all normality. Tell me, what are your first memories of this life?'

'I don't know… the lodging house at White Briar, I suppose. Why?'

'You were found in the forest,' Two Cups measured his words carefully. 'You were very young; some guessed at two years old, some at three. But no one knew for sure. No one knew where you came from, no one really cared. Except the young lad who found you and took you into town. He was only a pup himself.'

Her expression brightened. 'Who found me?'

'You don't know?' Two Cups smiled. 'The two of you have never talked about it? You've grown up together.' He gave a wry grin. 'You were recruited into the Order together.'

The revelation hit her harder than he'd expected. The colour drained from her face.

'Twelve Seven Two.' She almost whispered the words as the realisation sank in. 'Thank you for telling me. I didn't know.' She moved towards the door. 'I think I'll get that air now.'

They waited in silence until they heard the front door closing.

'Do you think she'll be all right?' asked Token with an air of concern.

'She'll be fine.' Two Cups refilled his cup. 'She has a strength about her.'

Token tapped his pipe on the arm of his chair. 'Doesn't look to me like she is going to accept her new destiny readily, if at all.'

'Alas, it is not my place to move the pieces,' sighed Two Cups. 'I can merely place them on the board.' He held a distant look for a moment, then smiled. 'Things will become what they must, Token. Whatever the outcome is to be, the Dragon Slayer will choose her path well.'

'You seem sure. How so?'

'Sanna Vrai of the Ra-Taegan.'

'The Sun Warrior?' Token's brows twitched. 'Yes, what of her?'

'She's in there somewhere. She has experienced being the Dragon Slayer before.'

Token ScriptScratcher took a long draw on his pipe. 'Well, I never. That is remarkable.' He crossed the room to his seat by the fireside. 'So, I've been wondering, our missing royal link, did you know it was the Dragon Slayer all along?'

'I was fairly certain of it.'

'Yet you let us believe that it was the Aaskrid girl.'

'Well, now, not really,' chuckled Two Cups. 'I'm afraid you all jumped to that conclusion by yourselves.'

'But you hinted at it here in this very room.'

'Aha, yes, I said that the change would come with the appearance of the Guardian of Elsor. I'm afraid you may have misinterpreted my words.'

'So it would seem,' mused Token. 'The girl's magic,' he continued. 'Was that all down to you?'

'I helped a little, but only a little. I merely sparked her skills

174

into life. A little encouragement was all that was needed. I have to say the crack in the sky was all her own doing. Very impressive indeed.'

'And the raven?'

'That was down to her too. I was touched by that gesture.' He smiled. 'Apologies if you feel I misled you, old friend, but I had to keep her identity concealed until I could reveal the hidden threat. I was certain that there was still a rogue element at work, and I was almost sure it would be one of the fallen High Council. I needed proof and confirmation and we got it, and right in front of all those witnesses. It honestly couldn't have gone any better.'

'And Elfin?' The Scribe's expression wavered. 'Please tell me he was acting on your instructions when he addressed Hawkers Square in that way.'

'Ah, young Fingle. Yes, he did exactly as I asked. And what a performance it was.'

The Scribe sighed. 'That is a relief to hear, believe me.' His eye followed a smoke ring up to the ceiling. 'Trask!' he gave a scowl. 'I never liked the fellow. I wouldn't be surprised if he was one of those behind the ploy to summon Osfilian down from the mountain.'

'I don't think there can be any doubt on that score.' Two Cups lifted a biscuit from the tray. 'And on that subject, it might be prudent to have a look at that mirror while I'm here. Let's make sure nothing is stirring in the Hidden Realm beyond.'

CHAPTER THIRTY-ONE

The light of the crescent moon flitted eerily among the branches. All was quiet in the forest. All except for the constant buzzing in her head.

From Bog-Mire she followed the stream south. There was no thought of keeping track of her route. Things could scarcely get any worse. It seemed inconceivable that she could feel any more lost than she already did.

She walked until her legs ached. Coming to a stop by a bend in the stream, she sat against a tree and looked up at the stars. Her mind was in turmoil. So much had happened. So much that made little or no sense. So many things she doubted she'd ever be able to understand.

The Messenger. From the moment they'd met for the first time at Bog-Mire, she'd felt comfortable around him. She'd sensed something familiar about him. Yet how could this be? And he himself had laid claims to being a wizard. Was he to be trusted? Despite her reservations, she liked him. But did she believe him? Part of her wanted to, part of her already did. She wanted answers so badly she was willing to believe anything.

The events in Hawkers Square were real enough. Real enough, yet impossible to comprehend. She'd killed Trask, without even knowing she was doing it. That was bad enough, more than enough for anyone to contend with, but what about the rest of it? Did she believe any of it? She didn't know.

The unlikely revelation that she was in some way connected to the royal line of Enntonia was difficult enough to accept, but the Messenger claimed she was an ancestor of Starrin, not a descendant. How was this possible?

Was there something in what he had told her?

Was it possible for someone to drift from one reality to another? From one set of circumstances to another? She knew of at least two occasions in recent days when she had lost all sense of awareness. Were there more? How many other times had this happened to her? The more she thought about it, the more she kept coming back to the same answer.

The Messenger aside, there was only one person who could help her make sense of it all. The one who had found her in the forest.

Twelve Seven Two. The bond between them now made sense. He had saved her life. A young child lost in the forest would have had little hope of survival. But where had she come from? And who had left her there?

Twelve Seven Two was the one she needed to help her find the answers. Problem was, Twelve Seven Two was missing.

An owl took flight from the branches overhead.

Ten Six Nine got to her feet and continued walking.

CHAPTER THIRTY-TWO

Detective Mickey Spades cursed his naivety.

He'd been so close; so close to the answers he'd been craving. His relentless pursuit of the truth had led him exactly to where he'd needed to be. Okay, so maybe he'd had a slice of good luck along the way but his hard work and dedication to the cause had reaped the rewards. He'd found the man he'd been tracking; the man who held all the answers.

The interrogation had proved to be more difficult than he'd expected but just when he felt he was making progress, those fools had let the author's legal representative intervene and, in a moment of inexplicable stupidity, Spades had let himself be tricked into leaving the room.

Sent on a wild goose chase through a confusing myriad of corridors, passageways, and doors, he'd eventually found himself wandering the deserted early morning back-streets only a few blocks from home, feeling disorientated, confused, and very annoyed. Quite how he'd ended up there was unclear, but then a lot of strange things had been happening lately.

One thing seemed certain, it seemed like his good luck had run out.

'So, no luck then, Detective?'

'What?'

'No luck finding Amy Coda? No clues as to what's happened to her?'

'No, none at all.' Spades looked at his watch. He'd been sat here for more than twenty minutes, listening to the chief forensic pathologist ramble on and on. Not that he was unsympathetic, the man was obviously deeply concerned for the welfare of his missing colleague, but Spades had heard enough. It was time to go. He had his own reasons for finding out what had happened to Amy Coda, and he wasn't making any progress on that front whilst sitting here. 'There's nothing more I can do,' he said with a feigned air of resignation. 'You'd best let the Missing Persons section know, as I suggested in the first place.'

The man nodded wistfully. 'That is what I'll do. I appreciate you looking into this for me.'

'No problem.'

'The café Amy mentioned in her work planner. Did you go there?'

'All closed up, just like your other colleague said it was.' Spades chose his words carefully. 'I went there a couple of times, just to be certain, but nothing. Been closed a long time if you ask me.' He drew a breath. 'It's a mystery. I've no idea what Coda's diary entry was all about.'

That part was true, at least. He had no idea why Amy Coda had scheduled a meeting with him at a derelict cafe in the Circus District of the city. A meeting he'd known nothing about, a meeting scheduled for two thirty on the afternoon of the day she was last seen.

Spades had been back to the Black Rose Café several times

since his ill-fated first visit when he'd found the cafe open for business. Despite their inexplicable nature, the events of that day were indelibly stamped on his memory. The woman with the flowing hair and the eyes that sparkled like diamonds. She'd led him seductively into the presence of the fortune-teller. Perhaps he should have followed the old crone's advice and ignored the lure of the café but if he had, he wouldn't have found the author Hans Rugen.

But, since that day, each time he'd gone back, he'd found the café in the same state of neglect; its paintwork flaking, and its windows barred by the weathered wooden shutters. The stone grotesque above the door held the same vacant expression on each occasion. On his first visit, Spades had been convinced its watchful glare had followed his every movement.

Amy Coda's diary entry had made no sense then and, even with what he'd gleaned from his investigations since, made even less sense now. Amy Coda was missing and didn't appear to be coming back. He gave an apologetic shrug. 'There's nothing more I can do.'

'Thanks, Detective. Perhaps Missing Persons department will be able to shed some light on it.'

Spades frowned as he pulled the door closed behind him. 'I wouldn't go holding your breath on that.'

Standing at the side of the busy street, he lit a cigar. Checking his watch, he contemplated his next move. There was time, just enough time, to jump on the train and make it across the city to the Circus District. Maybe today would be his lucky day.

Maybe today the Black Rose Café would be open for business. With a shake of his head, he dismissed the forlorn hope and waved for a taxi. His time would be better spent getting back to the office. Maybe he'd find something there to occupy his mind for a while.

The journey passed by in a blur. Re-lighting his cigar, he walked the short distance to the main entrance of the police headquarters and made his way inside. As he passed the office reception area, he waved a hand to the agent on duty.

Raised from his afternoon slumber, the balding man tapped the glass in response.

'No smoking in the building, Spades.'

'So you keep saying, Tubbs, so you keep saying.' He gave a cynical grin as he dropped the cigar to the floor, squashing it with his boot. 'Got anything for me?'

'You had a call when you were out.' Agent Tubbs flipped through the pages of his notepad.

'Who was it?'

'Just a second, it's here somewhere. Yep, here we go. Fellow by the name of Leif Skimmer. Says he owns a bookstore called Dog Ears.' Tubbs tapped his pencil on the pad. 'In the Eastern District, he says. Arch Lane, a little side street near the junction of Crown and Fifth. Never heard of it myself, and I'm a bit of a reader as you know.'

Spades shrugged his disinterest. He didn't know. He didn't care either. 'Did he leave a number?'

'No, he didn't. He said it was a personal matter and that you'd know what it was about.'

Spades frowned as he turned on his heels. 'Well, he's got that wrong.' With a shake of his head, he continued towards his desk.

A little over an hour later, driven to distraction by the mounting pile of mundane paperwork, Detective Mickey Spades left his office and boarded an eastbound train.

CHAPTER THIRTY-THREE

He found her in a run-down tavern at the end of a dark lane in the northern fringes of the city. The Last Straw was aptly named. The paint flaked from the rotting woodwork. The sign above the door swung alarmingly in the breeze; its rusted bracket looking ready to snap at any moment.

The interior was in no better state. Damp patches stained the crumbling plaster on the walls. The furniture was fighting a losing battle with the termites, and the floor wasn't keen to part with the sole of a man's boot. It was an effort just to reach the stained slab of decaying wood that functioned as the bar top.

The Last Straw was the kind of place you wiped your boots when you came out; that was if you were ever desperate enough to enter it in the first place.

It was empty. Hardly surprising really.

Well, almost empty. A figure, no more than a shadow, was hunched in the corner at the far end of the gloom.

'Over there.' The barkeep waved a crooked thumb. His greying hair was streaked with patches of pure white, giving him the appearance of a badger. A rough-looking badger at that. His withered face and dirty skin matched the feel of the place. 'Said she didn't want to be disturbed.'

'You let me worry about that,' he said dryly. 'Pint of the Rat

Catcher for me, and another bottle of whatever she's having.' He tossed a handful of coins onto the bar top. 'That enough?'

'Ought to do it.'

'Take them over when you're ready?'

'No.'

'Fair enough.'

The badger was a slow mover. Damnation, if he didn't have a thirst when he came into this rotten joint he sure had one now. How long did it take a man to pour a pint and uncork a bottle?

'There you go.' The badger thumped the bottle down next to the pitcher and hurriedly scooped the coins away.

'No change then?'

'We don't give change in here. Exchange rates. You know how it is.'

'No, can't say that I do.' With a shake of his head, he lifted the drinks and wandered across the room. Placing them down on the gnarled wooden table, he pulled a chair noisily across the floor and sat down opposite her. He wiped the rim of the pitcher with his sleeve and drank thirstily. Licking the froth from his lips, he eyed her warily. There was a calmness about her, but he sensed that she was poised ready to strike at any moment. She had the potential to be dangerous, this one. No doubt about it.

'Is this where you've been hiding these last two days?' He sniffed. 'Folk have been wondering where their new leader was.' His brow furrowed. 'Bit below the standards expected of one in your new position, ain't it?'

'I don't recall asking for your opinion.' She dismissed him without looking up. 'Or your company. Find yourself another table. There's plenty.'

'No, I reckon this seat here will do me just fine, at least until I've said what I've come to say.' He took another mouthful of ale. Her gaze stayed fixed on the dregs of the wine bottle in front of her. 'Figured you might want to know what's happening in the Twelve Bells right now.' He watched her carefully. 'There's some challenging your right to rule, and some are very vocal about it too… including some of your own kind.' He hesitated. 'By that, of course, I mean Dragon Slayers.' Still no response. He worked his gums patiently. One more prod would just about do it. 'Yup! It's all getting quite nasty down there. Just thought you'd want to know.'

That did it.

'Are you going to get another table or not?' As she lifted her head, their eyes met. She glowered at him. 'Why would you think I care what they are saying? What makes you think I want this?'

'You don't want it?'

'No! I didn't ask for it, and I don't want it.' She lifted the bottle and drained it.

He pushed the second bottle towards her. 'A fine wine, by all accounts. Surprised they have it in a place like this. You have good taste, at least.' He tapped the table. 'Drink!'

'I can buy my own wine.'

'I'm sure you can but humour me, it's not often I can afford it.'

With a scowl, she lifted the bottle to her mouth. 'I'd never have guessed.'

He hid a grin of satisfaction. Sarcasm, he liked her already.

'Yes, I had the good fortune to run into a fellow out there in the wilds. We did some business together, and he paid quite favourably.'

'Good for you.' She took another swig of wine. 'What do you want?'

'Just sharing information, like I said.'

'Why? What's in it for you?'

'That remains to be seen. For now, let's just say it feels like I'm doing the right thing.'

'Who are you? Who sent you to find me?' A frown crossed her face. 'The General? Or the Messenger?'

'No one sent me, I'm here of my own accord.' He snorted at the thought. He didn't take orders from anyone unless they were paying handsomely for the privilege. 'They call me The Weasel. Finest scout this side of The Barrens.'

'Modest too.' She rolled her eyes. 'So, why do they call you The Weasel?'

'Seriously? With this face?'

'Thought I'd ask. It's not always safe to assume.' She shrugged. 'Thought it might have something to do with your devious nature.'

'Devious?' He grinned. 'The old Weasel? Surely not.' He took another drink. It was time to move things along. 'You're sure you don't want it? I might be wrong, but if I had a friend who was missing, lost somewhere between The Barrens and the Old Kingdom, I'd be taking all the help I could get to find them.' He watched for a reaction. 'Seems to me,' he continued, 'that suddenly finding myself with an armed force at my disposal would be a damned fine stroke of luck.'

Her body language changed immediately. Suddenly she was interested in what he had to say. 'How do you know I have a friend who's missing?' She leaned forward. 'Who told you?'

'Nobody told me,' he replied. 'At least, not directly. Folk talk, The Weasel listens. It's amazing the things you hear.'

'If no one told you directly, then how did you make the connection?'

'A keen ear and a perceptive eye. I was working with your friend. He's the one I was just telling you about.'

'Twelve Seven Two?' Her eyes widened. 'You were with him?'

'Well, he didn't tell me his name, but your General said it was something like that. Dark-haired fellow, quiet-spoken too. I'd say he was more of a thinker than a conversationalist. Mind you, he had plenty good to say about you.'

'He did?'

'Yup,' he smiled falsely. 'He didn't mention you by name, but I sure got the impression that he had someone special in his life.' It was getting harder to hide his growing satisfaction. People were so easy to play. The old Weasel knew it better than any. If you wanted someone onside, you just had to tell them what they wanted to hear.

'Where did you see him?' Her mood had changed from annoyed to anxious. 'Was he okay?'

'He was fine when I last saw him, but...'

'But what?'

Anxious and impatient; a potent mix.

'Well, when I last saw him he was wandering off into the

187

distance with a boar-man from Ergmire.'

'Ergmire? What was a rider of Ergmire doing in Enntonia?'

Anxious, impatient, and concerned. All he needed now was a dash of anger. 'Seems there was more than just one of them,' he inspected the dirt under his fingernails. 'And they'd run into two of your Order. Things had gone sour. We found a Slayer's body. Your friend recognised him. Got me to take it back to the city myself.'

'And Twelve Seven Two?'

'Like I said, he went off with that rider. They were going looking for the others. Reckoned he could save the other Slayer. Bad idea if you ask me. Told him it would be a trap. I tried to warn him, but he wouldn't listen.'

'You say you were working with him? He had hired you?'

'Yup! That's about the size of it.'

She frowned disapprovingly. 'If he was paying you to be his guide, you were working for him not with him.'

'Ah, well now, I see it differently. If someone is prepared to give you their money, it's obvious they need you more than you need them.' He gave a sly grin. 'But I'm a fair fellow, so I compromise. I call it working together.'

Ignoring his response, she pushed him further. 'Why had he hired you? Twelve Seven Two is a skilled tracker. Why did he need your help?'

'Thing is, he didn't have much experience in what he was looking for.'

'And what was that?'

'He wanted me to take him to the Gateways.'

'Gateways?'

'Yup.'

'What are they?'

'Ways of moving from one place to another.' Her jaw tightened. He saw it. That reaction. Why was everyone suddenly so interested in the Gateways? Darned things had been around longer than time itself. Why now?

'Who'd told him about them?'

'I did. Way I see it, he knew something strange was going on. Reckon I was able to offer some kind of explanation. Anyway, things were going fine until we ran into that boar-man.' He sighed. This wasn't getting him anywhere. It was time to make his play. 'Thing is,' he continued dryly, 'maybe your friend is out there needing help. If it were me and I had an army at my disposal, I'd be putting them to good use round about now.'

Seemed like that was enough to do it. He watched as her face flushed. She reached for the wine. Yup, rage wasn't far away now. The full spectrum of emotion, in all its glory. He watched on in wonder as she emptied the bottle. It had been more than half full and she drank the whole lot down without stopping. Their eyes met again as she rose from the table. Hells! She was angry now.

'Where did you say they were?'

'The Twelve Bells Tavern.' Watching her stride towards the door, he drained his pitcher. 'And I'll be right behind you.'

Getting to his feet with a belch, he followed. Tossing another gold coin onto the bar top, he gave Old Badger, the barkeep, a nod. 'Wouldn't miss this for the world.'

CHAPTER THIRTY-FOUR

The Dog Ears bookstore hadn't been the easiest of places to find. Tucked away from view near the end of a cobblestoned lane, far from the city bustle, its appearance was reminiscent of days gone by. A time when, as a young boy, he had visited places like this with his grandfather. "Books, Mickey," he'd always told him, "books will give you all the answers you'll ever need." Pushing the nostalgic thought from his head, Spades flicked the cigar butt to the ground and went inside.

A brass bell jingled brightly as he closed the door behind him, its ring another ghost recalling the past. The intoxicating old-book smell, familiar even from all those years ago, was almost overwhelming. Spades' eye wandered round the shop. The space felt cramped, almost claustrophobic. The low ceiling allowed for little headroom and the walls were lined with fully stocked wooden bookcases. A narrow aisle weaved its way among the cluttered floor display; a dozen or more rustic crates, each filled to overflowing with a jumble of well-thumbed, pre-owned books. The counter, a thick chunk of live edge pine, was built into a recess, midway along the far wall.

As Spades approached it, a tall wiry man appeared from behind a tattered curtain.

'Good day to you, Sir,' his voice was toneless. 'Can I help, or are you just looking to browse awhile?'

'I got a message.' Spades was never one for idle chat. 'Leif Skimmer? That you?'

'Yes, that's me,' the man cracked the faintest of smiles. 'Proprietor here at Dog Ears.'

'I'm Mickey Spades.'

'Ah, yes, of course you are. Excuse my manners, Detective,' he adjusted his spectacles. 'I didn't recognise you there for a moment. I'm still trying to get used to these new glasses. Not sure if I like them at all.' He paused. 'My apologies, I'm rambling.' He tapped two fingers on the counter. 'The book you ordered has come in. I'll be right back.' Turning nimbly, he disappeared behind the curtain.

Spades shook his head. This was clearly a wasted journey. The man was confusing him with someone else. Spades hadn't ordered a book; he'd never even been here before.

'This is a mistake,' he said bluntly as the bookstore owner returned. 'You must have me mixed up with someone else.'

Leif Skimmer fired him a look of displeasure. 'I can assure you, Detective, there is no error on my part.' He placed a paperback book on the counter. 'There you go.'

Spades glanced at the book. It meant nothing. Why would it? 'Look, you've made a mistake. I've never been in your shop before. The book is not for me.'

'I'm sorry, Detective, but you were here. You ordered the book when you were here with your friend.'

'What friend?'

'Your lady friend, the woman with the auburn hair.'

Spades felt the hairs on the back of his neck tingle. 'Coda?' He almost whispered her name. The bookstore owner pursed his lips.

'No, that wasn't what you called her.'

'Amy Coda?'

'Yes, Amy.' Skimmer flashed a smile. 'That was it. Believe me, such beauty would be hard to forget. You are a very lucky man, Detective.'

'Lucky?' Spades was struggling to keep pace. 'Why?'

'Again, my apologies, one shouldn't make presumptions, but you made such a lovely couple. Miss Amy is not with you today?'

Spades ignored the question. 'See now, that proves you're wrong. Coda and I aren't a couple. Never were… not even close. Our paths crossed every now and again professionally, that's all.'

Skimmer seemed genuinely flustered. 'Forgive me, I did not mean to offend you. I should not have commented or speculated on the nature of your relationship, but one thing I do know for certain is that you and the lovely lady visited Dog Ears bookstore last week. You specifically asked for this book by name. I didn't have it in stock, but I ordered it for you. We arranged that I was to call you when it came in.' He pushed the book towards Spades. 'Two Thirty. Written by Phinton Marlo.' Reaching beneath the counter, Skimmer retrieved a brown-covered ledger. Flicking through the yellowing pages, he stopped suddenly and turned it towards Spades. He tapped the page. 'You signed here to confirm your order.'

Spades' jaw dropped open. He stared at his signature in disbelief. He was a rational man. He had to be. His profession demanded it. A rational mind could find sense in any scenario, but this? This was beyond explanation. He'd never been in this place before. He was certain of it. He'd never laid eyes on Leif Skimmer until five minutes ago. Yet if that was true, how had his signature ended up in the man's book?

If he had been here, why did he not remember it? And how could Amy Coda possibly have been here with him only a matter of days ago, when she'd been missing for several weeks?

He eyed the bookstore owner with growing suspicion. This was obviously an elaborate set-up, but why? And who was behind it? It struck him suddenly that he might have the answer.

'Did Coda put you up to this?'

'Sorry?'

Spades considered himself a good judge of character. The man was either telling the truth or was a very good actor. 'Has Amy Coda been here?'

'Only with you, last week.' Skimmer's expression changed to one of concern. 'Is everything all right? You seem more than a little confused.'

Spades snarled his annoyance. Turning, he waved a dismissive hand and made for the door. 'I don't know what's going on here, but I've had enough.'

'But your book, Detective.' Something in Skimmer's voice made Spades stop and turn. 'Your copy of Two Thirty. Don't you want it?'

Two Thirty.

Spades drew a breath.

Two Thirty. Amy Coda's message. The entry in her work

planner. He'd assumed all along that it was the time she'd planned to meet him at the café. Was he wrong? Had she been referring to this book?

'The book,' he began warily. 'What's it about?' He moved slowly back towards the counter.

'You don't know?'

'Wouldn't be asking if I did.'

'I see.' Leif Skimmer adjusted his spectacles. 'Well, it's a little-known title,' he began, 'I'll admit that I'd never heard of it before, but I've done a bit of research. One must strive to be as informed as one can.' He smiled. 'Two Thirty could best be described as a delve into the unknown. An investigation into the hidden world of secret societies. From what I can gather, the author was a big fan of conspiracy theories.'

'Was? What happened to him?'

'Now, that is unknown.' Skimmer rubbed his hands. 'Not too much is known about Marlo, seems he was a very private fellow. I suppose he had to be. Subject matter such as this can be very divisive. It can often stir up heated debates and arguments with derogatory language and threatening behaviour, on both sides of the argument.' Skimmer paused for effect. 'As far as I can tell, the author slipped from public knowledge not long after Two Thirty was released. But I did uncover something of interest. Turns out he had a second book published some years later entitled, Inside the Circle.' Leif Skimmer's eyes sparkled with enthusiasm. 'Perhaps you would like me to order that one for you too?'

Spades lifted the book from the countertop and studied it closely. Two Thirty. The embossed lettering brought the plain front cover to life. He turned it over. The back page was blank. No blurb, nothing. Secrecy, it made sense. 'No thanks,' he replied flatly. 'This one will do. What do I owe you?'

Leif Skimmer took a moment as he readjusted his spectacles. 'I like to think of myself as a fair man, Detective. I don't want you to think I have been disingenuous in our dealings. I'm not going to charge you for the book. If it fails to meet with your expectations, you can always pass it on to someone else, or if you find yourself in this vicinity again, drop in and I'll add it to the library here.' He raised an eyebrow. 'And, in the event it proves to be a worthy read, you can always call in and offer a donation. How does that sound?'

Spades gave a shrug. 'Sounds fair enough. Thanks.' He made for the exit. He was still no nearer to an explanation. Maybe he'd find something of interest in the book. Perhaps an answer? Or a clue? Secret societies and conspiracy theories. Nonsense, all of it. Still, it seemed like he had nothing to lose. Looking round, he saw that Leif Skimmer had disappeared once more behind the curtain. The bell jingled faintly beyond the door as he closed it behind him. Spades made his way back up the lane.

Tucked under his arm, the book felt strange. He couldn't quite describe the feeling. The prospect of reading it unsettled him, yet it had to be done. As much as he felt it would be a waste of time, he knew he had to find out for sure.

Spades didn't have much time for reading these days. This would be only the second book he'd read in the last ten years. He hoped it wouldn't be as disturbing as the previous one had been.

CHAPTER THIRTY-FIVE

Lost deep in his thoughts, Elfin Fingle blew the froth from the top of his beer. There was a lot to reflect on. It had been a momentous couple of days, and it wasn't often you got the chance to play your part in changing history.

His gaze wandered lazily round the room. The tavern buzzed with the noise of chatter. The main topic of conversation, understandably, was the Dragon Slayer. The nameless woman, believed by the Messenger to be a missing descendant of the long-departed King Starrin. Judging by the air of disapproval, it seemed few in the tavern were ready to believe it, far less accept it. Elfin felt sorry for her. His sympathy was compounded by the fact he'd misled her by misinterpreting the conversation he'd overheard between the Scribe and Messenger Two Cups.

The Scribe had warned him often enough about the perils of eavesdropping. Despite his best intentions, the warnings had never had much effect. He wondered if this latest misunderstanding would make any difference. Somehow, he doubted it.

He wondered where she was. Far as he knew, he might just be the last person to have seen her, two nights ago, when she'd left Bog-Mire Towers, under the light of the crescent moon.

Things had been quiet at Bog-Mire since that night. The Dragon

Slayer was gone and so too was Reen, the girl from the Aaskrid. They'd both left without the chance to say goodbye. According to the Messenger, Reen had left Enntonia with the carnival only hours after the events in Hawkers Square. Elfin had thought it strange at first that she hadn't come to speak with him before she left, but the company were well known for their sudden departures. He expected that, by now, she was back home among her own people, somewhere on the vast Plain of Elsor. As to the whereabouts of the Dragon Slayer, that was anyone's guess.

The room fell suddenly quiet. The chatter ceased as three Dragon Slayers entered the tavern and pushed their way through the crowd to the serving counter.

Elfin held his breath. They were clearly looking for someone. He felt sorry for them, whoever it might be. The tallest of the Slayers moved towards the fireplace and addressed the hushed room.

'We're looking for the Scribe of Bog-Mire's assistant.'

Elfin froze. He dropped his gaze to his feet.

'The Scribe's apprentice.' The Slayer rasped. 'Elfin Fingle. Does anyone here know where he is?'

Elfin slid slowly down in the seat. What did they want with him?

'He's over there,' a voice called out. 'He's in that booth, in the far corner.'

Shifting uncomfortably, he peered over the top of the booth. They were crossing the room towards him. Why him? He had done nothing wrong.

'Elfin Fingle. You are to come with us.'

'Why? What do you want me for?' His hands fumbled nervously at his pitcher. 'Can I finish this first?'

'No. This can't wait. You are to come with us. Right now!'

Their tone left no room for debate. Elfin gathered his things and crept from the safety of the booth into the glare of the crowd. It felt like the eyes of the entire tavern were on him. The shame. His cheeks flushed with embarrassment. What a situation to be in. Escorted out of a crowded tavern by Dragon Slayers, in full view of everyone. Dropping his head, he fixed his eyes on the flag-stoned floor. As he neared the door, he looked up momentarily.

A smug-faced Wilton Tarnley sniggered in his direction.

Elfin couldn't help himself. 'Tarnley!' He fumed. 'Big mouth!'

A firm hand guided him from behind. 'Keep moving.' With a shove he was pushed out into the cold night. 'This way.' The tall Slayer took the lead. 'You're wanted in the Twelve Bells Tavern.'

'Why?'

'You'll find out soon enough.'

It seemed they weren't the only ones heading towards the Twelve Bells and when they arrived, Elfin saw that a large crowd had gathered outside. Several of the onlookers were trying to push their way inside. What was going on?

'Stand aside!' The Dragon Slayers flanked Elfin as they pushed the jostling crowd out of their way. With a lot of barging and shoving, they forced their way through the door into the tavern. The crowd parted, grudgingly acknowledging the Slayers' commands.

Elfin stared in disbelief at the scene that awaited him.

The Dragon Slayer who only days before had been declared Enntonian royalty, was restraining one of her fellow Slayers in an armlock with her blade resting against his neck.

CHAPTER THIRTY-SIX

Tightening her hold, Ten Six Nine glanced towards the door. Things had spiralled quickly out of control. Driven by rage, she'd let matters escalate beyond the point of no return. The cause of her anger eluded her. It didn't matter. All she wanted was to find Twelve Seven Two. She needed help, and she wasn't prepared to let anyone stand in her way. There was only one way out of this now, and her means to do it had just arrived. She took a deep breath.

'Elfin Fingle,' she spoke loudly so all in the tavern could hear. For the second time in a few days, it felt like the eyes and ears of all Enntonia were focused directly on her. 'I'm glad you're here. We have a situation.' An understatement. 'I have a resolution in mind but need your help in achieving it.'

The crowd drew a breath as the Scribe's assistant moved warily across the room. 'What can I do?' he asked nervously.

'I'm wondering that myself,' snapped the General. 'What do you expect him to do? Let it go, Ten Six Nine. I think you've made your point.'

She shook her head. 'I disagree. I don't think my point has been made yet.' She loosened her grip on the Slayer's throat just a little. 'What do you think, Nine Three Five? Is my point made? Are you ready to accept my claim?'

'Never.' The Slayer growled his response. 'You're no different to the rest of us. Your actions prove it.'

Ten Six Nine hissed as she tightened her grip. His denial pushed her further into a corner. If she didn't make her move now, things would end badly for her. 'Elfin Fingle, as apprentice to the Scribe of Bog-Mire, you will be familiar with Enntonian history and the laws of our land. Am I right?'

'Yes.' His response was shaky. 'Some of it, at least.'

'Good enough. Better than most in this room I'll wager, and I include myself in that.' She glowered at the crowd as she continued. 'In your opinion, what would be the consequences of challenging a monarch's right to rule?'

'I imagine the consequences would not be good.' He replied far more convincingly than she'd expected.

'And defying their claim? Dishonouring the royal line? What charge would be brought against someone for that?'

Elfin's face paled. 'Treason, probably.'

The room gasped in unison.

'And what would the penalty for treason be?' she continued. 'Death?'

'Possibly…' His voice wavered. He cleared his throat. 'That would be one of the punishments available to the ruling monarch. The decision would be at their discretion.'

'Now, hold on!' The General waved an arm in protest. 'Don't be making this worse than it already is, Ten Six Nine. Some of us were just talking out loud. Just airing our doubts and concerns. Ain't nothing wrong in that. It may be that things are right, and this is the way things are meant to be. Maybe some of us are just looking for some reassurances…' He hesitated. 'Some proof that you're up to the task, that you have the bottle for it.'

'Maybe you're right,' Ten Six Nine nodded. 'Maybe that's all it is.' With a swift movement, she released the Slayer's neck and caught him by the hair. Leaning forward, she swung her blade in front of him. 'What do you say, Nine Three Five? Do you accept my right to rule?'

'No!' The hatred in his voice was clear. 'You're no better than the rest of us. A spineless drunk and a coward. You don't scare me with your idle threats. We all know you don't have the guts to go through with this charade. Let me go. You're going to regret this.'

'Maybe.' Ten Six Nine drew her blade across his throat and let him fall to the floor. The tavern crowd gasped its disbelief.

One solitary voice broke the stunned silence.

'Yup! Reckon that'll do it.' The Weasel had followed her. He grinned in her direction. 'I'm reckoning she's up to the task. She has my vote.'

'And mine.' Elfin Fingle offered his support as he drew his eyes away from the fallen Slayer's body.

Ten Six Nine nodded and addressed the room coldly. 'Does anyone else want to challenge my rule?'

No one spoke. Hardly a breath was heard. She braced herself. She wasn't done yet. There was one more obstacle in her way. And a big one at that. She turned to face him. His expression gave nothing away. There was no way to gauge how this would go. Not that it mattered. There was no way to avoid it.

'What about you? Do I need to find myself a new General?'

'Seems you're getting mighty fond of using that blade,' he began measuredly. 'First Trask, now you just killed one of your own, in front of all these witnesses. Just to prove your point?'

'Seems that way.' Her heart raced. Had she gone too far in challenging him?

'Takes guts, I'll give you that.' He raised his pitcher to his mouth and drank. She knew what he was doing. Drawing the moment out, making her wait for his answer. Her hand hovered over her blade; poised, ready. Draining the pitcher noisily, he threw it to the tavern floor and sneered in her direction. 'Either a lot of guts or just plain stupid.'

The room drew a collective breath. The Twelve Bells Tavern might well have had a long history, but none of its current clientele remembered seeing anything like this.

'So, which is it?' Her hand twitched. 'Does Enntonia need a new General?'

The silence was almost deafening. His expression hardened.

'No, I don't reckon it does.' The General moved towards her and clamped a hand on her shoulder. 'Didn't know you had it in you, Ten Six Nine. You have my backing, but I'm telling you now. There will be no airs and graces from me. I've known you too long.'

'Suits me fine. I don't want that from anyone.'

The General turned to the room. 'Right, you lot, she asked us all a question. Does anyone else want to contest her right to rule?' Again no one spoke. As he scoured the room, the General's eye settled on The Weasel. 'What are you doing here? Didn't I send you out with that party of riders?'

The Weasel shrugged dismissively and gestured towards Ten Six Nine. 'I've been helping the cause in other ways,' he flashed a wily grin. 'And it appears she outranks you.'

Scowling his contempt, the General turned to face her. 'It looks like you have your resolution, Ten Six Nine. What's next?'

'We have to raise our game, General. Our defences are a disgrace. The boar-men of Ergmire rode unchallenged into Enntonia, killing a Slayer and taking two others as hostages.'

'I'm aware of that,' he replied gruffly. 'I have sent…'

'We will discuss it tomorrow,' she cut him off bluntly. 'Assemble the Dragon Slayers. We meet outside the old High Council chambers tomorrow at first light.' Sheathing her blade, she cast her gaze around the tavern. The crowd parted willingly as she made towards the door, their expressions a mix of fear and disbelief.

Bracing herself against the chill breeze, she walked along the main thoroughfare and made for the safety of a side alley. She stopped to draw breath. A strange calmness descended over her as she replayed the events in her mind. It was crystal clear; every gory detail of it. Yet she felt no trace of regret. She felt completely in control. What had happened to her? Where had she found this new depth of character?

Keeping to the shadows, she continued along the alley. Arriving at the house, she glanced over her shoulder. Content that no one was following, she pushed open the door and went inside. The dim light of the streetlamps filtered through the dirty windowpanes. Flitting among the debris of the broken furniture, she climbed the wooden staircase. Creeping along the passageway at the top of the stairs, she glanced into the room to her left. Save for the bed frame and old wardrobe it was empty, just like she knew it would be. At the end of the passageway, she paused at the second door. Her hand hovered momentarily above the handle before she entered the room.

The bare floorboards creaked as she crossed to the window. Looking out onto the street below, she saw no sign of movement. Bending to inspect the fireplace, she ran her fingers through the cold ashes. Walking to the bed, she sat down on the crumpled sheets. Instinctively her fingers reached for the identification tag around her neck.

Twelve Seven Two. Where was he?

The sound of movement on the stairs focused her thoughts. Someone was coming. Moving back to the door, she listened to the footsteps in the passageway. As they drew to a halt, she held her breath.

The knock on the door was quiet, almost apologetic.

'It's me,' whispered a voice. 'It's Elfin Fingle.' With a sigh of relief, she opened the door. 'I'm sorry, I followed you.' He continued. 'I hope you don't mind. There's something I need to talk to you about.'

She beckoned him into the room and closed the door. 'It's okay. I think it's me who owes you an apology for putting you in that situation back at the Twelve Bells.'

'You were just doing what you had to,' he rushed his response. 'It was my duty to help.' He stood by the fire; hands clasped behind his back. 'And I should say sorry for misleading you at

Bog-Mire.' He squirmed visibly at the recollection of his error. 'I honestly thought the girl from the Aaskrid was to be the new queen. The Scribe has always lectured me about the dangers of eavesdropping… and you told me too… but…'

'Forget about it.' She couldn't help but grin at his discomfort. 'Old habits can be difficult to change.' She sat down on the bed. 'Relax, Elfin. You don't have to stand to attention like that. So, now that the apologies are dealt with, what did you want to talk to me about?'

'The men from Ergmire, the ones you were talking to the General about in the tavern.'

'Yes, what about them?'

'The things you said. When did they happen?'

'I don't know for sure, I only just found out about it tonight. Why do you ask?'

'Well, I know nothing about this recent event, but this isn't the first time that riders of Ergmire have been seen in Enntonia in the last few months.'

'Really? What happened?'

'There was a big group of them,' Elfin continued. 'They were camped in the foothills of the Hogback Mountains. A few of them rode into town.' He hesitated. 'I met with them, alongside the Scribe and the Defender.'

'The Defender?'

'Yes,' replied Elfin enthusiastically. 'They were led by a General called TrollGatten. They had been sent here to enforce the settling of old mining debts.'

'And what happened?' Ten Six Nine could scarcely believe

this latest revelation. How could this not have become public knowledge?

'They were slaughtered.' Elfin's face dropped. His tone rang with sadness. 'The Harbinger and I saw it happen. It was awful.'

'Slaughtered?' A shiver ran down her spine. 'By whom?'

'A group of hooded riders. The Harbinger called them Raiders. I don't know where they came from… or where they went.'

'Who all knows about this?'

'Apart from me? The Harbinger, the Scribe, the Defender, oh, and Messenger Two Cups.' He hesitated again. 'I know it sounds funny, but I thought he might be the Defender.'

'Really?' Ten Six Nine concealed her grin.

'Yes, it was before I realised that Two Cups was Scaraven. I even asked the Scribe if he thought Scaraven was the Defender.'

'What did he say?'

'He was a bit annoyed. Told me he'd never considered the possibility and that I should avoid discussing wizards' business.'

'Probably best.' Ten Six Nine rose from the bed. 'Thanks for sharing this with me. And don't worry, I'll not let anyone know that it was you who told me.'

'Thank you,' he looked relieved. 'But don't you think it's strange that Ergmire hasn't sought revenge for what happened? Or do you think that is the reason these riders are here now?'

'Possibly,' she frowned. 'The strangest thing is that no one else knows about any of this. You keep illustrious company, Elfin Fingle. But, as you are here, there is another favour I must ask of you.'

Elfin was quick to offer his help. 'Anything. Just name it.'

'There may be a need for some legal formalities tomorrow. When you return to Bog-Mire tonight, I want you to talk to the Scribe. He must prepare a document. Will you bring it to the old council chambers in the morning?'

'Yes,' Elfin agreed eagerly. 'I'll get going right now and catch him before he retires for the night.' He let his words hang. 'There's just one other thing. It's rather awkward.'

'What is it?'

'What should I call you? How are we to address you?'

Ten Six Nine brushed the question aside with a shrug. 'The nameless don't care about such things.'

'Really?' He looked up at her wide-eyed. 'You're sure?'

'I'm certain. Don't give it another thought.' She showed him to the door. 'I'll see you in the morning.'

Closing the door, she paused by the mirror and ran her fingers through her hair. A faint trace of a smile softened her troubled reflection. Reaching into her pocket, she took out the silver chain and trinket. Studying it closely, still unable to comprehend its bizarre appearance let alone its supposed significance, she placed it around her neck. So much had happened since she had done the same thing with Twelve Seven Two's tag. She'd lost count of the days. With one final glance at the mirror, she closed the door behind her and went back downstairs. Pulling up her hood, she stepped out into the night.

CHAPTER THIRTY-SEVEN

Keeping to the dimly lit lanes, side-streets, and alleyways, she moved unchallenged through the night.

Enntonia City's grid-like street system was as old as time itself. A dingy run-down remnant of ages past, designed to allow freedom of movement in the event of dragon attack.

Few noticed her movements, those that did were happy to give the sight of a Dragon Slayer's longcoat a wide berth.

The old clock tower announced the quarter to the twelve bells as she stopped under the weathered timber mortar and pestle sign. Candlelight flickered from beyond the steamed-up window. It was said that Old Hunchback the herbalist never slept.

The pungent smell hit her as she opened the door. As she reached the counter, she heard the shuffling of feet. Muttering his annoyance at being disturbed at such late an hour, he appeared from behind the cluttered wooden shelving.

'You again!' His haggard features twisted. 'You're not welcome here. I thought I made that clear.'

'I've had a change of circumstances,' she replied bluntly. 'Are you going to refuse my business?'

He gave a hiss. His conflict was obvious; his conclusion was grudged. 'More Devil's Eye, is it?'

'No. My shoulder is fine.' Fact was, it hadn't troubled her

since she'd met the girl in the forest, and she still had the little bottle of ointment Elemi had given her. 'I want something to darken my hair.'

The herbalist looked up at her in surprise. 'Really?'

'Is that a problem?'

'No,' his expression soured again. 'Just didn't have you marked as the vain type.' With a leer of contempt, he ambled slowly back behind the tower of bottles.

Ten Six Nine stayed alert as the shuffling and clattering amplified from beyond the counter. Following a crash of glass and a burst of expletives the herbalist returned, dragging his lazy foot behind him.

'Dark Rage.' He placed the vial on the countertop.

'Never heard of it.'

'Hardly surprising,' he sneered. 'I just named it. After you, as it happens.'

'I'm touched.'

'Don't be,' he grunted. 'It wasn't meant as a compliment.'

'Really? I'm hurt.' Gods, she wanted to punch him. 'Will it work?'

'It will work. Do you really need to ask?'

He looked genuinely offended. Such delusions of grandeur. His shoulder remedy had never worked very well. 'How much do I use?' she asked warily. Was it even wise to use it at all?

'Depends on what look you're after. It's a wild variant of the sage family. Potent stuff, I wouldn't advise drinking it.' His nose twisted. 'Even with a liver as strong as yours.'

'Flatterer. A convincing pitch, as ever. I'll take it.' She slipped the vial into her pocket.

'Is it true?' He eyed her cagily. 'What they're saying about you?'

'Maybe, maybe not.'

'Fair enough. That'll be four dragyr.'

'I had a different price in mind.' She returned his scowl. 'Dark Rage. I like the name. If I like the results, I'll consider putting the royal crest above your door. Imagine it, Apothecary by Royal Appointment. That should help business. Or I could close you down, and I already have a replacement in mind.' His wrinkled old face looked like it was about to burst. With a grin, she turned towards the door. 'Oh, and if you're thinking of calling for your friend Laris and his blade, I strongly suggest you reconsider.'

With a spring in her step, she headed for the north part of the city. The clock tower chimed the hour of one as she reached the end of the dark lane and entered The Last Straw.

'He's over there,' the barkeep gestured to the far corner of the empty tavern. 'He said you'd be back.'

She nodded. 'We'll need more drink. Wine for me…'

'And the Rat Catcher for him.' He flashed his blackened teeth. 'On the house. I'll take them over when they're ready.'

Ten Six Nine crossed the room.

'Definitely has its advantages, doesn't it?' The Weasel looked up from his pitcher, a wide grin on his face. 'Being of noble lineage, I mean. Table service from the old badger, and complimentary wine to boot.' Cackling his amusement, he took a mouthful of ale.

Ten Six Nine pulled up a chair. 'Hope you've not got any

plans for the next couple of hours,' she said quietly. 'Seems we have things to discuss.'

The Weasel wiped his mouth with his sleeve. 'No plans,' he replied. There was a noticeable glint in his eye. 'I'm all ears.'

CHAPTER THIRTY-EIGHT

Mickey Spades boarded the early morning train bound for the Eastern District. A return trip to the Dog Ears bookstore hadn't been in his plans two days ago, but that was before he'd read the book entitled Two Thirty.

It had begun just the way he thought it would. An enthusiastic introduction to the shadow world of conspiracy theories and secret societies, penned by someone who had obviously spent too much time alone living in a perpetual state of paranoia.

Spades had flicked quickly through the opening chapters, disregarding the ramblings and far-fetched plots that ranged from alien invasion and abduction to the beliefs that the world and everyone in it was being controlled by a small group of extremists who worshipped a demon. He'd been on the point of discarding the book and throwing it in the rubbish bin when the content had taken an interesting turn.

The author's investigations had put him on the trail of a secret society rumoured to have gained knowledge and control of passage between alternate realities. Until recently Spades would have dismissed the suggestion of such ideas as lunacy, but some very strange things had been happening of late. Unexplainable things. And the more he read about it, the more it seemed he might have stumbled onto a possible, if unlikely, explanation for at least some of these events.

After finishing the book he'd spent several hours on-line, researching the eye-opening subject of quantum mechanics. Despite being a self-confessed hardened sceptic, he'd gone to bed in a state of some confusion, unsure quite where the line between science fact and science fiction could be found.

He'd wakened early from a restless night with one clear goal in mind. The author's note at the end of Two Thirty had left him with little choice. It was either a last minute, hastily written addition to the manuscript, or a master stroke in marketing.

Marlo revealed that his efforts to infiltrate the group had been successful. He'd spent several months befriending a member of the organisation, painstakingly gaining their trust, slowly but surely working his way into their confidence, and it appeared his patience had finally paid off. The Circle, as they called themselves, had accepted him into their fold.

Spades silently vented his frustrations as the city trundled by. He desperately needed to get his hands on a copy of Marlo's second book, Inside the Circle. The bookstore owner had offered to order it for him, but he'd been too arrogant to accept. If he hadn't been so hasty, he could have been on his way to collect it now. He'd tried to contact Skimmer to let him know he was coming but, despite his best efforts, he'd had no luck in tracing a phone number for the Dog Ears bookstore.

He glanced at his watch. Not long now. Skimmer had already sourced the book so there shouldn't be any problems, and Spades was happy to pay extra for a quick delivery. The book was certain to contain revelations of the author's time within the group and it might well give Spades the answers to some of the questions that plagued him.

His thoughts switched to Amy Coda. He wondered how far along this trail she had come.

Was he still following in her footsteps?

Had she read Marlo's second book?

Coda had made the chilling discovery that someone was writing about them and the events in their lives long before Spades had. She'd tipped him off about the Black Rose Café, and the book entitled Two Thirty. Amy Coda had then vanished.

Leif Skimmer had told him that Phinton Marlo had disappeared. Was there some connection?

Was Marlo missing, or was he still operating incognito within the Circle?

The more Spades thought about it, the more he was convinced that he was on the right trail. The questions piled up as the train rumbled into the station.

What had happened to Amy Coda?

Where was Phinton Marlo?

Was there a connection between Marlo and the author Hans Rugen? If so, what was it?

One hour later Mickey Spades was back on the train, heading home with an even more disturbing dilemma on his mind. He'd been unable to find his way back to the Dog Ears bookstore. Admittedly, it hadn't been easy to locate at the time of his first visit but that was only two days ago. His failure to find any trace of the cobbled Arch Lane had him stumped.

He'd made the mistake of stopping passers-by to ask for directions. Their blank expression had said it all. Assuring him he was in the wrong part of the city, the three people he'd approached had all told him the same thing; they didn't know of a street called Arch Lane, and none had heard of a bookstore called Dog Ears. After much aimless wandering, Spades had admitted defeat and boarded the train for the journey home.

Strange things were happening with increasing regularity. He wondered if it was all in his mind. Had he been giving too much thought to this whole Coda thing?

Was he beginning to lose his grip on reality?

The strange concept of reality. He'd been thinking a lot about it since he'd first stumbled onto this trail. Seemed like the further he went, the further away he got from a solution.

Maybe it was time to drop the whole thing and forget about it, even if only for a short while.

A break from it might be just what he needed to clear his mind, even just to give some perspective. He could always re-visit it again later and take another look at it with fresh eyes.

Arriving back at headquarters, his plan changed when he saw Agent Tubbs lounging in his chair. Maybe there was just one more move to play; one more attempt to satisfy his curiosity. He tapped the glass. Tubbs jumped to attention.

'You got nothing, Spades. No calls when you were out.'

'That wasn't what I came to ask you. Remember that call I got last week from that bookstore owner?'

'Yes?' Tubbs frowned.

'You still got the details? I wanted to check it out.'

'Really? You serious?' Tubbs' eyes widened. 'You're talking about the wind-up?'

Spades expression dropped. 'What wind-up? What do you mean?'

'Quit joking around, Spades.' Tubbs glared at him. 'You went to check it out already. When you came back you told me it must have been a wind-up or a prank call, cos you couldn't find the place. Nobody had ever heard of it.'

Spades flinched. What was going on? 'No, that's not right, I found it the first time but...' His words trailed to a halt.

Tubbs eyed him with concern. 'You okay, Spades?'

Spades swallowed uncomfortably. Things were obviously far from okay. He turned away without responding.

CHAPTER THIRTY-NINE

'Is this it?' Dragon Slayer Ten Six Nine assessed the gathering from the steps of the defunct High Council chambers. It wasn't quite the show of force she'd been hoping for.

'This is it!' Standing by her side, the General flashed a sardonic grin. 'The Order of the Dragon Slayers. Least, all I could gather at such short notice. Seventy of Enntonia's finest, give or take.'

'Where's everyone else?'

'Well, let's see now,' he scratched at his greying stubble. 'There's the twenty I sent to root out this Ergmire problem. Two have been taken hostage, two are recently deceased; one at the hands of the boar-men, the other... retrieved from the floor of the Twelve Bells...' He noted her scowl. 'Well, you get the picture... anyway, the rest of them? They could be anywhere. Most likely in the lands west of the Terra Hydra Mountains. That's always been a favoured stomping ground, but who knows? Let's face it, until recently there hasn't been a lot to keep them occupied around here. It's hard to say how many are still active members of the Order.' As the realisation dawned, his expression changed. 'Hells, this is shambolic, Ten Six Nine. I'm the damned General, and I don't even know.'

His grim assessment did little to lift her mood. Ten Six Nine turned to face the grey stone building. 'Open it up,' she commanded. 'And bring Tauris inside.'

'Hand me that axe.' Fuelled by his own scathing indictment, the General attacked the door. Swinging the axe wildly, he brought the butt end of the blade down on the chains and, with a roar, sent his boot crashing into the timber. The doors burst open, swinging violently back on their hinges.

Ex-Councillor Tauris was led up the steps. He glared his contempt at the General. 'Couldn't you just have used the keys?'

'Could have, but where would be the fun in that?' The General grinned. 'Besides, we were looking for something more dramatic. A bold symbolic gesture. I think that did it.'

Ten Six Nine hid her amusement as she passed him.

'You shouldn't be going in here,' Tauris sneered in her direction. 'This is High Council property.'

'Shut up, fool.' The General playfully slapped the back of the man's balding head.

The musty air greeted them as they filed inside. The spiders had been busy. The grand reception area of the chamber was grey with cobwebs. Immediately in front of them, the sweeping staircase yawned its sleepy welcome. High overhead, the great chandeliers hung redundantly from the domed ceiling.

'Council meeting room, Tauris.' Ten Six Nine cleared her throat. 'Which way?'

'Corridor to the left.' His reply was grudged.

'Place could do with a freshen up.' One Slayer ran his finger through the dust on the wooden dado rail as she led them into the large wood panelled room. Daylight filtered through the trio of spider-webbed windows gracing the far wall, giving the room a ghostly atmosphere. A long oak table, with legs thicker than tree trunks, ran down the centre of the room. A dozen high-backed chairs, each carved with the High Council crest, surrounded the table. The walls were lined with a gallery of hangings; centuries of history scratched onto a sprawling mass of yellowed parchment. The room looked old and tired. But then, history could have that effect.

'Yep! A lick of paint wouldn't go amiss.'

'I think we should burn it all down.'

'In all the Hells, Five Eleven, if you had your way, the whole of Enntonia would be in flames.'

'I like watching things burn. Ain't nothing wrong with that.'

'You've a troubled mind, lad. You really do.'

'This dust is going to play hell with my sinuses.'

'I'd rather be here than in the royal residence,' quipped another. 'It's been empty a lot longer than this place has. Think how bad it'll be in there.'

'Gods help us,' bellowed the General. 'Listen to you all. You've all gone soft in the head. Since when were the mighty Dragon Slayers concerned with the décor of a place?'

'The Dragon Slayers are no more.' Ten Six Nine pulled back a chair at one end of the table. The room fell silent. The Slayers exchanged puzzled glances.

The General took a few steps closer. 'What was that you said?'

'You heard what I said. The Dragon Slayers are no more.' She slapped the cushioned chair, sending a cloud of fine dust into the air. The mood of the room changed instantly. As the dust settled, she saw the Scribe's assistant enter the room, accompanied by the white-whiskered Messenger. Boosted by their appearance, she sat down. 'I'm disbanding the Order of the Dragon Slayers, with immediate effect.'

The room echoed with a chorus of disbelief, protest, and opposition.

'You what?'

'You can't do that.'

'No!'

'What will we do?'

'You can't.'

Ten Six Nine thumped the table with her fist. 'General! Bring this rabble to order.'

Making no effort to hide his resentment, snarling his instructions, he brought the protests under control. Silenced, the Dragon Slayers grudgingly took their positions, forming a circle around the table.

'Take a seat, General.'

'I'll stand.'

'Please yourself.' Ten Six Nine turned her attention to the door. 'Elfin, come sit next to me.' The Messenger hung back, content to watch over proceedings from the periphery of the chamber. As Elfin Fingle approached the table, another figure pushed his way to the front.

'Make way, friends. Make way for a scrawny fellow.' The Weasel emerged with a wry grin and ambled towards the table. Wiping the chair with his sleeve, he took his place opposite the Scribe's apprentice.

Riled by the unexpected arrival, the General barked his opposition. 'What's he doing here?'

Ten Six Nine was in no mood for explanations. 'He knows things,' she replied dismissively. 'And it appears we need all the help we can get.' She sat upright in the chair. 'I'm disbanding the Order, and before anyone says different, I can, and I will. You all know it. Royal command. That's the only way it can be done. It should have been done a long time ago, the days of fighting dragons belong in the ancient past. We need to focus on the real and present threat facing us. As most of you will know, there are riders from Ergmire here in Enntonia. Accident or not, they took the life of a Slayer and have taken two others captive.'

A murmur ran through the chamber. She knew what they were thinking. It wasn't the only Slayer who'd lost their life recently. They were thinking it; but none said it.

The General let the moment pass before responding. 'I've already sent a group to deal with this, Ten Six Nine. They'll be reporting back soon. The threat has probably already been dealt with.'

'And what if it hasn't? We don't know why these riders are here. None of us know what Ergmire is up to. It could be a scouting party reporting back to a larger force, which could already be on its way.'

The General turned his frustration on The Weasel. 'Your friend here told us that these riders were a rogue element, and that they were not riding under the authority of Ergos.'

'And who told him that?' Ten Six Nine countered immediately. 'A boar-man.'

The Weasel steepled his fingers. 'Yup! It could have been a lie.' His nose twitched. 'Could have been a trap. It sure felt like a trap to me, and I told your Slayer so; right before he went marching off into the wilds.'

'Ten Six Nine, do you really think Ergmire is planning an attack?' The General's expression twisted. 'Seems unlikely to me.'

'I don't know, but we need to take the initiative. We have to find our missing people, and there must be some retribution. Ergmire will recompense our losses or face the consequences.'

The chamber drew a collective breath.

'Exactly what are you suggesting?' The General's tone matched the mood of disbelief in the room.

'We deliver an ultimatum,' Ten Six Nine continued, her determination unwavering. 'We head northeast, tracking Twelve Seven Two, Eight Five Nine, and the Ergmire riders. When the time is right, General, you will lead a party directly east to Ergos and deliver our demands in person.'

'I will?' The General gaped at her in wonder. 'And what will this ultimatum say?'

'The removal of all Ergmire's forces from our lands; the safe return of our two kinsmen, if we haven't found them by then, and full disclosure of what Ergmire have been planning.'

'Or else? What if they decline?'

'Then we'd have ourselves a war.'

The room quickly descended into chaos. Shouts of dissent and disapproval echoed among the rafters.

'War?' bellowed the General. 'Have you lost control of your senses, Ten Six Nine?'

'We can't wage war on Ergmire,' yelled a voice.

'It'd be the end of us,' shouted another. 'We'd be signing our own death warrants.'

'Enough!' Ten Six Nine jumped angrily to her feet. The chair grated nosily on the floor as she kicked it back. 'This is not a democracy.' Fury raged inside her as she circled the room. They were wasting precious time. 'You all had the opportunity to challenge my rule and declined. From this moment on, you are soldiers of the realm. Enntonia's Elite Guard. And I will not tolerate this insubordination.' Pacing the room, she sensed a reluctant acceptance in the air. It was a start. As she passed the General, he pulled a chair back from the table and sat down. They all saw it. It was a defining moment. His tone carried restraint as he raised their collective concerns.

'We do not have the resources, Ten Six Nine. We'd be outnumbered; grossly outnumbered.'

'War is expensive,' added Tauris gingerly. 'Enntonia does not have the finances to wage a war.'

'Typical,' snarled the General. 'First mention of war and the spineless politician finds his voice.'

'Yes, Tauris,' added Ten Six Nine. 'Enntonia's finances are in a bad state, and we all know where to lay the blame for that.' She continued circling the room, making eye contact with as many of them as she could. 'Enntonia may be bankrupt,' she continued, 'but Ergmire is not. The General will lead a party of ten riders to Ergos and deliver our terms.'

'Ten?' His face reddened. 'Are you mad? They won't listen to ten of us.'

'I don't imagine they'd listen to one hundred of you,' she replied calmly. 'It's irrelevant. While you are drawing their attention in Ergos, our main group will approach from the north and take control of the mines.' She paused as the enormity of her words sparked a new wave of incredulity. 'Ergmire's strength relies heavily on their wealth of their mining works,' she continued as the noise abated. 'Aside from the financial revenue, there are the raw materials for their weapons. If we control the mines; we control their power. Given time, the odds will swing in our favour.'

'They'll have a bloody great armoury in Ergos itself, fully charged with weapons,' the General protested.

'Not if three of your group has infiltrated it.'

'Three?'

'Three would be all you'd need.' The Weasel re-joined the debate with a wily grin. 'The armoury in Ergos is big enough, but poorly guarded. No need for it to be any other way in these times of peace. I can give you a sketch of the place. Two of you could deal with the guards whilst the other one sets the explosives.'

'You're suggesting we blow it up?'

Ten Six Nine grinned. 'Sounds like a job for Five Eleven.'

'Gods, yes!' came his reply. 'I'm your man. Let's do it.' A hesitant laughter rumbled round the room.

Ten Six Nine gestured towards The Weasel. 'As for the main party, our scout knows the terrain better than anyone. He has identified a route through the mountains to the north of the Barrens, into southern Tonduur. There is an entrance to the mines there and it is usually unguarded.'

Having circled the room, she arrived back at her chair and sat down. 'That's the plan. Are there any questions?'

The room fell silent. The plan had their attention. Glances were hurriedly exchanged. Eyebrows were raised. Beards and chins were scratched. But no one spoke. All eyes settled on the General as he cleared his throat.

'So, the Order of the Dragon Slayers is no more?'

'Disbanded, by royal command.' Elfin Fingle announced boldly. 'Sorry,' his face flushed, suddenly aware that everyone was looking at him. 'The Scribe told me to take notes.'

The General gathered his thoughts. 'Fair enough. So, Ten Six Nine. What did you say we are to be called now?'

'Enntonia's Elite Guard.'

'Enntonia's Elite Guard.' The General echoed the name. 'I like it.' Nods of agreement joined his appraisal. 'So, Enntonia's Elite Guard marches a two-pronged force into neighbouring lands, demanding retribution. It then blows up Ergmire's armoury and seizes control of its mining operations, regardless of the fact it will be heavily outnumbered, with little or no resources and even less military experience.'

'That sounds about right.'

The General grinned his best black-toothed grin. 'I think it's the most ridiculous bloody plan I've ever heard.' He drew a breath. 'When do we leave?' A nervous laughter echoed around the chamber. 'What do you say, friends?' he boomed. 'Ladies and gents of the Elite Guard, shall we take a foray into enemy lands?'

The gathering roared its approval in unison.

Ten Six Nine grinned her satisfaction. It was going better

than she could have hoped. The Weasel winked surreptitiously in her direction. She stood up again.

'Then we are agreed.' Her shout brought the room to order. 'Elfin Fingle, as you have been taking notes, you are our witness. You will report back to the Scribe of Bog-Mire. The records will show that as of this day, the Order of the Dragon Slayers ceased to exist. Do you have the document from the Scribe?'

'Yes. This is it.' Elfin pushed the parchment across the table. Ten Six Nine quickly read through it.

'Bring Tauris forward.'

The ex-councillor was harried to the table. 'You've all taken leave of your senses,' he snarled.

'No one is interested in your opinion, Tauris, but as you are here, you can represent the disgraced High Council. You need to sign this.' She pushed the paper towards him.

'What is it?'

'Your recognition of the change of governance in Enntonia.'

'I'm not signing that. I don't recognise your authority. And I'm not alone in that.'

'Sign it, or I'll cut your throat open and mark it with your blood.'

The room drew a breath. Tauris' hostility dispersed quickly. His eyes widened with fear. 'You're dangerous,' he whined. 'And you're out of control.'

'Half true,' she hissed. 'Not bad for a politician.' She held out Elfin's quill. 'Sign it!'

Tauris signed without further debate.

'Return him to the cells.' As they led him away, she delivered her final instructions. 'Prepare your troops, General. A dozen should remain to watch over the city in our absence. I want riders dispatched. Scour the settlements to the west of the Terra Hydra. Round up the Slayers, wherever they are. Inform them of what has happened and give them the same option you all had. If they choose well, they will return to defend the city. If they don't... charge them with treason and kill them.'

Another gasp filled the room. Holding their gaze, she couldn't help but wonder, yet again, where her newfound strength was coming from. She felt so alive. So in control.

The Dragon Slayers; an age-old Enntonian institution. A way of life for generations beyond count. She'd stripped them of their identity in the blink of an eye. Yet there they stood, eyes focused on her, awaiting her next command. The responsibility should have been weighing heavily on the shoulders, but she felt nothing. Her sense of urgency negated all other emotions.

Twelve Seven Two was missing. He was in trouble. She couldn't shake the feeling. She had to find him. Nothing else mattered.

'Soldiers of the realm,' she addressed them coldly. 'Make your preparations. We leave tomorrow at noon.'

CHAPTER FORTY

Messenger Two Cups watched with interest as events in the chambers unfolded. He was obviously not alone in his growing admiration for the Dragon Slayer. Despite their initial resistance, the acknowledgement of her peers was in little doubt. Respect might yet be a long way off, but it was a good start. A very good start indeed.

As she exited the room, Two Cups watched the shared nods of approval. True, there were still many expressions of disbelief. It seemed none in the room could quite comprehend the sudden change in the quiet unassuming Dragon Slayer known as Ten Six Nine.

Two Cups smiled inwardly. They might not know the reason for the seismic shift in their new ruler, but then none of them knew Sanna Vrai.

The Sun Warrior was blossoming in her new role. He had little doubt that her influence was driving things forward.

And things were moving quickly. Of that there was little doubt. Elfin Fingle had kept him fully appraised of the events of the previous night; events in the Twelve Bells Tavern, at least. Young Elfin had opted to omit the details of his meeting with the Slayer when he'd followed her to the house in the alleyway. Two Cups suspected he knew what had transpired, but it was best to have his thoughts confirmed. Leaving the gloom of the stuffy chamber, he followed the Scribe's assistant out into the morning sun.

'Well, Master Fingle, that was quite something back there, wasn't it?'

'Yes,' Elfin agreed excitedly. 'Yes, it was.' He was obviously quite taken with the whole thing.

'Yes, our new leader, she really is something. I was wondering, did you tell her about the things you saw in the woods when you were with Harbinger Talus?'

'Sorry?' Elfin's expression said it all.

'You told her about General TrollGatten and the Raiders, didn't you?'

'I... I didn't mean to... It just...'

'Don't fret, Elfin,' Two Cups patted him on the arm reassuringly. 'No harm done; no harm at all.'

Elfin sighed with relief. 'I just wanted to know if it was connected to these more recent sightings of the boar-men.'

'I understand.' Two Cups considered the possibility. 'I expect we will find out soon enough.'

'There's something else that doesn't add up though.'

'And what would that be?'

'Well, don't you think it's strange that she didn't mention it back there in the chambers. If the Slayers knew that Ergmire's forces were depleted and that their General TrollGatten was no longer alive. Wouldn't that have helped persuade them? Given them more hope?'

Two Cups smiled. For all his frailties, the lad was very

perceptive. 'I expect she didn't want to alarm them,' he countered. 'The revelation of what had happened right on their doorstep would have come as a shock to them all.'

'Yes,' agreed Elfin. 'I suppose that makes sense.'

'Splendid. I won't hold you back any longer. You have your duties to attend to.'

'Yes, I must get this document back to Bog-Mire right away,' he patted his jacket. 'The Scribe will be waiting for me.'

'Excellent work, Master Fingle. Enntonia is lucky to have your services.'

Elfin flushed with pride as he turned away. Two Cups scratched thoughtfully at his whiskers. The lad had raised an interesting point; one he hadn't picked up on himself.

The Dragon Slayer planned to leave the city tomorrow at noon. Messenger Two Cups felt it imperative that he talk with her again before she left.

CHAPTER FORTY-ONE

Mickey Spades didn't like where this conversation was going. He didn't like it at all.

The Chief glowered at him from across the desk. 'Well?'

'I don't know anything about it.' Spades shrugged.

'Jaxson Tiller seems to think differently.'

'Digger? What do you mean?' This was an unexpected twist. Spades liked the conversation even less. 'What's he got to do with it?'

The Chief tapped his finger on a bundle of papers. 'He's about to release this, it's almost ready to go to print. Luckily, he came to me first to see if I'd any thoughts or if I was prepared to make a comment.'

'What is it?'

'A piece he's written about Amy Coda. And I have to say, it doesn't look good. A prominent member of the district pathologist team's been missing for several weeks, and our Missing Persons department hasn't even been notified about it.'

'What's that got to do with me?'

'I'll tell you what it's got to do with you, Spades.' The Chief slapped the desk angrily. 'Your name is mentioned in here. Tiller seems to think you know more than you're letting on. He reckons you've been down to the Circus District several times these last few weeks, doing your own investigations into Coda's disappearance.'

'Lies!' Spades snapped furiously. What was Digger up to?

'Is it? Is it really?' The Chief's face reddened. 'I've been in touch with the Chief Pathologist, initially to see why he hadn't passed Coda's case on to Missing Persons. Turns out he had a few things to say when I pressed him. It doesn't look good. If this goes to print, it'll cause me a whole load of trouble; trouble I just don't need.' He sat back in his chair. 'Seeing as you don't want to talk to me about it, I'll give you another option. Talk to Tiller, sort this out. I have no issues with him printing a piece on Coda. He's a damn fine journalist, and he's one of the good guys. He's always been straight with us and has always done his bit to help the Force. When his piece comes back to me for review again, I don't want to see anything in it that upsets me. Got it? Sort this mess out, Spades. Go talk to him.'

Mickey Spades launched himself from the chair.

That was exactly what he was going to do.

CHAPTER FORTY-TWO

Jaxson Tiller stared smugly across the table.

Spades had never liked him much; Spades didn't like anyone much. That said, he'd always considered Digger to be one of the better ones, someone willing to pull in the same direction, just like the Chief had said. But now, Spades wasn't so sure. Now, Mickey Spades wanted to reach across the table, grab him by the throat, and strangle him.

'So, what's this all about, Digger? What's your take?'

'Reporting the truth, Mickey.' he grinned. 'Same as I always do.'

'The piece you gave to the Chief, what does it say about me?'

'He didn't let you read it?' Tiller nodded. 'Okay, that's good to know.'

'What does it say?'

'Not much really, only got the bare bones so far, but it's got potential and it's definitely in the public interest.' Tiller took a sip of coffee. 'But I'm glad you came to me. I was hoping to have a chat, maybe get your viewpoint on a few things before I go to print. I've always thought we got on well, Mickey, professionally I mean, obviously. Coda, too. I like her a lot. But then, who wouldn't? What's not to like about Amy Coda, eh?' He winked. 'Anyway, that's why I've been looking into her disappearance.'

Digger. The nickname suited him well. Spades might have to do some digging of his own to get out of this situation. 'I don't appreciate being followed,' Spades snapped. 'You should have been upfront with me from the start.'

'And you'd have told me what you were doing? I doubt that.'

'That's not the point.'

'Oh, come on, Mickey. We've always worked well together. You, Coda, and many others in the service. We've worked together on cases for years, sharing our information, gathering our resources. And it's always worked well. I'm always in the loop. I sometimes think I know more about your lives than you do yourselves, and that's what strikes me as odd. If you're looking for Coda, why not include me? Maybe I could help. It's strange that you kept me out of this one. Why is that? What are you not telling?'

Spades felt his blood boil. Tiller had him riled, but he couldn't let it show. If the journalist knew how he was feeling, he would know that he was onto something. 'There's nothing to tell, Digger. You're fabricating a story. You got nothing and you need to drop it. I'm in trouble with the Chief now because of you and I don't like it.'

Tiller pulled out a notebook. 'I don't believe you.' He flicked through the pages. 'The day Coda went missing, you two were scheduled to meet. What happened?'

'How do you know about that?'

'You don't deny it then?' Tiller scribbled on the notebook.

'What are you doing?' Spades felt his anger building.

Tiller ignored him. 'You've been to the Circus District several times in the last few weeks, seven times that I know of. Windmill Lane, I believe?' Tiller looked up from his notes. 'A derelict café called the Black Rose.' He pointed a finger accusingly. 'That's where you and Coda were scheduled to meet that day. Wasn't it?'

Spades cursed inwardly. This was getting worse by the minute. 'You've been talking to the Chief Pathologist, right?'

Tiller's eyes widened with interest. 'No, I haven't, as it happens.' Again, he scribbled eagerly on the pad. 'Sounds like it might be worth my while though?'

Spades took a deep breath. He had to try to limit the damage. Jaxson Tiller was one of the best in the business. 'Who told you all this?'

'Now you know I can't go revealing my sources. Even to you. Even if I wanted to. Which I don't.'

'Then I suggest your source isn't reliable.'

'I have to disagree. My source is good. Your reaction is all the confirmation I need. Something's going on, something you're keeping to yourself. But it's reflecting bad on you. You've got to admit it.'

'It wouldn't look bad if you weren't writing lies about me. I'm telling you to stop it.'

'I can't do that. Coda's missing and something's wrong here. You can't expect me to drop it.' Tiller closed the notebook and put it back inside his jacket. 'Look, I know you had nothing to do with Coda's disappearance, but something strange is going on. I know you're trying to find her, but why are you doing it alone? Why not let me help? Maybe if we work together, we can figure out what happened to her.'

The offer was tempting. It seemed genuine enough, but Spades quickly dismissed it. He had no other choice. There was a lot more to this than Amy Coda's disappearance. Things he wasn't ready or willing to share with anyone, regardless of how good an investigator they were. How would Tiller react if he told him the things he'd discovered recently?

Things he'd discovered with Amy Coda's help.

What would Tiller say if he told him that he suspected none of this was real?

That their lives were nothing more than the product of someone's imagination?

What would Jaxson Tiller say if he told him he could show him proof?

Spades had the proof; he had the book, the story of the previous two years of his life. There were seven other books, all written about him, but he'd avoided seeking them out for obvious reasons. Instead, he'd gone on the trail of the man who'd written them. And he'd found him! He'd been on the cusp of answers when that whiskered old fool had intervened and tricked him.

As things stood, there was no way he could take a respected journalist such as Jaxson Tiller into his confidence. Spades would be ridiculed. Locked up for his own safety, most likely. But maybe when he'd investigated further, if he could make some sense of things, maybe then he could let Tiller get involved. There was a lot to do before that could ever happen. Spades had only scratched the surface and if he was going to make any further progress, the first thing he had to do was get Tiller to drop his interest.

'Okay,' he began, 'I can save you the trouble of going to see the Chief Pathologist. He doesn't know anything. That's why he asked me to look into it before he contacted Missing Persons.'

Tiller hesitated at the sudden change of heart. 'Right. So, do you admit that the meeting between you and Coda was due to take place?'

'Yes,' Spades conceded. 'At least, according to Coda's diary. But I knew nothing about it. Not until he showed me her work planner.'

'Really?' Tiller eyed him suspiciously. 'So, why did it take you so long to report back to the Chief Pathologist? I've been to the Black Rose Café. It's all boarded up.'

'You've been there?'

'Yes, just the once. Didn't seem like there was much point in going back. At least, not to me. But you must feel differently. Why did you keep going back there? What were you hoping to find?'

'Seems like you know all my movements. You have someone following me?'

Tiller shrugged. 'I might have.'

Spades hissed his annoyance. He should have been more careful. This had gone far enough. 'Seems like you and me might have some trust issues to iron out, Digger. Call off your informant. It stops now.'

'Okay, consider it done.'

'Make the call. If we're going to work together. Do it now.'

Tiller picked up his phone. Spades listened as the instruction was passed on. Tiller hung up. 'There, it's done.'

'How can I be sure?'

'Believe me, he won't do it; not unless I pay him in advance. He's not the type to do favours.' Tiller stretched. 'So, what's the next step?'

Spades glanced at his watch. 'I've got to be somewhere. Are you free this afternoon?'

'For this? Definitely.'

'Okay, let's say we meet over in the Circus District. There's a coffee place on the way to Windmill Lane. It's not far from the train station, on a street corner by an ornamental fountain. Three o'clock suit you?'

'Three's fine. What do you have in mind?'

'Not sure yet,' Spades rose from his chair. 'But I'm sure we'll come up with a plan, and it seems like the logical place to start.' He rose from the chair. 'See you at three.'

Back outside in the sunshine, he lit a cigar and made his way towards the train terminal.

Boarding the cross-town train, he headed for the old market town area of the city known as the Circus District. He checked his watch. It was time for some serious planning. He had little over three hours to come up with a way to convince Jaxson Tiller to drop his interest in the disappearance of Amy Coda.

CHAPTER FORTY-THREE

Elfin Fingle's heart skipped. There it was again. The sound of shuffling and scraping in the side alley. Someone or something was following him; it had been tracking him every step of the way since he'd left the Messenger outside the Council chambers.

Pressing a hand against the contents of his jacket, he peered into the gloom. 'Who's there? I know you're there. Come out right now.' He held his breath anxiously as the sound of shuffling drew closer.

'Don't be worrying yourself, lad,' the shadow took form. 'I ain't interested in your paperwork. Nothing there of interest to the old Weasel.'

'Oh, it's you.' Elfin breathed a little easier. 'Have you been following me?'

'Yup! That I have.' The Weasel's nose twitched.

'Why?'

'Reckoned you an' me might have a chat, that's all.'

'Why the subterfuge? Couldn't you just have come and spoken to me?'

'Ah, well now.' The Weasel rubbed at his chin. 'Thought it best if we were discreet. You never know who's watching.'

Elfin glanced around warily. 'What do you mean? Why would anyone be watching us?'

'You an' me? The new monarch's most trusted advisors?' The Weasel flashed a grin. 'Important people now, you and me.'

'We are?'

'Sure we are.' He sidled a little closer. 'So, I got to thinking. There we are, us two fine fellows, back there sitting either side of our queen; two fellows obviously held in high regard, and rightly so I might add, and yet, we'd never been properly introduced. Figured it was time to put that right.' He extended a hand. 'They call me The Weasel.'

Elfin accepted the handshake nervously. 'I'm Elfin Fingle.'

'That you are,' grinned The Weasel. 'And the pleasure's all mine.' He wrapped a spindly arm round Elfin's shoulder. 'It's good to have a friend you can rely on, especially in these troubled times. I reckon you and me could become the very best of friends, don't you?'

'I suppose so.'

'No doubt about it.' The Weasel pulled his arm away. 'See, I'm not so sure about those Dragon Slayers. Unscrupulous lot, I reckon. It might look like she has their backing, but I'm just not sure how dependable they are.' He playfully slapped his forehead. 'Oh, listen to me; they're soldiers of the realm now. Yes, change can be a difficult thing to adapt to. Old habits an' all.' He winked mischievously. 'I'm a creature of habit, young Fingle, and I like to know who I'm dealing with. So, now that's us properly acquainted. We have those soldiers accounted for, and Tauris? I reckon he won't be around for too much longer.'

Elfin was aware that he was being circled. 'I don't suppose so.' The constant chatter was making him feel quite dizzy.

'There was one other fellow there though.' The Weasel continued. 'He kept himself in the shadows. I expect he went unnoticed by most, but not by the old Weasel. Keen attention to detail, very important as a scout and guide. It might just be the difference between life and death.' His jaw gave a loud click as he grinned. 'So, I'm wondering who that fellow might be. Saw you chatting with him outside, seemed like you two were acquainted?'

'Oh, Two Cups?' Elfin smiled. 'I don't know him very well. I've only met him two or three times. He's one of the Messengers.'

'Messengers?' The Weasel worked his gums. 'Never heard of them.' He scratched at his nose. 'Why was he in the chamber? He didn't say much. Quiet fellow, is he? Man of few words?'

Elfin chortled his amusement. 'No, quite the contrary... usually.'

'And why was he there?'

'He accompanied me from Bog-Mire Towers. He and the Scribe had business to attend to. I think he was just watching over things. He likes to...'

'Yes? He likes to what?'

'Nothing really...' Elfin flustered. 'He just likes to look out for people. I don't think it's anything more than that.'

'Sounds fair enough.' The Weasel backed away with a smile. 'Well, I'll not detain you any longer. Pleasure talking to you, Elfin Fingle. We'll meet again soon, I expect.'

'Yes, I'm sure we will.' Elfin nodded courteously. 'It was nice talking to you too. I'd best be on my way.'

'Right you are.' The Weasel grinned. 'Travel safe now.'

Elfin waved his farewell and continued on his way, glad that the disconcerting sounds of being followed had ceased. Reaching his pony, he mounted up and headed north along the Kings Highway. With luck, he'd be back at Bog-Mire in time for lunch.

CHAPTER FORTY-FOUR

The Weasel reflected on the brief exchange as the Scribe's assistant waved his farewell.

The Messengers? Who were they? What was their purpose and why had he never heard of them before? Should he be concerned about this Two Cups fellow's presence?

To what extent was he involved and what were his motives? What was he hoping to achieve?

Did it even matter? The Weasel didn't think so.

It ought not to impinge on his ambitions. If he played his cards right, everything would work out just fine. He already had his foot in the door, so to speak. Patience was what mattered now. His strategy was tried and tested. Make himself appear indispensable; didn't matter how long it might take.

The potential rewards were enormous. He'd already done the hardest part. He had gained her trust, at least to some extent, that much was obvious.

Even he had been surprised by how quickly she had taken control of the Dragon Slayers. She was a woman to be reckoned with and no mistake. It shouldn't matter who this Messenger fellow was, or what influence he might hope to yield. She wasn't the type to be controlled by anyone. She would make her own decisions. As long as he appeared loyal, and played the role of trusted confidante, everything would fall into place.

And the possible rewards? He was almost salivating at the thought. A title? A title for the old Weasel? Who'd have thought it? And land to go with it? One of them big rolling estates with one of them big fancy country houses? Or a castle?

Sure, he loved the outdoors. Life in the wilds was all he'd ever known, but he wasn't as young as he used to be and these days the damp and the cold seemed to creep into his joints the way it never could before. One of them fancy big houses with a nice soft bed would be just ideal. Servants too; lots of them, waiting on his every command. Now that was a life worth looking forward to. Yup! He reckoned this was his calling. Patience, that's what was needed.

Wiping the drool from the corner of his mouth, he cracked his jaw and scratched his chin. Strategy development could give a man a thirst; a thirst that needed to be sated before noon tomorrow.

CHAPTER FORTY-FIVE

Desperate times called for desperate measures. Mickey Spades glanced at his watch with mounting trepidation. Jaxson Tiller would be here in half an hour and Spades was no nearer to finding a solution to his predicament. He'd gone over it again and again. The more he thought about it, the more he came to the same uncomfortable conclusion.

Jaxson Tiller was an inconvenience.

While the prospect of getting fired and publicly humiliated was bad enough, Tiller's involvement would almost certainly end Spades' hopes of ever finding his answers; something he wasn't prepared to let happen, at any cost. He finished his fourth coffee, signalled for a refill, and stared out the window.

Time was running out, and his options were limited. If he failed to convince Tiller to drop all interest in Amy Coda's disappearance he would be left with a grim alternative.

Jaxson Tiller might also have to disappear for a while.

Desperate times, yes. But desperate measures? Was he really contemplating such action?

'You look troubled, friend.'

Startled by the interruption, he swung round. The owner of the voice's appearance unsettled him even further.

Spades swallowed uncomfortably. Just his luck, a circus freak.

Given his location, it was only to be expected. But he was in the minority here, there was no need to go upsetting the locals.

'No, I'm just having a quiet coffee.'

'Then please accept my apologies for the intrusion, Sir. I wanted only to enquire as to your well-being. I will trouble you no further.'

The actor's guise was magnificent. The face make-up was striking. Brilliant white, with black diamonds framing both eyes. Blackened lips completed a ghoulish appearance. His long dark coat, embellished with a spider's web design, swished eloquently as he turned away. What a costume. What an actor. That said, there was something unnerving about him and if it hadn't been for the hat, Spades would never have made his next move. But the hat had caught his attention. The hat, the white band that ran around it, and the image of the black rose.

'Wait!' Spades spoke without thought for the consequences. 'You just surprised me.'

The circus actor swung round gracefully. 'You did look deep in thought, Sir.'

'You could say that,' Spades sighed. 'Have myself quite a dilemma.'

'Is that so?' The actor wrapped his white-gloved hands around his silver cane. 'I've always been of the opinion that a problem shared is a problem solved.' He glanced fleetingly at the empty chair. 'I consider myself a great listener. I have a few moments to spare. If it would help?'

Spades nodded without hesitation. It couldn't do any harm; the distraction might even help.

The stranger glided into the chair with an elegance that defied his lofty stature. Removing his hat, he placed it on the table. Freed from constraint, his jet-black hair tumbled down over his shoulders. Spades' eye drifted to the hat. The black rose. What did it mean? Was it a coincidence, or did this stranger have some connection to the Black Rose Café?

If so, did he know about Spades' interest in the place?

'And so to your dilemma, friend.' The actor removed his gloves. The hairs on the back of Spades' neck tingled at the sight of the long, black-painted fingernails. Were they real? 'Your quandary, Sir.' The stranger's voice focused his thoughts. 'What is it that troubles you?'

Staying acutely aware of his surroundings, taking care not to mention the Black Rose Café, the author Hans Rugen, or the disturbing revelations that had ensued, Spades talked through his predicament. The circus actor listened intently and without interruption, his attention never wavering. Uncomfortable as he was, Spades stuck to his task. When he finished, he found that the man might just have been right. Whilst the problem was not yet solved, talking about it had definitely helped. Not only had it eased his burden, but it had also confirmed his earlier thoughts. There was no longer any doubt about the best way forward.

Jaxson Tiller had to disappear.

'Fascinating!' The circus actor purred his appreciation. 'So, if I may, to summarise, your friend is missing. You believe you are the person best suited and therefore most likely to find her and have already made some progress, but you are worried that sharing what you have learned with the journalist might well scupper all hopes of a successful outcome.'

'That sums it up perfectly.'

'A compelling dilemma, Sir. Tell me, has sharing it helped in any way?'

'It certainly has.' Spades took a sip of coffee and made his play. 'And I think you might be able to help with the solution.'

'Really?' The black lips pursed with interest. 'How intriguing. Tell me, in what way do you think I could offer assistance?'

Spades lowered his voice. 'The man in question, the journalist. He is in the way. He needs to disappear.'

The long fingernails curled round the top of the cane. 'How ghastly. Do you really think so?'

'I'm convinced of it. I wouldn't normally condone such an extreme course of action, but desperate times call for desperate measures.'

'I see. And what makes you think I could help such a macabre plan come to fruition?'

'You strike me as someone who might know how to get things like that done around here.'

'You flatter me, Sir.' The actor worked his fingers on the cane. 'But tell me, even if your notion was true, why do you think I'd be willing to arrange such a thing for you?'

Spades stalled. 'Well, because you offered…'

'I fear you may have misinterpreted my offer, friend. I was willing to listen as you shared your burden, but I don't recall offering to play any part in such an unspeakable act.'

Spades' mis-guided assumption had led him badly wrong. He jumped quickly to make amends. 'Apologies, I wrongly assumed that, given you are from the Circus District, you would know how to make it happen, or know someone who did.'

'You assumed I am from the Circus District?'

'You're not?' Spades shook his head. His blunder was worse than he'd thought. 'Then, where are you from?'

'Here and there.' The man's demeanour changed suddenly. 'Forgive me, friend,' the white-masked face stretched in a grin. 'I must confess to teasing you. You are quite perceptive. Were circumstances different I might well be able to facilitate your gruesome request but I'm afraid that here, in the Circus District, we can only look out for our own. We cannot interfere in the dealings of outsiders and incomers. The ramifications of such actions are unthinkable. But perhaps I could help in some other way.'

Spades glanced at his watch. 'What other way?'

'I detect that your time is precious, so I will be succinct. Perhaps I might offer a word of caution, something for you to consider before you take any action that you may well come to regret.'

'Yes?'

'Consider this. If the journalist were suddenly to go missing, would your predicament not become more precarious? Wouldn't such a scenario further fuel your commanding officer's suspicions about you? What then? Your Chief of Police, he knows so much already… would he also have to disappear? Where would it end? How many would have to be silenced before the web finally closed in around you?' The circus actor shook his head in judgement. 'It would be a dangerous road to travel, friend.'

Spades slouched back in the chair. The stranger's assessment was accurate. The idea was ludicrous. Was he really that desperate? Could he really have gone through with it? He doubted it. 'I guess you're right.'

'I fear so, Sir.' The man rose nimbly to his feet. 'The burden of carrying out such an undertaking would be heavy. The cost too high a price to pay.' He donned his hat.

Spades' eye was drawn once again to the image of the black rose. The opportunity to ask about it hadn't come up. The desire to raise the subject had, for the moment, left him.

The actor slipped his fingers into the white gloves. 'There's always price, friend. We must always remember that. And we must always ask ourselves... is this really what we want? Are we prepared to pay the price?' He offered a smile. 'I sense there is more to your dilemma than you have shared but that is your business, and your business alone. I will leave you to your deliberations and bid you good day.'

Spades nodded. 'Thanks for the advice.'

'An honour and a privilege, friend.' A white-gloved hand gave a flourish as the actor bowed. 'An honour and a privilege.'

As the door of the coffee shop closed behind the stranger, Spades gave an involuntary shudder. The guise, the movement, the chilling presence. Almost too real to be the work of an actor.

Spades checked his watch again. Five minutes. His time was almost up.

The stranger's words of caution echoed in his mind.

Did he really want something like that to happen to Tiller?

Was he really that desperate?

Yes, he was. And as much as he hated to admit it, he couldn't see any other way out.

He watched and waited.

The seconds ticked by agonisingly. Jaxson Tiller's arrival loomed ever closer, and he still had no idea what he was going to tell him.

He waited.

Three o'clock came and passed. Tiller didn't appear.

Spades ordered another coffee. He waited for more than an hour with a growing sense of unease. If Tiller been held up, he would have been in touch. But there was nothing. No call, no text. Digger had been desperate for this meeting. Why had he not shown up? Had he stumbled onto another lead? Or a breaking story? Even that seemed unlikely. He would still have contacted Spades to let him know and to re-schedule their meeting.
Was Tiller playing him for some reason? The more he thought about it, the more annoyed he got. He'd wasted an afternoon for nothing.

At four fifteen, with his mood a confused mix of annoyance and relief, he settled his bill and left. So, Tiller had wasted his time but, on the upside, he now had more time to devise a way forward. One thing was certain, he had to be more careful. He was making too many mistakes.

The temperature had dropped noticeably; the sun was now hidden behind the cover of brooding clouds. As he crossed the cobbled street towards the fountain, a young girl, carrying an ice cream cone, came running from nowhere and almost collided with him.

'Hey!' Spades snapped his annoyance. 'Watch where you're going.'

'Sorry, Mister.' The girl smiled up at him and pointed excitedly at the fountain. 'Isn't it beautiful? It's even grander than the one on the island.'

Spades watched as she ran, barefoot, across the cobbles and danced by the fountain.

'My apologies, friend. She's very excitable.'

The hairs on the back of his neck bristled at the sound of the voice. The white-faced man drew up alongside him.

'Isn't she just adorable?' Tipping the brow of his hat in greeting, he then called out to the girl. 'Come along, young lady. We must get you home before dark.'

Spades drew a breath. 'Your daughter?'

'No, but I do regard myself as somewhat of a guardian.'

The girl skipped back towards them. 'I've been on the most amazing adventure.' In her excitement she almost lost the contents of her cone. 'I wish it would never end.' She pushed the ice cream back into place.

'Dear child.' The white face widened with a grin as he wrapped an arm around her. 'Remember, we must all be careful what we wish for.' His eyes sparkled from within the black diamonds as he gave Spades yet another of his elaborate hand flourishes. 'Once again, it seems, we must say farewell. Good day to you, friend.'

Spades watched with a sense of relief as they rounded the corner and slipped from view. The encounter confirmed his earlier suspicions. The man was no circus act.

He took one last look at the fountain as he debated his next move. From here, it was only a short walk to Windmill Lane and the Black Rose Café.

With a shiver, he pulled up his collar and turned instead towards the train station. He'd had more than enough of the Circus District for one day.

CHAPTER FORTY-SIX

Wisps of cirrus clouds floated high in the bright afternoon sky. The Sea of Lucidity sparkled as a company of gannets bombarded the white-tipped waves. As she neared the rocky outcrop hiding the Haven from view, she saw Raddan waiting for her.

'Shadow.' He greeted her with a smile. 'All quiet at the Watcher's Stone?'

'Yes,' she replied. 'It feels strange to think I won't be back there for a while.'

'A break from routine does no one any harm.' They crossed the rocks and walked side by side along the beach. 'So, you leave in the morning. Have you made all your preparations?'

'I think I'm ready.' She wasn't at all sure that she was. 'At least, as prepared as I can be. I'm not sure quite what lies ahead.'

'We all are on our paths, Shadow. None of us know for certain what lies ahead. We can only take things as we find them.'

She was sure she caught his meaning. Lately, things had taken a very unexpected turn for them all. 'You are already a worthy warden, Raddan,' she smiled. 'Druan chose well.'

'Thank you. I'm doing my best, under the circumstances.' He quickly changed the subject. 'With your consent, I will accompany you tomorrow, as far as the Ash Woods.'

'Yes,' she nodded. 'I'd like that.' Given the choice, she would have his company for the entire journey. Little was known about what lay beyond the dunes to the east of the Ash Woods, and that which was known was rarely talked about. It truly was to be a journey into the unknown. 'Have you been to the dunes, Raddan?'

'No, I have not. That part of the island is a mystery to us all.' His mouth curled with the faint trace of a grin. 'Well, perhaps not all. Has Druan given you directions yet?'

'No, not yet. Tonight though.' As the melodic chimes greeted their arrival, they drew to a halt outside the grey walls of the Haven. 'We are to make our final preparations then. Would you like to join us?'

'Alas, I have my duties to attend to, but you are in good hands. Sleep well tonight. I will see you in the morning.'

Druan's map proved to be a revelation. She scanned the parchment in wonder, scarcely able to believe that so much of the island remained unknown and unexplored.

To the south of the Haven, lay The Forbidden, a stretch of desolate land peppered with fault lines and subterranean tunnels. East of this was The Mire, a treacherous area of bogland always best avoided.

'I always thought there was nothing beyond The Mire but sea.' She looked at Druan. 'This is so much more than I could ever have imagined. You knew of all this?'

'Some of it. It is a changing landscape, one that best remains unknown.' He tapped a finger on the map. 'To the south of The

Forbidden lies the Sea of Fools. Dangerous waters, and well named, for only a fool would even attempt to pass The Sentinels.' The map showed the sea littered with giant towers of rock. 'They guard the coastline well.' Druan rubbed his palms together. 'Your only safe route is to the east side of the island.' Her eye followed his instruction. 'Beyond the Ash Woods, you will reach the Sands of Intention. A wild expanse of inland dunes that appear to stretch all the way to the end of the world and back.' He pulled open a drawer in his desk. 'They can be hard to navigate, but this will help.' He handed her a silver locket.

'What is it?'

'A compass,' he replied. Shadow popped the locket open. The needle spun round gently. 'It is magnetic,' continued Druan, 'and is drawn to the rocks on Horizon's Ruin.'

'The Ruins of Old?'

'Yes. The compass should lead you through the dunes to the coastline. You'll get a good view of the ruins from the beach. By my reckoning you should reach there before dark on the second day.'

'It will take that long to cross the dunes?'

'If all goes well.' He smiled wistfully. 'Time passes differently beyond the Ash Woods.' He turned his attention back to the map. 'From the beach, continue south. A trail leads through the mountains. It can be difficult to follow in places, but as long as you don't cross the Ashrun River you will be fine. And before you know it, you will be back on the plains.'

Shadow followed the map south. 'The Pinnacles of Sorrow? I didn't know they were on the island?'

Druan gave a wry grin. 'Technically they're not, but you will see them, nonetheless. It is not only the nature of time that may seem distorted. You will see much on your journey that makes little sense.' He prodded the map enthusiastically. 'But no matter. From the Pinnacles south the terrain is hospitable, or so I'm led to believe. The Sea of Lucidity will be on your left and to your right, the Lake at the Point of Forever.'

'From the story? Tea at the Point of Forever?'

'The very same. Skirt the southern shore of the Lake and follow the River of Hope, all the way to Journey's End. A sight to behold, if all the tales are true.'

'Journey's End. The Seer will be there?'

'It is at his request that you go,' Druan cleared his throat. 'So, yes, he will be there.'

Shadow traced a finger across the map. 'How much of this landscape have you seen? Have you been there? To any of it?'

'I studied for a time on the islet of Horizon's Ruin, many lifetimes ago it seems. I always knew there was land to the south, but it was never my place to go there. It is his domain. It is the land of the Seer. Aside from him, you and I might just be the only ones ever to have seen this map. I only discovered it a few days ago, in amongst all his papers. Funny, it's as if it were hiding until the time was right.'

Shadow watched as he rose awkwardly from his chair and walked to the window. He seemed suddenly frail, as if she were seeing him in a different light. 'How long will this journey take, Druan? How long will I be gone from the Haven?'

'I honestly don't know, Shadow.' He answered without

looking round.

'But I will come back... won't I?'

He turned at this. A smile softened his aged face. 'Yes, I expect you will, one day, when you have played your part in all things.'

'Played my part? What do you mean?'

'Some say life is a journey and fate has already chosen our path. Others believe we create our own destiny. You are on your path, Shadow, that much is certain, but from here? Who knows what must pass? It is not for me to guess.'

'But I will see you again. Won't I?'

'Of that, dear friend, I am certain.' He moved towards her and offered his arm. 'Whether you will recognise me is another matter altogether. Perhaps we will both appear very different the next time we meet. But don't worry, I'll be looking out for you.'

Momentarily lost for words, she took him by the arm.

'Enough deliberation,' he smiled. 'It's a beautiful moonlit night. Come, let's walk these bodies barefoot on the sand one more time.'

CHAPTER FORTY-SEVEN

Mickey Spades wondered where the long walk to the Chief's office would leave him. He would be in trouble, that much seemed inevitable. But what else? Suspension? Or worse?

He hadn't fixed his issue with Jaxson Tiller. The Chief was not going to be happy.

And if that wasn't bad enough, he'd just had the worst sleep ever. A restless night of troubled dreams; disturbing visions of a white-faced ghoul haunting him, watching his every move, following him everywhere he went. His usual morning concoction of coffee and cigars wasn't working. He felt like he was in a daze.

A summons to the Chief's office this early in the day was the last thing he needed, and he knew it wasn't going to end well.

His footsteps echoed in the long corridor as he contemplated his best plan of defence. The Chief would ask him about Coda. He just knew it. How should he respond? Deny all knowledge, like he did before? Unadvisable.

Problem was, he was walking into this blind. Tiller hadn't shown up for their meeting, but did the Chief know about their proposed meeting in the Circus District?

Marching into the Chief's office without a plan was just plain stupid. But lately it seemed Spades was losing his knack of staying ahead of the game, something he used to be so good at.

Reaching the end of the corridor, he drew to a stop. He'd just have to wing it and hope for the best. There seemed little point in delaying. Best get it over with. With a shake of his head, he knocked on the door.

'Yes?'

He took a deep breath and entered the room. 'You wanted to see me, Chief.'

'Take a seat, Spades.' The Chief made him wait as he thumbed through his notes. After several minutes he pushed the papers aside and fixed him with a stare. 'I'll get straight to the point. This business with Amy Coda.'

Spades knew it. Gut instinct. Right every time.

'I don't know what you were up to, and to be honest, now, I don't care. I'll assume you didn't get the chance to talk to Tiller. Let's face it, you never were one for following my advice quickly.'

Spades wondered about the sudden and unexpected change of heart. 'Well...'

'This isn't a conversation.' The Chief stopped him bluntly. 'I'm talking, you're listening.' His fist hit the desk as if to emphasise his point. 'I don't want to hear any more about your involvement in anything related to Amy Coda. Got it? It's being dealt with by the right people now, so leave it alone. Do you understand what I'm saying?'

Spades nodded. 'Loud and clear.'

'Good! That's it settled then. That will be all.'

Spades stood gingerly. 'And what about Tiller? Is he dropping his interest in it?'

The Chief's expression changed. 'You didn't hear?'

'Hear what?'

'Well, that's a promising sign.'

'What do you mean?'

'I thought you'd be up to speed on the news from the Circus District. Maybe it shows you're conquering your obsession with the place. Good thing, too. That area is bad luck.'

'Why? What happened?'

'Jaxson Tiller. He went there yesterday. It happened when he was leaving the train station… he must have been preoccupied or something. He wandered out into the busy street, right in front of an oncoming delivery truck.'

Spades felt a cold shiver run down his spine. Now he knew why Tiller hadn't shown up. 'Is he…?'

The Chief shook his head gravely. 'He didn't stand a chance. Shame, he was one of the good guys.' Dismissing Spades with a wave of his hand he turned his attention back to his papers. 'Back to work, Detective. Close the door behind you.'

The walk back along the corridor seemed to take forever. This was bad. This was very bad. The more he tried to deny it, the worse it felt. Things had taken a very sinister turn. The knot in Mickey Spades' stomach suggested things might never be the same again.

CHAPTER FORTY-EIGHT

'And so, the Order of the Dragon Slayers is no more.' Messenger Two Cups could scarcely believe it.

Ten Six Nine faced him. 'You don't approve?'

'On the contrary,' he smiled. 'Under the circumstances, it is a necessary change and one that was long overdue.'

'I hope Enntonia doesn't come to regret my decision.'

'Dragons?' He shook his head. 'I don't think it's an issue. The only dragon ever likely to return here wouldn't be the kind to be defeated by men, women, and swords.'

'I hope you're right.' Her gaze returned to the sea.

'Are you not joining the others?'

'Maybe later.'

'It's awkward?'

'Yes. I don't think they're sure how to react towards me.'

'Seems to me you had their full attention earlier, in the chamber. Had them hanging on your every word by the end.'

'It went better than I'd expected. I didn't think they would concede so readily.'

'Sometimes all they need is something to believe in. A purpose, a cause, and someone to follow. You've given them all that and more.'

'Maybe.' She seemed unconvinced.

'So, you leave tomorrow.'

'Yes.'

'It's a bold plan.'

'Is it the right plan?' Her gaze stayed focused on the sea.

'It is not my place to speculate,' he replied. 'It is your destiny, not mine.'

'Would you do things differently?'

'I can't see the way ahead.'

'Even with your gift?'

'Sometimes,' he frowned, 'but not on this occasion.'

'Twelve Seven Two. I'd already decided that I was going looking for him before you told me those things.'

'I'd guessed that much,' he smiled.

Turning to him, she held his gaze. 'Do we know each other?'

'What?' The directness of her question took him by surprise.

'There is something familiar about you,' she continued. 'I've felt it since we met at Bog-Mire.'

'Ha! You know, I get told that a lot. I must have one of those faces.'

'You're sure there's not more to it?'

'What more could there be?' She wasn't convinced, that much was obvious. It didn't matter, there was no way he could tell her the truth.

'The Scribe's assistant told me things,' she continued.

'I'm aware of that,' Two Cups interrupted. 'He told you about the incident involving the men from Ergmire and the hooded Raiders. As unlikely as it sounds, it's all true I'm afraid. Ergmire's loss was real.'

'I need to know. What happened?'

'Ergmire's soldiers were here, camped in the foothills of the Hogback Mountains. I believe it was nothing more than a show of force. Our High Council had neglected their debts and Ergmire's patience had worn thin.' Pausing, Two Cups waved a hand in dismissal. 'I will cut the tale short. Ergmire's threat was real. So too was a darker threat. An army of hooded riders summoned by the Black Wizard. They slaughtered the men of Ergmire.'

'Black Wizard?' She shook her head. 'How is it that, save for a few, no one knows about this?'

'Alas, I could do nothing to save TrollGatten and his men, but I could save Enntonia. I hid both threats in a veil of deception and confronted the Black Wizard in Bog-Mire Towers. I defeated him and, with his threat nullified, his foul riders scattered.'

She waited a moment before responding. 'What does Ergmire know of this? If their loss was real, why have they not sought revenge?'

'I sent word to Ergos, informing them that TrollGatten and his men had fallen in battle, standing shoulder to shoulder with their allies, repelling a foreign invading force.'

'And they believed it?'

'They did, at least for a while. Now, I'm not so sure.'

She nodded. 'This ties in with everything The Weasel has told me.'

Two Cups' brows twitched with interest. 'Ah yes, your scout. This Weasel fellow, can he be trusted?'

'I've no reason to doubt him so far. He was with Twelve Seven

Two when they found the Slayer's body. He did as Twelve Seven Two instructed. He could have easily just discarded the Slayer's body and disappeared into The Barrens, but he did the right thing.'

'And Twelve Seven Two? Do you know what happened to him? Do you know where he might be?'

'The Weasel said he last saw him with a rider of Ergmire, one who claimed to have infiltrated the rogue riders at the request of the government in Ergos.'

'Maybe things are not as bleak as we thought. If those riders are in Enntonia without the consent of Ergmire's government, perhaps all is not lost. Perhaps Ergmire and Enntonia will not end up at each other's throats.'

'It seems unlikely. Especially given my plan.'

'Ah, yes, but plans can change.' Two Cups grinned. 'So, you are heading north, by Bog-Mire?'

'Yes.'

'Avoiding the Eastern Forest?'

'Time is against us. The last thing I need is to get lost in there again.'

'Indeed.' Two Cups toyed with his whiskers. He no longer felt the need to ask her why she'd not shared her knowledge of TrollGatten's demise with the others. It felt like he'd taken the conversation as far as he could. She was focused and determined. She held Enntonia's fate in her hands. If he had some greater insight of what lay ahead, he could offer his help and influence but, for now, it seemed there was nothing more he could do. 'You must have a lot on your mind. I will leave you to your thoughts.'

'What about the girl?'

'The girl? Ah yes, Reen of the Aaskrid.'

'She is gone?'

'Yes. I'm afraid she had to leave at short notice. Opportunities to switch between realities are not always easy to plan. They can crop up suddenly and without warning.'

'It would have been nice to see her before she left, to say goodbye.'

'She felt the same way, I can assure you.' He extended his hand. 'It has been a pleasure to meet you, Ten Six Nine. Perhaps when you return, we might get the chance to become further acquainted.'

To his surprise, she brushed his hand aside and put her arms around him. 'I'd like that, Scaraven.' The embrace felt familiar. His name even more so. But as he stepped back, he saw the distance in her eyes. 'Forgive me, Messenger, that was inappropriate.'

'Not at all. Far from it.' He smiled. Sanna had been there, he was certain of it. If only for a fleeting moment, she'd been there. Comforted by the thought, he said his farewell.

Leaving her at the seafront, he made his way back through the city. There was much to consider. The Representatives would have to be informed of the recent events.

He wondered just how much they already knew. They had their contacts within the city, they'd told him so, but did they know more than they'd let on? Was this the change they'd predicted, or was there more to come? He couldn't shake the feeling that something was amiss. Something was coming. He could feel it in his bones, but he just couldn't see what it was. The more he thought about it, the more the doubts crept in.

Reen of the Aaskrid had triggered his suspicions when they'd chatted just before the carnival's departure. Her questioning had raised the subject of the Fifteen.

The Guardians of the Gateways. Messenger Two Cups knew them by a different name. The Wise Ones.

The girl's interest in them was innocent enough. She'd heard their name mentioned several times during her short visit to the island and whilst she'd been happy with his explanation, he was the one now experiencing these niggling doubts.

Was there solid foundation to the simmering concerns of the Acolytes? Two Cups frowned at the possibility.

The Representatives would be informed of events in Enntonia, but he would not be the one to do it. He was not yet ready to make a return visit to the Hall. The thought of the precarious bridge crossing was enough to deter anyone.

On his return to Bog-Mire he would send for the Harbinger. Talus would ride to the Hall in his stead, leaving him free to investigate the cause of his concerns further.

Fumbling in his coat pocket, his hand settled on the glass sphere. As he whispered his incantation, an old tramp, cradling a wine bottle, staggered into view at the end of the lane.

Messenger Two Cups chuckled as the tramp's slack-jawed expression slowly faded, replaced by the cobblestoned courtyard of Bog-Mire Towers.

CHAPTER FORTY-NINE

Gallows Fall was a town just like any other. While its name was anything but inviting, the people seemed friendly enough; content to go about their business without sticking their noses into other folk's affairs. Not that it mattered much. He'd be gone before anyone had the inclination to ask about him or his uncanny resemblance to the face on the posters that would soon be winging their way into town.

The tavern bustled with activity. It had a homely feel. A warming fire blazed in the open hearth and whilst the ale might not have been the best, the food was well above average. A man could do worse than getting a room here and putting his head down for the night.

A bed and a mattress; a comforting thought. But there was no need to rush the decision. It appeared safe, but he'd review the situation as the evening progressed before making a final decision. Better safe than sorry.

Hendrick Stanner watched the room as he pondered his latest disaster. The bank job in Sleeping Firs should have been so simple. An early morning strike; in and out. No dramas, no hitches, and definitely no casualties. He shuddered at the thought of it. The latter seemed inevitable.

How had things gone so wrong? How could he have made such a catastrophic blunder?

He'd checked the strength of the powder several times. The mix should only have been strong enough to cause a small blast in the garbage accrued in an alley a block away from the bank.

It should have been a diversionary tactic, nothing more.

But instead of casually walking into the bank amidst the ensuing melee and instructing the teller to part with the contents of the safe, he'd watched on in horror and disbelief as the explosion blew half the street sky high.

With a shake of his head, he took a mouthful of ale. Things were going from bad to worse. These days it seemed like everything he touched went wrong. All his plans were going awry, his dreams were turning to dust. His trail west was descending into chaos and disaster; a catalogue of errors, drawing far too much attention. He was no longer considered a petty thief of little or no consequence. He was fast having to come to terms with an uncomfortable truth. He was running out of places to go, and things were looking bleak.

His sudden, catastrophic decline in luck might have been easier to accept if his finances were growing in tandem with his notoriety. They weren't, and, as glamourous as it might sound, being infamous alone wasn't enough to buy the new future he longed for.

He watched with disinterest as one of the serving girls approached his table.

'Want some company?'

'Me?'

'Yes,' she smiled. 'You.'

Stanner glanced quickly round the room. Was it a trap? He

shook his head. His paranoia was becoming worse.

'Sure, okay. Pull up a seat.'

'Not here,' she winked suggestively. 'Five minutes. Room twelve. Upstairs, at the far end of the corridor.' Turning with a smile, she merged with the bustle of the room.

Stanner drew a breath. Maybe his luck had just changed for the better. Best to be on his guard, just in case. He scanned for danger as he drained his pitcher. Content that the risk was low, he crossed the room and climbed the wooden stairs.

A solitary oil lamp flickered on the wall. The floorboards creaked noisily under the threadbare carpet as he made his way along the corridor. Room twelve was right where she'd said it would be. So far, so good. He tapped on the door and waited. After a moment he knocked again, opened the door, and entered the room.

In the half-light he saw the shape of a bed against the far wall.

'Are you in here?' No response came. Maybe she'd got held up with her duties downstairs. He crossed the room, took off his jacket, and sat down on the bed.

A lamp burst into life, throwing a new set of shadows onto the gable wall. There was someone in the room waiting for him, but it wasn't who he'd been expecting. His jaw dropped open in astonishment.

The bearded man with the strange eyes raised a hand in greeting. 'And so we meet again, Hendrick Stanner. Just like I told you we would.'

'You? What are you doing here?' Stanner jumped to his feet. 'Where's the girl?' He'd been duped. Her invitation had been a

271

trick, just as he'd suspected. Why had he fallen for it?

'She said you wanted company, so here we are. Perhaps not the company you had in mind but, if you will humour me, it might prove beneficial.'

'I doubt that.' Stanner groaned. 'Why are you following me? What do you want?'

'A few moments of your time, nothing more.' The weathered face remained stolid. 'You've been busy, caused quite an upheaval in Sleeping Firs by all accounts.'

'How do you know about that?'

'Let's just say I've been keeping up with events. I see that the price on your head has increased considerably. Only to be expected. People can't be allowed to go around blowing up buildings, no matter how desperate things become for them. But you will be glad to learn that there were no serious injuries. By good luck, everyone seemed to have been elsewhere at the time of the explosion.'

'Makes no odds to me.' Stanner bluffed his response.

'Oh, come now, such bravado.' A gnarled finger pointed at him. 'I see the relief in your eyes. You are no killer, Hendrick Stanner.'

'I've done my share.'

'No, you haven't. Your conscience is clear on that count at least. Except perhaps for that one night, the night your partner in crime met with his undignified end. But you shoulder no blame for that. It had to be done. It was unavoidable.'

Stanner's unease heightened. How was this possible? Had he been following him that long? Watching him all this time?

'How do you know about that?'

'You saved that woman's life that night, Hendrick Stanner.' The voice floated hauntingly across the room. 'That night in the settlement of Creek. The injured woman, she survived and recovered from her wounds. All thanks to you.'

The revelation hit Stanner like a freight train. Reeling back, he sat down on the bed.

Creek.

The wounded woman in the alley.

The night he'd ended his partnership with Drake.

As the memories came flooding back, his gaze wandered across the room and settled on the old man's rust coloured coat. 'It was you!' The words almost stuck in his throat. 'That day on the plateau. That was you!'

'There now.' The stranger clapped his hands together. 'I knew it would come back to you.'

Stanner's head flooded with questions. 'That settlement. Creek. Why did you tell me to go there? Did you know what was going to happen?'

'In my defence, you were already on your way there regardless of my intervention. Sometimes fate throws us a fork in the path, offering us an opportunity. I merely helped ensure you made the right choice.'

Stanner scowled his annoyance. 'The right choice? Right for who?' Things were quickly falling into place. 'Not for me, I reckon. When I think about everything that's happened since that day, seems things have gone from bad to worse for me.'

'Come now,' the old man chortled his dismissal. 'Your bad

luck started long before the day we met. You'd been making bad choices for a long time. I've merely presented you with the chance to take a different route. To forge a new reality for yourself, and that is why I'm here. To make you an offer.'

'I'm not interested in anything you have to say.' Stanner growled as he got to his feet. 'And as for choices; if I have a choice, this will be the last time we cross paths.'

'That is your prerogative but first, let me say my piece. The reward for your capture has risen steeply. The bounty hunters are still on your tail and, unfortunately for you, they have doubled their resources by adding a couple of accomplices. Given their progress, I expect them to be here in Gallows Fall before dawn.'

Stanner cursed. Looked like he wouldn't be getting that bed for the night after all. Despite his reservations, the old man's warning had been genuine the first time and there was no obvious reason to doubt it now. He could put a full night's ride between him and his followers, but this stranger's persistence was troubling. His warnings might be genuine, but what did he expect in return? As far as Stanner was concerned, Creek hadn't turned out to be such a good idea. He'd maybe doubled his haul by eliminating his partner, but it had been reckless. Interfering in other people's business rarely ended well.

'I want the truth, old man. What are you up to? Why are you following me? And why are you giving me these warnings?'

'Just looking out for a friend.'

'You're no friend of mine,' Stanner hissed. Damn it, those eyes were unsettling.

'Everyone needs friends,' the man tapped the table firmly. 'My motives are clear. As I said, I'm here to make you an offer. Be honest, you must be getting tired of the chase. How long do you think you can keep this up? You are running out of places to go.'

'As long as I need to.' His response sounded less than convincing. It seemed the old man had the ability to read minds.

'Your path is a lost cause, Hendrick Stanner, but you are not. I can offer you the chance to change everything. Imagine that. A new reality, a new life.'

Stanner shook his head. There was no way he was agreeing to anything this stranger offered. 'I'm not interested.' He pulled on his jacket and moved towards the door. 'I appreciate the warnings but, whatever it is you're after, I'm afraid you're out of luck.'

The old man rose slowly from the table. 'Very well. Perhaps next time.'

'No offence but see to it that there isn't a next time.'

'None taken, but there will be a next time, Hendrick Stanner. I think you know it just as well as I do.'

Stanner hurried along the corridor and went downstairs. Downing three shots of liquor in quick succession, he left the comfort of the busy tavern and went out into the night.

He had plenty on his mind as he rode under the stars.
Who was the old stranger with the glass-like eyes?
What was he up to? And what did he want?
Was there truth in his words?
It seemed like there was. Seemed like there was a lot.
He had to admit it.
The man's words had echoed many of Stanner's thoughts.

Time was running out. He could feel the proverbial noose tightening around his neck.

Against the growing feeling of resignation, he spurred his horse onwards. Gathering speed, he rode long into the night.

CHAPTER FIFTY

The early morning dew glistened in the bright sunlight.

Shadow's breath hung in the cold air as she allowed herself one final look back. Home. It was all she had ever known, at least, all she could remember. For now, all memory and awareness of other lives were hidden from view. She wondered if this might change on the journey ahead.

Beyond the grass-covered roof of the Haven, the waves rolled gently into the bay. It was a view that warmed her heart. Blocking all thought of when she might see it again, she turned and nudged her horse into a gallop.

She caught up with Raddan at the brow of the hill. Riding silently, side by side, they made steady progress across the tiered plains of the Uplands. Shadow had ridden here many times before, on her way to exploring the hills and mountains to the north-west of the Ash Woods, but today, everything felt different.

With the sun high in the morning sky, they stopped for a rest by the side of a stream. Shadow scanned the way ahead for sign of movement, but all was still.

'We're doing well.' Raddan gave his assessment. 'I'd say we are halfway to the Ash Woods.'

She nodded, and her thoughts drifted. There had been no sight of Druan this morning and though she hadn't expected to see him it had still come as a disappointment, especially given the enormity of his words the previous evening.

They chatted for a while as they rested but before long they were on the move again. Not long after the sun passed its zenith, the ghostly vision of the Ash Woods came into view crudely piercing the lush green of the landscape. Riding towards it, Shadow watched as the anomaly grew in stature. Though she'd seen it several times from a distance, she had never ventured into the woods. She'd never had cause to and, truth was, the thought of going in there filled her with dread.

Named after their ghostly pale appearance rather than any species of tree, the Ash Woods was a mix of oak, pine, and silver birch which, for reasons unknown, had taken on their pallid appearance and had never recovered. Some said it was because of the sandy nature of the soil, others blamed the frequent blasts of wind from the neighbouring dunes. Whatever the reason, the forest looked sick and entering it made for a daunting proposition.

As they neared the edge of the woods, Raddan drew them to a halt. 'This is where I must leave you, Shadow. I must be back at the Haven before dark.'

'I understand.' She took a moment to check her provisions, then fussed over her horse. The dunes were no place for him. She handed the reins to Raddan. 'Take good care of him for me.'

'I will. Good luck, Shadow.' Their farewell was brief. There was no need for it to be any other way. Raddan turned the horses and mounted up.

'Goodbye, Raddan.'

She watched as he galloped into the distance. When all sight of him was gone, she hoisted her pack onto her shoulder and turned to face the ghostly forest.

The trees seemed held in the grip of an eternal winter. The birch and oak were little more than bare stalks of silver and white stripped of all their greenery. Though it still held on to some of its needles, the pine looked like it had been the victim of a vociferous forest fire, as if the flames had ripped through the trees, turning everything ash grey. There was no point in putting it off; delaying the inevitable would only make it worse. With no small measure of apprehension, she entered the Ash Woods.

All the tales might well be true. This place might well be cursed. A forest of lost souls, held prisoner in a spell of constant discolouration, watching her every step. Try as she might, she couldn't shake the feeling of being watched. She knew there was no life here. No birdsong, no sign of wildlife. Yet the feeling remained with her.

As she moved further into the forest, the light began to fail. Struggling to break through the gloom, the pale sunlight took on a supernal haze as if a mist had descended surreptitiously all around her. She lost all track of time as she picked her way through the grey monotony.

Her surroundings barely changed. Here and there a sporadic pine offered a fleeting glimpse of green, but they were few and far between.

A further dramatic decline in the daylight signalled the onset of evening.

The sun had dipped below the treetops. It would soon be time to find somewhere to rest for the night, before the darkness took hold.

Not long after, her mood lifted as the trees gave way to a clearing with a grassy knoll at its centre. Dropping her pack to the ground, she began a hasty scavenge for firewood.

The pickings were plenty. The dry branches broke easily from the trees, and a warming fire was soon cracking merrily in the clearing.

With her hunger pacified, wrapped in her blanket, she watched as the Ash Woods succumbed to the night. Tomorrow, if all went well, she would be clear of the sallow forest and would begin her crossing of the Sands of Intention.

As she closed her eyes, her mind danced with visions of ghostly trees, sun-bleached wastelands, and great pillars of age-old rock. She was now truly in the throes of her journey.

She was a day nearer meeting the Seer Magister.

CHAPTER FIFTY-ONE

Waking early, she watched the first slithers of dawn creep among the trees. Spurred into action by the sudden drop in temperature, she continued her passage through the ghostly forest.

Though its source remained hidden from sight, the pale glow of the rising sun guided her east. Onwards she walked through the grey stillness.

The hours dragged slowly by.

Life on the island was, for the most part, one of solitude. Despite this, the sense of loneliness was something she had never experienced, until now. She felt it now. The isolation of the Ash Woods made her want to scream out loud. Anything to break the silence. She longed to hear a voice, any voice. Anything to breathe life into the void.

And yet she knew it was unwise to wish for such things. Daunting as it was, the silence of the forest might prove infinitely better than the sudden appearance of life when she least expected it. And who knew what form life might take in this strange place. Taking control of her fears, she focused her thoughts and kept moving.

As the daylight improved, she began to see the first signs of change in her surroundings. Pockets of sand emerged here and there from the vegetation of the forest floor. Her mood lifted as momentary glimpses of pale blue sky danced teasingly among the trees. Her pace quickened in anticipation, in the hope that the bleakness might soon come to an end.

Not long after, with a further change in terrain, the land began its striking transformation.

The descent was gradual at first, the slope barely noticeable, but she quickly gained momentum. The trees thinned as she stumbled down the steep banks. Overhead, the blue sky ripped great holes in the ash-coloured veil. Her heart raced in expectation.

The Ash Woods came to a sudden and dramatic end in the form of a great bank of sand which had consumed many of the trees, leaving only a few skeleton tops exposed. Eager to leave the forest behind, Shadow scrambled to the top and saw her first glimpse of the wilderness ahead. The sense of elation at being freed from the stagnant grip of the dead woods might easily have been dashed by the prospect of what still lay ahead.

Pushing all such negative thoughts to the back of her mind, she paused for a rest before opening Druan's locket. The compass needle spun back and forth for several seconds before finally settling on its course. Buoyed by the clear view of the sky and the feel of the gentle breeze on her skin, she bundled her way down the embankment and began the trek towards the coast.

The Sands of Intention were a daunting stretch of sand dunes; an ever-changing landscape of erratic chaotically formed ridges and hills of sand blown far inland from the sea. A vast undulating expanse of desert, peppered with sporadic clumps of sharp grass and even fewer clusters of dead sun-bleached trees.

Guided by the compass, its needle now firmly fixed on its

target, she walked on determinedly.

A myriad of quarries and craters, blasted and sculpted by the wind, were interspersed with open stretches of wind-rippled sand. Druan had been right. Without the aid of the compass, navigation of this landscape would have been hopeless.

In places the sand banks towered high overhead. Dwarfed by their presence, she strengthened her resolve. As the hours slipped by, her hopes of seeing sign of life diminished. Nothing, not even the sight of a bird scouting the skies above. The desolation of the dunes almost matched that of the Ash Woods.

Again, she felt the sting of loneliness. Was it to be like this for the entirety of her journey? Though she knew the folly in such thoughts, part of her craved to talk to someone, anyone, even if only for a few minutes.

Onwards she trudged, reminding herself constantly that she had much to be thankful for.

As repetitive and as void of life as they were, the dunes were a far more appealing proposition than the ghastly forest in which she'd spent the night.

As the sun began its slow descent towards evening, after what seemed like an eternity in the wasteland, the banks became noticeably smaller and less imposing. Crossing a flat stretch of coarse sand, her gaze fixed on the splash of green lining the crest of the slope ahead. She broke into a run. Reaching the incline, she ploughed her way upwards, her boots sinking and sliding in the shifting sand. As she neared the brow of the hill she heard it, the unmistakable roll of the sea.

A flurry of seabirds called noisily overhead.

Clutching at handfuls of the sharp grass, she pulled herself up to the top of the climb. The compass had served her well.

She had reached the coast.

Great banks of golden sand rolled down to the beach. The curved bay seemed to stretch for miles in both directions. She looked out to sea. The jagged landform of Horizon's Ruin was well named. Rising sharply from the water, it dominated the view. The grey-walled ruins where Druan, along with many others, had studied, were just visible, the towers and turrets sitting proudly atop the steep cliffs. Her view did not stay unhindered for long. As she took in the scene, a great rolling bank of cloud appeared. Within minutes the island was gone from view. She made her way down onto the beach and sat for a while, her eyes closed, listening to the gentle breaking of the waves.

The last few hours of daylight were spent walking on the beach. The sands ended abruptly at the foot of the steep cliffs. Climbing the rock shelves, she found a great notch in the lee of the overhanging headland. Crawling inside, she found ample shelter for the night ahead. The gathering clouds hid all signs of sunset. Sometime later she fell asleep to the sound of rain falling heavily on the rocks outside the cave.

CHAPTER FIFTY-TWO

Beyond the rise on the far side of the frozen lake, the snow-covered mountains stretched far into the distance. The biting wind nipped relentlessly. Watching the clouds as they raced across the sky, Amy Coda zipped the fur-lined jacket up as far as it would go.

'Nallevarr.' She said the name again, as if repeating it would bring a better understanding of her whereabouts and how she had come to be here. 'You say this was once a great forest?'

'Some of what you see was once covered in trees,' his response was sombre, 'before the rising of the seas and the coming of the ice. But the archaeological teams suspect that much of what was once Farnwaar Forest still lies hidden beneath the ocean.'

'And you work with them on the excavation sites?'

'Yes, as a guide. We should keep moving. We'll find shelter down in the cove.'

He led the way, navigating a safe route among the frozen pools and jagged spears of rock. The two dogs paced faithfully behind him. Dogs or wolves? She was unsure. Perhaps they were something in between. Despite their size, they had a gentle nature. Each stopped in turn, as if checking on her progress, all the while sniffing the air in expectation.

Three days had passed since her inexplicable arrival in this strange land. Hopelessly lost, she had wandered for hours along the rugged coastline before seeing any sign of life. Desperate for help and for answers she'd followed him, unsure of the danger involved or how he would react to her sudden appearance. But there had been no cause for concern. If he'd been surprised by her arrival, he hadn't shown it. He had been understanding of her predicament, even claiming that the same thing had happened to him. From their subsequent conversations, it was obvious he'd experienced the phenomenon more than once. They had a lot in common; it was undeniable.

The time had passed quickly. He'd mentioned a settlement when they'd first met but instead had taken her to an isolated stone building in the hills. The structure bore semblance to an ancient long-forgotten hunting lodge, similar to the ones she'd read about in her childhood folk tales. The interior of his sanctuary, as he referred to it, boasted a grand banqueting hall stamped with all the hallmarks of eminence and regality. A long feasting table and wooden throne, walls adorned with tapestries depicting great battle scenes and an eye-opening display of cob-webbed weaponry: rusting spears, swords, and axes.

Adjoining the main hall, several smaller rooms offered basic sleeping arrangements and in one, best of all, there was a large open fireplace. Sitting either side of a roaring fire, sheltered from the snowstorm that had raged for much of the previous two days, they'd talked at length, comparing the similarities in their experiences.

Though she found him easy to talk to, she sensed he was shielding her from the true scale of her predicament. That suited her just fine. She knew she would have to face the harsh reality of her situation soon enough. Whilst he had spoken much of Nallevarr's history and discussed the subject of his odd encounters with strange new landscapes, she had the feeling there was a lot about himself that he was reluctant to share. She could hardly blame him for that. There was plenty she hadn't yet told him, but that was all about to change.

It wasn't that she owed this stranger any explanation, but she had to tell someone. She didn't know how much longer she could carry the burden alone. Her worry was how he would react when she told him. What would she do if he took it badly and asked her to leave? How would she survive in this bleak land without his help?

As they neared the coast, they joined a track leading down a precarious ridge. Weakened by the timeless pounding of the waves, the crumbling cliffs had slipped forward to confront the surging swell of the sea. The descent to the shoreline was rapid and airy. Reaching the scattered coastline, the rocky ridge gave way to a stretch of white sand that appeared to stretch forever into the distance. The cove formed a natural stone amphitheatre, its walls were gouged with great yawning caves and black notches. Sheltered from the buffeting wind, all was quiet save for the occasional cry of the seabirds watching from their perches in the rock-face high above. Sitting by his side on the rocks, she watched the unrelenting roll of the sea as it met with the sand.

'The strange tides of Nallevarr.'

She caught the distant look in his eyes. 'Strange, in what way?'

'High tide happens here only once a day. It's believed the regional geography was shaped by a massive tremor in the seafloor plates long ago.' He looked towards the horizon. 'The tides are strange but consistent. They follow a thirty-day cycle, their characteristics changing little from one day to the next. But on the thirtieth day, with each full moon, at low tide, the sand stretches further than the eye can see. When the ocean returns the following day, the high tide fills the largest cave there in the cliffs right to the top.' He turned to face her. 'This cove holds a special significance, and I believe it is your best chance of finding your way home.'

'Why? What is its significance?'

'Legend tells that a brave few have walked out there at low tide, in search of the ocean… to find out where it goes. None ever returned. Popular belief is that they run out of time and the ocean swallows them on its return journey. True or not, high tide at the end of the cycle signals a great shift. Nallevarr and everything that happens here is bound by this timeline.' He hesitated for a moment. 'We've talked about the archaeological digs, but you must be wondering why I've not mentioned the settlement again or taken you there.'

She noted his reluctance. 'A little.'

'We are already well through this cycle of the moon. Come to the cove each morning. Wait a while, walk on the sand. Do this each day. If you are still in Nallevarr ten days from now, I will take you to the excavations and it will then be safe for you to visit the settlement.'

'Why is it not safe to go there before that?'

'We don't get many visitors here. The folk will ask questions about who you are and where you come from. It would be easier for me if I didn't then have to explain your sudden disappearance. But if you are still here after that time, we can tell them you have come from the southern lands to join the explorations.'

Amy Coda drew a deep breath. 'So, if I'm still here in ten days...?'

'If you are still in Nallevarr at the next full moon, if you visit the cove and see nothing but sand when you look out to sea, it's likely that you will never leave.'

CHAPTER FIFTY-THREE

Taro Brook watched her reaction closely. If she was alarmed by his revelation, she was hiding it well. Her measured response took him by surprise.

'Maybe that would be for the best.'

'You surely don't mean that?'

'I don't know what I'd be going back to.' She held his stare. 'Is that what happened to you? Were you not able to leave this place?'

'Nallevarr is where I belong.'

'I see.' Her frustration was obvious. 'This is all my own fault. This is what I get for meddling in things that should have been left alone. I should have never interfered.' A sadness tinged her voice. 'Believe it or not, being stranded here isn't the worst thing that can happen. This isn't the lowest point for me...' She hesitated. 'There's no easy way to say this... I killed someone.'

Aside from the obvious implications of her predicament, Taro Brook had sensed that something was troubling her. Something bigger, something she needed to share. But he hadn't expected this.

'It was an accident,' she continued. 'I didn't mean for it to happen. I'd just wanted to talk to him, but everything spiralled out of control. It all happened so quickly.' Her eyes welled up. She looked away.

Brook took a deep breath. 'Maybe we need to rewind?'

'Yes,' she nodded. 'Maybe I should start at the beginning.'

'As good a place as any.'

Wiping her eyes, she began cautiously. 'You've told me that you've often found yourself in unfamiliar surroundings.'

'Yes.'

'As you know, this isn't the first time it's happened to me but it feels different.'

'Different in what way?'

'I always felt someone else's presence around me, like they were part of me and I was part of them. But not this time... It's just me. When you shift to these different places, are you still fully aware of things or do you feel disorientated? Do you feel like someone else?'

'A bit of both,' he replied hesitantly. 'And it differs each time.'

She nodded. 'I kept finding myself in some other place, as if I were having a recurring dream, but it was so real, I was still fully aware of who I was. I knew that everything around me looked different and that everyone looked different, but yet I still knew them. Does that make sense?'

'It does.'

'I was still me, I was still Amy Coda, but these people were calling me something else. Then it all became apparent, one day, when I saw myself in a mirror.'

'You looked different.'

'Yes. I looked different because I was someone else, but I was always more aware of myself than I was of that other person.'

'It sounds familiar. So, this other place. You went there a lot?'

'Yes. I can't say how long it went on for. I don't remember much about her, but we shared a common interest. We both loved reading, and when I was there, I came across a book, a fiction detective story. The name of the main character was Mickey Spades.'

Mickey Spades? Taro Brook winced. Why did that name sound familiar? 'And?'

She hesitated. 'Sorry, at this point I should probably say that in my work as a forensic pathologist, I often have dealings with a detective called Mickey Spades.'

'Really?' Detective Spades. Brook rolled his shoulders. 'A coincidence?' There was no such thing as coincidence. Experience had taught him as much.

'That would be the logical conclusion,' she continued. 'And that's what I thought until I read further and found my name in the book, along with the names of several others I know and work with.'

Brook's eyes widened. 'How is that possible? Who wrote the book?'

'An author called Hans Rugen.'

Brook flinched. 'Hans Rugen?' The conversation had taken a disturbing twist.

'Yes, and the things he wrote about Spades and me, the events in our lives, the details of the cases we worked on, it was staggering. There's no way he could have made it up. It was as if he was with us, working alongside us, it's the only way he could have known it all. The only explanation I could come up with was that the writer, Hans Rugen, must have been shifting between places too.'

Brook nodded his understanding. 'He was writing his memories of someone else's experiences?'

'Yes, and I think I know who it was.'

'You do?'

'A journalist by the name of Jaxson Tiller. He worked with the authorities on many cases, sharing information and such. He's the only one I know who had that level of clearance.'

'So, Hans Rugen was drifting into the world of Jaxson Tiller.'

'Yes and writing accounts of his experiences, portraying them as fictional stories. Possibly even unintentionally. He might not even have been aware that they were based on real events.'

'Did you talk to Tiller?'

'And say what?' She frowned. 'It's not exactly an easy subject to broach. Not unless you want people to think you're crazy.'

'A fair point.'

'I did talk to Hans Rugen though.'

'Really?' Brook felt his pulse quicken. 'How did you manage that?'

'I bluffed my alter ego's way into an investigation.'

'Is that legal?'

'Probably not.' She dismissed the notion with a shrug. 'A friend of Rugen's, the editor of his local newspaper, had been found dead in a forest. It appeared he'd fallen from the cliffs. It seemed straight forward but something about it didn't add up.'

'How so?'

'There was a strange wound on his body, an arrow wound but not one made by any conventional arrow. I talked to his widow, but then the authorities closed the case down. I didn't give up though, it just made me even more determined.'

'It sounds like you were very in control of your drifts.' Brook felt a tinge of envy. It rarely worked out that way for him. 'Nearly all of them happen completely at random. How did you manage it?'

'By good luck I'd found a place, a location connecting these two different worlds. It was in an old part of my home city; it was called The Black Rose Cafe. By going there and entering the alternate reality by a different door, I was able to control my visits. I left a trail for someone to follow in case anything happened to me. I photocopied a few of the pages from Rugen's novel, pages mentioning Spades and myself, and left them at the scene of a case I was working on. Detective Spades was working on the same case, and I knew he would find them. I'd only had a brief chat with him about all of this. It was cagey. Neither of us wanted to say too much. I don't think he even realised that it was me who'd left the pages for him, but he said enough to let me know that he'd found them.'

'How much did you tell him? Did he believe in the whole concept?'

'Spades is one of the biggest sceptics I know.' she smiled. 'But he has an inquisitive nature. He wanted to know everything I'd uncovered, but I told him the bare minimum. I told him to keep following the trail at his own pace. Meanwhile, I continued my own investigations in both realities. Rugen was a very reclusive individual. After some work I traced his agent but then when things took a twist, I no longer needed to talk to him.'

'Why not?'

'Something unexpected happened. Back in my home world, I researched the concept of alternate realities and discovered an interesting book written on the subject. It was called Two Thirty. And not long after I'd read it, the author contacted me.'

'What did he want?'

'It was bizarre. He told me he could arrange a meeting with Hans Rugen. He said that they were old acquaintances, and that Rugen was in hospital after having had a bad accident. He said that he had been rescued in the same forest that his editor friend had died in. Incredibly, they'd both fallen from the same cliffs.'

'Now that is peculiar.' Brook could barely keep pace with the unfolding tale. 'So, the author, did you accept his offer?'

'Yes, and that's where it all went wrong. I should have walked away and taken no further part in it. I left a note for Mickey Spades in my work planner. It referenced the Black Rose Café and the book Two Thirty. It had to be cryptic. I knew that if anything happened to me, if I didn't return, my boss would check my work planner, so I made it look like Detective Spades and I had scheduled a meeting for that afternoon. I was certain he would contact Spades, who would then follow my trail.'

'What happened? Did you meet with Rugen?'

'Yes. I found him at the hospital.'

Brook guessed they'd reached the crux of the story. Her expression said it all. 'What happened?'

'It was all a terrible accident. I only wanted to talk to him, but everything got so confusing. My mind started to play tricks on me. I almost forgot who I really was. I think I even believed for a few moments that Rugen had actually created me. I asked him what he had done to Spades. He tried to deny all knowledge of it. He had a notebook, I snatched it from him and quickly read it. He'd written a page about killing off Mickey Spades.' She hesitated. 'For that moment I believed he had that power. Everything became so blurred. I couldn't think straight. The lines between fact and fiction disappeared completely. I panicked. I lost control. We struggled, he hit his head and fell... then I panicked even further... I held the pillow over his face...' Her words trailed off to nothing.

Taro Brook swallowed uncomfortably. 'Do you think he's dead?'

'Hans Rugen? I'm certain of it.'

'And your detective friend? What about him?'

'I don't know for sure, but I just can't shake the feeling that something has happened to him. I know that Rugen has no influence over us, but the trail should have been easy to follow. And there's one thing I'm certain about; sceptic or not, Spades isn't the kind to give up easily.' She put her hands to her face. 'But how is he going to find me now?'

Brook looked towards the horizon as a silence fell between them. He waited a few moments before speaking.

'So, what happened after the hospital. Where did you go?'

'I ran. I just kept running. I tried to find my way back to the café but, in my confusion, I lost my way. I remember being so tired, so upset. I don't know... I ran until I couldn't run any further. I wandered aimlessly. I found myself by the sea... And I found myself here.' She held his gaze. 'Why did I come here?'

Taro Brook shook his head. He didn't know why she was here. 'Maybe the reason will show itself, maybe it won't.' He glanced to the sky as he got to his feet. 'Those clouds are gathering pace. We should start making our way back to the sanctuary.'

'So, I should come here every morning?'

'I think it's your best chance of getting back home. And let's face it, going back is probably your best chance of finding your answers. If you stay here, you'll always wonder.'

'You'll come with me? To the cove, I mean.'

'I'll walk with you some of the way, but I won't come down to the beach. Last thing you need is me disappearing and you being left here alone.'

She managed a half smile. 'That wouldn't be ideal.'

'Let's get going.' Brook took the lead as they began the climb back up from the shelter of the cove.

'Taro Brook.'

'Yes?' He turned to face her.

'Thank you for listening, and for not judging me harshly.'

'That's okay. I wish I could give you more of the answers you seek.'

As they made their way back up the ridge, he had plenty to think about. He meant what he said. He wished he could give her some of the answers, but he couldn't. Not yet at least.

He liked her; it would be difficult not to. Her reasons for being here appeared genuine, but he couldn't tell her the things he knew. Not yet. He couldn't tell her he had met her detective friend, and that Mickey Spades had wrongly interrogated him.

Detective Spades, that was his name. He remembered it all too well. Brook's white-whiskered legal representative had exposed the man's identity when he'd entered the room and interrupted the inquisition.

Taro Brook sighed.

He couldn't let her know that he recognised the name of the writer Hans Rugen, and he wasn't prepared to tell her that Detective Spades had believed that he, Taro Brook, was Hans Rugen. And he definitely wasn't about to tell her that she might well have killed him in another reality.

CHAPTER FIFTY-FOUR

The persistent drizzle matched the mood of the day. The cloud hung low; so low in places, it hid the tops of the trees.

They watched from the rooftop balcony of Bog-Mire's old bell tower as the procession rode silently by.

Messenger Two Cups' mood was despondent. The party were less than an hour's ride from the city and were already looking a bedraggled bunch.

'Enntonia's Elite Guard,' he sighed. 'The soldiers of the realm.'

'Not exactly the stuff of legends.' Harbinger Talus hawked a spit to the ground and scowled his grim assessment. 'This isn't going to end well, Scaraven.'

Two Cups gave his measured response. 'No, I don't expect it will.' There seemed little point in false optimism. 'But things are as they must be and besides, there is always darkness before the dawn.'

'Father had a saying,' Token ScriptScratcher tapped his pipe on the parapet. 'What happens is best.'

'Not much sense in that, if you ask me,' grunted Talus.

'On the contrary,' Token offered a smile. 'I recall once asking him about it. If it was true.'

'And what did he say?' Two Cups turned to the Scribe.

'He said that it probably wasn't true but if you thought it and believed it, things would be easier to accept.'

Two Cups grinned. 'I like it.'

'Might be something in it,' Talus conceded grudgingly.

'What happens is best.' Two Cups whispered the words as the riders slipped from view beyond the trees. He said it, but he wasn't sure if he believed it. 'I am in need of your services, Talus.'

'Figured that much when you summoned me, Scaraven. Folk rarely go calling on me for my wit and charm alone.'

'Quite.'

'What do you need?'

'The Hall of the Representatives.'

Talus frowned. 'Yes?'

'They are expecting me to keep them updated on events. I want you to ride there and inform them of all that has happened here.'

'As you wish.' Talus adjusted his stance. 'Anything else?'

'Yes, I have another favour to ask. You will be welcomed at the Hall by the Acolytes.' He pulled a sealed envelope from his pocket. 'Can you deliver this for me?'

Talus skimmed an eye over the scrawled handwriting. 'Attention of Shroo or Moxi.' The corner of his mouth curled. 'Acolytes?'

'Yes,' Two Cups nodded. 'Discreetly. Please.'

'Discretion it is.' The Harbinger tipped the brow of his hat. 'I'll take my leave.' He made towards the tower door. 'Fare ye well, Scaraven. And you, Master ScriptScratcher.'

'Safe journey, Talus.'

They watched the door close behind him.

'You look troubled, Scaraven.' The Scribe eyed him keenly.

'Niggling concerns, old friend, surrounding Trask's involvement in things. For him to know about the Aaskrid girl, we must assume that he was working for someone very well informed. I'm wondering how much they knew about the role she had to play in the unfolding events. And what else do they know? Bog-Mire hides a dangerous threat beyond the mirror. We must double the guard here. Better safe than sorry. Troubled times, I fear. I suppose you might say I could do with some good news.'

'And if I might ask? The letter to the Acolytes?'

'Just a few lines to let the little fellows know I haven't forgotten their concerns. Far from it.'

'I'm sure they never doubted it, Scaraven.' Token ScriptScratcher's nose twitched as he adjusted his spectacles. 'I have it on good authority that Mrs Burrows was to be baking this morning. My pipe is fairing badly in this weather. Let's go inside.' He motioned towards the bell tower door. 'Tea and fresh scones in the drawing room by the fire? How does that sound?'

Two Cups grinned widely. 'That sounds like very good news indeed.'

CHAPTER FIFTY-FIVE

'Hey, Spades!' Tubbs knocked on the glass and slid open the panel. 'You got another prank call when you were out.'

Mickey Spades drew to a sudden stop. 'What?'

'The bookstore fella. Leif Skimmer. Remember?'

Spades remembered it all too well. 'What about him?'

'He called again.' Tubbs tore a page from his notepad and waved it through the hatch. 'Called about an hour ago. Says he has another book for you.'

Spades felt the hairs on the back of his neck tingle.

'Dog Ears bookstore,' continued Tubbs. 'Isn't that the place you went looking for and couldn't find?'

'Yeh! That's the place.' Spades wheeled towards the exit. 'Throw the note in the bin, Tubbs.'

'What's it all about? What a joker, eh? Do you want me to file a report?'

'Don't bother. I reckon I know who's behind it. I'll go and sort this out right now.'

Spades exited the building, lit a cigar, and headed for the train terminal. This was it. His watershed moment. He couldn't lose either way. If he found the bookstore, he'd be one step closer to unravelling the mystery. And if he didn't, he was prepared to give the whole thing up. This would be the last time he went looking for answers in places that were abandoned, derelict, or couldn't be found at all. His grip on reality had been stretched to its limit. He'd barely slept in the last two weeks. His search for reason in the chaos had almost driven him crazy, and he'd had enough.

Enough of the Black Rose Café. Enough of the white-faced ghoul who stalked his dreams. Enough of the endless questions concerning Amy Coda and Hans Rugen, and the constant nagging feeling that he was partly to blame for Jaxson Tiller's untimely demise. If he hadn't invited Digger to the Circus District maybe the journalist would still be around.

And now, to top it all, the bookstore owner, Leif Skimmer.

What a name! The more he thought about it, the falser it sounded. Skimmer's message was that he had another book for him. What would it be this time?

As the train rattled noisily towards his moment of reckoning, his mind wandered randomly. Skimmer's message. This was the second time he had invited Spades to his bookstore. Was that the key? Did the bookstore only show itself to those who had been invited?

Spades shook his head at the ridiculous notion. This kind of nonsense was exactly why he needed to give this whole damned business up. He was dangerously close to losing all sense of reality.

Reality. There it was. That word again.

Cursing inwardly, he closed the thought process down as the towering spires of the Crown Cathedral signalled his arrival.

The grey sky hung heavily overhead as he stepped from the train and fumbled for his matches. Striking life to the flame, he fired his cigar and began the short walk to Arch Lane.

It didn't matter what happened next. He'd either find the bookstore or not. Either way, he was ready. He was prepared for anything. Whatever the outcome, he would finally be able to move on. Propelled by the thought, he soon found himself at the end of the cobbled lane.

With a puff of smoke, he surveyed the scene ahead. It looked just the same as when he'd first seen it. But then why wouldn't it? He continued walking.

To his left, the little tearoom with the yellow sunflowers in the window. To his right, the bakery and the draper's place. The quaint little candle shop, with its sweet aromas, stood right across the lane from the drab-looking antique store. The bright-coloured frontage of the gemstone shop, the bric-a-brac place. It all looked just the same. The clockmaker's...

Spades drew to a sudden halt. Dog Ears bookstore.

His insides twitched at the sight of it. Evidently, he wasn't as prepared as he thought he was. There it stood. Just like the first time. He stood transfixed as the minutes ticked by.

The door of the clockmaker's shop stood slightly ajar. From within, a clock chimed the half hour.

Spades gathered his thoughts.

The bookstore was to be the deciding factor. That was how he'd planned it. That was how he'd prepared himself for either outcome. Now, he had to stick with the plan. Ignoring the voice in his head that yelled caution, the one that urged him to forget all about the peculiar bookstore and go home, Spades flicked his cigar to the ground. It was time to take control of the situation. It was time to see what Skimmer's latest invitation was all about.

The bell jingled merrily as he made his way inside and as the door swung closed, Leif Skimmer appeared from behind the curtain.

'Good day to you, Sir.' With a momentary frown, he adjusted his spectacles. 'Ah, it's you, Detective.' His face lit up. 'How nice to see you again. You got my message?'

Spades took a few tentative steps towards the counter. 'Yeah, I got a message. Care to tell me what it's about?'

'Give me one moment. I'll be right back.' As Skimmer slipped behind the curtain, Spades glanced round the shop. Everything looked just the way it did the first time.

'Here we are,' Leif Skimmer reappeared, holding a book in his hand. 'I know you said you didn't want this one, but I took it upon myself to order it. Call me impulsive, but I just had the feeling that you'd want it after you read the first one.'

Spades eyed the book warily. 'What is it?'

'Inside the Circle.' Skimmer smiled smugly. 'Phinton Marlo's second book.'

Spades drew a sharp breath. Maybe things were picking up. Had his luck just changed for the better? 'Well, as you've gone to the trouble…'

'Oh, it was no trouble at all.' Skimmer's mouth curled with a grin of satisfaction. 'Just doing my job. That's what I'm here for.' He pushed the book across the countertop.

As Spades reached for it, the bell rang behind him.

'You have another customer,' he said without looking round. 'I'll not hold you back. How much do I owe you?'

'Oh, there's no rush,' Skimmer brushed the remark aside with a wave of his hand. 'Time passes slowly here in Dog Ears. My customers usually like to browse awhile, and there was something else I wanted to share with you if you have a moment?'

'And what would that be?'

'Well,' Leif Skimmer peered over his glasses. 'When I ordered the book, the strangest thing happened.'

Spades frowned. He'd had his fill of strange occurrences lately. 'What happened?'

'I had a communication from the author.'

'Really?'

'Yes!' Skimmer's eyes sparkled. 'Phinton Marlo, the reclusive author himself. He got in touch to say how much he appreciated the fact that I'd ordered two of his books. But I wasn't going to take all the credit, Detective. I told him all about you.'

'You did?' Spades didn't know how to feel about that.

'Yes, I did.' Skimmer grinned triumphantly. 'Turns out that Mister Marlo has just had a third book published. As we chatted, one thing led to another. He was very interested in you,' he hesitated, 'and I hope you don't mind, but I have arranged for you both to meet.'

'You have?'

'Yes, I have.'

'When?' Spades couldn't believe his luck. This time he'd make sure he got his answers. This author wouldn't escape his questioning. 'Where?'

'Here,' smiled Skimmer. 'Now.' He rubbed his hands together excitedly. 'He's right behind you.'

As Spades spun round in expectation, his heart sank to the pit of his stomach. 'You?'

Leif Skimmer struggled to conceal his delight.

'Detective Spades,' he cackled gleefully. 'Meet Phinton Marlo.'

'Hello, friend.'

That voice. That face. The white-painted face with the black diamonds.

'You!' Spades struggled for the words. 'You are Phinton Marlo?'

The circus actor doffed his hat with a grand flourish. His jet-black hair tumbled free.

'A pseudonym, Detective,' the blackened lips curled with the faintest trace of smile. 'One of my many aliases. Forgive me, but when we last talked I wasn't aware that you were a keen follower of my work.'

'I didn't know who you were.' Spades' anger boiled inside. Skimmer had tricked him. The bell signalled another arrival. As he glanced towards the door, his mood turned from anger to despair. Seemed his luck had changed all right, but not for the better.

'Hey, Mister,' the woman with the flowing dark hair and the jingling bangles crossed the room provocatively. 'Do you want to know your future?' Her eyes still sparkled like diamonds, even in the gloom of the bookstore. Behind her, the burly tattooed man from the fortune-teller's place barred the door and with it, Spades' chance of escape.

'I'm sure you'll remember my friends,' the white-faced ghoul donned his hat. The image of the black rose looked down mockingly. Somewhere in those black diamonds, a hunter's eyes closed in on their prey. 'Allow me to introduce myself, Detective. My name is Pysus Mythrap. And it seems you are not one to heed fair warning. I believe Mister Skimmer has already alluded to my new book. Perhaps you'd be interested? I'd like to talk to you about it and its content. It's entitled The Price to Pay.'

CHAPTER FIFTY-SIX

The baying of the hounds echoed loudly across the plain.

They were getting closer by the minute. Time was running out and there was nowhere left to run. Crouched in the rocks at the top of the cliffs, Hendrick Stanner prepared himself for the worst.

Unarmed, bereft of hope, and out of luck. Hardly the ingredients for a heroic last stand. But then Stanner had never really been the heroic type. He'd never wanted to be. He'd always kept his aspirations low. A small-time petty thief could get by nicely, keeping his head down, staying under the radar, not drawing any unwanted attention. How had everything gone so wrong?

Sleeping Firs had been bad enough. The bungled explosion in the failed bank job should have been a low point but just when he'd reckoned things couldn't get any worse, he'd reckoned wrong. When he rode into the town of High Springs, things got much worse. It should have been so easy. How could a simple robbery have gone so awry?

Some people just couldn't hide their wealth, some even went out of their ways to flaunt it. Having identified his target, Stanner had prepared well. He'd watched the place for five days. He knew all the comings and goings, and he knew when the place would be empty long enough for him to get in and out safely. Problem was, he hadn't reckoned on how bad his luck was about to get.

He hadn't planned for the unlikely scenario that someone else might be in the house for the same reason he was, and that they might be armed and trigger-happy. He hadn't planned on the owners of the house breaking with their normal routine, returning unexpectedly to find him on the stairs laden with a bag of their most valuable possessions.

The shooter had emerged from a room on the ground floor and all hell had broken loose. Instead of slipping quietly unseen through the backyard as he'd planned, panicked into action, Stanner had made his escape via an upstairs window.

His exit was poorly planned. The sound of gunfire had drawn onlookers onto the main street. Landing among them in a shower of broken glass, he'd put a face to the perpetrator of the heinous crime.

Hendrick Stanner was the man responsible. More than a dozen witnesses could testify to that. It didn't matter that he wasn't the one to blame. The killings had nothing to do with him, but it didn't matter. He was already a wanted man. The price on his head was now even greater.

The pursuit into the wilds had been relentless. As the evening sun dipped in the west the plain had given way to the rocky terrain offering him a brief glimmer of hope, only for it to end in the precipitous drop behind him.

There was no way out.

It was the end of the road for Hendrick Stanner.

Movement in the shadows to his left caught his eye. As the figure emerged from the gloom, he cursed his luck. His rotten luck that seemed to deteriorate further at every turn.

Even in the half-light, there was no mistaking the identity of his unwanted company.

'We meet again, Hendrick Stanner.'

'Old Clear Eyes.' Stanner could scarcely believe it. He hissed his contempt. 'I thought I made myself clear last time we met. What are you doing here?'

'I'm here to repeat my offer.'

'I told you before, I'm not interested.'

'Really? Even with the current decline in your fortunes?' The old man shook his head. 'This is not your destiny, Hendrick Stanner. You must surely realise that you are on the wrong path. I offer you the choice once again.'

'How could you possibly know what my destiny is?'

'The dogs have your scent. They are getting closer by the second. You don't have long now. Are you too proud to accept my offer of help?'

'Pride has got nothing to do with it,' growled Stanner. 'I don't know what you want, old man, and I don't care. I know how these things work. If I accept your help then I'd be in your debt, and I'll not be tricked like that.'

'Very well, I will not force you. It must be your decision, your choice alone. However, if that were my motives I fear you'd already be in my debt. I've given you fair warning on more than one occasion but be assured, my help was given with no conditions attached. The choice is still yours to make, but I will not stand aside and watch you condemn yourself to such a pointless fate.'

'What do you mean?'

'I can't force a choice upon you, but I can save you from the hangman's noose.'

The old man lunged forward unexpectedly.

Caught off guard, Stanner was unable to block the move. The blow to his head sent him spinning to the ground.

His eyes felt heavy. Seemed he wouldn't be getting to his feet anytime soon. As he lay looking up at the stars, the bearded face leaned over him.

'Until next time, Hendrick Stanner.'

CHAPTER FIFTY-SEVEN

Mickey Spades wasn't happy. He didn't like being on the wrong side of the interrogation table. He re-assessed his situation with a growing sense of gloom.

The room beyond the curtain of the Dog Ears bookstore offered only one way out; a door barred by a toned mass of tattooed muscle. The woman with the sparkling eyes and jingling bangles sat nearby, idly filing her long fingernails. Leif Skimmer had left the room in answer to the call of the doorbell. The white-faced ghoul from Spades' troubled dreams stared back at him from the far side of the table.

Downing a mouthful of coffee, Spades gave voice to his fears.

'So, what's this all about? What do you want from me?'

Pysus Mythrap twisted his black-lined lips in response. 'Seems I might very well be asking you the same question, friend.'

'What do you mean?'

'Come now, Detective. You are the one who has being pursuing me.'

'What? That's ridiculous…'

'Forgive me, but it is the truth.' A gloved hand waved his protest aside. 'Perhaps you just didn't realise it. I've been aware of your interest in our little secret for quite some time. I watched on from a distance in the hope that you would lose heart but when it became obvious I'd underestimated your determination,

I began leaving a trail for you to follow.'

'Your books?'

'Indeed. And I deployed the same tactic with Miss Coda.'

'Coda? You've seen her? You know where she is?'

'I know where she is, but we have never met in person. I believe that to be my loss. By all accounts, Miss Amy is enchanting company.'

'What have you done to her?' Spades clenched a fist in anger. 'Where is she?'

'All in good time, Detective. I will come to that, but I'd rather if we conclude our business first.'

'What business?'

'I have an arrangement to discuss with you.' A trace of a grin flashed across the white face. 'One I think we will find mutually beneficial.'

'I'm not interested in your offers.' Spades fired his response.

'Ah, I think you may have misunderstood me.' The gloved hands wrapped around the cane. 'This is not an offer.'

'What do you mean?'

'The time for choice is past, I'm afraid. You've been given plenty of opportunities to back away from all of this, but you've declined.'

Spades fought the stifling feeling of entrapment with a newfound vigour. 'You're deluded. Why would I have anything to do with you after what you did to Jaxson Tiller?'

'The journalist? I hope you are not suggesting that any responsibility for that lies at my door. Believe me, Detective, that was nothing to do with me. You will have to talk to your conscience about that.'

Spades hesitated. It was hard to read what someone was thinking when their eyes were hidden deep within black diamonds. 'You didn't make that happen?'

'A terrible accident. You have my word on it.'

Spades took a moment to gather his thoughts. 'Okay, so let's say I believe you, and the jury's still out on that, what did you mean by the price to pay? If you're not responsible for Tiller's demise, why would I owe you anything?'

'Ah, my new book.' The black lips parted in a smile. With a flash of white teeth, Pysus Mythrap rose to his feet. Spades shuddered as the ghoul circled the table. 'A concept far too many take for granted. I will get straight to the point, Detective. I want you to work for me.'

Spades fought the urge to laugh out loud. This was preposterous. 'Thanks, but no thanks. I already have a job.'

'As I said, this is not an offer. You will work for me whilst continuing your present profession.' Mythrap returned to his seat, doffed his hat, and placed it on the table. The black rose winked surreptitiously in Spades' direction. 'Let me give you a little background. I belong to an Order that works tirelessly to guard an ancient secret. A secret Miss Coda, you, and countless others down through time have stumbled upon. Despite our best efforts, too many have come close, dangerously close, to knowing too much. I need help, Detective. I need someone like you, someone in your position, working to keep others away. To thwart their investigations, to stop them uncovering the very truth we work so hard to protect.'

'What truth?'

'The knowledge of alternate realities and the ability to move between them. I believe you've familiarised yourself with the concept in my first book?'

Spades drew a breath. 'I read it. I'm not saying I believe it though.'

Mythrap grinned. 'And yet, here you are. I think you believe far more than you would readily admit.'

'Maybe. Maybe not.'

'Believe it, friend. You experienced the phenomenon for yourself when you took your small foray into the world of Hans Rugen.'

Stunned by the revelation, Spades held his breath as the pieces fell into place. So that was why everything had looked so different beyond the back door of the Black Rose Café. He struggled for a response. 'How do you know about that?'

'I've been watching, Detective. And if you needed further proof, Arch Lane. A little side street that doesn't even exist in your world. But yet, here you are.'

Spades nodded slowly. 'So, that's why I couldn't find it the last time.'

'Yes, it seems your ability is limited. To leave you to your own devices would be negligent, dangerous for both of us, and that is why you would serve our cause best from the safety of your own world.' Mythrap tapped the table with his gloved fingers. 'You will work for me. You will do all you can to keep others away and, in return, I will grant you access to the answers that have plagued you for months.'

Spades hesitated. Sure, he wanted the answers, more than anything, but at what cost. 'Have I got an alternative?'

'No. I'm afraid you haven't.'

'What if I refuse?'

'I wouldn't recommend it, and why would you? You will have your answers and no further need to worry yourself about our little secret. And I'm certain you will come to look on me as an appreciative employer.'

'So, I am trapped?'

'Think of it as being enlightened.' Pysus Mythrap got to his feet. 'Come, let us not begin our new collaboration on a negative note.' He walked towards the door. 'My colleague, Mister Stamforr, will accompany you. Last thing we want is you losing your way again, not when you are so close to achieving your goal.'

Spades' eye settled on the burly tattooed man. 'Accompany me where?'

'To your answers. Isn't that why you are here?'

'I thought you were going to give me the answers.' Spades scowled. 'And you were going to tell me what happened to Coda.'

'And I am a man of my word. I could share it all with you, but I have someone better in mind. Someone who can offer you a more personal perspective on this most daunting of subjects. I think she will be able to answer all your questions, better even than I could. Stamforr will take you to her.' As Spades' escort opened the door, Pysus Mythrap gave an eloquent swish of his hat. 'We will talk further when you return, Detective, but a word of warning. No matter how tempting it seems, you must resist the urge to run. If you stay within reach, I can protect you.'

With a gentle nudge, Spades was directed out into the grey drizzle. Stamforr ushered him into the back of a waiting car. As the blackened windows rolled up, Spades caught a glimpse of the tall buildings. The architecture was unfamiliar. Holding his silence, he checked his watch as the car sped through the quiet streets.

Ten minutes later they drew to a halt. Seconds later, Stamforr opened the rear door. 'We're here.'

Spades got out and stretched. At least the rain had stopped. He looked up at the daunting grey-stoned building. 'What is this place? What are we doing here?'

'You wanted answers.' Stamforr sneered his indifference. 'Go up to the second floor. Ask for Claudia Bankz.'

Spades frowned. 'And who is she?'

Stamforr folded his arms in a gesture of dismissal. 'You go in now.'

Spades shook his head. Was this to be his moment of truth? Would he finally get his answers or were things about to deteriorate further? It seemed hard to believe that things could get any worse. With a sigh of resignation, he entered the building.

The high-ceilinged foyer had a strange feel to it and wouldn't have looked out of place in an old mansion from a horror movie. Spades shook the image from his head and quickly made his way towards the grand staircase. Taking the steps two at a time, he drew puzzled looks from the three men huddled in conversation on the first-floor landing.

Access to the second floor was barred by a door. Stopping short of it, his thoughts drifted back to that fateful day; his first visit to the Black Rose Café and his brief exchange with the fortune-teller. The old crone had warned him that his answers lay beyond a door and that there would be consequences if he chose to walk through it. Her prediction had been easy to dismiss at first, but recently he'd been ready to concede that she'd alluded to the secondary door in the Black Rose. Maybe he was wrong.

His hand gripped the door handle. He reckoned the time to worry about consequences was long past. So, were his answers waiting on the other side? There was only one way to find out.

The door creaked loudly as it swung shut behind him. At the end of a short corridor lined with doors on either side, he was greeted by a smiling woman seated behind an oval-shaped reception desk.

'Good afternoon, Sir. How can I help?'

'I'm here to see Claudia Bankz.'

'I'll let her know you are here. Can I ask your name?'

'He is Detective Mickey Spades.'

Spades spun round at the sound of the voice. A dark-haired woman stood by one of the doors he'd passed. He glanced back to the receptionist.

'Is that her?'

'Yes,' she nodded. 'That's Claudia. She must have been expecting you.'

CHAPTER FIFTY-EIGHT

She knew it was him. Strange, given that she'd never set eyes on him before. But then strange things had been happening a lot lately.

'Detective Spades,' she motioned him forward. 'Would you like to come in?' Moving back to her desk, she sat down as he followed into the room. She waited until he was seated.

'My name is Claudia Bankz. I'm a research assistant here at our Foundation for Scientific Studies.' She paused. 'It's strange being in a different world. Strange and confusing. You're probably finding the whole concept difficult to accept. I understand completely. Safe passage between alternate realities isn't something I'd have believed in either until recently. Until your friend showed up.'

'You mean Coda? Amy Coda? You've seen her?'

'No.' She shook her head ruefully. 'I haven't seen her. She is in my head.'

'What?'

She almost laughed at his reaction. 'It sounds ludicrous, doesn't it? Believe me, it takes some getting used to.'

'I... I don't understand.'

'Infinite numbers of realities, Detective.' She took a deep breath. 'An infinite number of everyone and everything. Infinite versions of you, me, and everyone else. In case you are in any doubt about what is going on here, you are experiencing a view of an alternate reality and you are talking to this world's version of Amy Coda.' Leaning forward, she steepled her fingers on the desk. 'Spades, I know it's hard to believe, but it's really me. I'm Amy.'

Amy Coda held her breath as the confusion lifted. Her gaze settled on the figure sitting on the far side of the desk. Mickey Spades. He had found her. He was here, but he was obviously struggling to take it all in.

'Spades, I know it's hard to believe, but it's really me. I'm Amy.'

'Coda?' He shook his head. 'How can it be you?'

'Everything Claudia has told you is true. I know that I look different, but it's really me.' She reached across the table and caught him by the hand. To her relief, he didn't pull away. 'I'm so relieved you're okay, Spades. It's so good to see you. How long has it been?'

'Several weeks.' His response was staggered. 'Where have you been? Where is the real you, Coda?' He frowned. 'What happened to you?'

'I don't know…' She hesitated as the memories came flooding back. The white sand, the cove. Taro Brook, Nallevarr. All so vivid and yet, so confusing. 'You followed the trail I left for you, Mickey. How far did you get?'

Spades shrugged his shoulders. 'Pysus Mythrap.'

'Who?'

'The circus freak. You don't know about him?' Spades pulled a face. 'He said that you two hadn't met, but he knows all about you. Until this minute, I reckoned he'd put you up to this. He's the one pulling all the strings. He more or less admitted it to me.'

Coda shook her head. 'I've not heard of him.' She hesitated again. 'Did you manage to find the book I told you about? Two Thirty, did you read it?'

'Oh, yeah.' Spades grimaced. 'I read it. It was written by Mythrap.'

'No. The author was Phinton Marlo.'

'It was Mythrap, he wrote it under the pseudonym of Marlo.'

Coda held her breath. 'But... Phinton Marlo contacted me by email, he told me where I could find Hans Rugen.'

Spades leaned forward. 'Mythrap! Like I said, he's pulling all the strings. Wait... Hans Rugen? You met with him?'

Amy Coda sat back in her chair. 'Yes,' she sighed. 'I met with Hans Rugen.'

'I found him too, I had him right where I wanted, at least I thought I did? What did he look like? Describe him to me.'

As she gave her description, Spades' enthusiasm waned. 'Doesn't sound like we found the same person. Where is he, Coda? Rugen, where is he?'

'You won't get any answers from Hans Rugen, Mickey.' Her tone dropped to a whisper. 'He's dead. It was an accident... but I killed him.'

Spades clenched his teeth. He hadn't found Rugen, and he wasn't going to now. 'I thought I had him. He was doing everything he could to deny it, but I was certain it was him. He'd started some new book, about a walker in a forest. Dammit, it wasn't him.'

Amy Coda steadied herself. 'We have a lot of catching up to do. Have you talked to Jaxson Tiller recently?'

'Yeah, but I won't be talking to him again. Digger is gone too… he was run down by a delivery truck in the Circus District.'

Amy Coda drew a breath. Jaxson Tiller had met with the same fate Hans Rugen had planned for Spades. She'd read it in his notebook, seen it with her own eyes. Her train of thought raced. 'Did Leif Skimmer contact you? The bookstore owner?'

'Yeah!' Spades sneered. 'He tried to tell me we had visited his bookstore together to order the damned book. Tell me I'm not going mad, Coda. We were never there, were we?'

'No. We weren't. He pulled the same stunt on me.'

'How did my signature end up in his ledger?'

'I don't know,' she hesitated, 'but the Circus District, the Black Rose Café, Jaxson Tiller. I can probably help with some of that. I think it's time we started filling in the blanks.'

As she began, her thoughts drifted once again to the land of Nallevarr. It seemed like only moments had passed since she'd told the same account to Taro Brook.

'Turns out,' she began, 'that Jaxson Tiller had an alter ego who was drifting between worlds. An alter ego who wrote books for a living, crime fiction mostly. His main character was a detective called Mickey Spades.' She offered a smile as she watched the revelation hit him. 'Jaxson Tiller was Hans Rugen in another reality…'

CHAPTER FIFTY-NINE

Mickey Spades listened intently as Claudia Bankz shared her tale in graphic detail. It was staggering; unbelievable, but yet the only explanation that made any sense.

Was it really Amy Coda telling the tale? Far as he could tell, it was and, as disconcerting as it was to hear it from the mouth of a total stranger, the more she told him, the more everything fell into place. And loathed as he was to admit it, Pysus Mythrap had stood by his promise.

Mickey Spades finally had his answers. His life was his own. Not the creation of some unknown fiction writer concocting his life events. Everything was real. True, things were becoming harder to believe, far-fetched even, but still real.

As Claudia Bankz fell quiet, Spades drew his mind away from his own dilemma and shifted his concerns towards her. The question had to be asked, even though he knew he wouldn't like the answer.

'Where are you now, Coda? Let's just say I accept that this is another version of you...' He paused. He had to accept it; how could it be any other way? 'Where is the version of Amy Coda that I would recognise?' His voice wavered slightly. 'What happened to you? Where are you?'

The woman stared back blankly, as if searching for an answer.

Her response, when it came, sent a chill rushing through him.

'I don't know, Mickey. I'm lost. I don't know where I am. I've tried, but I can't find my way back.'

Spades swallowed uncomfortably as she continued.

'It's okay though, I've accepted it. I've seen the most amazing things, and I've been to the most amazing places…'

Her words came to a sudden halt.

'Coda?' Spades leaned forward. 'Coda?'

Claudia Bankz rubbed at her eyes. 'I'm sorry, Detective… she's gone.'

'Gone?'

'I'm sorry, I can't help you further. She's been around for some time now and I've got used to her ways. Her presence has been fading over the last few days. I don't know if it is her choice or if I'm getting better at shutting her out.'

Spades sighed as she rose from her chair and moved towards the door.

'I'm glad you had the chance to catch up. I know it would have meant a lot to her. It's time for you to leave now too.'

Spades moved slowly. He felt like he'd been hit by a train. He grasped the woman's hand as he paused in the doorway.

'Thank you.'

He descended the stairs and made his way outside.

Standing by the car, Stamforr opened the door as Spades approached. Stooping to climb in, he found Pysus Mythrap waiting for him in the back seat.

As the car eased into motion, Spades stared at the blackened windows.

'So, Detective.' Mythrap's tone did little to ease his gloom. 'I trust you found your answers?'

Spades surprised himself with his response. 'Isn't there anything you can do to help her?'

'I'm afraid not, friend.'

'Don't you feel responsible?' Spades snapped. 'It was you who sent her to see Hans Rugen, it was you posing as Phinton Marlo.'

'Alas, I can't be held responsible for how people react. Miss Amy would have found her way to Rugen with or without my assistance. I tried to help but she was determined, just like you. Seems neither of you were prepared to let it go. I gave her the same warning I've given you. Phinton Marlo told her to advance with care. At least she took precautions; she left a trail for you to follow, and you found her.'

'Yeah, maybe, but not in time to help her. That woman, Claudia Bankz… is she working for you too?'

'No,' Mythrap considered the thought for a moment. 'Not yet at least.'

'She says Coda is gone. That her presence has been fading for a while. What's happened to her? Where is she?'

'I am sorry for what you are feeling, Detective, I truly am. But things can't always stay the same forever. Miss Coda's time in this world may have come and gone but surely you must find some solace knowing that she is still out there, somewhere in the great unknown?'

'Doesn't seem much comfort in that. You're really telling me she is gone. That she can't come back?'

'Gone from your reality at least. Perhaps you will find more enlightenment in my book, Inside The Circle. And if I may offer some further reading material for you to digest.' Mythrap reached inside his black coat and presented Spades with a large notebook.

Spades eyed it warily. 'What's this?'

'Your very own copy of my new book. The Price to Pay.'

'Doesn't look much like a finished book to me.'

'I agree.' Mythrap's white face stretched with a ghoulish grin. 'Some of the best books ever written are the ones that never get finished.' He wrapped his gloved hands around his cane. 'So, I trust our agreement is in place? I ensured that you got your answers. In return, you will guard our secret to the best of your abilities?'

Spades sighed inwardly as the car rolled to a halt. 'Do I have an alternative?'

'Not really. You could run but then you might get lost, like Miss Amy. Lost, with no way back. Not an appealing option.'

Spades tapped on the hard cover of the notebook. 'No, I guess not. So, what's in here?'

'A reminder of our terms, along with a few helpful ideas. We will keep a watchful eye on things from a safe distance. You'll not know we are there; I give my word. But we will be watching.' He pointed a gloved finger at the book. 'In there you will find directions to a burned-out warehouse. I'm afraid a macabre discovery awaits you there. The charred remains of a missing person. Identification will be tricky, but I'm certain with the advancements in today's scientific field they will be able to help you draw a suitable conclusion.'

'Coda?' Spades' reply came out little more than a whisper.

'It's not her, but that is what you will have them believe. It's what you do. You close cases. And in this case, it is the best for all concerned. In the notebook you will also find the details of a fellow willing to confess to starting the fire. It was an accident. The unfortunate individual was merely trying to eliminate all traces of his connection to a smuggling gang, and he thought the warehouse was abandoned. He'd no idea a vagrant had been sharing the rats' accommodation. Wracked with remorse, he is eager to share information which could take the entire smuggling network down. A notable coup for a hard-working investigator, a man dedicated to the cause. Like I said... I think you'll find me an appreciative employer.' As the car door swung open, Pysus Mythrap flashed his white teeth. 'I believe this is your stop, Detective. First stop on the way to becoming Chief, I shouldn't wonder. Good day to you, friend.'

Stepping from the car, Spades watched as it sped into the distance. Reaching for his cigar pack, he took in his surroundings.

He was back in familiar territory, only a short walk from Headquarters. Striking a match, he blew a smoke ring into the air. Things hadn't gone the way he'd expected. They'd turned out considerably better than he could have hoped. He had the answers, most of them at least.

He still wasn't sure how he felt about his enforced arrangement with Pysus Mythrap or his involvement with Jaxson Tiller's fate. And if the man he'd tracked down wasn't Hans Rugen, then who was he?

Mickey Spades shook his head. It now seemed like he had a choice after all. He could further test his sanity by trying to make sense of the answers he'd found, or he could just get on and make the best of the situation. It didn't seem like a difficult decision to make. Taking out his phone, he scrolled through the contacts list and made the call.

'Hey, Tubbs. It's Spades. Put me through to the Chief. I've had a breakthrough on a couple of cases. I think he'll be impressed.'

CHAPTER SIXTY

'This is it.' The Weasel wiped the rain from his face. 'This is where I last saw him. Headed in that direction, with the boar-man.'

Ten Six Nine dismounted. The visibility was poor, same as it had been all day. Drawn to the peaks of the Hogback Mountains, the cloud hung thick and low.

'Lead them on, General. Make camp by the lake, as planned. We'll follow when we've searched the area.'

'You'll find no clues here, Ten Six Nine,' The General scowled. 'The rain will have seen to that.' With a shrug, he waved the group onwards.

Her chain of command was simple. As General he was responsible for the men and women of the Guard, but she'd made it clear she would overrule him whenever she felt the need. It wasn't an arrangement he was over-enamoured with, that much was obvious, but it was one he was prepared to put up with, for now at least. She watched them as they trooped past, riding three abreast. Despite the constant rain, a day and a half's worth of it since they'd left the city, the mood among them seemed upbeat. A few of them even acknowledged her with a nod. Seemed most of them were content to have something to do; to have some kind of purpose. Whether the cause would prove worthy remained to be seen.

'He's right, you know.' The Weasel pulled a face. 'Damn rain is a tracker's worst nightmare.'

'I know.' She began scouring the area. 'This is where you found the body?'

'Yup!' The Weasel stayed on his horse.

'And they went that way?'

'Yup!'

'Okay.' She mounted up. 'Let's split up. That way we can cover more ground between here and the lake.'

'I'm not sure that's a good idea.'

'Why not?'

'What if we run into them boar-men?' His nose twitched anxiously. 'I mean, if we're dealing with ordinary reasonable folk, the old Weasel can talk himself out of any situation, but these riders from Ergmire. They don't strike me as being the reasonable type.'

Ten Six Nine sighed. 'Fair enough. We'll search together.'

His grin returned. 'Now that's an altogether much better idea.' He wiped his nose with his sleeve. 'Yup! Much better.' His jaw gave a click as she took the lead. 'I'm thinking you an' me are becoming quite the team. A formidable pairing, don't you agree?'

'If there are any boar-men out there, your inane chatter will lead them right to us. That's what I'm thinking.'

The Weasel fell silent. Accompanied by the constant patter of the rain and the splashing of the horses' hooves, they widened the search area. They found nothing. As the light failed, she drew a halt to their efforts and changed course.

The shout that food was just about ready echoed among the tents as they rode into camp.

'Good to hear.' The Weasel found his voice again. 'Stomach feels like my throat's been severed.'

'Find anything?' The General emerged from a tent as they dismounted.

'Nothing.'

'Any sign of the boar-men?'

'No.' Her expression hardened. 'They're probably long gone, but we need to be on our guard. Alert everyone, General. We'll need people on watch throughout the night.'

'Already done,' he grinned his satisfaction. 'All prepared. I'm quite good at this, you know. Been doing it a long time.'

'You have that,' she replied. 'Just making sure you haven't got complacent.'

The General's face reddened. 'Think I'll go get some food.'

The Weasel cackled his amusement. 'That told him, eh, Chief?' Her scowl caused him to change tack quickly. 'Anyway,' he cleared his throat, 'I'm thinking, maybe I'll just go join the big fellow at the grub queue.'

'Maybe you should.'

With her eyes fixed on the forest, she circled the encampment several times before helping herself to some stew. As darkness fell, she found shelter beneath a stand of tall fir trees by the shore of the lake and fell asleep to the sound of the rain.

CHAPTER SIXTY-ONE

'Daybreak by the Nameless Lake. Got a poetic feel to it, don't you think?' The Weasel scrambled to the top of the bank and stood next to her. 'See anything, Chief?'

From a vantage point like this, there was plenty to see. The day had dawned bright and clear. In the distance, beyond the far shore of the lake, Ten Six Nine saw that the mountain tops glistened with a fresh covering of snow. 'Nothing bad.'

'Glad that rain stopped,' he sniffed. 'Didn't half dampen a fellow's spirit.' He folded his arms knowingly. 'It's a fine view and no mistake. According to legend, it was round these parts that the Order of the Dragon Slayers first came to be. King Anthusar, think it was, he'd be one of your ancestors. Yup! All them ages ago. Story has it he met a witch in the woods by the lake, the Crow Witch some called her. Seems he was almost at his wit's end with them dragons and the witch came to his aid. Some say that's where your curse started.'

'I wouldn't know.'

'No, 'course you wouldn't,' he eyed her closely. 'It's only legend, but it would make sense. The Nameless. They probably got the idea from the lake.' He clicked his jaw with a yawn. 'Yup! It might explain a lot. Might explain how every now and again your lot leave for the lands in the west, returning years later wanting folk to think you're the next generation of the accursed ones. Not all folks are so easily fooled, mind you. There's plenty who reckon they know why you all look the same and answer to the same strange numbers.' His eyes widened. 'Immortals.' He almost whispered the word. 'That's what some folk think.'

'And what do you think?'

'Me? The old Weasel?' He gave a snort of indifference. 'Don't matter what I think now, does it? I'm just a scout and a guide.' His eyes narrowed again. 'Ain't my place to say what's true or false, right or wrong, and besides, it won't matter much now either way.'

'What do you mean?'

'Well, you'll have broken the witch's spell now. You being royal blood an' all. And that's what's got the old Weasel to thinking, maybe that's why you have the support of the Slayers. It doesn't really matter how foolhardy your plan seems, doesn't even matter if it's a lost cause. You've lifted the curse, so to speak. You've given them the chance to go out in one last blaze of glory.'

Ten Six Nine looked away. 'You talk too much.'

'Might be that you're right on that score too, Chief. Don't mean I'm wrong though.' He smacked his lips sarcastically. Noting her silence, he turned away. 'Fair enough. I'll wait for you back down at the trees.'

Ignoring his conjecture, Ten Six Nine returned her attention to the view. She pictured the bridge at Callinduir, only a few hours walk west from where she stood. It seemed so much further. So much had happened in the days since she'd been there. The Messenger had told her she would be there again. She recalled his words with clarity. What did they mean?

'You coming, Chief? Rest of them will be well ahead by now.' The Weasel called out from the bottom of the slope. With a groan, she turned her back on the lake and began her descent.

By the time they'd re-joined the rest of the group, the sun was high in the sky. Their search had been fruitless. No signs of Twelve Seven Two or the men from Ergmire.

The tree coverage had thinned. Leaving the woodlands far behind, they now rode across an open plain heading towards the mountains. Tucked in behind the General and his two flanking riders, Ten Six Nine rode in silence and deep in thought. The Weasel rode alongside her. Like the rest of the party, he too was quiet for now at least. Thankful for the respite, she reviewed her plans.

It would soon be time for the General and his riders to leave for Ergos; time for her to lead the rest of the group north, through the mountains to the west of the disputed lands of The Barrens, and into Tonduur. The hope that they would find Twelve Seven Two before they went their separate ways was fading fast. It looked increasingly like the riders of Ergmire had returned home with their captives. Should she be changing her plan? If that was where they'd taken him, shouldn't she be the one going to Ergos? As the mountains loomed closer, a dot on the horizon began to take shape.

'Get a glass on that rider!' The General snapped his instructions. 'Who is it?'

'Think it's one of our scouts returning, General.' The flag bearer delivered his verdict.

'Let me see.' He grabbed the spyglass as all eyes focused on the approaching rider. 'Ready yourselves!' The General's expression soured. 'It's Seven Ten, and he's in a hurry. Looks like bad news might be coming our way.'

Ten Six Nine held her breath as the rider drew up alongside.

'We've found something, General.' His tone was grave. 'In the hoodoos beyond the plain.' His attention centred on Ten Six Nine. 'It's not good.'

'Right!' The General roared his commands. 'Keep formation. Ride close, and keep your eyes peeled.' Nodding to the scout, he motioned ahead. 'Lead the way, soldier.'

Nudging their horses into a gallop, they covered the ground quickly. As the plain gave way to the arid badlands, the terrain steepened quickly. Sporadic remains of dead trees and scattered clumps of shrub dotted the rust-coloured landscape. Surrounded by an army of tall spires of eroded rock, some the height of ten men or more, some higher still, they climbed single file towards the weathered sandstone cliffs.

'How much further?'

'Not far, General.'

'Wait!' With a wave of his fist, he drew them to a halt. 'That's far enough.' The General turned in his saddle. 'No need for all of us to go up there.' He motioned to his flanking riders. 'You two with me. Ten Six Nine, you and your guide fall in between us. The rest of you stay here, get into position. Eyes and ears focused.' Turning to the front, he gave the signal. 'Lead the way, Seven Ten. Let's move.'

The horses toiled in the eerie setting. Ten Six Nine eyed the totemic pillars vigilantly, half expecting a hidden foe to launch an attack at any second. She wondered with trepidation what awaited them at the top of the climb. What had the scouts found?

'Eyes peeled!' The General scanned the overhanging rock chimneys.

'The ground levels out again soon, General. A dry riverbed, most likely. That's where we found them.'

Approaching the top of the slope, they found the rest of the scouting party waiting among the pillars.

'There's someone in the rocks above, General.'

'What?' Seven Ten frowned. 'Thought there was none left alive?'

'They have a bow. There's been arrows raining down on us since you left.'

'How many of them?'

'Just the one, far as we can tell.'

'Let me at him, I'll give him arrows...' The General barged his way to the brow of the slope. 'In all the Hells!' He dropped to his knees.

Ten Six Nine pushed the scouts aside. 'Let me see.' She stopped dead in her tracks. Her insides lurched at the sight of the massacre. 'The boar-men of Ergmire?'

'What's left of them.' Seven Ten answered coldly.

Ten Six Nine eyed the scene in disbelief. The ground was red with the mutilated remains. The bodies had been ripped to pieces. Panic coursed through her.

'Twelve Seven Two? Is he there? Have you looked?'

'He's not there.' A scout shook his head gravely. 'But Eight

Five Nine is.'

'How in the Hells can you tell?' The General had turned white as a sheet.

'We searched through them before the arrows started coming down. Difficult to be certain but reckon there must have been twenty or thirty of them. All boar-men, all but one.'

'Eight Five Nine? How can you tell?'

'It's Eight Five Nine all right. He was real proud of his three gold teeth. Showed them to everyone, he did.'

Ten Six Nine's head spun. Any relief that they hadn't found Twelve Seven Two was short lived.

'Gods save us all!' The Weasel had crept up to join them.

'Who's that up in the rocks then?' The General scowled. 'Who's the one with the bow?'

'A boar-man. Reckon he's the only survivor. And he's scared out of his wits by the looks of it.'

'Well, he ain't helping anyone by firing arrows at us.' The General got to his feet and stepped forward. 'Hey, you up there...' An arrow whizzed past and clattered into the rocks behind them, missing his head by mere inches. He dropped to his knees with a curse. 'Hells!'

'We need to talk to him.' Ten Six Nine took control. 'He's the only one who can tell us what happened here.'

'Get up there two of you,' growled the General. 'Flank him, take him down.'

'Keep him alive.' Ten Six Nine reaffirmed her authority. 'We need him alive.'

'And there was us thinking the boar-men were our problem.'

338

The Weasel sniffed. 'Looks like we all might be needing us a change of plan.'

'What in the Hells could have done that to them?' The General shook his head. 'I've never seen anything like it.'

'Looks like you picked a bad time to take over, Chief.' The Weasel eyed her with a genuine look of concern. 'Hope you have a good back-up plan in mind.'

'Shut it!' The General scowled.

'Just saying!'

'Don't bother.'

'Fair enough.'

'Quiet, both of you!' She hissed her annoyance. 'They're nearly there.'

Moving swiftly among the rock spires, the scouts closed in on their target.

'He suspects something.' The Weasel's nose twitched. 'It's all gone too quiet.'

'A diversion should help.' Ten Six Nine jumped to her feet. Waving her arms in the air, she strode into view of the hidden bowman.

'In the name of the Fallen Kings, woman!' The General roared at her. 'Get down!'

'Hold your fire!' Ten Six Nine swerved as an arrow flew past her right shoulder. 'No harm will come to you. Not from us.' Another arrow missed her by the thickness of a hair. 'Hold your fire!' She yelled again. 'Tell us what happened here.'

A shout came from above, an anguished cry for help, followed by the sounds of a struggle. Ten Six Nine held her breath. A second shout helped slow her racing pulse.

'We got him. General.'

'Then bring him down here.' The General roared his response. 'Let's hear what he has to say.' Turning to Seven Ten, he fired his instructions. 'Get back down there and inform the others of what's happened. Bring half a dozen men back with you, get them into position. Make sure our perimeter is safe.'

Ten Six Nine paced anxiously among the bodies as they waited. The Weasel was right. On this evidence, they had big problems ahead. The perpetrators of this brutal attack were still at large, roaming the wilds of Enntonia.

The scouts bundled their prisoner down the scattered slope and along the old river basin towards her. Hands tied behind his back, he struggled in vain to break free from their grip. Ten Six Nine eyed him cautiously as he approached. He was a boar-man all right. She'd never seen one in the flesh before, but she'd heard enough and read enough about them.

She felt torn. It was hard not to feel sympathy for him as he stepped gingerly over the gory remains of his companions, but her over-riding emotion was a potent mix of anger and contempt. He was part of an invading force; an element who had entered Enntonia for reasons as yet unknown. The reason didn't matter. Two of her kin were dead and Twelve Seven Two was missing.

The scouts forced him to his knees in front of her. Even then he was near as tall as she was. The boar-man's eyes darted left and right. He bared his fangs in a show of defiance, but she wasn't fooled. He was scared; he was terrified, but she didn't reckon it was them he was afraid of.

'What happened here?' she asked firmly. 'Who carried out this savagery?'

His rounded eyes widened. His rasping tone sent a shiver down her spine. 'Demons!'

'Demons? What do you mean?'

'Devils!'

'Enough of this.' The General lunged forward and grabbed the boar-man by the scruff of the neck. 'Who did this?'

'Leave him!' Ten Six Nine clasped the General's shoulder. 'Look at him. You can't scare him any more than he already is. Let him talk.'

As the General freed his grip, the boar-man held her gaze.

'Demons, devils, monsters… they had no shape or form. Invisible… they came from nowhere.'

Ten Six Nine and the General exchanged a glance.

'Invisible?' He grunted. 'How can that be?'

The boar-man continued his ramblings. 'Invisible… at first, then I saw them. Demons.'

'He's making no sense.' The General snarled his frustration.

'Don't seem like he needs to say much more.' The Weasel offered his raw assessment. 'Makes sense to me. Whatever did this, man or beast, it was possessed by something.'

'Demons.' The boar-man's tone grew desperate. 'Empty faces, black holes for eyes. They smelled of death.'

Ten Six Nine put her hands to her head. 'I've heard enough. We're not going to learn anything like this. Whatever did this might still be close. The Weasel is right, we need a change of plan.' She motioned to the scouts. 'Untie him.'

'Wait!' The General eyed her. 'You sure about that? He still has lots to answer for.'

'Release him.' She repeated her command. 'Seems to me Enntonia and Ergmire have a common enemy.'

As the boar-man got to his feet and took a step back, Ten Six Nine nodded in his direction.

'He is no threat. Pick three riders to accompany him to Ergos, General. He needs to let his homeland know what's happened.'

'The plan's changed? You still want me to go to Ergos?'

'No. You need to return to the city.'

'You think whatever did this will go there?'

'I don't know.'

'What about you?'

'I'm going to continue the search for Twelve Seven Two.'

'The Hells you are! It's too dangerous. There's no way I'm leaving you out here on your own.'

'I won't be alone. I'll have my scout with me.'

'Whoa!' The Weasel bristled. 'Hold on a minute, Chief. I'm tempted to agree with the big fella on this one.'

'It's not happening, Ten Six Nine.' The General scowled. 'You're coming back with us. I'll put guards on you if I have to.'

Ten Six Nine quickly changed the subject. There was no point in arguing. 'What will we do with the remains?'

'Leave them for the birds,' growled the General. 'A fire would only attract attention. Let's put some miles between us and this mayhem. Maybe that way we can forget what we saw here.'

Ten Six Nine knew it was a false hope.

CHAPTER SIXTY-TWO

The sights and sounds of the colourful travelling show faded quickly from view. The carnival was gone. In its place, the vast plain stretched all the way to the horizon.

Reen smiled at the familiar scene. She was home.

Hurrying to the edge of the hill, she looked down excitedly on the camp. Smoke filtered from the flaps at the top of the conical tipis. Though dusk was still some hours away, the perimeter lanterns were lit in preparation for the night ahead. Her heart skipped with joy at the sight of her kin. It felt like ages since she'd seen them.

How long had it been? How many days and nights had she been gone? She'd lost count. She began her descent with apprehension. She was home, but she might be in big trouble.

What an adventure it had been; the best adventure ever. But it would probably be her last for a while. She wouldn't be allowed to wander off on her own after this, not for a long time.

The prospect of her impending interrogation grew more daunting with each step. Where had she been? Who had she been with? And what had she been doing?

What was she going to tell them?

The truth didn't seem like a very good idea. And anyway, no one would believe it.

So, what was she going to say? What would her excuse be?

Reaching the plain, she moved quickly through the herd, jumping up every now and again to run her fingers through the soft dark fur. The Seyk gently rolled their heads in response. Dodging the great swinging antlers, she ran towards the tipis... and bundled headlong into a herdsman.

'Reen!' Her father glared down at her disapprovingly. 'Why are you running in the herd?'

'Sorry, Fah.' She caught her breath. This was it. There was no point in delaying the inevitable. 'I'm sorry I was gone so long.'

'What?'

'I don't know how it happened, Fah.'

'You don't know how what happened? What are you talking about, girl?'

'My reason for being gone so long. I'm really sorry...'

'Oh, I understand.' He gave her a big smile and ruffled her hair. 'It's another one of your games. Very good, Reen.' He pulled her close and hugged her. 'But haven't you got chores to do before dinner?' He winked. 'And where is your brother?'

Reen's confusion mounted. 'He's not here?'

'Ah, there he his.' Her father motioned over her shoulder. 'I'll see you both at the fire.'

Reen turned to see her brother running red-faced towards her.

'How did you do that?' he puffed.

'Do what?'

'How did you get back here before me? I was well ahead of you.' He shot her a look of suspicion. 'You knew a short-cut. You tricked me, didn't you?'

Reen frowned. This was an unexpected twist. No one had

missed her. How was this possible? Had no one even noticed she'd been gone? Had she imagined the whole thing?

Closing her eyes, she quickly pictured their faces, each and every one of them. She hadn't imagined them; they were real.

The Carnival Master with his black diamond eyes. The adorable Scribe of Bog-Mire, and his inquisitive apprentice Elfin Fingle. The Dragon Slayer: the woman she had helped become queen. The dark-haired angel from the stories of legend, and Messenger Two Cups, the tea-drinking wizard…

'Reen! Was it a trick?'

Opening her eyes, she looked up at the sky and wondered, just for a second, what would happen if she pointed a finger to the heavens. Deciding against it, she threw her arm around him.

'No, little brother.' she smiled. 'It was no trick.'

CHAPTER SIXTY-THREE

'We didn't know what they were, or where they came from. They appeared without warning, first as a contortion of the air and then as sunlight reflecting on a blade. Cloaked by evil sorcery, they stalked their prey unseen. But I saw them. I saw the face of The Formless, and I will never forget it. The memory of it haunts me every moment of my days.'

Dragon Slayer Twelve Seven Two shuddered at his own recollection of the face. Shifting uncomfortably, he pulled the coarse blanket tightly around his shoulders. 'I think I've heard enough.'

Clutching the handwritten journal, the young boy looked up at him eagerly. 'Will I read some more?'

'No.'

At the far side of the cave, the old man scratched vigorously at the ground with his rustic walking stick. The boy's eyes danced excitedly.

'Smmuga, Last of the Skree, thinks I should read a few lines more.'

'Does he?' Twelve Seven Two glanced to the cave entrance. Outside, the snow was still falling heavily. 'Well, I can't stop you. And I'm not going anywhere in that weather.'

To his obvious delight, the boy continued reading. 'They kill without prejudice, slaughtering everything in their path, but for all their mystery, one thing about The Formless is known. They will not take the life of one of their own kind.'

Twelve Seven Two felt the weight of their stare. Stung by the insinuation, he jumped to his defence. 'I am not of their kind. I am nothing like them.'

Throwing the blanket aside, he stomped to the mouth of the cave. Through the swirling snow, he caught glimpses of the rocky buttress jutting from the landscape like the backbone of some prehistoric beast guarding its lair.

The mountainous chain formed the boundary to his peculiar incarceration. He didn't know where he was, or how he had come to be here. He'd been here eight days. Eight he was aware of, at least. He'd spent the first four days trying to leave; trying to find an escape route. But each time, he found himself back at the foot of the escarpment looking up at the cave where the old man and the boy stood awaiting his return.

He'd climbed the ridge to the top of the cliffs high above the cave. On the far side of a deep gully an imposing wall of snow-covered mountain loomed threateningly, its summit lost in the clouds. There seemed no way out.

On the fifth day he stayed at the cave and listened as the boy told him all about the geography of the land, assuring him that the caverns were no prison. This was their sanctuary.

Smmuga would let them know when it was safe to leave.

On the sixth day, the snow came.

Twelve Seven Two didn't remember coming here. The last thing he remembered was the face of the apparition bearing down on him, just before it knocked him unconscious.

He had wakened here, to see the old man and the young boy watching over him. They'd offered no explanation; he'd asked where he was but had been given no satisfactory response. He was meant to be here. That was all the boy would say.

The boy had no name. Least, if he had one, he claimed to not remember it. The old man was called Smmuga. That's what the boy had told him, and Twelve Seven Two had to take his word for it. In the eight days since his arrival, the old man hadn't uttered a single word.

According to the boy's book, Smmuga, Last of the Skree, had taken a vow of silence in honour of his fallen kin. As means of communication, the old man had written everything down for him. The boy had no recollection of how long he'd been here in the company of the old man. He said it didn't matter. The journal told him things were the way they were meant to be.

With his anger quelled by the cold, Twelve Seven Two dragged his gaze away from the snowstorm and walked back to the fire. On the far side of the flames, the old man scratched a quill hurriedly across the pages of the book. As he looked up, his stare landed on Twelve Seven Two. Taking the book, the boy studied the page closely and returned to the fireside.

'The Formless.' He looked up nervously. 'You have seen them?'

'Yes.' Twelve Seven Two nodded. 'I've seen them.'

'Can I read more to you?'

'I suppose so.'

The boy flipped the book open excitedly and began to read. 'Smmuga advises against jumping to conclusions as it can lead to misinterpretation.' His finger traced along the yellowed page. 'Smmuga believes that The Formless come from another world and can move back and forth between worlds at will. He believes that by cloaking their appearance, by not fully materialising in either world, they can remain almost invisible. Smmuga, Last of the Skree, knows of a name given to beings with the ability to shift between worlds. They are known by some as Drifters. Smmuga says that he has seen this happen. Smmuga believes that you are a Drifter. He says that you will know he speaks the truth.'

Twelve Seven Two met the old man's stare. Who was he? How could he claim to know such things, and what gave him the right to make such assumptions? Even if they felt right. Even if they made sense. Even if they offered Twelve Seven Two a glimpse of the understanding he'd been craving for so long. Who was he? And how could he know these things?

The answers might lie in the journal. The boy had offered to read the old man's story several times. Twelve Seven Two hadn't wanted to hear it, until now.

'Seems Smmuga has a lot to say about others, what has he written about himself in there?'

'You want me to read it to you?'

'Yes.' Twelve Seven Two nodded. 'Let's hear what the old mute has to say about himself.'

'I will read it, in his own words.' The boy flicked back through the pages to find his place, and the tale began. 'I am Smmuga, Last of the Skree. Cave dwellers and goat herders, and I fear I am the last of my kind. They are all gone. I have not spoken since the day they were taken from this world, and I will not speak again until the time is right. Like so many others we were innocent victims caught in the midst of an apocalyptic battle between warring dark forces. The great firebirds came from the south, scorching the lands. The Scavengers followed; flesh eaters, legions of them, feeding on the survivors. Fleeing for our lives we were driven higher into the mountains. There was nowhere left for us to go. It was hard to imagine anything worse than those soulless damnations, but then we encountered The Formless. Summoned to repel the scourge of the Scavengers, they slaughtered all in their path. There is no right and wrong in war; no good and bad.

Their attack came in the high mountain pass. We were trapped. With no warning, with no time to prepare, and nowhere to run, they took form right in front of our eyes. Only Smmuga survived.'

The boy steadied the shake in his voice. On the far side of the cave the old man stared blankly into the flames. 'I wandered aimlessly for days without number,' the boy continued reading, 'lost, bereft and alone, wondering how and why I had survived. Then, one day, I found it. The blurring of the shapes; the great rift in the mountainside. Smmuga moved between worlds. Smmuga knows this to be true.'

The boy closed the book quietly, wrapped himself in his blanket, and curled up by the fire. Beyond the flames the old man sat hunched in silence, his face directed to the floor of the cave.

Twelve Seven Two stoked the fire, lay down in the gathering darkness and waited for sleep. It was slow in coming. The old man's tale weighed heavily on his mind.

350

His indifference towards the stranger shifted slowly towards empathy. It appeared they had a lot in common. Twelve Seven Two might not be the last of his kind but they were both lost, and they shared a common enemy.

CHAPTER SIXTY-FOUR

Twelve Seven Two had wakened to the welcome sight of a clear blue sky. A thick blanket of snow had transformed the landscape. Rising starkly from the white canvas, the black jagged backbone of the prehistoric guardian was more striking than ever.

'A fine day to explore.' The old man emerged from the cave behind him. 'Perhaps today you will discover a way out.'

Twelve Seven Two faced him in astonishment. 'You're speaking?'

'Smmuga has stayed silent long enough.' The old-timer brushed the white hair back from his wrinkled face and zealously inhaled the fresh air. 'Today, Smmuga feels good.'

Twelve Seven Two shook his head at the sudden change. 'I haven't seen the boy today. Where is he?'

'The boy is gone.'

'Gone? Gone where?'

'He no longer needed to be here. You should be pleased.'

'Why?'

'You helped him, more than you'll ever know. To show his appreciation, he left a gift for you.' He took the boy's journal from the folds of his blanket. 'He wanted you to have this.'

Twelve Seven Two held the book in his hands. 'Why did he leave it for me?'

'So that it can help you, in the same way it helped him. He

wrote a message in it for you.'

He opened the book tentatively. 'Shouldn't we go looking for him?'

'You will not find him. Read his message. It's near the back.'

Twelve Seven Two leafed through the pages until he found it. He read through it silently three times. The words themselves were simple enough. With each reading, the enormity of their meaning intensified.

'What does it say?' Grinning knowingly, Smmuga prodded his arm impatiently. 'Read it to me.'

Twelve Seven Two read the message aloud, barely recognising the sound of his own voice. 'It pleases me to know the man I will become. I hope you will come to see the old man in the same way.'

Smmuga gave a cackle. 'I wonder if you will.'

It felt like the ground had shifted beneath his feet. 'The boy?'

'You didn't recognise him?'

'You?'

'I recognise you.' The old man wrapped his arms around him. 'I think it's time.'

Twelve Seven Two felt the cold breath on his neck. 'Time for what?'

Tightening his hold, the old man's words came out little more than a whisper. 'We are Smmuga, Last of the Skree. We can go now.'

CHAPTER SIXTY-FIVE

Sunlight pierced the storm clouds. Spears of light illuminated the sky, like a host of celestial stairways linking the rolling sea with the heavens high above. Accompanied by the hypnotic crashing of the waves, Taro Brook followed the footprints in the white sand until they came to an abrupt stop. The seabirds circled noisily overhead as he scanned the empty beach for sign of life.

Amy Coda was gone.

Whilst the outcome was far from unexpected, the timing of it unsettled him. They'd visited the cove only the previous day. Having looked forward to the opportunity to discuss things further with her over the coming days, her sudden absence troubled him greatly.

Her presence in Nallevarr had offered invaluable insights; revelations which had fallen into place like missing pieces from a giant puzzle. But much of the puzzle remained a mystery and although some of what she'd shared had given reassurance, he found elements of her disclosure disturbing. Hans Rugen and Mickey Spades; their names evoked memories too complex to fully comprehend. The little white-whiskered man who'd claimed to be his legal representative; who was he? And why did he haunt Brook's subconscious?

Amy Coda being here had presented an understanding of some things but had also raised some serious questions.

Why had she come to Nallevarr?

What had drawn her here? Was it him, or something else?

Rugen and Spades aside, what was the true scale of their connection? Was there more to it?

Amy Coda was gone. So too was his opportunity to find the answers.

More would come to Nallevarr. He would have to remain vigilant. It was foolish to believe he was the only one with questions; the only one seeking to unravel the truth. Amy Coda's divulgement was evidence enough of that. How many others were gathering the fragments of a scattered past?

Turning his attention back to the sea, he fixed his eyes on the far horizon. In only a matter of days, with the full moon, the great ocean would recede leaving a vast white desert in its wake, and a new cycle would begin.

CHAPTER SIXTY-SIX

Amy Coda tapped the brass nameplate by the doorway and entered the building. Climbing the narrow stairway to the third floor, she knocked on the wooden door.

'Come in!'

As she entered the room, a spectacled man flicked cake crumbs from his shirt and stood up from his cluttered desk.

'Larry Taskin?' She knew it was him. Though he would never know it they'd met once before, in Hans Rugen's hospital room.

'That's me,' he made a momentary clicking noise with his tongue. 'Literary agent extraordinaire.'

She took a deep breath. Her conversation with Mickey Spades had convinced her of the need to come here, and to talk to Hans Rugen's agent. She proceeded with caution.

'My name is Claudia Bankz. I'd like to talk to you about one of your clients. Hans Rugen.'

Taskin bristled at the sound of the writer's name. His expression paled as he quickly sat down. 'I'm sorry. Hans Rugen is no longer with us.'

'He's gone to another agency?'

'No. You misunderstand. He is no longer with us.' He paused awkwardly. 'He died a few weeks ago.'

Steadying her voice, she continued with her deception. 'What happened to him?'

'Very sad,' replied Taskin. 'He passed away peacefully, during a hospital stay.'

'Peacefully?'

'Yes, a small consolation.' Taskin's colour returned as he picked up a muffin from the desk. 'He'd been admitted to hospital after falling from the cliffs in Greenhill Forest. But he had been making good progress, he was recovering well… then he just slipped away.'

'Just slipped away?'

'Yes. In his sleep.'

'In his sleep?' She couldn't quite believe what she was hearing. 'In bed?'

Taskin raised his brows in response. 'Yes, that's usually the best place.' With a shake of his head, he bit into the muffin.

Amy Coda took a deep breath. Things had taken a sinister turn. In her panic and distress, she had left Hans Rugen lying on the floor of his hospital room with a pillow covering his face. So how had he been found in bed? Someone must have moved him, without reporting his cause of death. Why would someone do that? Were they aware of her involvement? Was someone covering her tracks? If so, why? She backed slowly towards the door. 'I'm sorry. I didn't know. I'll not trouble you any further.'

Taskin wiped his mouth. 'Wait! You wanted to talk about Rugen. If you didn't know about his passing, what was it you wanted to talk about?'

And there it was, her opportunity to salvage something from this visit. She quickly regrouped. 'I'm somewhat of an agent myself,' she began. Spades had offered a slither of hope; she recalled his words with care. 'Hans Rugen had contacted me with the bones of a new novel he was exploring... a walker in the woods?'

Taskin sat forward abruptly. 'Rugen contacted you?'

'Yes.'

'About the walker in the woods idea?'

'Yes, you knew about it?'

'Oh, I knew about it.' Taskin's cheeks flushed with anger. 'I didn't know he was fishing around for another agent though.' He thumped the desk. 'I told him it was a non-starter; told him he should stick with what he knew. The Spades series was tried and tested, a winning formula...' He held her stare. 'A crime fiction series, are you familiar with it?'

'I've heard of it.'

Taskin nodded his satisfaction then continued his rant. 'But he was becoming obsessed with the walker story.'

'I don't suppose you have a copy of it lying around?' She softened her stance and smiled. 'I know it's a lot to ask... but he did promise me I'd get to see it.'

Her smile worked its charm. Taskin's fury subsided. She could tell he was still annoyed, but his manner was much calmer. 'I don't know what Rugen was playing at. We had an arrangement; he shouldn't have been talking to anyone else about his books. I'm sorry, but I can't share anything on his walker in the woods idea. There was no first draft, only a few pages written on his old laptop computer. He ran out of inspiration early in the process. I don't know why he was speaking to you or anyone else about it. He had nothing, and I told that private investigator the same thing.'

'What private investigator?'

'Fella who came to see me when Rugen was missing in the forest, right before they found him.'

'Who was he? What did he want?'

'He offered to help look for Rugen. He wouldn't leave his name. I thought he reminded me of Mickey Spades, the detective in Rugen's crime series. I told him so too.'

Coda's skin tingled. Spades had been here. 'What did he say?'

'Didn't say much,' Taskin tutted. 'Laughed about it. Anyway, I never saw him again. I assumed he'd heard that Rugen had been found.'

'So there is nothing you can show me that relates to that book?'

'No. Hans asked me to take his laptop to him in the hospital but when I went to his cottage, I couldn't find it. He was darned annoyed and when I told him about the investigator fella, he got even more fired up. He reckoned he'd stolen it. Looking back now, it's obvious all wasn't well with Hans.'

'Why would you say that?'

'He was convinced that the P.I. was Mickey Spades. That he'd somehow come to life, and that he was coming after him. Crazy, right? He even went as far as writing a scene where he killed off Spades. I persuaded him not to be too hasty, got him to agree to delay his decision and take a few days to think about it.' Taskin paused for a moment. 'That was the last time I saw him, when I showed his next visitor into the room.'

'Someone else came to see him?'

'Yes, she said she was from the pathology department. I figured she had come to talk to him about a case involving a friend of his who'd died a few weeks earlier.' Taskin held a cookie in his hand and eyed it longingly. 'She'll likely never know it, but I reckon she was probably the last person to talk to Hans Rugen.'

Claudia Bankz had heard enough. It was time to go. Mickey Spades had been here, and her hunch had proved to be right. Hans Rugen had been a trail worth pursuing. 'I've taken up enough of your time, Mister Taskin. Thank you, and again, I'm sorry for your loss.'

Taskin handed a business card across the table. 'Let me know if you find anything out, Claudia. I'm afraid it looks like your interest in the walker story is over. Sorry I couldn't do more.'

'On the contrary,' she flashed a smile. 'You've been a great help.'

She'd lied to the detective. Amy Coda's presence wasn't fading. If anything, it was becoming stronger. All attempts to shut her out had been unsuccessful, but now a resolution seemed obvious. They both wanted the same thing. Amy Coda was lost; working together, they just might help her find her way.

CHAPTER SIXTY-SEVEN

Shadow's day had begun brightly. After the rain ceased shortly before sunrise, a fresh breeze had whipped the clouds into order, leaving large swathes of blue sky in their place.

Her route south, through the rolling foothills, had led her into a woodland of high canopy pine. Following the gloom of the Ash Woods and the hardships of the sand dunes, the walk had been a welcome and uplifting experience. But now, it seemed her luck had taken a turn for the worse.

At the foot of a gently sloping hillside awash with blueberry, a track had led her to the head of a gorge. She'd followed the trail carefully as it zig-zagged its way downhill, dodging between the overgrown windblown trees and broken branches. The river at the foot of the gorge, a dizzying drop below, wound its way noisily among the timber debris and abandoned boulders. An old wooden railing, broken in places and rotting in others, offered little in the way of security. Several short sections of wooden footsteps and walkways had been erected to negotiate the precarious voids where the land had slipped away. She'd wondered who had built them, just as she wondered about the creator of the little wooden bench that marked the fork in the trail. Staring at it, her frustration heightened. This was the third time she'd seen it. The same bench, under the same fir tree, next to the same flat-topped rock.

She'd followed the path in both directions, with the same outcome. Both had led her back here, with neither trail offering any deviation or alternative.

It wasn't a circular route, it couldn't be. In both directions the path worked its way downhill, yet at no time gave any impression of climbing back up again.

With a sigh, she sat down on the bench. Her options appeared limited. Try again or retrace her route back up the side of the gorge. As she debated her next move, a scuffling noise came from behind the rock. Jumping quickly to her feet, she swallowed uncomfortably and, at the same time, regretted the previous day's desire for company.

An odd-looking fellow, only half her height, clambered into view at the top of the rock. Rubbing his hands on the front of his faded green jacket, which appeared far too big for him, he sat down cross-legged and eyed her keenly.

'Having trouble with the trail, Miss?'

The honeyed tone of his voice did little to mask his dubious appearance. His bare feet were proportionately too big for his body, his hands were bigger still. His tattered grey trousers came to a ragged stop just below his knees, a look that mirrored his rolled-up sleeves. Reaching into a bulging jacket pocket, he pulled out a handful of walnuts. Arranging them with precision at his feet, he picked one up and began tapping it against a flat piece of stone held in the palm of his left hand. The shell cracked open after only a few blows. He repeated the process several times before reiterating his greeting. 'Having trouble with the trail?' His eyes widened. 'I could help you with that.'

He stuffed a handful of the crushed nuts into his mouth and began crunching noisily. His stumpy nose twitched animatedly as he chewed. Little pointed ears poked out from beneath his hat, a conical conglomeration of bark and twigs which seemed to rest atop his bushy eyebrows.

Shadow wasn't sure if he was cute, repulsive, or something in between. Either way, she had the feeling he was not to be trusted. 'Who are you?' she asked warily.

'Faramus Thorn,' he replied. 'Keeper of the gorge. You're having trouble with the trail. I can help if you'd like me to?'

'No, thank you.' Shadow declined the offer. 'I'll be on my way. It was nice meeting you.'

'I doubt that.' With a flash of his yellowed teeth, he scooped the remaining nuts up in one hand and began bashing them furiously one by one against the rock.

Spurred into motion by the wild flailing of his arms and the flying pieces of shell, Shadow hurried down the short slope to a bend in the trail. With the sound of manic nut-cracking fading behind her, she continued briskly through the trees.

There had to be another path, an alternative route, something she'd missed earlier. Fully focused on her surroundings, eyes scanning left and right, she searched for signs of where she'd gone wrong. After a short while the ground levelled, just as before. She kept walking, watching for a change in the terrain, but saw nothing, no hint that she was climbing again. Maybe this time, without realising it, she'd found her way out.

Rounding another bend in the trail, she drew to a sudden halt. She hadn't found her way out.

She was back at the wooden bench again.

'How is this possible?' She voiced her disbelief.

Perched atop his stone, Faramus Thorn looked up from his nut bashing. 'Having trouble with the trail, Miss?' He spat out a piece of shell. 'I can help with that if you'd like?'

Shadow looked around in frustration. There seemed no logical explanation for this strange anomaly. Her situation was becoming desperate. 'Why do I keep finding myself back here?'

'Obvious, isn't it?'

'Not to me.'

'Obvious to me, Miss.'

'Would you like to share with me?'

'Share what?'

'The reason I keep ending up back at the same place.'

'Oh, that!' Relief flashed across his little face. 'I'd be happy to. You're having trouble with the trail. That's why.'

Shadow took a deep breath. Getting annoyed wouldn't help the situation. 'Would you care to elaborate?'

'Not really.' He tapped a nut against the stone in his left hand. 'Do you want help or not?'

If it was a matter of choice she would have declined, but she didn't have that luxury. Whether she liked it or not, she needed his assistance. 'Yes, please. Help would be good.'

His expression lightened. 'Great!' He took a celebratory swing at the rock. The shell shattered instantly, sending pieces flying in every direction. He studied the nut carefully before popping it in his mouth. 'Goes without saying,' he chomped, 'there will be a price.'

'A price?'

'A fee. A small recompense. I help you with your dilemma, you pay a fair price for my trouble. That's fair, isn't it?'

Shadow hesitated. 'How do I know I can trust you?'

'You don't.' He glared at her. 'We only just met. You wouldn't trust a stranger you'd just met, would you? That would be stupid. And it would be stupid for me to trust you, especially with that sword hanging at your side but, as we both have something to gain from our transaction, I'd say it's a risk worth taking. Wouldn't you agree?'

'Yes, I suppose so.'

'Great!' He swung a thumb in the direction of the bench. 'Take a seat, Miss. I'll be with you shortly.'

'I'm happy standing.'

'Please yourself.' He pulled another handful of nuts from his pocket.

Shadow watched him for a moment. 'So?'

'So what?'

'What's the fee?'

'What you got to offer?'

'Shouldn't you name your fee?'

'No! No! No!' He shook his head vigorously. 'That's not how it works. If I was to name my price straight away, I might miss out on what you might be prepared to offer. I might miss out on the chance of something better.'

There was a strange but fitting logic to his argument. 'Sorry, but I'm afraid I don't have much with me.'

Faramus Thorn straightened himself on the rock. Clutching

the fistful of walnuts tightly, he tapped them gently against the palm of his left hand. 'Got any nuts?'

'No.'

'Pity.' He frowned. 'What else you got to offer then? What you got in your pack?'

'Water?'

'Water?' He threw her a look of disgust. 'I got my own gorge with a river running through it. I got all the water I'd ever want. What else?'

'Not much,' she replied cagily. 'Fruit? Oat biscuits?'

'Oats? Disgusting! And definitely not fruit. The seeds get stuck in my teeth. What else? Got any nuts?'

'No. I told you I don't have any nuts and I have nothing else to offer in exchange. And anyway, I need my supplies for my journey.'

'Journey?' The pointed ears bristled with interest. 'Where are you going?'

'Journey's End.'

'That's not fair.' He slapped the rock. 'You're being cryptic. Stop it! Every adventure would finish there.'

'I'm not being cryptic.' Shadow took a step back. This wasn't going well. 'Journey's End is the name of the place I'm going.'

The little fellow's eyes narrowed. 'Sounds interesting. What's to see there?'

'I don't know, I've never been there before.'

'So, why are you going there?'

Shadow held her breath. She couldn't tell him any more about where she was going. She'd probably said too much already. 'I...'

He jumped on her hesitation with glee. 'Well, Miss,' a strange gurgling noise accompanied his obvious delight. 'It appears we have found our resolution.'

'We have?'

'Yes.' He grinned mischievously. 'I've just decided, I like you.'

'You do?' Her alarm bells rang loudly.

'Yes, and because I like you, I'll make an exception. For you, I will name my fee.'

'You will? Very well, what is it?'

'I'll agree to help you find your way out of the gorge and in return,' he pointed animatedly, 'you will take me with you on your journey.'

Shadow's heart sank. She couldn't take him with her to Journey's End, even if she wanted to. And she didn't. His dubious nature aside, the constant crunching and smashing of nuts would drive her crazy. 'No, that's not possible. I can't take you with me.'

'Why not? Secret mission, is it?'

Shadow frowned. 'I can't say.'

'Even better. I love secret missions.'

'I'm sorry, but you're not coming with me. You can't.'

'Then you have a problem, don't you?' He folded his arms and glowered his contempt. 'Doesn't look like you're going anywhere either. You can find your own way out of the gorge. Good luck with that!'

It seemed their discussion had come to an end. Turning away in frustration, Shadow walked down the slope to the turn in the trail. There had to be a solution to this. Something she was missing. Walking to the edge, she looked across to the far side of the narrow ravine where a small stream tumbled from the ledge down into a swirling pool some thirty feet below. Though she knew instantly that something wasn't right, it took her a moment to process her discovery. There was something odd about the birch trees overhanging the pool. It might only have been a slight discolouration in the leaves, but its meaning was unmistakable. An orange tinge, a yellow burst. The first signs of autumn.

All she needed now was confirmation.

Hiding her satisfaction, she marched back up the path.

'Back so soon?' Faramus Thorn grinned impishly. 'Still having trouble with the trail?'

'We're not on the island, are we?'

His expression changed in a flash. 'What island?' He glared at her suspiciously. 'What are you talking about?'

'I didn't think so. Goodbye, Faramus Thorn.' She grinned at his consternation. 'It was nice meeting you.' Turning swiftly, she hurried back down the trail. As she moved towards the edge, she glanced over her shoulder.

The manic nutcracker was standing upright on the rock, stamping his foot and waving a fist in anger.

'You'll be back,' he screeched. 'You can't leave this place without my help.'

His shouts of protest faded as she jumped.

Closing her eyes, she held her breath...

But she never reached the water. There was no impact, no awkward landing.

She opened her eyes slowly. Her intuition had led her well. At some point, in the woodland above the gorge, she had drifted between worlds. The pool had been her way out.

Now she was back in the clutches of summer. A lush green meadowland, mottled with scattered stands of trees, stretched into the distance. Adjusting to the sudden change in surroundings, her eyes settled on the host of towering rock pillars dotting the landscape in the near distance.

Shadow drew a breath at the sight of the age-old monuments.

She had arrived at the Pinnacles of Sorrow.

Approaching the towering giants she looked up in awe, scarcely believing she was here walking among them. Some said they were Guardians of the Gateways, whilst others claimed they were lost souls in limbo. The less imaginative of folk reckoned they were nothing more than remnants of ages past when the land had slipped.

Despite her sense of wonder, she stayed focused. Druan's words of caution remained uppermost in her mind. Ignoring the urge to explore the noises emanating from beyond the imposing stone columns, she kept her eyes fixed straight ahead. Creaks, cracks, and groans; the dragging of rocks; the sound of falling stones and the echoes of distant voices all pulled at her imagination. Dismissing them all without hesitation, she walked on resolutely. Druan had also warned how time might appear to move differently here. His words rang true.

Dusk came quickly. The daylight faded rapidly. Onwards she walked through the hours of darkness, her determination unflinching. Overhead, the black canvas of sky shimmered with the lights of a billion stars and moons too many to count.

Marvelling at the celestial show she stuck to her task, shunning the scratching and scraping noises that threatened the serenity of the night.

By early morning, as daylight edged steadily across the sky, the Pinnacles of Sorrow were far behind her. When they were little more than dots in the distance, she climbed to the top of a grassy knoll and watched the sunrise. Dawn chilled the air. Wrapping herself in her blanket, she slept for a short while but was soon on the move again.

The hours slipped by unnoticed. Just short of midday, with the sun reaching its peak, the rolling grasslands reached the shingled shores of a glistening lake. Feeling a rush of both excitement and expectation, she took out the map. Not that she needed confirmation. There was little doubt about her location. The Lake at the Point of Forever was well named.

An infinite expanse of blue; greater than all the seas and oceans combined, stretching far beyond the realms of imagination. The tales, magical as they were, did this place little justice.

Lifted by the experience, she followed the edge of the lake for several hours until the changing terrain forced her to change direction. Rising steeply from the water, the mountains and cliffs reached for the sky. There was no way around.

She kept to the lower slopes until, concerned that she was being led too far from her intended route, she began climbing.

As evening approached, she picked out a narrow ledge running at an angle up the side of the mountain. Ascending the airy shelf cautiously, she came to a great notch in the rock-face. Undaunted, she clambered into the gloomy recess. Hidden from the warmth of the setting sun, she followed a steep-sided gully as it wound its way between the overhanging cliffs.

As the water-gouged chasm widened, the ground levelled and she entered a conclave of age-old oak trees. A flag-stoned path emerged gradually from the greenery of the forest floor.

Entering a clearing in the trees, she came on the overgrown ruins of an ancient stone structure. A procession of crumbled stone pillars flanked her on either side as she walked towards the centrepiece of the ruins; a gaping circle of vertically built, time-bleached stone blocks. Beyond the strange portal the light danced with an unnerving ethereal glow.

Shadow stopped short of the archway. This place was not mentioned on Druan's map.

Had she strayed from her true path? Should she turn and retrace her route back down the mountainside? She looked up in search of inspiration… And there it was.

An inscription carved into the face of one of the stone blocks.

Reaching up, she ran her fingers over the symbols. An ancient text, chiselled long ago judging by the worn nature of the stone. Though how this was possible she couldn't quite comprehend. She read the inscription aloud, hoping that hearing the words might offer some better understanding.

'Welcome, Shadow of the Seers Watch.'

The shimmering light beyond the arch beckoned her forward.

Would this lead to Journey's End?

Was she about to meet the Seer Magister?

There was only one way to find out.

CHAPTER SIXTY-EIGHT

Funny thing about dreams. More often than not you're just getting to the good bit when you get disturbed, and the moment is gone forever.

There he was at the royal palace to receive his award, his commendation for services to the realm. As the crowd cheered his name, a hand clamped down over his mouth.

'Wake up!' Shaking him by the shoulder, she roused him from his slumber. 'It's time to go.'

Sitting up abruptly, he rubbed the dream state from his eyes. It was dark. Not so dark that you couldn't make out the shapes of the mountains in the distance, but still dark enough. Patting the warmth into his shoulders, he lurched to his feet. 'Go? Now?'

'Yes. Quietly.'

With a stretch and a yawn, he followed. They climbed steadily up through the trees, stopping at an outcrop overlooking the camp. He looked down on the sleeping company. All was quiet. The General had wanted to keep going, to ride on through the night, to reach the city as soon as possible. She'd convinced him otherwise. Her motives were now becoming apparent.

'Another change of plan, Chief?'

'No. Same plan I've had all along.'

The Weasel rolled his gums thoughtfully. 'Well now, ain't this a turn up? You an' me, we were never going to Tonduur?'

'No.'

'We were going looking for your friend.'

'Yes and before you go casting any judgements, remember this was your idea.'

'Wouldn't dream of it, Chief. Thought never even crossed my mind.' He yawned again as he surveyed their surroundings. 'Obvious now why you told me to sleep at the edge of the camp. But I reckon we still got some guards to get past.'

'Already taken care of.'

'You knocked out your own men?'

'Only two of them...' She rolled her eyes. 'And one woman. I took them tea several hours ago. They appreciated it at the time, maybe not so much when they wake with sore heads.'

'Laced tea!' The Weasel tutted his disapproval as she retrieved two laden packs from behind a rock. 'Provisions too. I'm impressed.' He slung a pack over his shoulder. 'You've been busy.'

'Best to be prepared.' She motioned ahead. 'Let's go.'

As she led them further away from the camp, The Weasel considered the ramifications of this latest twist. 'Don't imagine the big fella is going to be happy with you when he wakes up.'

'The General? He's got enough to deal with.'

'Still, he's going to be annoyed.'

'He's always annoyed about something.'

'True, but I'm reckoning he'll send someone after us.'

'Then it's a good thing I've got my guide with me, isn't it?' She stood to one side. 'Take us north. And make sure no one can follow.'

'Right you are, Chief. The Bridge at Callinduir?'

'No. Keep to the forest to the east.'

'Fair enough.' Tilting his head, he looked to the sky. Clouds veiled many of the stars, but there was enough there for him to take his bearings. Leading the way, he gave voice to his thoughts. 'So, the Tonduur plan? The mines of Ergmire? All that work we put into drawing it up. What was the thinking behind it?'

'It was a good plan. We had to be seen to take action.'

'But you'd no intention of going there yourself?'

'Not until we found our missing people.'

'Seems like you kept that part of the plan to yourself when we discussed it.'

'Seems that way.'

'Fair enough,' he shrugged. 'You're the boss. But what if them boar-men had taken your friend to Ergos?'

'They didn't.'

'Nope! They sure didn't.' He shuddered at the thought of the carnage in the hoodoos.

'We'd no way of knowing how things might go. The General's message might have been well received in Ergos.'

'You reckon?'

'It depends how strongly they felt about their rogue riders. There might have been no need for us to even attempt to take control of the mines.'

'Could have ended badly though. Ergmire's superiority could have crushed Enntonia.'

'It wouldn't have come to that. I told the General to be prepared to surrender. Enntonia would have been safe under

Ergmire's rule. That's what a good leader should do. Do what's best for the people. But it doesn't matter now. Judging by what we saw yesterday, I don't see how things could have turned out any worse than they already have.'

'Fair point.' He scratched his chin. 'So, it wasn't on your mind to lead your force into Tonduur. Shouldn't you be leading them back to the city to prepare them for what might be coming?'

'And do what? Sit around idly, waiting for something that might never happen?'

'Just thinking, maybe now's the time the people need their leader. Maybe now's the time for you to be watching over your kingdom.'

Landing her hand on his shoulder, she spun him round fiercely. 'I don't want to be their leader and I don't want a kingdom. I told you that the first time we met. This was your suggestion, Weasel. Not mine.' Releasing her grip, she stepped back and looked away.

This was awkward. Still, she made a fair point. He'd overstepped his mark. 'You're right, Chief. Apologies, but I'm reckoning it's my place to say these things. Just trying to do my job proper. I mean, what kind of advisor would I be if I didn't raise such topics for discussion?'

She faced him again. Her anger had passed, but there was a steely determination in her eyes. 'When I want your advice, I'll ask for it. Until then, just guide. Okay?'

'Crystal clear, Chief.' His nose twitched. Seemed like he'd diffused the situation. Things were back on track. 'Crystal clear.'

His route north took them through the forest and up into the mountains to the northwest of the Nameless Lake.

They traversed the knife-edged ridge at Crow's Lair and entered the Forgotten Caves; a winding series of inter-linked tunnels and chambers hidden far beneath the Etched Mountains. The Weasel knew this place like the back of his scrawny hands.

Night or day made no difference in here. Didn't matter when you had the finest snout this side of The Barrens.

For the most part, they journeyed in silence. It seemed they both had a lot on their minds. Her intentions were clear enough, and The Weasel? Well, he had a decision to make. And he'd have to make it soon. Things had changed. They'd changed dramatically.

Question now was, did he stay with her?

Her actions, which many would view as reckless, not to mention pure selfish, might just have undermined her authority. She risked losing control of the kingdom.

What bounty would she then be able to offer him as payment for his services? Way he saw it, his dilemma was simple.

Stay with her or cut his losses and head for home.

Emerging from the caves, they saw the eastern sky glow with the colours of dawn. It was then that he noticed. He'd thought there was something different about her but hadn't been able to put his finger on it.

'Your hair.'

'What about it?'

'Looks darker. You changed it before we left camp? Herbal?'

'Yes. Dark Rage. Least, that's what Old Hunchback called it.'

'Dark Rage, eh?' He reckoned it might be a good name at that.

'Suits you, Chief... the colour I mean, not the name.' Quickly changing the subject, he pointed to the valley below. 'Fool's Gully. From here, there's only one way down. You ready?'

'Jump?'

'Yup! Jump. And you'd best get ready to roll.'

They jumped.

The drop was deceiving. They hit the grassy slopes sooner than expected.

From impact, the tumble down to the valley floor took only a matter of seconds. Catching their breath, they looked back up at the cave entrances nestled in the rocky escarpment.

'Where are we now?'

'That's us through the Etched Mountains.'

'I don't recall ever seeing mention of them on any map.'

The Weasel grinned. 'You wouldn't have. We like to keep them on a need-to-know basis, that's kind of how the Forgotten Caves got their name.' He winked casually. 'Anyway, we'd best keep moving. Word is goblins roam these parts.'

'Goblins?' She scanned their surroundings.

'Never seen them myself, just saying. That's what I've heard.'

'You don't believe in all that nonsense, do you?' She glared at him.

'Things I've seen lately, I'm about ready to say anything's possible.' He cracked his jaw and gestured ahead. 'Let's get moving.'

After a while, again spent walking in silence, the ground steepened gradually as the lush greenery of the dry valley gave way to scattered clumps of sharp, pale brown grass. Climbing to the brow of the hill, they found themselves high on a ledge at the top of a boulder-strewn slope. A bleak and arid landscape stretched out before them, far as the eye could see.

The Weasel turned to her with a frown. The time had come for him to make his decision. 'This is it,' he eyed the scene wistfully. 'Furthest north I've ever been.' He pointed towards the peaked horizon. 'That there's the Old Kingdom, in all its glory. Somewhere out there, beyond those distant hills, will be the Old Ruins, and beyond that, the Northern Wastelands.' He worked his gums. 'From there, far as we know, ain't nothing but a whole big lot of nothingness, all the way to the Sacred Mountains.'

'And beyond that, Sacra.'

He looked at her with surprise.

'What?' She scowled. 'I can read maps too.'

The Weasel gave a dry chuckle. 'Fair enough. So, how far you planning on going?'

'As far as I need to.'

'Until you find him?'

'Until I find him.'

'What makes you think he's out there? No one goes there. No one has gone there for centuries. What makes you think he's there?'

She stared quietly at the great expanse as if searching for her response. 'Intuition.'

The Weasel drew a breath. Intuition? Was he about to risk his life on her gut feeling?

'You don't have to come any further.' she said quietly.

'What's that now?'

'If this is the furthest north you've been, you probably can't help me anymore.'

'Ah, well now. I'd have to disagree there, Chief. I may not be familiar with the terrain, but I can still track and scout better than any man. Or woman, for that matter.'

'I don't doubt your abilities. All I'm saying is that you shouldn't feel obliged to accompany me any further.'

The Weasel winced. Problem was, he did. All this effort, all his patience. If he left now, it would have all been for nothing. And what then? Back to square one. His dreams of land and titles; his big house with the comfy beds and all those servants. All gone.

'We've never discussed payment.' It seemed like she might have read his mind.

'What's that you say?'

'Your payment for helping me. What's your price?'

He waved a hand in mock dismissal. 'Oh, I hadn't really thought about it…'

'Liar.'

Was she grinning? At his expense? 'Just been happy to help, Chief,' he cleared his throat. 'What with you being royalty an' all… reckon the old Weasel's just been doing what's right.'

'I don't believe you. Name your price. Anything you want.'

'Anything?' His whiskers twitched uncontrollably. Damn if they weren't doing their whiskery best to expose him.

'I rule over a kingdom. I can give anything.'

'Thought you didn't want it?'

'I don't. Doesn't change the fact that it's still mine to rule.'

'But, what with you taking off like this… maybe it will undo your claim.'

'Maybe, but you said it yourself. I've given them all something to believe in. And a ruler who risks their life by venturing into the wastelands to save one of her kin? Nothing short of heroic. They'd respect me even more for that.'

'That they might.' His nose twitched. 'But all that rigmarole of ruling a kingdom. It's not for you, is it?'

'No, but the mark of a great leader is their ability to delegate. I'm not familiar with all the different roles and titles but I imagine I'd need a Lord High Chancellor, or something like that.'

The Weasel felt a shiver of excitement run down his spine. 'I imagine you would, Chief.'

'One thing's for certain though,' she continued dryly. 'I wouldn't envy the role of Lord High Chancellor at a time like this. Imagine being in command of the city right now, with the threat of whatever did that to those boar-men hanging over us.'

The Weasel grimaced at the thought. 'A task best left in the hands of the big fella, if you ask me, Chief.'

Things suddenly seemed much clearer. Seemed like he'd reached his decision. Seemed like it was the only obvious choice to make.

CHAPTER SIXTY-NINE

'I agree.' Ten Six Nine hid her amusement. 'The General is the best qualified to deal with that threat. The best qualified by far.' With their discussion concluded, her thoughts quickly turned to the daunting prospect ahead. Did she really think Twelve Seven Two was out there, somewhere in the sprawling desert wilderness? Intuition? Was she prepared to risk everything on nothing more than a gut feeling? It appeared so.

'Looks like there's a lot of ground to cover,' she said with a sigh of resignation. 'I'd best get started.'

'Wait! Hold up!'

The Weasel sidled up next to her. 'Can't let you go out there on your own, Chief. Wouldn't be right. What with you being royalty an' all.' He tilted his head. 'And besides, your friend an' me, we have unfinished business to tend to. You know, I wasn't with him for long, but I felt we bonded… that make sense?' His expression twisted with an air of self-importance. 'Yup! It felt like him and the old Weasel had the makings of what might become a fine partnership. Not in the same league as you and me, of course, not anything like it, but…'

'You're coming with me?' She feigned her surprise.

'Yup! That I am. You can rely on the old Weasel. I mean, what kind of guide would I be if…'

'Right! I get it!' Ten Six Nine held up her hand. 'I still say you talk too much.' For a fleeting moment she thought about telling him she was glad to have his company but decided against it. 'Okay then,' she nodded. 'To the Old Kingdom.'

'You're the boss, Chief.' The Weasel's jaw gave its trademark crack. 'Old Kingdom it is.'

CHAPTER SEVENTY

Elfin Fingle hurried along the hallway towards the front door. The knocking was getting louder by the second. Whoever it was, they were impatient. 'Yes,' he shouted. 'Yes, I'm here.' He pulled open the door. A stern-looking man, wrapped in a dark grey coat, pulled back his hood and glowered his greeting.

'Good day to you. Is the Scribe of Bog-Mire here?'

Elfin didn't like the look of him, not one bit. 'No. The Scribe is in town, on business.'

Leaning forward, the man peered over Elfin's head. 'Then, perhaps I should come in and wait for his return.'

Elfin tightened his grip on the door. This wasn't proper conduct at all. It was good manners to wait to be invited. 'I'm not sure that's a good idea. He might be a while.'

'No matter.' Shoving Elfin's arm out of the way, the man pushed his way inside.

'Wait. You can't barge in here…'

'It seems I can. And you would be foolish to try stopping me. Would you really refuse welcome to an envoy of the Wise Ones?'

Elfin's eyes widened. 'Wise Ones? Oh…'

'Oh, indeed. I came here from the Hall of Representatives on pressing business.' He turned his attention to the far end of the hallway and then back again. 'Is Scaraven here?'

'Scaraven? No, he's not here either.'

'How tiresome. We have an arrangement to meet here at Bog-Mire Towers.'

Elfin frowned. 'We weren't informed. Scaraven mentioned nothing of this.'

The man shook his head in annoyance. 'Very well. If you would do me the courtesy of arranging refreshments, I'll wait.' He began walking along the hallway.

Elfin braced himself for confrontation. 'Now hold on a minute. This is totally inappropriate. I can't let you wander around freely in here…'

The man turned on him in a flash. 'And you would try to stop me, would you? A little doorman? I think you might have ideas above your rank.' He flashed his teeth in anger. 'I don't have time for this. I have urgent business to attend to.' He towered menacingly over Elfin. 'The banqueting room. Where is it?'

'Leave him alone.'

Elfin spun round in response to the shout. A small figure stood by the front door, shaking his fist angrily.

'Leave him alone, Nevias. Or you'll regret it.'

'Regret it, will I?' The man turned his fury on the new arrival. 'And who will make me regret it, Acolyte? You?' He stormed towards the door. 'What are you doing here?'

As they disappeared into the courtyard, Elfin summoned his wits and ran after them. He reached the door in time to see a third figure join the fray; a big-framed bulk of a man, cloaked in black. Elfin looked on in disbelief as Harbinger Talus swung a shovel and struck the man on the back of the head.

As he hit the ground, a blinding flash of light flared across the cobbled yard accompanied by a deafening blast of noise. Throwing his hands to his ears, Elfin looked away from the light. When he looked up again, the man was gone.

'What the…? Where did he go?'

The Acolyte poked his fingers in his ears. 'Blimey! That was loud.' He looked up at the Harbinger. 'Thanks, Talus. That showed him.'

The Harbinger hawked a spit to the ground. 'Are you sure that was necessary?'

'Absolutely!' The little fellow bounded towards Elfin. 'Are you okay?'

'Yes,' Elfin replied hesitantly. 'I think so. I'm Elfin Fingle. Who are you? And what is going on? Who was that man?'

'My name is Moxi. One of the Acolytes of Sycamore Glade.'

'I've heard of you. I've read about your people in books.'

'I'm sure you have. I now live at the great Hall along with many others of my kind. That man was Representative Nevias. I followed him here from the Hall.'

Elfin looked to the Harbinger. 'What is going on? Why would someone representing the Wise Ones come to Bog-Mire in such an aggressive manner?'

'Beats me, Fingle.' Talus scowled. 'Scaraven sent me to the Hall to inform them of events here in Enntonia. As requested, I also passed his letter to the Acolytes. Next thing I know, I'm halfway back to Enntonia when I realise this one is following me.'

'I was following Nevias,' Moxi grinned. 'Just so happened we were all going the same way. Figured a big fellow like yourself would be helpful.'

'Why were you following him?' Elfin frowned. 'And why did he come here?'

'I followed him because I don't trust him, and I'm not alone in that. When the Harbinger delivered his news, Nevias was in such a rush to leave the Hall I just knew there was trouble ahead. And after what I've seen here, I'm more convinced than ever.'

'Convinced of what?'

'The Representatives are up to no good. I'm certain of it. And who knows how far up the chain the corruption goes.'

'The Wise Ones?' Elfin gasped. 'The Fifteen? Surely not.'

The Acolyte nodded. 'We have our suspicions.'

Elfin found it hard to believe. 'But the man, where did he go? The light and noise? What was that all about?'

'Sorcery at work there if you ask me.' Talus sneered.

'The Representatives do command some skills in that area,' agreed Moxi. 'He shouldn't have been here. And when things went badly wrong for him, he transported himself away.'

'But why was he here? Why was he asking about the banqueting room?'

'He wants the mirror.'

'The mirror? In the banqueting room? What would he want that for?'

'You don't know about it?'

'Know what?' Elfin's nose twitched.

'Osfilian, the Black Wizard. You've heard of him?'

Elfin shivered. 'Yes, I've heard of him.'

'He's in there. Scaraven banished him to the Hidden Realm, using that very mirror.' He hesitated. 'I'm surprised you didn't know. I wonder why they didn't tell you?'

Elfin winced. 'Probably because of my curiosity. If they told me, no matter how hard I tried, I wouldn't be able to resist the urge to go in there, just to have a look.'

'Ah! Right!' Moxi of the Acolytes grinned. 'Then we are kindred spirits, Elfin Fingle. I believe there's no better way to unravel the truth than by eavesdropping and snooping. I do it all the time.'

'Osfilian.' Talus focused the conversation with a growl. 'He was the one responsible for the Raiders.'

'The Raiders.' Moxi hissed. 'What a fiendish creation.'

'They were awful.' Elfin shuddered at the recollection. 'Talus and I saw them attack the boar-men of Ergmire, some weeks ago. Their savagery was beyond belief.'

'What did they look like?'

They turned to see a Dragon Slayer standing behind them.

'Where did you appear from?' Talus challenged.

The new arrival ignored the question. 'These Raiders,' he continued. 'What did they look like?'

'Skeletal fiends,' Elfin replied. 'Cloaked in black.'

'And what happened to them?'

'They vanished,' answered Moxi. 'With Osfilian's banishment to the Hidden Realm, their presence ceased.'

'And the Black Wizard, he is still banished?'

'Yes.'

Talus aired his thoughts. 'Why are you not with the others?'

'The others?'

'The Elite Guard.'

'Elite Guard?'

Talus frowned. 'You do know that your Order has been disbanded?'

'Disbanded?'

'Sounds like you've a lot of catching up to do.'

Elfin Fingle clicked his fingers excitedly. 'You're Ten Six Nine's friend. The one who was missing.'

'And the last of your kind by the looks of it.' Talus scowled.

'You're right in that. My name is Smmuga.'

'Thought your lot were nameless?'

'So did I. The rest of them, where are they?'

'She led them north.' Elfin replied.

'She?'

'Ten Six Nine.'

'Ten Six Nine was leading them?'

Talus grinned widely. 'A lot of catching up to do.'

Elfin hurried the conversation on. 'They went looking for you and another Slayer, and to investigate reports that boar-men of Ergmire are in Enntonia.'

'I was taken hostage by several of the boar-men. A larger group may still be out there somewhere. We'd wandered into unfamiliar territory, and that was when we were attacked.'

'Attacked?' Elfin's heart jumped a beat. 'Who by?'

'The Formless, things far worse than those Raiders you mentioned. They cut the boar-men to pieces, none survived.'

'And yet you did?' Talus eyed him with suspicion.

'I did.' He paused. 'I can't believe it's her. You say Ten Six Nine is leading now?'

'You've missed out on a lot.' Elfin added cagily. 'She now rules all of Enntonia.'

'She what?'

'Enough chat.' Talus cleared his throat and hawked another spit to the ground. 'Scaraven needs to be informed of what happened here today. Prepare the ravens, Fingle. Send a summons. I'll ride north, let the others know one of their missing friends is back safe.'

'Wait, Harbinger! I'll come with you. Two of us can cover more ground. When we find them, she cannot change her plans. As long as she keeps going north, Enntonia is safe.'

Talus eyed the Slayer keenly. 'What do you mean?'

'I think it is her they are looking for.'

'What?' Elfin panicked. 'Then she is in great danger. We have to warn her.'

'On the contrary. She might be the only one who can control them.'

'And how come you're such an expert on these things?' Talus questioned.

'You might say I've had a glimpse of my future. As Twelve Seven Two I knew nothing of this, but Smmuga has seen the face of The Formless and survived… twice.' He turned to Elfin. 'Who is this Scaraven?'

'A wizard,' replied Elfin.

'The best there is.' Moxi added eagerly. 'He will know what to do. This assault on Bog-Mire will come as no surprise to him. The letter he sent to Shroo and I outlined his concerns. Nevias was one of a Council of Three who met with him at his recent visit to the Hall. In his letter, he likened Nevias to a wolf and didn't like his manner at all.'

'Then the Harbinger is right. We need his assistance. When he arrives, tell him everything.'

'But I don't understand,' Elfin quizzed. 'Why do you think these creatures you call formless would answer to Ten Six Nine?'

'I have seen writings, passed down from the days of the Old Kingdom. Recent events must have triggered their return. I may be wrong, but I think she might be the one who summoned them centuries ago.'

Elfin's jaw dropped in astonishment as he watched Talus and the Slayer mount up.

'He's an interesting one, that's for sure.' Moxi nudged him as the two riders merged with the trees.

Elfin snapped his fingers. 'I think I've just figured out why those two former Slayers have been hanging around these last few days. Scaraven must have asked them to keep watch over the place. But where were they when we needed them? I hope that Representative didn't harm them.'

'Maybe they went north with the others?' Moxi offered. 'Nothing we can do about it anyway. Come on, I'll help you with the ravens.'

Elfin looked down on his new ally. 'Shouldn't you return to the Hall? You would be safe there. And you need to let your fellow Acolytes know what's happened.'

'I'm staying. Can't wait to see what Scaraven makes of all this.'

'Okay.' Elfin nodded his assent. 'Let's go send the message.'

CHAPTER SEVENTY-ONE

Hendrick Stanner slowly opened his eyes. A dull pain ached in his neck and shoulders. Gingerly rubbing the back of his head, he sat up on the bed. Where was he?

Looking to his left, he saw the iron bars on the window. He glanced quickly round the room. He had his answer.

They'd caught him. It was hardly a surprise. It had been unavoidable.

'Ah, I see you are awake at last.'

As if the bars on the window weren't enough, Stanner's gloom deepened at the sound of the familiar voice. Turning his head, he saw the old man in the rust-coloured greatcoat sitting at a table on the far side of the room.

'How are you feeling? Apologies for the bump but I had to do something, and time was running out.'

Stanner despaired. It didn't seem as if he would ever get rid of this crazy old fool. 'I take it your plan didn't work.'

'On the contrary. It worked exactly the way I intended it to.'

'Really? Then why am I in a prison cell?'

'You'd have ended up here either way. That much became inevitable when you turned down my offer. This way, I've bought you some time.'

'Time for what?'

'Time to save you from the gallows.'

'And how exactly do you think that is going to happen? Have you got some grand escape planned?'

'No, even to attempt it would be folly. You're a dangerous man in the eyes of the law now, Hendrick Stanner. A harsh judgement perhaps but it is the case, nonetheless. Escape is no longer an option for you. But as it happens, for now at least, being here is probably the safest place for you.'

'So, you let me get caught for my own sake. What a stroke of genius.' Stanner got to his feet and paced towards the window. 'What happened? Collect the reward yourself, did you?'

'I took you in. It was the only option. I couldn't have left you to the mercy of that lynch mob. Who knows what might have happened? I didn't take the money though; it didn't feel right. I told them to put it towards some of the damage you've caused.'

'How very noble of you.' Stanner walked back to the bed and sat down. 'Okay, so I'm locked up. But why are you in here?'

'To keep you company, old friend. It's the least I can do.' The man got to his feet and dragged his chair to the centre of the room. He sat facing Stanner, his seemingly translucent eyes fixed on his prey. He was an imposing figure. The big-framed shoulders: the beard mingled with the mass of tangled hair; the weathered, time-worn face and those damnable eyes. Stanner shuddered as his nemesis continued talking.

'At some point in the coming hours and days they may question you. They may go through the motions, but the whole procedure will be nothing more than a charade. You're a condemned man, Hendrick Stanner. Any trial will be a foregone conclusion. There's no hope for you.'

Stanner threw himself back on the bed. As dire as his outlook was, the situation was almost laughable. 'Great! It's the gallows for me and as if that wasn't damnation enough, for my last few days in this miserable existence I have to put up with you.' He sat up and pointed angrily. 'Well, I'm not having it. I'm telling you now, you need to leave.'

'I'm sorry, I just can't do that.' The man's expression never seemed to change. 'I won't leave you to face this fate alone.'

Growling his annoyance, Stanner scrambled to his feet. He crossed the room and thumped loudly on the door.

'Hey! Is anyone there?' He waited a few moments, but no response came. He walked towards the mirror on the wall and tapped a finger against it. 'You in there! I know you're watching. You need to come and get him out of here.'

'They won't come,' the old man sighed. 'You are in no position to make demands.'

Stanner slid to the floor and held his head in his hands. Why wouldn't this old fool leave him alone? What had he done to deserve this kind of harassment? 'Why are you doing this?' He looked up. 'Why are you so determined to get me to agree to your offer?' He hesitated as the notion struck him. Maybe that was his way out. 'If I agree, will you leave me alone?'

'Mister Stanner, please.' A hand waved his plea aside. 'I couldn't possibly take advantage of you under such circumstances.'

'So, your offer? Are you now telling me it no longer stands?'

'Let's just say it is temporarily withdrawn. I know how vehemently opposed you were to accepting it. If you were to accept now, it would undoubtedly be for the wrong reasons. A decision you might very well come to regret in the future.'

Stanner got to his feet and raised a clenched fist in annoyance. 'I'm tired of your games, old man. You need to get out of here. I'm not sure how much longer I can put up with you.'

'Come now, we've been through this before. You are not a violent man, Hendrick Stanner.'

Stanner marched to the door and thumped it angrily. 'Get him out of here.' Venting his anger, he turned to the mirror. 'I want out of here! Now!'

It was useless. He knew it was useless. He wasn't getting out of here and it didn't look like he was getting rid of his tormentor either. Deflated, he walked back to the bed and lay down.

He closed his eyes. Maybe it was all just a bad dream. Maybe, any moment now, he would open his eyes, and it would be over.

Sleep came quickly.

When he woke several hours later, starlight filtered through the barred window. The form in the shadows by the table confirmed his worst fears. True to his word, the old man was still there. Hendrick Stanner closed his eyes again and wondered if the nightmare would ever end.

CHAPTER SEVENTY-TWO

Sheriff Konrad Blaine shook his head in disgust. The scene in the room beyond the two-way mirror was playing out the same way it had for the last three days. It wasn't good. It wasn't good at all. With a sigh of resignation, he cast his glance sideways.

The white-suited man, partially hidden by a cloud of cigar smoke, returned his stare blankly. Blaine waved the smoke aside. He knew full well what was coming.

'So, what do you think, Judge?'

'I'd say your concerns are well founded, Sheriff. Has he been like this since you apprehended him?'

'Yes, same every day. He's convinced there's someone in the room with him. When he's not sleeping, he's talking to himself. Keeps banging on the door and the mirror, demanding that we get his imaginary friend out of there.'

'Not an act?'

'Definitely not. I've seen all the tricks in my time, but never a show like this.'

'Have you questioned him?'

'I don't see the point in trying. We'll not get a coherent dialogue with him, not in that state. He's guilty, beyond doubt. We've got all those witness accounts. No, we've just been monitoring his behaviour.'

'Delusional disorder.' The Judge gave a shrug of dismissal.

'You'd be wasting time and resources pursuing it any further. You're not going to get the verdict you want on this one. Let's get him assessed, evaluated, and certified as soon as possible. I'll make the necessary arrangements at my end. We should have him out of your hair in a few days.'

Blaine nodded his agreement. 'Thanks.'

'Happy to help. I know it's far from ideal but it's best to wrap cases like these up quickly. I know they leave a bad taste in the mouth but best not to dwell on it.' With a puff of cigar smoke, he motioned a thumb towards the glass. 'You'd never win a case against that; it would be a complete waste of time and money trying. It's got insanity defence written all over it.' His expression lightened. 'We have a little poker night lined up for Friday. You in?'

'Yeah,' sighed Blaine. 'I'm in.'

'Excellent! See you at the club around eight.'

Sheriff Konrad Blaine took one last look into the room beyond the glass and shook his head. The Judge was right.

Shame this one wouldn't get what he deserved. At times like these Blaine hoped that a lifetime stuck in a padded cell with only the voices in your head for company was a far worse sentence than a quick visit to the gallows. That way, there might still be some justice left in the world.

CHAPTER SEVENTY-THREE

From high in the star-speckled sky, the full moon's glow bathed the night in charcoal grey. Across the bay, a jagged silhouette of lofty mountain peaks rose steeply from the sea.

A light breeze ruffled the branches of the mighty firs as, prompted from her trance by the territorial call of a hunting owl, Shadow left the cover of the forest and followed the track down the gentle slope to the shoreline. A small stone bridge, lit-up by pale lanterns, spanned the narrow stretch of water separating a small island from the shore.

Sharing the company of a solitary fir tree, a gathering of dwarf conifers, and a scattering of berry bushes, the grassy islet's main feature peered out from beneath its sweeping two-tiered, slate-tiled roof. The homely-looking wooden building beckoned invitingly. Light flickered from beyond the eye-shaped window above the arched doorway, and a plume of chimney smoke rose lazily into the night sky.

Her boots scrunched noisily in the gravel as she crossed the bridge. Climbing the stone steps set into the grass bank, she arrived at the wooden door. The ornate doorknocker, a winged grotesque, yawned its silent welcome as it came into contact with the old timber, and the door swung slowly open. Holding her breath in expectation, she waited a moment before stepping inside.

Moonlight streamed in through the rounded windows on either side, guiding her progress across the flag-stoned floor. She moved into the adjoining room. To her left, a series of small crescent-shaped windows looked out onto the glass-like water. On her right, four large oval windows offered a stunning view of the moonlit bay. Beyond, the dramatic profiles of eroded rock towers speared the night sky. Shadow turned her attention back to the room's interior.

The walls, bearing an array of lit candle sconces, were a soothing mix of white plaster and varnished timber. Two circular chandelier candle holders hung from the wooden ceiling and, at the far end of the room, a fire blazed in the recess beneath the rustic oak mantel. Midway between the fire and the furthest window, a wooden staircase spiralled its way to the upper level. The air hung heavy with the calming smoky fragrance of burning sandalwood.

She sat down on a low sofa looking out over the bay. Easing back into the soft cushions, she yawned contentedly. Her eyes felt heavy; she suddenly felt so tired.

When she woke a short while later, it was still dark. The moon shone in through the oval windows. Rising to her feet, she rolled her shoulders and stretched. Casting her gaze across the water, she added a log to the fire and climbed the stairs.

The room at the top of the stairs was everything she hoped it would be. After a long soak in the steaming bathtub, she sipped a cup of elderberry tea and climbed into bed. As the soft mattress enveloped her, she closed her eyes and fell asleep.

CHAPTER SEVENTY-FOUR

Situated high in sprawling woodlands, Rose Falls Asylum commanded a stunning view of the valley below. The view from Hendrick Stanner's room might just have been perfect were it not for the steel bars on the outside of the window. Those cursed bars. Not only did they ruin the view, they were also a constant reminder of just how rotten his luck had become.

That said, whilst it might not be perfect, the view was all he had. In the two days he'd been here, he hadn't seen or spoken to anyone. His food and water arrived whenever he was asleep. Coincidence or not? He couldn't say for certain.

Two days? He wasn't sure about that either. Everything was merging into one long blurred nightmare. He had only a faint recollection of being led from the police cell. He remembered the Sheriff advising him of what was going to happen, and he remembered rudely telling the lawman he didn't care what happened as long as they made sure Old Clear Eyes disappeared. Ignoring his outburst, the Sheriff's blank stare had been a damning judgement. Was he crazy? He didn't think so, but then wouldn't denial be the first line of defence in such a condition?

As he watched from the window, two eagles soared into view above the trees. Right at that moment, Stanner would have given anything to wander freely; to explore the forest and the vast open spaces beyond. Funny how things like that were taken for granted until the opportunity was gone. The pang for freedom gave way to a surge of regret and a realisation that he had wasted much of his time on all the wrong pursuits. Now here he was, locked up. How long was he going to be here?

The thought scared him. No one was telling him anything. No one was coming to talk to him. But then why would they? They considered him deranged and incapable of rational conversation. And why did they think he was crazy?

One simple reason.

Old Clear Eyes. The messenger from the plateau.

Stanner shook his head ruefully. He didn't think he was crazy but if he was, he knew who to blame. The old fool had been haunting him for months. Desperate for some light in this darkest of tunnels, he clung to the hope that there might be at least one small shred of comfort to be found in this solitary confinement. Disturbing as his current predicament was, Rose Falls Asylum had one big thing in its favour. Since coming here, he'd had no visits from his maddening bane.

The time passed slowly. Day turned into night and then back again. Still no one came to talk to him. Twice a day his food tray appeared whilst he was sleeping. Didn't matter how hard he tried to stay awake, he kept missing the opportunity to question anyone about their plans for him. What had they done to him? Were they putting something in his food?

Would he have to avoid eating?

Paranoia? Wasn't that another symptom of a troubled mind?

On the morning of the sixth day, least he thought it was the sixth day, it was becoming increasingly difficult to keep track of time, he woke to find he had a visitor. His nemesis had returned. Old Clear Eyes had found him.

'Good day to you, Hendrick Stanner.'

Stanner rubbed the sleep from his eyes as he sat up on the bed. The sight of his visitant would normally have invoked a surge of contempt and hatred. Yet strangely, he felt nothing.

No feelings of anger, or frustration. What had this place done to him? Had they drugged his food as he'd suspected? Had the sense of isolation taken its toll? Or was he finally accepting his condition? Did he even have a condition?

Yet again it seemed the old man had read his mind.

'Things don't look good, Mister Stanner. The consensus seems to be that you've lost control of your faculties. Delusional. I believe that is their prognosis.'

'Am I?' Stanner asked the question outright. 'Are you a figment of my imagination?'

'No, I am not. You are perfectly sane.'

'Then why were they not able to see you?'

'Because I made it so.'

'You can do that?'

'I can do a lot of things.'

Stanner grimaced. 'Pity you didn't share that one with me in the high ground above the plain.'

'I did offer, but you refused my help. I regret that things had to come to this, but something had to be done. I saw no other feasible way out of your predicament.'

'What do you mean?' Stanner frowned. Things weren't becoming any clearer.

'By concealing my presence from all others, I created a scenario that would ensure you evaded the gallows.' The old man eased towards him, grinning wryly as he pointed a gnarled finger. 'You are a very determined fellow, Hendrick Stanner. I greatly admire your tenacity; a gift that could be put to great use were you to choose a different path, but I'm not going to force you or attempt to influence you any further. This will be the last time I come to you.'

Stanner didn't find the prospect as favourable as he might have expected. 'You'd leave me here to rot?'

'Who knows? Without me around you might convince the authorities you are actually still of sound mind.'

'And then what? That would mean the noose for me.'

'You might escape. Go back to a life on the run?'

'And if I don't manage to escape?'

'Then you'll face the consequences. After all, we should all be held accountable for our actions. Don't you agree?'

Stanner scowled his disgust. 'I can do without your reprimands. Why are you here?'

'I'm here to repeat my offer, one last time.' The old man fumbled inside his coat.

Stanner watched as he placed a small contraption on the table. He eyed it warily. What trick was the old clown playing now? 'What's that for?'

'Some refer to it as a device for measuring the passage of time.'

'I know what an hourglass is. Why do we need it?'

'To give you an opportunity for reflection before making your decision. You should, however, be aware that this is not your typical sandglass. When the top bulb is empty, the mechanism will rotate automatically with no need for assistance and the process will begin again.' The old man's tone darkened. 'The glass will turn thirty times before coming to a stop. When the sand settles, a period for final deliberation will follow. Shortly after that, an opportunity to leave this place will present itself to you and that is when you must act in accordance with your decision.' The old man's hand hovered above the hourglass. 'If you are ready? We will begin.'

Stanner swallowed uneasily. As uncomfortable as he was with the ultimatum, it appeared he had finally run out of options. If this was to be his last encounter with his aged tormentor, there seemed little point in delaying. 'Let's get this over with.'

With a fatalistic nod and a flick of his finger, Old Clear Eyes tipped the glass and the countdown began.

'Thirty turns of the sand, Hendrick Stanner.' The old man retreated slowly from the table. 'Thirty turns of the sand.'

Engrossed by the glass, Stanner watched the sand for several minutes. When he looked up, he saw that the room was empty.

He was alone again.

Old Clear Eyes was gone.

CHAPTER SEVENTY-FIVE

The hourglass was an impressive piece of craftsmanship the height of four spanned fingers. Carved from dark-hued wood, its base resembled the scaled-down design of a ship's wheel. Daylight danced on a miniature-sized glass orb at its centre, throwing a kaleidoscope of colour to the drab walls and ceiling. The upper section of the device encasing the glass bulbs, sat suspended an inch above the base and was attached to the slender wooden uprights by two threaded brass pins no thicker than matchsticks. The wooden disc atop the hourglass bore the etched symbol of a navigational compass.

Stanner watched the white sand trickle slowly through the narrowing of the glass. Each time the top bulb emptied, the brass pins clicked into motion and the glass spun slowly round to begin the process all over again. Resisting the urge to pick it up, he leaned in and studied it closely. Driven by some hidden force or mechanism, its movement was precise, smooth, and seamless. Following its progress attentively, he counted the first few rotations without distraction but, mesmerised by the hypnotic nature of its repetitive process, he soon became lost in contemplation.

The time passed unnoticed. Transfixed with wonder, his gaze stayed with the hourglass until, summoned from his catatonic state by the loud click accompanying the conclusion of the cycle, he realised it was over. The sand lay still. Breath held, he watched it closely, waiting, almost hoping for it to click into motion again. But he waited in vain. The sand had settled for the last time.

Dragging his eyes away from the hourglass, he glanced round the room. Nothing had changed. He rose stiffly from the table. Stretching the feeling back into his limbs, he walked to the window. The sun was now high in the sky. His thoughts drifted. How long had he been sitting there, watching the strange timepiece, oblivious to the passing of time? And for what? Did he honestly believe the old man's words? Had he really been naive enough, desperate enough, to think this far-fetched nonsense could lead to some form of salvation?

The moments slipped slowly by. His frustration grew. What was he waiting for? He was foolish to have expected any outcome other than this. As he turned his focus to the source of his disillusionment on the table, the door of the room swung open and an officious-looking woman, clutching a clipboard close to her chest, entered the room.

'Hendrick Stanner?' She ran her deep-set eyes over him in judgement. She was evidently less than impressed. Adjusting her dark blue blazer, she clicked her heels to the centre of the room. 'My name is Doctor Morelle. I've been assigned to your case.'

Taken aback by her sudden and unexpected appearance, Stanner took a moment to catch up. 'About time someone was,' he mumbled. 'I've been here for days and haven't seen a soul.'

'These things can take time, I'm sure you can appreciate that.' Her expression suggested she didn't care whether he did or not. 'I believe you've been made aware of the protocol?'

'What protocol?' Stanner looked at her questioningly. What was she talking about?

With no further explanation, she lifted the hourglass from the table and turned towards the door. 'If you'd like to follow me?'

Stanner eyed her suspiciously. 'Follow you?' What was she doing with the hourglass? Was this some kind of test? 'Where are we going?'

She frowned impatiently. 'Mister Stanner, I have other patients and matters I must attend to. Have you made your decision?'

'My decision?' The old man's words rang suddenly in his head. Stanner's gaze darted to the open door. 'I can leave?'

'If that is your wish.' She turned away. 'It is your decision to make.' As she left the room, the door slowly began to close behind her.

Stanner's heart raced. An opportunity would present itself, that's what Old Clear Eyes had told him. Was this it? Or was it a trick? Aware he was almost out of time, he sprang towards the door and caught it with only seconds to spare. 'Wait!' He followed her into the corridor. 'I'm coming with you.' It appeared he'd made his decision.

'Very well,' she pursed her red-lined lips. 'Follow me, Mister Stanner.'

The long walk along the windowless corridor passed with neither of them speaking. Her cold demeanour was more than enough to keep him from asking any further about where they were going or what was about to happen to him. Was he going to be released? Was he free to leave? Was Old Clear Eyes' offer going to prove to be genuine? If so, what would he have to pay in return? His jumbled thoughts came to a crashing halt as they stopped in front of a grey door.

'Wait here, please.' She offered a half smile. 'I won't be a moment.' Closing the door firmly behind her, she left him alone with his doubts. Stanner waited, heart in mouth, wondering what might happen next. Was his luck on the turn? Or were things about to go from bad to worse?

True to her word, he didn't have to wait long to find out.

The door opened and with a wave of her hand she beckoned him inside.

The darkened room was empty. No table, no chair, and no window barred or otherwise. Stanner glanced nervously at the solitary wall lamp. 'What is this?' He turned to her anxiously. 'What's going on?'

'This is where I must leave you, Mister Stanner.'

'What?' Stanner panicked. 'I thought you said you were taking on my case?'

'I did.' Her expression showed no sign of emotion. 'And I have concluded my assessment. In my professional opinion, there is nothing wrong with you. You are free to go.'

Stanner glanced worriedly round the room. 'This doesn't look like freedom to me.'

'Perceptions can vary, Mister Stanner. I bid you farewell.'

As the door closed behind her, Stanner heard movement in the corner of the room. Spinning round, he saw Old Clear Eyes step from the shadows.

'Hendrick Stanner.' The old man's expression was the closest

Stanner had seen to a smile in all their encounters. 'I see that you have made your decision.'

Stanner nodded. Sometimes the wise man is the one who knows when to admit defeat. 'Yes.'

'Wonderful. I'm pleased. Very pleased indeed.' He pulled a small glass sphere from his pocket and offered it to Stanner. 'Shall we get out of here?'

'What is that?'

'It's for you. Think of it as a gift. From an old friend.'

Fitting snugly in the palm of Stanner's hand, the sphere had a warm reassuring feel. 'What is it for? What does it do?'

'It makes for an excellent form of transportation.'

He studied the glass carefully. 'Really?' More tricks? 'Okay, so what happens now?'

Reaching out, the old man placed a firm hand on his shoulder.

'Now, Hendrick Stanner, we meet your destiny. Close your eyes. It's time to go.'

CHAPTER SEVENTY-SIX

The yawning grotesque stared back blankly as she pulled the door closed behind her. With a smile, Shadow crossed the gravel path and walked down the steps to the little wooden jetty as the early morning sun crested the jagged mountain ridge on the horizon. The eleventh morning of her stay at Journey's End was to be her last. For now, at least. She would return, it was inevitable.

In keeping with the majority of her journey, her time here had been spent alone. Although the Seer had not appeared in physical form, she'd felt his presence strongly. It resonated in every fibre of the place; in the house and in its surroundings and though she had been alone in his dwelling, she hadn't felt awkward or uncomfortable. At no time had she felt like she was intruding or invading his privacy. Far from it. She'd felt right at home.

It was like he'd been guiding her, pointing out notable curios dotted around the house; directing her to suggested reading material hidden among the troves of literary gems catalogued in the library on the upper level of the house. Books from every corner of every world imaginable, accompanied by his detailed translations of each.

Following an early morning walk in the forest or along the shoreline, her days had been spent between the library and his study; the room with the eye-shaped window that watched over the little bridge, reading through his stash of handwritten journals, all the while building her knowledge of his writings. She'd passed her evenings reading by the fireside, before walking to the beach in the moonlight for her nightly meditation.

As if in preparation for her visit, the larder had been fully stocked with supplies; a fact that didn't seem to ever change.

As much as she had looked forward to meeting him in person, she felt no sense of disappointment. Everything felt right, just the way she thought it should. She no longer held any pre-conceived ideas of how things should be, or how things would turn out, and had no lingering doubts or questions about her journey. And although there had been no specific instructions left for her, she instinctively knew what she had to do next.

The journal she'd discovered in the old carved trunk at the rear of the study the previous evening had provided the final piece in the puzzle. The journal's account, and the tarnished silver button she'd found in the trinket box on the shelf above the fireplace.

Sitting on the jetty, deep in thought, she watched the turn of the tide. The time had come.

As the warmth of the sun permeated the day, a mist rose from the surface of the water. As it began to disperse, she saw a wooden craft glide into view some distance away. She thought about her oaths as she watched it approach. Everything now seemed so obvious. The oaths had never been a bind. Part of her would always be on the island, for the island reached everywhere.

As the craft neared the boardwalk, she saw a familiar figure tending the oars. Instead of his oversized green jacket, he now wore a smart blue blazer, and a peaked boatman's cap had taken the place of his twig-covered hat. Though unexpected, his appearance didn't surprise her as much as it ought to have. As the boat nudged against the jetty, he jumped to his bare feet.

'Have no fear, weary traveller. Your chariot is here.' As their eyes met, his mouth dropped open. 'Oh, it's you!'

'Faramus Thorn.' She smiled at his startled reaction. 'Keeper of the gorge.'

'It's you?'

'Yes, it's me,' she grinned. 'You didn't tell me you were also a boatman.'

He threw a pained expression. 'A fellow's got to have more than one string to his bow these days,' he hesitated, 'not that it's any of your business, but then…' he paused again, 'maybe it is.' With a self-assuring nod, he flashed a smile in her direction and beckoned her forward. 'Welcome aboard, Miss. Pleasure to have your company for the crossing.'

'Thank you.' Shadow embarked and made her way to the front of the boat as he busied himself with the mooring rope.

'Tide's a' turning, and the wind is with us.' Pulling a little gold chain from the breast pocket of his blazer, he studied the watch face quizzically, turning it one way then the other, before slipping it back into his pocket with a shake of his head. 'We'll have you on the other side in no time at all.' His impish grin was never far away. 'And begging your pardon, Miss,' he tipped his cap. 'But I never would have delayed you in the gorge if I'd known you were coming here.'

'But I told you I was going to Journey's End.'

'Ah, see, I thought you were being cryptic.' He frowned as he gave his chin a rub. 'Thing is, I ain't never heard it called by that name before.' His grin returned. 'It don't matter though. Anyway, enough of my chatter. Let's get this old girl moving.' He slipped a hand gingerly into his blazer pocket. 'Curses! Wrong jacket. I don't suppose …'

'No!' She cut him off quickly. 'I don't have any nuts.'

'Didn't think so.' He winked playfully as he took his seat and dropped the oars into the water. 'Thought I'd ask anyway. Enjoy the crossing. Best view is at the front, right there where you are. Glad to have you aboard.'

Shadow watched the house at Journey's End fade into the distance.

'How was the old place?' he asked. 'Did you find everything as it should be?'

'Yes,' she replied softly. 'Everything is as it should be.' Merging with the morning haze, the bay faded from view. Shadow turned to look ahead.

'Journey's End, eh?' The oarsman spoke as if thinking aloud. 'Never heard it called that before. A fitting name for a place of such beauty. But only a name, of course. I don't expect such a place exists for the likes of us, Miss?'

Shadow smiled inwardly. 'No, Faramus Thorn, I don't expect it does.'

The remainder of the crossing passed in silence, each of them apparently content with knowing the other's secret. Emerging gradually from the mist the jagged mountain range ahead loomed ever closer, growing in stature with every stroke of the oars.

As the ragged vertical coastline came into focus, the boat

steered towards a narrow stretch of grey-coloured shingle.

As they neared land, Faramus Thorn pulled in the oars and jumped to attention.

'Mind your step as you disembark, Miss.' The craft drifted gently into the refuge. 'There's some dangerous rocks here hidden beneath the surface. This is as close as I can get you.'

She stepped from the boat to find that the water was only a few inches deep. 'It's shallow.'

'Everything's relative.' He grinned in reference to his own lowly height. 'The mountain trail, is it?'

'Yes.'

'Well, it's a fine day for it. Safe travels, Miss.'

'And to you, Faramus Thorn.'

She watched as he pushed away from the shore. Within minutes the wooden craft had slipped from view, hidden by the rolling mist. She took one last look at the sea.

Crossing the mass of rounded pebbles, she found her way to the foot of the trail and began the steep ascent of the basalt cliffs.

Noon found her walking the meadows of the headland. Further inland, lined by a guard of alder trees, the trail followed the course of a winding river. By late afternoon she had passed through a scattered settlement of stone houses. She sensed life beyond the shuttered windows but saw no one. Her presence went unchallenged.

Dusk found her climbing steadily through the scattered pine, up into the green-clad foothills.

For two days and nights she followed the trail, high into the misty mountain tops. On the morning of the third day, in the shelter of a small cave, she woke to cloudless blue skies and her first view of a jagged white mountain ridge that sparkled in the early morning sunlight.

By mid-morning on the following day, she had begun her final ascent of the airy ridge towards the man-made stack of stones on the skyline.

CHAPTER SEVENTY-SEVEN

Messenger Two Cups toyed thoughtfully with his whiskers.

'And where is she now?'

'She is heading north.'

'Into the Old Kingdom. Is she alone?'

'No, she has company. The Weasel.'

'So, she thinks that her friend, the missing Dragon Slayer, is somewhere in the Old Kingdom?'

'That's what her instincts are telling her.'

'And you, Sanna. What do you think?'

'The lines between us are blurred, Scaraven. It's hard to say. It could be my influence driving her further north.'

Two Cups reached for his pack. 'Your drive is certainly helping her but, from what I've seen, Ten Six Nine knows exactly what she is doing.' He twisted the flask open. 'Another brew?'

Sitting by the cairn, they watched the sunshine dance on the sea far below. As Two Cups' gaze wandered along the shattered white ridge, his eye settled on a figure moving steadily towards them. 'Aha! I thought I recognised that feeling. You know the one I get just before a new adventure?' With a chuckle, he got to his feet and drained his tea in three quick mouthfuls. 'Best be prepared, Sanna. Looks like we have a visitor.'

Sanna stood next to him and watched as the figure crested a spur on the ridge. Relaxing her stance, she glanced down at him.

'There is no danger, Scaraven. It is the blue-cloaked woman from the island.'

'Seers Watch?' Two Cups' eyes widened with excitement. 'Good heavens!'

'But her oaths? I thought she was unable to leave the island?'

'Indeed!' Two Cups waved a finger. 'You raise a fair point, one that suggests this is going to be important.' He grinned. 'This looks like official business to me.' He waved an arm in greeting. 'Welcome, friend,' he bellowed. 'Welcome to the Cairn of Scaraven.'

As the blue-cloaked woman drew to a halt, Two Cups drew a breath. By the stars, she was beautiful. The stories were true. And she had the voice of an angel, a dark-haired angel at that.

'And you would be Scaraven?'

'Yes, that's me.' He bowed eloquently. 'Also known in some circles as Messenger Two Cups. And I am delighted to make your acquaintance.'

'And the Sun Warrior?'

Sanna bowed her head slightly in response. Two Cups watched them closely. They made for a formidable pairing.

'My name is Shadow…'

'You are Shadow of the Seers Watch.' In his excitement, he couldn't help but interrupt. 'My trusted friend here can vouch for that.'

'She can?'

'We met on the island.' Never one for saying more than was necessary, Sanna's explanation was brief and to the point. As was often the case, Two Cups took it upon himself to elaborate.

'This is Sanna Vrai of the Ra-Taegan. The Sun Warrior as you rightly say, but she would have looked very different when you met on the island. Blonde hair, long brown coat. Ring any bells?'

Shadow of the Seers Watch took a moment before responding. 'I remember. Three came to the distant shore and my journey began. The girl. She is safe?'

'She is safe.'

'And the third? You nullified their threat?'

Sanna nodded gravely. 'I saw to it.'

'Then everything is as it should be.'

Two Cups couldn't contain his enthusiasm any longer. 'Much has happened since your last meeting, Shadow, but be assured, Sanna speaks the truth. Reen of the Aaskrid is safe, back home with her tribe. And the horrible business of Trask has been dealt with. I am itching to share everything that has happened with you but first, my curiosity is almost at breaking point. Can I ask your reason for coming here?'

Shadow of the Seers Watch stood to attention. 'I carry a message from an old friend of yours. In his writings he refers to you fondly as his finest student. You studied together at Sumarren before he had to leave unexpectedly for the island.'

'The Seer Magister.' Two Cups' voice wavered slightly.

'He very much regrets leaving without being able to say his farewells but knows that you will understand.' Stepping towards him, she reached into her pocket and held out her hand. 'It was his intention that I give this to you, and to tell you that the time has come.'

As the silver shank button landed gently in the palm of his hand, the revelation hit him like a train. Two Cups reeled as the memories came flooding back. Visions of a past existence, a life long forgotten, flashed before his eyes.

'Scaraven.' Sanna voiced her concern. 'Are you all right?'

'Yes, yes, I think so. Taken aback, you might say.'

'By an old button?'

'Yes,' he smiled. 'By the button, and the vivid memories it evokes.' Gathering his thoughts, he sat down by the cairn.

'What is its significance? What does it mean?'

'It means, Sanna,' his face broke into a grin. 'That we are bound for another adventure.' Rolling the button between his fingers, he held it up to the sunlight. 'The old rascal,' he snorted his amusement. 'He never did reveal his secret.'

'What secret?'

'His identity. Who he really was. And I had no idea.' He slapped his knee in delight. 'Shadow, please join us. Take a seat by the cairn. And, Sanna, if you will grab the flask and pour the tea, I'll share with you both a tale from ages old.' He grinned his satisfaction. 'I'll tell you the story of how the Seer Magister came into possession of this button.'

CHAPTER SEVENTY-EIGHT

Hendrick Stanner felt the breeze on his skin. Savouring the moment, he then opened his eyes. Sunlight filtered down through the trees from a cloudless blue sky. His spirits soared.

This felt like freedom. Like a freedom he'd never experienced before. A buzzard swooped into view, circling several times before dropping out of sight. A short distance away, a conspiracy of ravens chattered noisily in a field beyond the trees.

'Where are we?'

Old Clear Eyes wore a satisfied grin. Though mostly hidden in the tangle of beard and hair it was unmistakable.

'Dipper Mill Forest, on a fine spring morning. There's no better place to begin a new journey.'

Stanner's feelings of resentment towards the old devil were gone. In their place was a calming sense of acceptance. Sure, he had questions, lots of them, but if experience had taught him anything it was that asking questions often led to confusion and the need for further questions. Sometimes it was better to just let things roll. Reaching inside his pocket for reassurance, his hand settled on the little glass sphere. Yes, sometimes it was better just not to ask. Could the manner of their passage here from the Asylum be easily explained?

He doubted it. Avoiding raising the subject, he turned his thoughts to the woman who'd played her part in his liberation.

'My release seemed very straightforward. I hope Doctor Morelle isn't going to be judged too harshly by her superiors for letting me walk out of there so easily.'

'I shouldn't imagine that will be an issue.' The old man suppressed a laugh. 'Doctor Morelle doesn't work at Rose Falls Asylum.'

'What? Then how? I don't understand…'

'She works independently. She answers to no one. She is a bit like me in that respect. Our paths cross from time to time and well, let's just say she owed me a favour. She liked you though, she was very interested in you.'

'Why? She said there was nothing wrong with me. Said I was perfectly sane.'

'Your state of mind had nothing to do with it. Her interest centred on your gift.'

'What gift? I have no gift.'

'Really? Then how do you explain your arrival here?'

Stanner eyed him warily. 'That was down to you. You made that happen. And come to think of it, you've been doing a lot of weird inexplicable things ever since we met. Just who, or what, are you?'

'Think of me as a messenger, nothing more. But believe me you do have a gift, one which I will not attempt to explain to you here and now.' He gave a muffled sigh. 'I fear neither of us would enjoy the complexities of such a task. Suffice to say, you are now a free man and now that your journey of discovery has begun, I'm certain the answers will begin to present themselves to you. A new outlook, a change of perception, that will be all you need.'

Hesitating for a moment, Old Clear Eyes wagged a gnarled finger. 'The past, however, can be a cruel mistress. Might I suggest a change of name? The name Hendrick Stanner no longer does you justice.'

'I can change my name, but people will still recognise me. My face is plastered all over those posters.'

'Your appearance will no longer be an issue; I can assure you of that. And so, to a name.' Lifting his head, he cupped a hand to his tangled hair. 'Ah, listen to them. I have always loved the kraa of the ravens. Such a joyous sound.' Clapping his hands together in delight, his gaze drifted Stanner's way once more. 'I think I have it!'

'Have what?'

'A name for you.' Old Clear Eyes rubbed his palms together in anticipation. 'Scaraven.' His brows twitched. 'There's a name with a ring to it. What do you think?'

Stanner glanced in the direction of the field. A change of name made sense, and one name was as good as any other. As if in confirmation, the ravens took to the air in a sudden flurry of activity and flew from sight beyond the treetops. Their sudden absence left a haunting silence. Stanner reckoned if he needed a sign, he'd just got it. 'Scaraven it is then.'

'Excellent! And so, your journey begins.' The old man nodded his satisfaction. 'There is a little cottage not far from here. The young lady who lives there will be looking out for you. She is a delightful soul and makes a rather splendid cup of tea.'

'I'm not much of a tea drinker.'

'You will be. Farewell, Scaraven. Until we meet again.'

'You're leaving?'

'Yes. My work here is done.'

'But what am I to do? Where am I to go?'

'I suggest you start with that cup of tea. Everything else will fall into place.'

'Why did you do this? Why did you help me?'

The old man's eyes widened. Striking as they were, they no longer instilled fear or intimidation.

'Fate is a strange thing. You never know when it's going to creep up on you. Who knows, perhaps you will return the favour one day.'

'We'll meet again?'

'I'm certain of it. Though whether we will recognise each other is another thing entirely. Perhaps a memento will help.'

Reaching out a hand, he tore a button from Stanner's coat.

'I'll keep this. Don't worry, you'll be needing a new jacket. That one looks too big for you now.'

The old man bowed his retreat. 'If I need you, I'll send for you. If you see this button again, you'll know it's me.' His aged features broke into a grin.

'Until the next time, Scaraven of the Messengers.'

CHAPTER SEVENTY-NINE

'And with that he vanished, right in front of my eyes.'

Messenger Two Cups took a mouthful of tea and smiled.

'Old Clear Eyes, that's what I called him back then. And when we were at Sumarren he never once gave a hint of our past. I had no idea we shared such a history.' He glanced down at the button as he rolled it between his fingers. 'Of course, he looked completely different, just like he said he would... or did he? Is it possible that because it had all happened in a previous incarnation, I'd just forgotten?' With a chuckle, Two Cups got to his feet.

Sanna looked at him with a new sense of wonder.

'Hendrick Stanner? I've not heard mention of that version of you before, Scaraven.'

'No, it seems he'd escaped my memory.' He gave a mischievous grin. 'Oh, I think he was a harmless fellow on the whole. A little misguided perhaps, but our old friend put him on the right track.'

'I'm curious.' Shadow of the Seers Watch cut in. 'The name Two Cups?'

'Well, Old Clear Eyes was right about the tea. I've developed an insatiable habit for the brew. Don't get me wrong, I like the name Scaraven, but someone else picked that for me. So, when this little flask of mine came into my possession it brought with it the idea for the perfect alias.'

'A fitting name.'

'Indeed! I always thought so.'

As Two Cups bent to retrieve his pack, a thought struck him suddenly; a notion so obvious he wondered why it took so long to present itself.

'Scaraven?' Sanna noticed the sudden change in his expression. 'What is it?'

'It just dawned on me. I never asked who she was?'

'Who?'

'The woman I saved in the settlement of Creek.'

'Creek?'

'It all makes sense now.' He felt a rush of enlightenment as the pieces tumbled into place. The strong connection he shared with Ten Six Nine. He'd thought it was merely down to the fact she was another reality's version of Sanna, but it was so much more than that. The revelation chilled the back of his neck.

Ten Six Nine's identification tag; he now understood why he'd hesitated when he'd held it in his hand in Hawkers Square. That was why it had unsettled him so much. Because he'd recognised it. He'd seen it once before. The woman he'd helped in Creek had worn it around her neck.

The woman he'd saved was Ten Six Nine; the woman he would help bring to the throne of Enntonia centuries later.

She was a Drifter; she would have survived with or without his help. The reason for his involvement back then was obvious. It had been a lesson in hope and belief, and it had been his first step on the road to salvation. But now?

With a puff of his cheeks, he scratched his forehead in contemplation. He didn't believe in the concept of coincidence, so why was the Seer sending for him now?

Was it connected to Ten Six Nine and the recent changes in Enntonia? Was there some connection to the Fifteen, and the Representatives? He gave a shake of his head. If the reason was there, he couldn't yet see it.

'Scaraven?' Sanna eyed him with concern. 'Are you all right?'

'Yes, yes, I am. Forgive me, I am merely trying to catch up with my thoughts.' Fumbling with the flask, he hurriedly refilled his mug. Taking two mouthfuls of tea in quick succession, he regained his composure and sat down by the cairn.

'My friends, there is much to discuss and much to be shared. Perhaps then, the road ahead will seem clearer. New adventures await us at every turn, and I am eager to begin. But first, if you will allow me, there is another tale I must share with you both.' He grinned contentedly. 'And it is a fine tale, even if I say so myself. It all began one day long ago, on a windswept plateau.'

Thank you for reading *Thirty Turns of the Sand.*

If you have a few moments to spare and would like to leave a review on Amazon, it would be much appreciated!

ALSO BY THE AUTHOR

THE SEA OF LUCIDITY